FEEDING TIME

ADAM BILES

FEEDING TIME

Illustrations by Melanie Amaral and Stephen Crowe

GALLEY BEGGAR PRESS

First published in 2016
by Galley Beggar Press Limited
37 Dover Street, Norwich NR2 3LG

Paperback ISBN: 978-1-910296-68-4
Black-cover edition ISBN: 978-1-910296-73-8

Text design and typesetting by Tetragon, London

Printed and bound in Great Britain by Clays Ltd, St Ives plc

For Darran

Thus walke I lyk a restelees kaityf,
And on the ground, which is my moodres gate,
I knokke with my staf bothe erly and late,
And seye, 'Leeve mooder, leet me in!'
(Chaucer, The Pardoner's Tale)

Book One

1

Dropping the key through the letterbox, just as the boy from the estate agent's had instructed her, Dot (*née* Dorothy, aka Dotty to some, most of them dead) wondered, for a moment, if anyone had ever drawn a line under life in quite such a don't-mind-me manner as this.

'We'll take care of the rest, Mum,' the boy-agent had assured her, shifting about beneath his suit, his back broad enough to support just one of the jacket's shoulder pads at a time. 'Leave the worrying to us.'

That Dot couldn't do. She forced a smile.

The storm had started during the night and hadn't let up. The rain whipped earthwards from the charcoal heavens, churning in the potholes of the driveway and coursing along the gutters of Trapp Street in miniature white-water drifts.

No chance, it seemed, that the driver would brave the storm to help Dot with her cases. Since the battered Cortina had rolled to a stop outside the bungalow and the man behind the wheel had honked – three hopeful pips to begin and then, a minute later, a single insistent blat – the only movement from the car had been the determined flapping of the wipers.

When, trout-wet, Dot opened the door, tumbled her cases, her handbag and then herself onto the back seat, the driver's greeting caught her off guard:

'You filthy motherfucker!'

She wasn't shocked. The utter incongruity of the outburst forbade that. She simply felt as if she'd been goosed, emotionally.

'I…'

The driver turned, his shirt covered with sweat; the material creased like a walrus's paunch. He gestured with his index finger, killing two birds by using it first to suggest she pause, and then to indicate the black plastic tongue curling from his ear, the tip of which was pulsing with a pin-prick blue light.

'Uh huh... No, no. Go on.'

Dot waited as the driver continued his call, for the most part a symphony of grunts, snorts and harrumphs dropped to reassure his interlocutor that he was still listening. After a couple of minutes he paused. In the rear-view mirror Dot saw a flare of panic in his eyes:

'The Aristocrats? Ha! Wait... What?' Another pause. 'No, no. I get it... It's just... *What?*' He flicked the ignition and the car choked to life. Then, with a lurch of acceleration they were away, out of Trapp Street and onto the main road, refusing the slow and poetic farewell between herself and the receding bungalow that she'd played out so many times in her mind since deciding to sell it.

'No, no, Mike. That was a good one,' the driver said. 'Who've I got up next? Jenks? The old cun...' His eyes collided with Dot's in the mirror. 'The old *guy* with the colostomy bag? Jesus, Mike! Last time I drove him he leaked all over the seat. Took me a fortnight to... What's that? Bin liners? Well I could, Mike, but I'm not sure I'll be able to convince him to climb into one!'

His meaty hands crashed onto the dashboard as he wheezed his satisfaction with the joke. The driver was a big man. Not fat exactly, but solid – an ancient standing stone spirited to life. He dragged his sleeve across his nose. Dot ached to intervene, to reach forward and clip the rogue behind the ear. They're never too old to fear the sting. But she couldn't. What had happened to her? Had forty-five years of classroom hardening drained away overnight?

Dot thought of the formidable specimen she had become by the time she'd retired at the age of seventy: a smoky, combative old dame, with a line in dry wit that was two parts Wilde, three parts London Gin. She'd been the kind of teacher only appreciated several years down the line, when a safe distance had been achieved and maintained. Her pupils might remember how she would shy her *Collected Shakespeare* across the room, clocking the crown of a classroom gossiper, but they would also jolly well remember every word of Macbeth's dagger soliloquy until their dying days. Unless of course…

No. The woman Dot had been when she retired would never have put up with such insolence from a taxi driver. But a lot can happen in four years. She'd been dry most of that time, and had even given up the smokes.

'Yeah,' the driver said. 'Shouldn't be too long now, anyway. Take it easy, Mike.'

Then, spying his chance to join the beetling rows of cars, he flung the Cortina into the outside lane.

After about a quarter of an hour, the traffic slowed, then stopped. The driver started beating a dislocated drum solo on the steering wheel and sighed, the air whistling through his dry lips to the accompaniment of the thumping wipers.

Dot pulled the brochure from her handbag and flipped through it. It had the same vaguely chemical odour as the expensive fashion magazines in her doctor's waiting room, the same way of flopping open in the hands, the same luxurious heft. She traced the gold-embossed logo on the cover: the silhouette of an acorn that seemed, perversely, to be smirking. There wasn't much text, just the name of the place – Green Oaks – in a childish font and below, in squint-or-you'll-miss-it grey, the words 'A West Church Holding'.

Behind the acorn was a photo of an old manor – Tudor? Georgian? Leonard would have known – roosting atop a verdant hillock, flanked by two wizened oak trees, their foliage a tapestry of the ochres and rust reds of cliché's autumn. The cloudless sky shone with the gilded blue of late afternoon, although the sun and its long contemplative shadows were absent, lending the scene an uncanny lack of depth.

Dot got the message. Even the most addled of her pupils could have. It was hardly subtle: *You may have reached the autumn of your life, the twilight of your years*, it crooned, in that flashy, mercantile tone everything seemed to have these days – *but you needn't be afraid. Because look, not only is this the natural way of all things, of the day, of the seasons, it is also, in some way, quite beautiful, something to be cherished.*

Codswallop! Bilge, bosh, bunk and blarney! No, anyone who had reached the age of admittance to a place like this and could still be manipulated so easily was a dupe who had learnt almost nothing from life.

Inside were more sugar-blasted photos of the grounds, along with floating testimonials from several residents. What a handsome bunch of eeries! There was an extra-terrestrial glassiness to their eyes, as if they had been imported from the propaganda of some futuristic dystopia, or an advert for some Japanese video game for retraining flaccid, geriatric brains. A world from which dirt and other imperfections had been meticulously, but brutally, erased. A TV world, in which even the uglies were beautiful.

They were all smiling, of course. Not at the camera, but at something just beyond it. And they could smile, looking like that! Whereas Dot had rotted and shrivelled over the years, an old plum with her own patina of bluish mould, these models had been matured in oak caskets. Whereas her skin was desert-cracked, theirs had softened and creased like fine Italian shoe-leather. Whereas her hair had thinned out into a substanceless scaffold of a do, theirs was as vigorous and bushy as squirrel tails.

Strangest, though, was not what their faces showed, but what they didn't. Where was the sadness, where the pain of loss that she saw etched into her own face? Where the resignation? Where the runnels carved by the unquenchable tears shed over the 'For Sale' stakes planted in the gardens of *their* bungalows?

A question nipped at her mind. That voice again: *Why do you think any of these fine specimens of humanity – so much finer than you, by the way, so spared, coddled and closeted by life – would have chosen to enter the purgatorial world of residential care?* Although she also knew that she'd been lied to by the brochure. These were not the faces she would meet at Green Oaks.

But Dot didn't care. She was done with illusions. She was going to Green Oaks to expire. Rattling off to die, however long it took. Her life was over, and she no longer regretted the fact. Not since everything that had happened to Leonard. She had no more ambitions, no more hopes, and all of her dreams were backwards looking now.

She might have just died at home of course, saving even more money for Thomas's inheritance, but it wasn't as easy as it sounded. In the six weeks since Leonard's internment at Green Oaks, there had always been something to do, someone to see, some appearance to keep up or obligation to fulfil. Something always drawing her back to life.

Not least Thomas's phone calls from Cologne. They were dutiful, regular (he had never called her so often) – and short. He would press her for reassurance that she was 'alright' without Dad. Well she wasn't alright. Never would be again. Although she didn't say that to Thomas. Hilde was behind the calls, Dot knew. It wasn't about Thomas or Dot, but about Kristofer, their son, and the lessons he would learn concerning how a man should treat his ageing mother. This was long-term planning at its most Teutonic. It grieved Dot that Thomas felt obliged to call her – he was off living his life, just as he should be, he owed her nothing – but it was always nice to hear his voice.

She had thought, and in some way hoped, that Thomas would be cross with her when she told him she'd sold up and checked them both into the home. And he had tried his best to play the part. But what she'd heard beneath the pleas for her to reconsider was an unmistakable note of gratitude. And Dot couldn't blame him. Institutions like Green Oaks existed as much for the young as they did for the old. Nobody should have to see that.

So, she might have been determined to let go of life, but that was just the half of it. Life, it seemed, was a kind of celestial compact and the universe clearly wasn't ready to let go of Dot. She was going to have to wrestle herself from its clutches, its petty exigencies, hop off its hamster wheel and just lie down beside Leonard and let the whole sorry joke run to its punchline without her.

Part of the problem, she suspected, was that life, in all its prickly realness, just doesn't fit the narrative arc we demand of it. It is an arc she'd taught every year, *to* every year, during their composition lessons.

'Exposition,' she would intone as the chalk inscribed the beginning of the arc on the blackboard, a line, almost horizontal, rising slowly from left to right. 'Complication,' she would go on, as the line began its steep ascent. 'Climax,' she would stress as the line peaked, and then, as if it came as a blessed relief, 'Resolution' she would almost sigh, the squeaking chalk giving her emotions voice. Exposition, Complication, Climax, Resolution, and perhaps, if you were lucky, a Denouement. It seemed funny to her now that she had never thought, and none of her pupils had ever asked, what came after the Resolution, after the Denouement. Were we just supposed to imagine that the characters froze in time or ceased to exist? Was the Happily-Ever-After assumed without debate? At least now she had an answer to the question.

What came after the Resolution? Simple: Green Oaks.

'Finally!' the cabbie exclaimed as his turn to accelerate came. Then, because it was apparently beyond his control, his whole being having attained at-one-ment with the spirit of Platitudinous Guff: 'Life goes on, eh?'

Oh no you don't! Not that old sentimental chestnut! Life goes on. Or how about: You only live once. Or why not: *Carpe Diem.* Dream as if you'll live forever, live as if you'll die today. Life is what happens when you're making other plans... *Ach!* The whole tide of hackneyed phrases, long debunked by the keen scalpel of experience, surged across Dot's mind like a diarrhoeal wave. And she sensed the driver was itching to loose a sequel. Well, too bad for him! She could feel the old Dot – the brassy matron who had divided the staffroom as much as the classroom – rising up.

'Shut your trap and drive!' she hissed.

Not dead yet then. Not quite.

2

Half an hour later, as the car farted over the cattle-grid onto the winding driveway, Dot was beset by a peculiar feeling. She thought of the rare occasions on which she had flown, visiting Thomas in Germany, of the ear-popping moment the descent began and pressure in the cabin struggled to keep up. The rain had stopped too, quite abruptly, as if the car had passed between weather fronts or even – Dot indulged herself – between worlds.

The driver left the headlights trained on the front porch as he unloaded the vehicle, first of its human charge and then of the three small cases – brown leather oblongs, stolid and battered. The door of the manor house – Edwardian? Oh, who cares! – was opened by a thick-set skinhead in a dirty overall, the stump of a burnt out rollie planted in the corner of his mouth.

'You made it then?' offering neither his name nor his hand. 'I'm not even supposed to be working now.'

He eyeballed Dot's cases on the porch, then turned and walked back into the dimly lit hallway. A thick black claw curled up above the overall's collar, the crown of what must have been a hideous tattoo. After a couple of steps he stopped and without turning said:

'It's an insurance thing. Ain't covered for lifting when off duty. Besides, I'm not the bellboy.'

His drift caught, Dot stooped to pick up her cases and followed him into the hall. She couldn't make out much of the decor. What light there was glanced off the moulded doorframes, hinting at the bourgeois grandeur of the place while revealing nothing about its conservation. Her sense of smell was not equally spared. The cabbagey miasma, flecked with intimations of laboratory-contrived bouquets, pricked at her throat. She licked her lips and swallowed hard.

It was the smell of decay – animal and vegetable. All too familiar to someone with as many years chalked up as Dot. The *pot pourri* of human life. The memory dredged up by the smell was not, however, of her last days with Leonard. Instead it was of a walk she'd taken with Thomas, past Palmer's Weir and along the river, before he moved to Germany. They had come across the rotting carcass of a badger and Dot had almost fainted because of the stink. Thomas had taken her by the arm and led her away to a nearby bench. Her breathing had become fitful, scissoring up and down a musical scale of her own invention. Thomas had tried, in his scientist's fashion, to reassure her, explaining that it was just nature's way of recycling the energy pent up in the badger's body, that everything, from the actions of the tiniest bacterium, to the movements of the largest stars, could be described as energy in motion, as the universe tending towards its natural equilibrium. As if, at the moment of its birth, it had been like a tightly wound spring, and all of this was just the spring unwinding, the universe running down. He'd given her the word for it too: Entropy. It wasn't a new word to her, but she had remembered and cherished it as she would any gift from her little boy. The comfort he'd seemed to find in his explanation though, had eluded her then as it eluded her still.

Not-the-Bellboy was waiting next to an open door at the end of the hall, beside an impressive grandfather clock. On the other side of the clock a white metal gate blocked access to an elegant stairwell.

'Ward B. Third cot on the right,' he said when she caught up with him, indicating with a nod that he considered his duties well discharged.

'Third on the right?' Dot mumbled. 'I was under the impression my husband and I would have private rooms.'

'Under that impression, were you? Funny how that happens. No private rooms here, lady. Should've read the brochure closer.' The unexpected assonance of his last sentence clearly satisfied him and he chuckled. 'Easy mistake.'

Dot wanted to protest but realised she just couldn't summon the fight. Not after today. Not after the last few months. Not alone.

Now she just wanted to find Leonard, to check how he was, to take hold of his hand and lie down to sleep… well, if not beside him, then at least much closer to him than she had done of late.

'Third on the right,' he said again, impatient now. Perhaps, anyway, he was right. Perhaps she should have read the brochure closer. She couldn't now recall any specific mention of private quarters, only of 'privacy'. No mention of independent rooms either, only of 'independence'.

Dot walked past him and into Ward B. Even in the poor light she could see how barren it was: seven metal cots, five of them occupied, four up one side of the long rectangular room, three up the other. It was cold too, architecturally, the original mouldings stripped away. Beside each cot was a cabinet, just a small cupboard and a couple of shelves. All of the bodies, but one, were still. The one that wasn't – on the left nearest the door – writhed and squirmed as if doing battle with an incubus.

Dot's gut buckled – Leonard wasn't there! She hadn't examined every cot, she didn't need to. She had ESP for her husband's presence that could put a Scotland Yard sniffer dog to shame. None of these blanketed bundles was him…

'Wait,' Not-the-Bellboy hissed behind her. Dot stopped, anticipating the correction of some grave error. Savouring the moment, she turned slowly.

'Yes?'

'Your watch?' he whispered.

'My what?'

'Your watch. I'm going to need it.'

'For what?'

'For nothing. Choking hazard.'

Oh, how Classroom Dot would have roasted this young upstart. *Choking hazard, my eye!*

'Here,' she said, loosing the strap and handing him the watch. What did it matter? It was just a five-pound quartz from the catalogue. Nothing sentimental. He turned it over in his hand then slipped it into his overall pocket.

'Excuse me?' Dot said, hoping her cooperation might have lubricated the exchange. 'I'm sorry to be a bother, but it's just, my husband…'

He looked away from her, scratched his stubble.

'What about him?'

'Well, and as I said, I really don't mean to be a bother but… well… he's not here.'

A few seconds passed before he turned his gaze back.

'What am I?' he said.

'It's just he's supposed to be… Excuse me?'

'What. Am. I?'

'You're…'

'Am I the bellboy?' He took a step closer to Dot.

'Excuse me?'

'Am. I. The. Bellboy?'

'No, you're…' Her voice cracked. She cursed herself for the display of weakness.

'No,' he said. 'Because if I was the bellboy I'd have helped you with your cases, wouldn't I? So try again.'

Dot gathered herself:

'You're the…' Actually, what the *hell* was he?

'Am I the manager?'

Classroom Dot saw an opening.

'Not bloody likely!'

If her barb found its mark, he didn't flinch.

'Do I have a shirt with sweat stains under the armpits, a polyester tie, trousers two sizes too small, and a pathological fear of the residents?'

Dot shook her head.

'No, I don't. All of which means I'm not Mister Cornish and therefore have no idea concerning the whereabouts of your husband. He could be in Vegas for all I care, getting married to a stripper by a Big Bopper lookalike, because all the Elvises are *h'*otherwise *h'*engaged. I know that's where *I'd* rather be. But I'm Pat. I'm nobody. I change sheets. I empty bedpans. And my only rule – my only *fucking* rule – is that when I'm not on duty, I don't *do* residents.' He started walking back to the door, then turned. 'I mean. Administrative error? Administrative arse! One, two, three, four, five, six…' – counting off the cots with his pointer – 'And the Indian made seven… how hard was that?'

Harder than it should have been for a boy of your age, Dot thought.

'So, for the last time, third cot on the right.'

Dot was trembling. From fear, humiliation or anger, she didn't know. *This* – she told herself – *is not over.* But even though the thought rose up within her, the fight didn't. She felt hollowed out, a lone matryoshka doll with nothing inside. She told herself it would be better in the morning. Perhaps then she would raise hell until her husband was returned to her.

She walked towards her cot. Of the empty two it was the second on the right, not the third, that looked as if it had been prepped for her arrival. The sheets and blanket had been tucked in with an almost military precision, whereas those on the third cot – hers, if the boy was not mistaken – were twisted into a cone. She stopped in front of the second and craned round to see if he was still there. He was. Catching her gaze, he shook his head and motioned that she was to continue on. And indeed, the cabinet belonging to the second cot wasn't empty. There was a small stack of old magazines and a crushed packet of cigarettes on the upper shelf, and a tattered pair of mud-caked slippers tucked just underneath.

Dot looked again at the third cot. She wasn't a demanding woman, but it seemed wrong that on her first night here she should be obliged to make her own bed fit for sleeping in.

She heard the door close behind her, then keys rattle, bite and turn in the lock. For a moment she considered climbing into the immaculate cot and to hell with the consequences. But the well-raised girl in her intervened. She set her cases on the floor and punted them under the cot she'd been assigned. A groundswell of tiredness swept through her body.

Letting her overcoat slide from her shoulders and pool on the floor, she fell forward onto the mattress and entwined herself in the sheets and blanket.

A new odour assaulted her now. A rotten, nitrous, male odour, all too familiar. A warmth too – animal again – but her tired brain refused to grapple with that. While she loathed emotional indulgence in novels, real life could be more tolerant of the occasional rampant cliché:

'Oh, Leonard, Leonard, Leonard!' she whispered. 'Leonard, my darling. What have I done?'

A fat tear escaped from her eye, cementing the scene.

'*Shut it!*' someone across the ward hissed, shattering it.

10 SEX FAULTS THAT MAKE YOU DISGUSTING TO WOMEN

AIR SOULS!

THE BELLY OF THE WHALE
A CAPTAIN RUGGLES NOVELETTE

25¢

THE BELLY OF THE WHALE

A CAPTAIN RUGGLES NOVELETTE

*The hardest battle a Limey commando
had to fight was against the ghosts of his own mind!*

I

Captain Dylan Prometheus Ruggles, British army first airborne division, was born at twelve hundred feet, through a slit in a sky measled with stars. A naked manikin, a hand span in height but fully matured, a search-and-destroy mission hardwired in his genes. A foundling, a celestial bastard, an orphan charged to the universe's care. A military experiment. A character in a bad novel.

Not yet burdened with consciousness, Ruggles drifted across the starscape as his body sprouted. A rootless tree possessed. Skin stretched, gave, wrinkled. Bones lost density, knobbled and arced. Hair greyed in chalky streaks. From his backpack a cord wound umbilically back to the birthing slit; a vertical wink of light against the inky darkness. His mind looped with partial thoughts and unanchored memories.

His mouth spoke, 'I...' and gravity interrupted with a jolt. He dropped, but only to the length of the cord. A yank at the pack, a whip crack, and the furled membrane of a parachute blossomed over his head. A ridged silk placenta softening his descent, a canopy barring the heavens from view, barring his retreat forever.

Easing earthwards Ruggles felt himself into his body, into the world. The air at this height was cold and his bare skin crawled. His feet throbbed, laced into paratrooping boots – calf-high, beetle black. The ground below flashed with toy explosions, phosphorescence in the gloomy, uncharted sea. Distant mechanical thunderclaps rumbled asynchronously with the flashes. His mud-green trousers flapped and snapped in the breeze, his combat jacket rippled.

Nascent thoughts ran first *Dulcie*, then *search-and-destroy*.

At eight hundred feet he could make out treetops and hedgerows and a river. In a clearing he saw three rows of huts, long and thin, witheringly institutional. Padding his uniform he felt a folded map, a book of some sort and a packet of *Gaspers*. He plucked one, crumpled it against his tongue, chewed it into a wad, then stuffed the pack into the band of his helmet. His kaleidoscope mind sharpened.

Spiralled and tossed like a dandelion seed – 'angels' Dulcie called them – his trajectory the whimsy of the eddying air. He was headed for the trees, for the huts, for the trees again and then for the banks of the river. At three hundred feet, the wind's last caprice snapped him back into line with the huts and whisked him into the final plughole vortex.

He saw fences and a watchtower. Beyond the fences were two monstrous figures, nightmarish sentries, five times the height of any man. Giants. Their *Stahlhelme* shoving skywards, two raging steel *glandes penium*. He pedalled against the void, swam. Imagining himself a bird, he flapped. No use! Fortune, that mischievous bitch, had played her hand, marked him as a prisoner. A hundred feet, seventy, fifty. A tube of light from one of the watchtowers swept across his path. Thirty, he slackened his legs for landing. Fifteen, ten, five.

Contact.

His feet sank into the churned soil and – he could have sworn it! – the earth rippled, pulsed with concentric circles. The huts juddered, skipped, and for the briefest moment, a single frame spliced in this disaster film, his mind mocked him with a vision of England, of tumbling hills, of a strange manor house, of an ambulance, its back doors leering open.

His body crumpled and he lost consciousness. Far, far above the white slit blinked once, flexed as though smiling, then closed forever.

II

Captain Ruggles awoke naked in a puddle of cold urine. The smell, camphoric and sweet, tickled his nostrils but was not unpleasant. He was alone in a small cell, barren and not much larger than a closet, with a barred window at one end and a door at the other.

His thoughts were muggy, as if he'd been asleep for some time, or drugged, and his throat pricked. No matter how much he ransacked his mind's outlying regions, Ruggles couldn't locate any scrap of intelligence concerning what had happened to him after he'd landed, how he'd been stripped and transported to the cell, and by whom. The forgotten events simply would not be located, as if they had been detached from his memory, torn out, victim to a coupon-cutter's need for (thorough and gentle, no shock!) Bowellax pills. Otherwise he was unhurt, tired certainly, but that was to be expected after the previous night.

What rotten, rotten luck that the wind had sabotaged his mission before it had even started. He knew that the Krauts had some formidable allies, but if they had now inveigled Zephyrus into the Axis, the war was as good as lost.

Whatever was going on, his priority was to contact HQ. To let them know he was alive, that the mission had been an abysmal failure, but that he was fit, and ready to do whatever they required of him from his newly compromised position. He was also keen to make contact with any other detainees, to pool intelligence and orchestrate an escape. But all of that would have to wait. At least until he could find a way out of this cell.

The shriek of a whistle warbled through the window, piercing to the heart of his ruminations. The window had been built high up into the wall, giving the cell a disjointed aspect, accentuated by the way it tapered towards the door. A room conceived to taunt its occupant with its unabashed, chew-up-and-spit-out, machinal inhumanity.

Despite being a stately six-foot-two, Ruggles was a good twenty inches shy of being able to see through the window and out into the yard. Still, twenty inches were nothing to a man of military bent. A quick spring and grab manoeuvre saw him hanging from the bars, his body right-angled, a perfect weight distribution between his ropy arms and equine legs, planted five feet up the wall. His soldier's body could be twisted to almost any request Ruggles made of it, make any habitat its own. Just then, he'd channelled the grimping powers of the koala in its eucalyptus tree, and felt at home at once. He could dangle so for hours if need be. He could even allow himself to free one hand to disentangle and scratch his slingshot genitals, perhaps the only part of his body over which he had limited dominion.

The yard was populated by his fellow inmates, harlequin-like in their tattered fatigues. What struck him at once was the good number of women – almost unheard of on the battlefield. None of the Allied powers recruited women to serve on the front line, as far as he knew. He had heard the rumours of the American Vixen Assassin Squads – what red-blooded Tommy hadn't? – but he'd never actually believed in them. Hadn't they just been conjured up by propagandists to inject fire into the bellies of the lower ranks – the delicious, though distant, prospect of encountering one of these burlesque princesses being enough to harden the wavering resolve of any tail-starved squaddie. But if so, where had these damsels in the yard sprouted from, and why had they not been segregated from the men?

Neither was the physical condition of the detainees encouraging. They were being put through their paces by one of the camp guards, an insipid slapstick of stretches that even the most vigorous among them struggled through like sorry old acrobats. Where was the Anglo-Saxon vim that the newspapers back home bragged of every day? Had that – like the Vixens – been merely another flake in the confetti shower of desperate propaganda scattered from the bunkers of Whitehall?

He turned his attention from the yard and out past the high wire fences. On the horizon he again saw the tall figures which, in the delirium of his descent, he'd taken for giants, horrifying progeny of the Nazi laboratories. In the truth-loving light of morning, he saw them for what they were – the skeletons of ruined smock mills, with timber caps he'd mistaken for *Stahlhelme* and shattered sails in place of the bolt action rifles. He had thought he was being dropped into ██████████ ████████████████████████, but now suspected the pilot had veered off course and chucked him out somewhere over Holland. More rotten luck. While he spoke French with ease, *il parlait néerlandais comme une vache espangole.* Any escape plan would have to grapple with this hobbling reality. Releasing the bars, he kicked off against the wall, turned a double somersault in the air, and punched his feet into the floor – a perfect stuck landing.

His uniform was folded in neat squares just beside the door – jacket, trousers and handkerchief piled in order of size. He picked them up, pressed his face into them and inhaled the scent of industrial springtime. Someone had taken, laundered and pressed his fatigues. What a strange thing for Jerry to have done! He had been instructed in the queer old-maidish tendencies of certain Nazis – a quality that somehow made their equally reputed sadism shimmer with enhanced grisliness – and he attributed this quirk to that. Their perverse spirits being excited in direct proportion to the dapperness of their torture victim. It made sense in a way: the more dignified, the more human, the captive, the further he could be dragged down and debased. Still, this treatment could perhaps be the quirk of a single, prudish guard, a man repulsed by the sight of grime, a fairy perhaps, and if this were so it might be something Ruggles could later use to his advantage.

He slipped into his fatigues, looser than he remembered them. The jacket bagged about his abdomen and the trousers, its buttoned waistband limp, hung from his hips as though pegged on a washing line. He tugged on the collar and checked the name inked inside. Ruggles, D.P. – his uniform alright. He lifted his jacket at the waist and went to pinch an inch of skin, but was shocked when four pallid inches came. The grotesque attenuation of his body meant he would have to start reckoning on his delirium having endured more than the eight or so hours he'd previously assumed. But how long? Two days? Seven? Forty? Really, he had no way of knowing, and such ignorance was dangerous for a soldier. When the balance of a war might tip in a matter of days, none of the intelligence he had been briefed on before boarding the Whitley could now be assumed to hold.

'So' – Ruggles thought – 'in this vile snakes-and-ladders conflict, I have paratrooped directly onto a serpent's head and slithered down to…' Well, he couldn't even be sure he was back to square one. At least with square one, you knew where you were and what lay ahead. Ruggles was lost, compass-less and alone on this vast bomb-pocked tundra. And worse, no matter which direction his honed soldier-sense might wish to lead him, he was cooped up in this prison camp, as flightless as a pinioned bird.

Ruggles waited for a long time, how long he couldn't fathom, and when still nobody came, he permitted his heavy head to loll and sleep to rise over him once again.

III

The young girl's voice warbled as if being channelled through a tin whistle.

'Daisy, Daisy, give me your answer do…'

Prising open his eyes, Ruggles lifted his head.

'I'm half crazy, all for the love of you…'

'Dulcie?' His voice barely scratched the air of the cell.

'I'm sorry Daddy,' said the girl. 'I didn't mean to wake you.' Ruggles shook his head and batted away the girl's apology.

'Dum-de-dum-dum marriage.'

'I can't afford a carriage.'

'But you'll look sweet, upon the seat of a bicycle made for two!' Ruggles lifted his leaden arms and clapped. The young girl, who until this moment had been sitting in a chair across the cell from him, stood and bounced a dainty curtsy. Ruggles ground the backs of his bruised wrists into his eyes. His vision cleared and he swallowed back a thrust of emotion.

She was here. His angel. Her robin's-egg eyes, her ruddy cheeks, her gossamer hair, that chipped tooth, cried over for days then worn proudly as a badge of creeping maturity. All here.

'Pinch yourself, Daddy,' she said and laughed again. He did, on the back of his hand. She was right to recommend it. Such apparitions were the stock-in-trade of dreams or heat-oppressed minds. The feeling of fingernails scoring crescents into flesh was blissful. He was awake, percipient. This was no dream, no hallucination, then. She was here. She had come for him.

'Dulcie,' he said again, for he could think of no other word nor had any desire to do so. Dulcie crossed the cell and took his head in her arms. Ruggles lolled into her grasp, allowed his head to be cradled against her ribs. She toyed with a tongue of his hair, twisting it about her fingers.

'It's so good to see you Daddy. It's been so long.'

'I know. I know,' trying not to sob in front of his daughter. 'But Daddy's got some things to do right now. Important things.'

'What things?'

'Just…' He flicked at the air with his hand. 'Just this. The war. England.'

'What war, Daddy? There is no war. Not anymore,' a hairline fracture to her voice.

'No war?'

'No, Daddy.'

'No Germans?' He could feel her small body trembling against his skull, then the patter of tears on his crown. His angel was crying.

'No Germans either.'

Ruggles' mind waltzed. Someone must have been trying to protect the poor girl, hiding the truth from her these four long years.

'But the Germans...' he tried again.

'*Shhh*,' she said. 'That's enough of all that now. It's that kind of nonsense that got you transferred here in the first place.' Was that impatience edging into her voice? A voice which, come to think of it, was not quite the voice he remembered. He wriggled from her embrace and eyeballed the girl. She looked like Dulcie, more or less, though perhaps her chin was a little more pointed, her skin a little more mottled than...

'Who are you?' he thought or said. The girl took a couple of steps away from him.

'I can't take all this. Not at the moment. ██████████████ ██████'

'Who are you?' No doubt he had spoken this time. The whole cell trembled with his frustrated insistence.

'Forget it!' she said sadly. 'You're halfway there already.' At this, the skin of Dulcie's face turned a very dark grey, powdered and cracked, becoming a kind of living sculpture of baked earth. Then, like a column of unflicked *Gasper* ash losing its battle with gravity, the apparition collapsed in a tsunami of dust, engulfing Ruggles and revealing what had been imprisoned inside: an intense blue ball of gyrating light, a Catherine-wheel apparition, spitting sparks and smoke as it whirled in the gloom of the cell. The brilliance of the light forced Ruggles to squint, but he could have sworn that as the light burnt itself out, the smoke took on different forms ending with the silhouette of the Führer, a defiant smile contorting his monstrous gargoyle's kisser.

Ruggles lay on the floor, his rib cage waxing and waning, double time, matching his sawing breath, and clutching a black and white photo of a young girl, smiling in front of a swing.

IV

How long after this Ruggles was released from solitary was impossible to know, but released he finally was, billeted to *Zellenblock B*.

The ruinous condition of his cellmates was quickly confirmed. They were a miscreated, dilapidated squadron, if ever he'd seen one. And more distressing even than that was the presence of Karmacharya, his old Hindoo friend, so far from his natural habitat. It had been many years since Ruggles had seen him, not since a disastrous mission they had undertaken together in the Kush when he was still a Private. And what a toll the years, or the prison, had taken on him – he was almost unrecognisable! Whereas before his thick, dark hair had shimmered like celluloid, now it hung in lustreless hanks. Even worse, his eyes, once so sharp, so alive, so possessed with scientific wonder, stared blankly, as if at nothing. But worst of all was that he gave no indication that he recognised Ruggles, as if everything they had lived through together had been wiped from his brain's slate.

He was further disheartened to realise that there was not a single one of his fellow prisoners he could count on to be physically or spiritually robust enough to act as his batman when the moment came to orchestrate an escape. The camp had broken them. It wasn't just that their bodies had cracked and curled in on themselves, prematurely aged, for even here that could be corrected with a little discipline. It was their spirits that he most despaired of, their hangdog passivity and pitiful cooperativeness with the regime. What fight they once may have possessed had been catheterised, sucked out by the guards as a wolf laps marrow from the bones of its kill.

Ruggles inhabited this predicament, this Gordian knot writ prison-size, for more than a year, isolated in his struggle. At times he was again the victim of cruel hallucinations, taunted with visions of rural England, of manor houses and oak trees, and of devils dressed up in gross parody of family members and friends – though never again Dulcie – urging him, as he had been urged in that first cell, to give up the fight, to lower his dukes. But he never caved, always resisted, cast the evil spirits out with insults and violence. And after a while he was victorious... they simply stopped coming.

During the months that followed, some of his fellow prisoners disappeared, and new ones arrived, but the tight-knit quiescence held.

Then, at the end of his thirteenth month in the camp, everything changed. One grey morning, when he was tumbled back into the canteen after another night in solitary, Karmacharya had vanished and a new prisoner sat in his chair. A woman, but with a masculine, donkey-like hardiness. She wore the uniform of a Tommy, and wore it well. In this lowly private, Ruggles at once intuited the Answer, the Knot-cutter, the Yin to his Yang. An alliance with this woman, Ruggles saw, was his best, his only chance of freedom. The question was, would she see this herself?

*Will Brit soldier Ruggles pull off
a spiffing, can-do escape?*

*Will he convince the reluctant
lady Private to join him?*

*And what became of
the ailing Hindoo?*

All this and more, only in the next issue of:

AIR SOULS!

On newsstands the 5th of EVERY month.

Her first morning at Green Oaks, Dot's eyes weighed heavy and were gounded shut. The night had been restless, punctuated with dreams. They had washed over her like the black waves of an oil spill – swelling, crashing, then receding to make way for the next. All that remained, now she'd been pitched onto the shores of wakefulness – albeit with the water still lapping at her arthritic ankles – were a handful of blurred images and the clipped flutter of anxiety. Coming to a little more, Dot felt something fleshy, calloused and warm resting on her forehead. A hand! Its clamminess suggested it had been there a while. Despite her surprise, Dot felt comforted. She decided to lie still for as long as the hand was there, for as long as it took to unpick the events of the previous night…

But her body intervened, a clod of mucus slumping into her throat. She coughed. Gently, the hand shifted, the thumb and middle finger searching out and massaging her temples.

'Stirring at last, Lord,' a voice said to itself. 'Hello? Hello my darling? Can you hear me?'

Dot blinked through the gum of sleep. The hand was affixed to the end of a clubby arm, and the arm to the largest woman she'd ever seen: a planetary black lady in a baby-pink sleeveless nightgown, her naked, football-sized paps floating weightlessly underneath. Their eyes met and the woman smiled, her whole face creasing amiably along familiar, well-worn lines. For a moment, Dot wanted nothing more than to burrow down into the rolling folds of flesh. Make a nest of the woman. A home.

In the daylight the ward looked even more barren than it had the night before. Seven cots, seven cabinets. Four folding chairs. Three windows along one wall. Six neon strip-lights. Four bedpans in the corner. And that was it. The bare minimum to fulfil some bean-counter's definition of a ward, to make it feel real.

And no Leonard.

Dot made to sit up but the hand held her firmly in place. The woman shook her head and shushed.

'We're in no hurry, darling,' she said. 'No hurry at all.'

You may not be – Dot wanted to say – *I, however, have...* But she held her tongue. The woman was right, of course. What were a few minutes when there was nothing left to hurry for, nothing to get up for, get dressed for, put up a front for? She had planned things that way, of course, but how odd it now felt.

'What are they calling you?' the woman asked. Dot snagged on the peculiar construction, but attributed it to one of those creases of foreignness that can never be fully ironed out.

'Dot... Dotty... Dorothy...'

The woman arced her eyebrows, as though to say she got the joke but disapproved of it nonetheless. She lifted her hand from Dot's forehead and balanced it on her ballooning bosom:

'Welcome to Ward B, Dot. They call me Betty.'

Before Dot could indulge in any pleasantries, a terrierish yelping erupted in the hallway. A woman skittered into the ward, moving with the chopstick awkwardness of a wading bird. A broom-head waved and prodded after her. Moments later a hand grabbed hold of the knob and yanked the door shut.

'I know what you're doing!' she shrieked at the closed door. 'You may have the others fooled but not me...' She turned away from the door and gobbed a fountain of pills onto the floor. 'Fuckers!'

'Olive!' Dot knew Betty's tone. It was laced with all the school ma'am authority she had built up herself over the decades and which, these last months, seemed to have evaporated. 'You know they're for your own good.'

Olive crushed a pill beneath her unslippered foot.

'For there is no authority except which... except which God has established? Romans what is it, Bets?'

'Thirteen, one to seven, clever-clogs.'

Olive cackled.

'Stop it, now. You're upsetting our new friend.'

Dot waved off Betty's concern, true as it was. Olive weedled a final capsule from under her tongue and hurled it at the door. She froze.

'New friend?' she asked, without turning around.

'That's right. Come meet Dotty.'

Olive peeked over her shoulder, caught Dot's eye, then snapped her gaze back to the door.

'Hullo,' Dot attempted.

Olive thumped to the floor. Dot's greeting had apparently had the effect of a well-trained bullet. Dot sat bolt upright. Betty put a hand on her shoulder.

'What happened to old Kalka?' It was Olive, calling from the floor, apparently unperturbed by her new horizontal alignment.

'Shouldn't we help her?' Dot said to Betty.

Betty shook her head, whispered:

'Don't encourage her, Dot. It only makes things worse.'

'She fell really hard—'

'It happens all the time,' Olive interrupted. 'Dropsy!'

Betty rolled her eyes.

'How many times, Olive? They diagnosed you with catalepsy, not dropsy!'

'But I *drop*, don't I?'

Betty's hands flew up in defeat, but there was affection to her exasperation.

'Just ignore me,' Olive called over to Dot. 'I'll be right as rain in a minute or two.'

'If you're sure,' Dot said.

'You didn't answer my question, Bets,' Olive went on.

'Which question?'

'Where's Kalka gone?'

Betty's nose wrinkled.

'Tipperary, Olive,' she said. 'Where does anyone here go?'

'Out?' Dot tried. 'Home?'

'Unthinkable!' Betty said, somewhat tersely.

Olive had started hoisting herself up the leg of a cot. Her arms were operating now, but her legs were dangling from her hips, as lifeless as a ventriloquist's dummy's.

'No, no, no... No!' she trilled. 'Kalka wasn't sick... No more than the rest of us, just ask Lanyard, he'll check his notes. And he didn't touch the meat, so it can't have been that.'

'Perhaps,' Betty said, unconvinced. 'But it wasn't only the meat he didn't touch. He hadn't touched any of his food for weeks. It's no surprise he...'

'But he was *here*...' Olive was back on her feet, though shakily. 'Last night. In *this* bed!' and her long arm extended, not towards the empty cot beside Dot's, but to the very one she was in. Remembering the twisted sheets she'd crawled between the previous night, the warmth they had given off, their smell, a chill ran through her.

'Oh God, you don't mean I...'

'Ward C, then!'

'Stop it with that Ward C nonsense, this minute!' Betty barked, a flash of anxiety in her eyes.

'Excuse me,' Dot tried again. 'Whose bed is...'

'Poor devil if it's true. Just the thought of Ward C makes me shudder.'

'Poor devil?' Dot tried, and then stopped. *Leonard*. Was he in Ward C? 'What's wrong with...'

'You look okay, I suppose,' Olive interrupted. 'Just rough enough around the edges to be convincing, but then, they're clever bastards. Cleverer than before... But can we trust you? We don't know who you are, where you've been, who you're with...'

'Enough!' Betty hauled herself to her feet and lumbered across the ward. Olive shrank away at first but upon seeing Betty's outstretched hand, took it.

'Dotty doesn't need to hear this yet,' Betty said.

Olive, as unsteady as a newborn foal on her reactivated legs, let Betty lead her to bed. Tucked in, Olive pulled the sheets over her head.

'She means well,' Betty said, sitting down again. The chair whined its protest. 'But ever since she stopped taking the Phlegmolax she's been a little…' – she paused, searching for the most diplomatic of adjectives – '… mercurial.'

'Rule one, Bets!' Olive's voice muffled from under the sheet. 'Don't swallow their poison.'

'Heaven forbid they might give her something to help with the catalepsy.'

Olive popped up for air, putting on a show for Dot as she rolled her eyes at Betty and mouthed *dropsy*.

'Her problem?' she said. 'Too trusting. That's rule two: Trust nobody. Except Betty. And maybe the Captain too. And, okay, perhaps Smithy. But the rest…' And, catching herself, she scowled distrustfully at Dot and disappeared below the sheet again.

'What was Olive saying about Ward C?' Dot asked.

'Oh, pay no attention to that.' Betty said. 'She'll get used to you soon enough. And you'll get used to her. The others too. Funny thing about this place, people forget quickly.'

Dot smiled thinly: 'One of the few blessings of age.'

'No,' Betty said. 'It's not the same kind of forgetfulness. This seems almost… almost wilful. Take Kalka…' she gestured at Dot's bed.

'Who was he?' Dot asked, feeling a keen desire suddenly to know a little more about the one whose spot she'd usurped. Betty bit her lip:

'He was a Hindu. That I do know. Nice fellow. Didn't say much. But you see so many passing through…'

Olive chuffed loudly.

'Oh you go ahead, lady, make all the noise you want!' Betty shouted. Then, turning back to Dot: 'She thinks it's because of something in the medicine. Or in the food. Something the attendants do to us.'

'The CareFriends, you mean!' Olive sneered.

CareFriends? Dot's soul shrank from the word.

'And what do you think?' she asked.

Betty looked very tired suddenly.

'Unfortunately, my dear, I think it's probably something we do to ourselves.'

4

A <u>SINCERE</u> AND <u>HEARTFELT</u> APOLOGY

STAFF:

Due to circumstances BEYOND MY CONTROL, being, as it is, a dictate IMPOSED from above by WCH management, it is with great professional sadness and more than a modicum of PERSONAL DISTRESS that I must be the MESSENGER of bad news, to whit: a diminution in the number of CareFriend effectives was DEMANDED and has been implemented with IMMEDIATE EFFECT.

Despite FURIOUS REMONSTRATIONS on my part, the BOARD'S DECISION was upheld and the AXE HAS FALLEN.

Follows, an EXHAUSTIVE LIST of those spared its keen edge:

1. Tristan Jenkins – Henceforth, Supervisor
2. Francesca Smithson
3. Patrick Hamilton

— ENDS THE LIST —

This decision is FINAL, NON-NEGOTIABLE and (vitally) <u>WAS NOT</u> MINE TO TAKE. No further discussion will be entered into. It is OUT OF MY HANDS.

Forever yours at this moment of great torment,

Fondly your DIRECTOR,

Raymond Cornish

POST SCRIPTUM:

CLARIFICATION: IF YOUR NAME IS <u>NOT</u> LISTED ABOVE, YOUR SERVICES ARE NO LONGER REQUIRED AT GREEN OAKS. YOU SHOULD HAVE RECEIVED A LETTER.

★

'Uncuntingbelievable.'

'I can just picture him typing that screaming – *Not the face! Not the face!*'

'How can such a massive coward still have such a brass neck?'

'Ally's letter came straight from West Church. Not a word from Corn-nuts himself. And making you supervisor. You? Fucking College Boy!'

Tristan smiled, turned away from Cornish's notice and sat down on the couch. The way its ancient springs received and cradled his body made him feel like he was nestling into a protective exoskeleton.

'Yeah, well I only sent off the applications last week, and I haven't told Cornish yet, so…'

'So you'll swagger around for nine months with a Cheshire cat grin on your fucking puss, while poor Pat and me do the same fucking work for fifty quid a week less?'

'Pat and *I*. And it's a hundred a week less actually,' Tristan said.

'How so?'

'Because with only three of us left, it'll be double shifts all round now.'

'Jesus!' Pat hissed. He was still glaring at the notice, as if he hoped he might pan a nugget of good news from amongst all the gravel.

'And then you'll flounce off to college leaving us to mop up your shit?'

'University,' Tristan muttered. Then, louder: 'That's about the size of it, Frank…'

Before he knew what was happening, the girl had pounced… sailing over the coffee table and thumping down on top of him, her hands zeroing in on his neck. Frankie played like an alley cat – a little too rough, a little too much like she meant it. Tristan could feel his head turning purple.

'Take that back!'

If any other girl had pinned him down like that, he would have got very hard, very quickly. And chances were that was exactly the response any other girl would have been after. But this was Frankie, and it wasn't because her face was rattishly ugly, or that she was a lesbian (he assumed), or that her blonde dreadlocks hummed with a perennial bouquet of mould and weed, or even that her body – dryly muscled, veined with DIY tattoos – made him think of a cabin-boy on a pirate ship, that she produced no sexual response. All those elements might have been negligible if there wasn't something else, something he couldn't put his finger on. It was as if Frankie belonged to a separate species, as if the creature he was wrestling with was not a fellow human being at all, but something more baboon-like… a cousin, but a distant one. Totally unfuckable. Even if she had been displaying swollen, fluo-pink buttocks for his gustatory pleasure – which she wasn't and would have flayed him for even thinking she might – millennia of meticulously constructed taboos would have seen off the slightest rise downstairs.

He pitched her off to one side.

'You fucking ape!'

Frankie laughed.

'I can't believe Ally's gone,' Pat said, only now turning away from the notice.

'Good riddance,' Tristan said.

'You didn't really know him,' Frankie said. 'He was a giggle.'

'A giggle? The guy was a psychopath.'

'Wasn't always,' Frankie said with a shrug. 'Only recently.'

'Seems I missed out on his pussycat phase,' Tristan said.

'And making you Supervisor,' Pat went on. 'I mean, no offence mate, but you're not even full-time. At least, you weren't. Why didn't he give it to Frankie or me?'

'Frankie or *I*,' Tristan whispered.

Frankie leaned forward on the couch, her legs spread blokishly wide and the tongues of her unlaced para boots leering open. She smirked.

'Excuse me, Patrick. I just want to be clear. Are you saying Cornish should've gave it to one of *us*?'

'Why not?'

Frankie inhaled a rasping, derisive laugh.

'Why not? Fucking hell! I'll go easy on you and start with myself. Look at me, Pat. Look. At. Me. I'm a fucking thug. I'm five foot tall in my boots and people still clear out of my way as I walk down the street. Of course, you and me both know I'm a regular little Winnie the Shitstain, right? But I terrify people. I can't believe they even made me a CareFriend, to be honest.' She shook her head: 'Christ, *I* wouldn't have given me the job.'

'Why not me then?' Pat asked. Tristan, winced. This wasn't the first time he'd watched the lamb offer itself up for the slaughter. Wasn't even the first time today.

'Pat, my darling,' Frankie said. 'You've got a good fucking heart, you really have. A good, strong heart. But making you supervisor would be like giving the fucking nuclear codes to a retarded labrador puppy...'

And Frankie rolled off the couch, landed on all fours, and began imitating said puppy, flopping against Pat's legs, her eyes rolling and her tongue lolling out of her mouth.

It would have felt wrong to smile, so Tristan tried not to, but it was hard. Like it or not, when you ran in a pack self-esteem came in a limited supply, and what one person lost got divvied up between the rest. Pat kicked Frankie hard in the ribs.

'I'm going for a shit,' he said, clumping out of the staffroom.

'Aww mate...' – Frankie pulled a face – '... *rank*!'

'Go easy on him,' Tristan said, once the door had closed behind Pat. Frankie rolled onto her back then hopped to her feet with push-puppet agility. She shook her head:

'You don't mean that,' she said. 'So stop pretending.'

Christ though, Tristan was pleased Ally had got the boot. That, more than his promotion, had already made his day. Since he'd started at Green Oaks nine months earlier – when his exam results hadn't quite come good – Tristan had lived in constant fear of this seething colossus. It was fear for himself, primarily, for his continued physical integrity. Ally scattered insults like confetti – about his drainpipe jeans, about his skateboard, about the 'faggot New York' novels he read – but would brook no dissent or counter-repartee, responding with the disproportionate ferocity of a cornered wolf to even the slightest barb. Tristan's only option had been to grin as insult after insult had slapped him in the chops.

But he was also relieved for the Greys. All the CareFriends resented them, but Ally had actively detested them and made no attempt to hide it. His had been a regime of physical punishments, of positive and negative reinforcers, of psychological trickery. And then there was that catchphrase, that he would lisp triumphantly after every hollow victory: '*Child's play!*'

Tristan had already decided he would be more laissez-faire, more live-and-let-live. Minimum contact, minimum interference. Get everybody through it all and out the other end as painlessly as possible. Under Ally, Green Oaks was heading to the edge of a yawning canyon… and if Ally had fallen, he would have pulled everyone down with him. In jettisoning Ally, Cornish – in a flash of what could only be accidental wisdom – had likely spared them all from calamity and disgrace. And Tristan could read his novels in peace.

Still, Frankie's '*Only recently*' had wormed itself in. Could Ally really have been so different before?

'You don't actually give a fuck about me being made supervisor, right?'

Frankie, was standing at the washbasin now, glaring at herself in the mirror, picking something from her teeth with a straightened paperclip.

'Fuck no, suits me down to the ground. More shifts means more money. But I couldn't hack the responsibility.'

'Still paying off the debts?' Tristan asked.

'The fashionable word's *servicing*, mate. Though to be honest, it feels more like it's the debt what's servicing me… day in day out, reaming my puckered little arsehole like it's drilling another Chunnel right through me. And I just can't seem to hold on to what's left because, you know, a girl's got to live…'

'Lipsticks, miniskirts, handbags and tampons, right?' Tristan said.

Frankie turned from the mirror, grinned:

'Fucking tell me about it!'

From her trouser pocket she pulled out a small ziplock bag stuffed with multicoloured pills and tossed it onto the coffee table. Tristan recognised the Phlegmolax and a few of the other low-rent painkillers. But there was one, a bright blue, spherical pill he had never seen before. Shiny and translucent, it almost seemed to glow with an inner light. Frankie slumped into the armchair. Tristan picked up the ziplock bag and held it up to the light.

'Who's this little fella?'

'Which one?'

'The shiny blue bastard.' Frankie looked confused for a moment, then smiled so widely her grey gums – top and bottom – got an airing.

'That, *Mein Führer*, is OxyNyx. One word. Capital O, Capital N.'

'Never heard of it.'

'Right! Neither had I till yesterday, but my friendly street-corner pharmacist says it's going to be *huh-yuge*! It's the new fucking Goliath of opioids, apparently.'

'Is that right?' Tristan said, tossing the bag back to Frankie. She plucked a few of the pills out and lined them up on the table-top.

'Think your pussy psyche will be able handle the new job?' she said. 'It ain't easy going from part-time to double shifts. That's four times the hours, meaning four times the arses to wipe…'

'And four times the corpses to shift…' Pat was back. 'Plus, there's last night's mess to deal with. Job for a virgin supervisor to cut his teeth on, if ever I saw one. Don't know what Cornish was thinking accepting a new resident like that.' He sat down next to Tristan on the couch.

Shit! Kalki. It had been Pat's dumb idea to shift him to Ward A to make room for the new resident, but he couldn't stay there long. If one of the Preemies regained consciousness and realised there was an intruder in their ward – and a dark-skinned one at that – they were done for. Contracts would be lost, heads would roll. But where could they put him? There was just no bed-space.

Ten minutes earlier Kalki had been Ally's problem, not Tristan's. But now… Now he just didn't want to think about it.

'And you skipped the newbie's baptism too,' Frankie said. 'Fucking sloppy.'

'Screw you,' Pat said, though without much malice. 'I wasn't even supposed to be working last night. Now come on Doctor Frankie-stein? Dose me up. There's a long road to travel before home-time.'

'Great,' Tristan said, standing up and walking over to his locker. 'So now I'm going to have two nodding imbeciles on my hands this afternoon, not just one?'

'We could be three nodding imbeciles,' Frankie said. 'If your arse wasn't so fucking stapled up.' Then, she flashed him an inscrutable half-smile and began crushing the pills with the back of a teaspoon.

Tristan opened his locker and pulled an envelope from the inside pocket of his jacket. He had caught the postman in the driveway that morning. His father also being a T. – Tanguy, in his case – gave him the perfect excuse to open Tristan's post, and then to comment on it, casting aspersions on his son's wilting trajectory. Bank statements were examined and tutted over, paperbacks were met with hammily arced eyebrows, and the one time he'd received a love letter... the one *fucking* time! Tristan still seethed when he remembered his father's smirk, that blend of condescension and satisfaction, as he gloated over Annie's florid clichés and unwieldy grammar. ('*From the lowest bottom of my hearts deepest depths...*' – stabbing a soldier into his soft-boiled egg – 'Poor girl couldn't get any lower if she tried.'). His father's implication had been clear: sewage seeks its own level. Tristan had liked Annie too, but could barely speak to her after that. Because, really, how stupid does a girl have to be to pen a romantic missive then address the envelope to Mr T. Jenkins?

Frankie was chopping at the powder with her bankcard now, beat-boxing in time.

This morning it was just an anonymous-looking brown window envelope. He turned it over in search of a clue, but found none. His chest tightened. What if it was a rejection, already? Christ, it *had* to be that! How crappy must his application have been for one – or all! – of the universities to dispatch him so quickly to the waste paper bin of life? How his Dad would fucking love that! Wallowing like a stoned hippo in his phoney disappointment... *I always dreamed my only son would be more successful than his father. What a fool I was.*

He slid his thumbnail under the flap, lifted it and pulled out the letter.

Ha! Fuck them all!

'Frankie,' he said, slamming his locker door. 'Give us a hit.'

'You've changed your tune,' Pat said. Tristan shrugged.

'First time for everything.'

'Tell you what,' Frankie said, screwing a rolled-up fiver into her nostril, embedding it in the snot, then kneeling to pray over one of the lines. 'I'll grind up an OxyNyx just for you.'

We acknowledge the receipt of your application and have forwarded it to the appropriate institutions. Fucking meaningless verbiage. He was still in the game.

Tristan was almost embarrassed in his own presence. What a pussy he'd been! He smiled, and kneeled down next to Frankie.

5

'**I** agree with Windsor.'

'Well, bugger me with Schloss Neuschwanstein!'

'Smithy!'

'By which you mean?'

'By which I mean that it wouldn't hurt having a bloody – Sorry, Bets, pardon me! – a bleeding opinion of your own for once, old man.'

From the hallway, hiding behind the doorjamb, Dot strained to hear the voices over the static assault of a badly-tuned television.

'I have many opinions of my own, thank you very much.'

'You do? I'd really love to hear one.'

'Well, for one that it was the crab that carried Kalka off.'

'That's the same as bloody, as bleeding – oh bugger it! That's *his* blasted opinion! He just said so, thirty seconds…'

'Smithy, would you have me invent an opinion, fabricate one, just so as not to be in concordance with Windsor?'

'Best not ask what I'd have you do, old man. Best not ask…'

'Could it have been his gout?'

Dot recognised Betty's voice. She recognised the tone too – of a woman stepping in between the jousting lances of two rowdy males.

'It wasn't the gout that made him moan like that, love. It was constipation.'

'Constipation?'

'Tommyrot!'

'Tommyrot, is it? Call it that again after you've been shitting like a rabbit kitten for more than a fortnight.'

'Please!'

'It's the food they give us here.'

'Well, *I'm* fine.'

'At least that explains your nocturnal moaning and raving.'

'Moaning and rav—? I do no such…' the speaker paused. 'Oh damn your eyes! The lot of you! Are we talking about me or Kalka?'

'Kalka. If you'll let us…'

'And that's what I'm saying. He hadn't taken a crap in weeks.'

'He hadn't eaten in weeks, either. Why would he need – as you so floridly express it, Smithy – to take a crap?'

A hand crashed down on sheet metal, silencing them.

'It. Was. The. Crab. I know its stink. Once you've lived with that stink inside you, you can smell it a hundred yards off. And the ward has been full of it recently.' The voice was a newcomer to the conversation. Its owner spoke with difficulty. 'And I beg you all to please stop using its name so liberally. We don't want to invite it amongst us.'

'Superstitious claptrap!'

'Smithy!'

'Well!'

'What're you doing?' Olive startled Dot.

'I'm…'

'You're spying.'

That wasn't fair, not really. She *was* eavesdropping, but only to delay her own entrance into the dayroom. She'd fallen asleep again after her conversation with Betty, and when she awoke, Ward B was empty. She had wasted no time in getting out of bed and going in search of Leonard, but her investigation had been thwarted almost as soon as it had begun. There were five rooms leading off of the hallway, all of them labelled – Ward B, the bathroom, the staffroom, the dayroom and a padlocked closet. At first she'd thought there was a sixth door, but as she'd approached it, she realised that, while it may once have been a door, all that remained was the moulding, wallpapered over long ago. Leonard had to be upstairs. But when she'd tried the metal gate she'd found that padlocked too.

So for now Dot had decided to join the others in the dayroom. But when she'd reached the door she'd frozen. They would want to know her background, her story, about her life before she came to Green Oaks. About Leonard. How would she be able to explain that she'd come here precisely to escape that story, to put an end to it, draw a line?

'I didn't want to interrupt,' she said to Olive. 'They seemed deep in conversation.'

Olive squared up to Dot, tilted her head, squinted. Their noses were almost touching.

'Well, if you're not spying…' – grabbing Dot's arm and yanking her into the doorway – 'let's make introductions now…' before letting go and thumping to the lino, in another cataplectic collapse.

Everyone turned and looked at Dot. The racket from the television flared up. Dot wondered about thumping to the floor herself, just to puncture the awkwardness she felt.

The dayroom was as barren as the ward. A metal card-table looked lost at its centre, surrounded by four ratty, mismatched armchairs, and a scattering of sludge-green plastic garden seats, three around the table, and half a dozen others in a teetering stack in the corner. The only other furniture was the huge cathode-ray television – an ancient beastie of faux-wood and black plastic dials.

'New girl!' Olive yelped.

'Dotty, you're up!' Betty said, warmly. Then, to the others, three men: 'We've already met.'

Bafflers of graves – that's what Walt Whitman would have called them. And how they were. What a wreck! Appalling! One, a short butlerish character, with a slick helmet of hair and large-lensed glasses that made a kind of Venn diagram of his thinly smiling face, had already slid off his chair and was shuffling towards her.

'My, my…' – he was muttering, like Alice's White Rabbit – '… a new girl, already. This is decidedly irregular. Decidedly…' He paused, whipped a handkerchief from his dressing gown and kitten-coughed into it. '… irregular. Lanyard.' He thrust his hand at Dot.

'I'm sorry?'

'No, no, dear lady. *I'm* Lanyard. Seventy-seven. Peripheral neuralgia. Arthritis. Cataract left eye. Suspected kidney stones. Forty per cent hearing loss, left ear. Thirty per cent right.'

Dot shook his hand.

'Add hypochondria to that,' Betty muttered.

'It seems you've met Betty – seventy-one. Diabetes, type B. Hearing loss fifty per cent left ear, chronic obesity…'

'Lanyard!' Betty snapped.

'And Olive, seventy-four. Cataplexy, very rare! High blood pressure, high cholesterol… But let me introduce the others.'

Lanyard formed a loop with his arm and nodded for Dot to hook hers into it. She knew what he was up to, had seen it done before, though rarely as brazenly. Cram enough old codgers into the same small space and a hierarchy of ailments was always quickly established. Quantity was important, but so was quality. Parkinson's trumped heart disease, but was itself trumped by osteoporosis. Cancer trumped everything, but only if you were beating it. Start losing your battle and people just didn't know what to do with you. As for dementia, that was hoodoo, *hors competition*. Nobody wanted to speak about that.

'Now, this old carthorse…' Lanyard began.

'Smithy,' the old carthorse interrupted. He stood, cupped the Calabash pipe from his mouth, and offered Dot his free hand. For a man of his age he was physically magnificent, his skeleton clothed in a suit of tired, but still viable muscles. How bodybuilders would age if any of their steroid-ravaged hearts ever made it past fifty without imploding. The fact Smithy had made it to this age was a victory alone, and yet in his eyes all Dot could read was defeat. As she shook his hand, Betty placed a proprietary index finger on Smithy's hip. 'I would say welcome, but, well, you've already seen the place, so I'll just say *bon courage!*' Betty tugged him back into his armchair.

'Seventy-six, high blood pressure and…' – Lanyard was determined to complete the inventory – '… we've just discovered chronic constipation. And this…' A hint of wonder crept into his voice, a throb of love, as he angled Dot towards a cracked old bust who appeared to have dropped off to sleep. 'This is Windsor. He's a survivor.'

'The camps?' Dot asked, impressed.

Lanyard coughed, shook his head. 'No, no,' he whispered. 'You misunderstand me dear woman, I meant the, *ahem*, you know, the…' He coughed again, then pressed his hands into pincers.

'Lobster attack?' Dot said, mischief rising out of her like a burp.

Smithy smiled.

'No, no,' Lanyard said, unaware, or at least unsure, if they were making a fool of him. 'The crab.'

'Will you stop it!' Windsor slapped the table-top a second time.

'I'm sorry sir,' Lanyard grovelled. 'I thought you had nodded off.'

'What difference does it make if I've nodded off or not? It's not me you're invoking. Now help me over to the window, will you? It's so bloody stuffy in here.'

Despite Windsor's impeccable grooming – his moustache was still runnelled from a recent combing and his hair was whipped up with lacquer – his cheeks glistened like greased paraffin paper, revealing a map of blue veins and red arteries beneath. He was the illest looking of the lot, and the tracheal tube jutting from his neck only confirmed how tenuous his hold on life was. Still, if he was going down, he clearly planned to do so smelling of roses… or at least of his tear-inducingly pungent rose-flecked cologne.

'With the greatest pleasure, sir,' Lanyard said, releasing Dot's arm. 'Although before I do… Dorothy, dear, perhaps you might?'

'Might?'

'Introduce yourself. Age, afflictions, etcetera.' Dot smiled. He was joking, wasn't he?

Oh, not if his expectant eyes were anything to go by. And he wasn't the only one. All of them – from Olive, almost vertical now, to Betty, Smithy and Windsor – they were all waiting.

'Erm. Well. I'm Dorothy. Or Dotty. Or Dot. Whichever you... really. And, I'm, *erm*, seventy-four... At least I was the last time I checked.' Ugh! She hated herself at once for the nauseating stab at levity. But they weren't satisfied yet. If she didn't feed them something, she was afraid they'd encircle her and, like rabbit mothers confronted with their sullied young, eat her face off.

But there was nothing wrong with her. A few aches and pains, perhaps. Hearing loss too, of course, but that little weasel would demand percentages and she had none to give. Or else she could lie...

'That's it,' she said. Lanyard leaned in towards her.

'Your afflictions,' he whispered, as if prompting a child.

'I don't have any. Not really.'

Lanyard took a step back, squinted at her.

'None?'

'Nothing that I know of. Unless rack and ruin is an affliction?'

'That is most unsatisfactory. Are you sure you don't have a small hernia? Or diabetes – any type will do. Or perhaps a little fistula somewhere personal?' His liverish complexion was making her queasy.

'No, I...'

'Why on earth would you come here then?' Smithy said, more to himself than Dot.

Should she tell them about Leonard? Could she? While she'd picked up on some complicity between Betty and Smithy, the others seemed like resolutely unpaired atoms. How would they react to the knowledge that she was not?

The grandfather clock chiming in the hallway spared Dot from an immediate decision. She counted its hollow knells...

Four? Nothing more? Four o'clock already? Where had the day gone? She'd assumed it was still morning, and was upset that she could have got it so wrong. Her consternation was interrupted by another chorus of chimes, two this time. Then a pause, then one. Then some yobbish cackling. She turned to look. Three attendants, in full scrubs, were gathered around the clock, a fairytale castle of thick smoke constructing itself in the air above them. One of them, the girl, handed the cigarette to one of the boys then turned the hands with her outstretched index finger. The chimes rang again – seven meaningless clangs – and all three of them disintegrated into a standing heap of giggles.

'What right do the little buggers have to do that?' Lanyard whined. 'Don't they understand how disorienting it is?'

'Oh they understand,' Smithy said. 'Why do you think they do it?' Betty laid a hand on his thigh.

'Not your high horse,' she said. 'Not now.'

Smithy whistled through his teeth like a pressure release valve.

'Who are they?' Dot asked. And suddenly they were all fixing her again. Even Windsor managed to arc the craggy cornices of his eyebrows.

'The CareFriends,' Betty said. 'Surely you met them last night? During…'

'Perhaps I met one of them,' Dot said, gunning for half a point. 'The fat one, with the tattoo.'

'Most, most irregular,' Lanyard said.

'She doesn't remember, that's all,' Olive said. 'I forgot too, at first…'

'Excuse me, but what don't I…'

'Shhh… Shhh…' Betty took hold of her hand. 'I know. There's so much to take in right now.'

Feeling a little dizzy, Dot perched on the arm of Lanyard's chair. She didn't know if this was allowed, if chair occupancy was inviolable here or not, but nobody complained. She decided to let the last exchange go. She had to choose her battles, and understanding what these loons were banging on about didn't seem too important just then.

Lanyard had recruited Olive to help Windsor clump to the window upon his rickety Zimmer. An odd choice considering her tendency for full physical collapse. But then what wasn't odd around here? It was as if Dot had walked into a nightmare of clunky Dickensian archetypes: Windsor? Lanyard? Smithy? As much as she disliked herself for it, she'd already found their pigeonholes: Windsor was the Faux-Aristo-John-Bull, Lanyard the Tuppenny-Ha'penny-Bureaucrat and Smithy the Broken-Spirit-Out-To-Pasture. As for Olive, she was an extraneous character, no doubt about it, thrown into the mix to hammer home a point about something or other, at some time or other, but with little direct impact on the narrative. She was having more trouble with Betty, although give her time... She'd nail her as well.

She knew it was a bad habit, but people did have the dreadfully depressing tendency to live up to the archetypes prescribed them. As if they were complicit in it, somehow. It came from school, the habit, from a game the teachers used to play. With every new intake they would race to identify which boy fitted through which hole. There were holes for them all, for the Worker, the Shirker, the Mummy's-Boy, the Daddy's-Boy, the Doesn't-know-his-Daddy-Boy, the Only-Child, the Lonely-Child, the Smart-Pet, the Dumb-Pet, the Rebel (Posh-and-Unhinged), the Psychopath, the Polymath, the Fatty (Vicious-/Depressed-/Vicious-and-Depressed), the Future-Baldy, the Little-Hitler, the STD, the Serious-Operation-in-his-Past, the Serious-Operation-in-his-Future, the Smoker, the Choker, the Pre-Eighteen-Croaker, the Carpetbagger, the Lab-Assistant-Shagger...

'It's strange how quickly he left us, though...' Dot had lost track of the conversation for a moment. 'They've let bodies lie in state for days before.' She was about to confirm she'd heard Smithy right, when Betty said:

'But aren't his lot into quick burial?'

'You're confusing him with a Mohammedan there, Bets,' Smithy said, clearly enjoying his vocabulary.

'And what was he again?'

'Hindu,' Smithy said. 'Or Sikh.'

'We're all sick!' Lanyard chirruped from the window.

Smithy waved him off.

'And besides, what other possibility is there? Other than Ward C?'

'The one ward that never gets full,' Betty said.

Smithy nodded, sadly.

'Is Ward C upstairs?' Dot asked, exploiting the lull.

'I suppose he could have gone to Ward A,' Betty said, ignoring Dot. She turned in her chair, a sly grin ripening on her face. 'Here, Windsor? Is it possible they transferred Kalka upstairs?' Windsor ignored what was, apparently, a provocation.

While Betty and Smithy continued their speculations, Dot tuned out of their conversation and into the one by the window. Had she just heard her name?

'... arrived in a storm, I'll bet...'

They were speaking loudly, to counteract their mutual deafness, but not loud enough for Dot to make out everything.

'... Not in Kansas anymore.'

'But where is Ward C?' she insisted, turning back to Betty and Smithy... But they'd gone. She didn't know how they had pulled off their vanishing act so quickly, although she thought she understood why. For a crooked silhouette – right hand on hip, left stroking the remains of a thickety anchor-beard – had materialised at the door. His face was cragged and chipped, like a flint hand-axe, and his striped pyjamas draped straight over his emaciated body as if they were arranged not on a human being at all, but on a wooden valet stand. His feet were bare, except for a caking of mud. He was scanning the Dayroom with narrowed eyes, turning words over on slate-grey lips, fluttering beneath his catfish moustache. When his gaze met Dot's, his eyes dilated and a frown chevroned his brow. He strode up to her:

'Name and rank. Chop chop!'

'I'm sorry?'

'No time for apologies, soldier. Name and rank?'

'Dor...' she began, before capitulating. 'I... Dotty.' She tried a smile. 'I don't believe I have a rank.'

'Private, eh? Private Dotty.' He said it slowly, as if testing it for a fit. 'Brigade?'

'Wh... What?'

'Captain Watt? Infantry, third battalion? Trained alongside him in the Raj. A fine soldier. Any man of his is a man of mine. Or woman! Captain Ruggles.' He proffered a knobbed hand. 'Where did you say they picked you up?'

'Picked me up? I didn't...'

'And you shouldn't, quite right. Careless talk costs lives and all that. Just as important in here as it is on the home front. Even in the hole I'm careful not to let anything slip. The walls have ears...' The walls weren't the only one. This man's ears, two huge gnarled oyster-shells, were so big they almost flapped when he moved his head. 'I know what you're thinking, Private. Same as us all: What have they done with the Hindu? Fear not. I have some of my best men on the case. Smoke?' He brandished a packet of candy cigarettes. Dot smiled and took one, as if humouring a child.

There was a kind of hyper-lucidity to the way he spoke, and a gleam to his eye that gave the impression, at least, of a certain clarity of thought. More than she had felt from any of the other residents.

'The fact is, Private,' he said, candy stick twitching at the corner of his lips with every word. 'I've been on the lookout for a batman for some months now – or a batwoman if circumstances demand it.'

A wave of fatigue rose up and broke over Dot. Was this loon trying to recruit an accomplice? If so, then she'd resist. She didn't have the spirit for this kind of caper.

'I don't think I could...' she said, trying to remain cordial.

'Of course you could. I haven't been soldiering for all these years not to be able to identify potential in one of my men...' He hiccuped. 'Women! You don't have to give me an answer now. You'll be rewarded handsomely once the war is won, that I assure you. Batwomen always are.'

'No,' Dot said, firmer this time, denying him with a shake of her head. 'I'm sorry. I just can't.'

She could, though. And, despite her best efforts, she would. She felt it in her gut. Step by arthritic step, she would fall in line behind this fruitcake. 'No' would not be a word that found much purchase in his feverish mind. He would remain unwounded by her recurring rejections too. He seemed convinced she would prove a willing accomplice, and maybe she would. Right now, what she saw in this man's delirium – indeed in the deliriums of all her new ward-mates – was the chance to disappear.

For the moment she had feared, of having to tell them her story – their story – hadn't come. They just hadn't asked. And now she knew, with an odd certainty, that they would never ask. So she resolved not to mention Leonard – not yet anyway – and to conduct her hunt for him in secret. The others seemed to prefer her storyless, anyway, disconnected from the world outside, the world that had abandoned them long before they abandoned it. And in truth – after everything she'd been through – being storyless in the eyes of others was perhaps what Dot needed right now. To be a blank canvas, set free from the crippling weight of memory. Cut adrift. Not so much to reinvent herself, as to let her edges blur until she dissipated into the ether. Without a story to define her, to imprison her, to hold her together, entropy would finally be free to get to work. And perhaps, if she tried hard enough, she might even start believing she was storyless herself.

Dot popped the candy cigarette into her mouth and crunched it to nothing. Captain Ruggles grinned his approval.

Book Two

1

'**T**oo-wit!'

'…'

'*Too-wit!*'

'…'

'*Tsst!* Private? Are you awake?'

'…'

'Dotty. It's time.'

A dog-eared copy of Captain Combat arced across the shaft of moon-light and slapped against Dot's face, waking her up.

'*Wha*… What? Captain?'

A pair of twiggy fingers, reeking of tobacco and solvent ink, pressed against her lips. After more than six weeks at Green Oaks, she knew those fingers well, could see their archipelagoes of discolouration despite the darkness.

'Apols for the rude awakening Dotty, old girl.' The whisperer was so close that his moustache tickled her ear. 'But I too-witted and I didn't catch your too-woo, and I thought maybe Jerry had rumbled us. Carted you off for a probing.'

'Go back to bed,' Dot said, turning away. She heard a shuffling from below her cot and, within seconds, the Captain was in front of her again.

'To bed? Are you out of your mind, soldier? Have you forgotten what night this is? The weeks of planning? All your surveillance work?' A spindly arm pointed at the barred window. 'Dotty, there's a car out there waiting to take us across the border.' Squinting to make out her friend in the dark ward, Dot reached out a hand and ran her fingers through his thin hair.

'Are you sure, Captain? Are you sure it's not tomorrow? Because I'm dog tired tonight, old man.'

'Listen Dotty,' the Captain whispered. 'As a private, there's a lot of intelligence that you're just not privy to. It's not because we don't trust you. Jeepers, Dotty, I'd trust you with my life, you know that. But we need to know you won't crack under torture and you just haven't spent enough time in the field for us to be sure. Though you have to believe me, Private, I would never send you into danger unless King and country absolutely demanded it. This is the moment, Dotty. It's our only chance. The tooter the sweeter!'

Dot sighed. Yesterday night had also been 'the moment'. And the night before that their 'only chance'. Both nights she'd had to talk the Captain to sleep before he was able to enact his absurd scheme of breaking out of Green Oaks. She shifted to one side of her cot and paddled the empty space beside her. The Captain clambered on. Dot draped her thick arm over him. No meat at all.

'Well then,' she whispered in his ear – the chance for her own moustache to do the tickling. 'You'd better remind me of the plan again.'

Just as she had expected, Dot had been unable to resist the Captain's advances. The old dog had charmed her from the off. Better just to admit it, at least to herself. Such elegance, almost graceful, how she imagined Nijinsky might have been if he'd ever reached that age. It wasn't a sexual thing, not exactly. She'd just never seen someone so close to death attacking life so hard, with so much conviction that he might actually win. He was off his rocker, of course. His mind had been overheated by those ridiculous war comics he spent all day reading. Or perhaps it had been over for his mind long before, and the comics had merely found fertile soil in his brain.

A few days after meeting the Captain, starved of her library and a little jealous of the time he spent reading, Dot had tried them. The first she picked up had a hole cut right the way through it, about two thirds up and an inch or so away from the spine. She'd recognised it at once: a spy-hole newspaper, the ultimate Boy's Own reconnaissance tool. From a second, a cascade of origamis had fallen into her lap: water bombs. How many had she confiscated in her career? The Captain's were tiny and fussily made, their drenching power limited – a minor irritation to their target, nothing more. The third comic was intact, although not undamaged. Dot had been wondering about the Captain's hands, where the stains came from, why they never seemed to wash off. She'd found her answer. The Captain had been redacting the stories with black marker, barring words, sentences, sometimes entire paragraphs from view. The ink had blotted through the pages, making whole chunks of the stories unreadable. And it wasn't just one. Every single magazine Dot had leafed through was a victim of the Captain's pen, to differing extents and with differing levels of meticulousness. Dot thought how she could have done with applying a marker-pen approach to parts of her life, too…

Although perhaps she already had. Or if not a marker pen, then a solvent. She was not striking things out, but letting them fade – loosen, untie, *release*, as the word's Latin origin would have it. Six weeks she'd been here. Six weeks already! And she'd seen neither hide nor hair of Leonard in that time. The fact that she had decided to conduct her investigation in secret, combined with the communal life on the ward, meant actions were limited to her rare moments of solitude. But it wasn't just that. Something else was underway. Something internal. It felt like such a long time since her arrival, and yet it also felt like almost no time at all had passed. It was urgent she see Leonard and yet… he could wait too. It was dizzying, as if time's arrow had lost its markers, as if she fallen into, and got stuck between, the spaces of an ellipsis.

'Dot… Dot… Dot!' The Captain was grinding his elbow into her ribs.

'Sorry, old man. Go on.'

'So, as you see, its genius is its simplicity. A classic washerwoman ruse updated to match the formidable efficiency and organisation of the modern industrialised enemy. Here are your papers…' He fumbled beneath the sheets and pressed something into Dot's hand. Her fingers traced its edges and turned it over, blindly examining its faces. A small rectangle of roughly cut card. This was new. On previous nights there had been nothing to add meat to the Captain's bluster.

'And you'll find the uniform in your pillowcase.' Dot slipped her fingers inside it. There *was* something in there: a thin garment of some kind, the material familiar to the touch, but unplaceable nevertheless. My God, he was really up to something tonight!

'Captain? What…?'

'No more questions, Private. Let's just say I had to trade a lot of *Gaspers* for these. I'll also be sporting an officer's cap, of my own creation. We're less likely to be stopped if they think we're of rank.'

'But what about the door?' she asked. 'They lock us in.'

'Most of the guards do, but not the one on duty tonight. He's a grunt, Private. Locking the door takes time and risks waking up the prisoners. So he leaves it unlocked and just sits in the mess all night, drinking coffee, with one eye on the door to *Zellenblock B*.'

'Won't he see us leave?'

'You're not paying attention, Private. I just told you he was drinking coffee.'

'So?'

'Coffee, Dotty!' The Captain's voice warbled his exasperation. 'One of Mother Nature's most powerful diuretics. And he drinks it by the pint! On the hour, every hour, he leaves his post to pass water. The sound of piss on porcelain at one o'clock sharp will be our cue. If we – quiet as mice, Dotty – can get out before he buttons himself up, he'll only see us from behind and, if we're lucky, be unable to tell us from any of his filthy comrades. After that, it's an open run to the glade at the bottom of the hill, where a car will be waiting to get us to the border.'

'And what about the alarms?'

'I've already disabled the alarms,' the Captain said.

Dot yawned. She didn't believe him, but it didn't matter.

'Then I suppose you've covered everything. But it can't be later than midnight. Why don't you rest up a little before the big push?'

'Not quite everything, Dotty. There is always a risk things will turn nasty, and if they do, I want you to have this.' He hooked something up from the floor and pressed it between her hands. It was cylindrical, plastic and quite heavy.

'What now, Captain?'

'Secret weapon, Private. You'll know what to do with it if the moment arises.' With that, the Captain slipped out of Dot's cot. 'I'll keep watch and give you the signal when it's time to move out. In the meantime, you get changed. And Dotty…' The Captain paused.

'Yes, Cap?'

'I just want to say. When this whole terrible, cursed show is over. When we've beaten off Jerry, I mean, and Albion's sovereignty is secured…' He paused again, as so many leading men used to in so many Hollywood films. Dot bit her fingers to stop herself giggling.

'Go on, Captain,' she managed.

'Well, old girl… I mean, perhaps you could come up to the Cotswolds and meet my daughter. We live in a little cottage up there. Thatched roof, white picket fence, probably. You know the kind of thing.'

Dot was surprised. 'Captain? I didn't know you had a daughter.'

'Why do you think I'm so darned set on getting back to Blighty? Tea and cricket? Look.' He thrust a folded photo under her nose. She took it from him, unfolded it and held it out to catch a blade of moonlight. She could just make out the silhouette of a young girl, surely no more than four-years-old, picked out in tones of grey. She was standing in front of a tree with a swing, flanked by two startled-looking teddy bears.

'Dulcie,' the Captain said, taking the photo and tucking it into the waistband of his pyjamas. Not knowing what to say – the intrusion of some sort of reality into this charade had destabilised her – Dot settled upon: 'She's pretty.' The Captain sniffed his agreement.

'What about you, Private? Isn't there someone waiting for you to come home?'

Dot pulled the bed sheet tighter about her.

'No,' she said. 'Not anymore.'

The Captain began shuffling across the lino on his knees, towards his own cot. Perhaps he'd just go to sleep, she thought, and forget about his plan for another night. Perhaps not, though. There was a new agitation to him tonight, a reckless edge.

Just as she was hoping she'd heard the last of him, the Captain called out again:

'Dotty! *Tsst!*'

'What now?'

'Quiet as mice, remember.'

'Quiet as mice,' Dot said.

2

'**P**rivate!'

A cymbal crash invaded Dot's dreamless sleep.

'Run!'

She couldn't be sure if it was the Captain's cry or the colander rolling on the floor that woke her. Everything was so confused, and happening so quickly, and she was still a little punch-drunk from her evening Phlegmolax.

Struggling upright, she saw the Captain streak past her, his knees thrusting so high they almost struck his chin – first towards the door then, after he cawed with surprise, back into the ward, hurdling the upturned colander. This second flypast revealed the true extent of the 'uniforms'. Not the promised guard's duds, but flimsy Johnny-gowns. The Captain was wearing his back-to-front and open, exposing his macerated body, his skin hanging in folds from his toothpick bones. His impossibly dangly genitals, stretching near half the length of his thigh, were swinging like pendulums possessed.

The lights were tripped from outside. Dot covered her eyes, blocking their icy inundation. She heard the door open and, a few seconds later, was able to make out two figures standing in the doorway. There was Tristan, the head CareFriend, and Pat, who Dot had met the night she arrived. She'd been surprised first by how young all the staff seemed – barely out of college by the looks of them – and then by how little interaction there was between them and the residents. Contact was functional – feeding, cleaning, drugging – and little more besides. She was also still yet to set eyes on the director, but he, she supposed, must have a lot on his plate.

Tristan and Pat were crabbing slowly towards the Captain. Her friend – for all his sartorial indiscretion – still struck the noblest pose of the three, presenting his flank to his pursuers with the taut-bow dignity of a Manolete poised for the *suerte de matar*.

'*Achtung Fritz! Achtung!*' he bellowed as the boys drew nearer. 'One more step and I shan't be held responsible for my actions. *Achtung*, I say!' Tristan and the Pat swapped slanting smiles.

'*Wo is die Toilette, bitte?*' Tristan said, incongruously.

'*Ja! Natürlich,*' joined Pat, even more so.

'Final warning! *Letzte*… err… *warnung!*' the Captain squawked, lifting his clenched right hand high above his head. Something in the fist caught the light. His assailants exchanged fretful looks. The Captain's reputation preceded him here. Might just save him. Both knew what he was capable of.

Just then, Dot remembered the Captain's earlier talk of secret weapons. Rummaging beneath the sheet, her hand lit upon the cylindrical object. Lighter than before.

Since the tableau had slumped into a fragile deadlock, she lifted the sheet and peeked beneath. A rippled yellow bottle of sunflower oil, its screw top punctured and a drinking straw planted in it. Along the length of the bottle, in smudged black ink, the word SLICK. The bottle was almost empty.

'What in the name of Jumping Jehovah?' Windsor was awake, his tremendous Prussian lip-slug twitching with annoyance across his death mask. 'Oh bugger me! Him again?'

'Shit!' Tristan said. 'He's raising the dead with his racket.'

'Ruggles! Now you just pack it in and go back to sleep, right away. Do you hear me?' Windsor rattled.

'No can do, Field Marshall,' the Captain said. 'My orders come all the way from the top.'

'The top?'

'High command, Sir. From the Big Man. *La Baleine Blanche*. The Bulldog himself. From Winnie.'

'Winnie? Oh for buggering-f...' Windsor adjusted the valve of his tracheal tube, spat a wad of sputum onto the floor and assumed the bullheaded expression of a toothless someone feigning himself to sleep.

Dot looked to see if any of the others were awake. Lanyard and Smithy, nearest the door, were both notorious heavy sleepers, and true to form neither had been stirred by the Captain's shenanigans. Dot couldn't see Betty's face, but the regular cadence of her breathing suggested she too had, thus far, slept through the storm undisturbed. Nearest the Captain's grandstanding was Olive. She was awake and drinking everything in, the fervour of an end-times preacher glistering in her eyes.

'Come on, Captain, you fractious old bastard,' Tristan called across the ward. 'Back to bed now, or it's the rubber room for you again.' Dot winced. The rubber room was kept almost as a private suite for her friend. The Captain scoffed, shook his fist. Whatever was inside rattled.

'Never alive, Fritz!' he yelled back. Pat, visibly bored with the whole adventure, took another step towards the Captain. A grave misjudgement.

'*Aïe-aïe-aïe-aïe-aïe-aïe-aïe-aïe-aïe!*'

Hopping on his right foot and beating the O of his mouth with his palm, the Captain windmilled his closed fist three times about his head, then liberated its charge...

The shower of coloured glass marbles twisted through the air like a swarm of insects. Some sailed past the Captain's assailants, others bounced off their bellies, but most just skittered sadly off their boots before gathering around the metal drain in the centre of the ward.

Tristan and Pat looked at the marbles, then at each other... and erupted with simultaneous, mocking gut-laughs.

The Captain didn't move. His shoulders looked suddenly less square, his eyes rheumier than before. He seemed to be looking at nothing, squinting as though at a horizon far beyond the walls of the ward. He turned to Dot:

'Now... Private...' he croaked. Dot held up the plastic bottle and inverted it. A defeated Morse signal of oil choked through the drinking straw onto the floor beside her bed.

'Sorry,' she mouthed, shaking her head.

The Captain slumped against the wall and slid into a jagged heap. Dot couldn't tell if he was even conscious anymore. Was that how it ended, then? Was the Captain's escape little more than a damp Bonfire-Night firework – retire to a safe distance, hiss, sputter, spark... then nothing? Dot squinted to bring the Captain's face into sharper focus, to divine his future from the crags. At first, he gave her nothing. It was as if his body was an empty shell, shucked off by his soul as it made a quick, and embarrassed, getaway.

However, as she continued looking... was that... could he be... smiling? It was barely noticeable at first, a light tugging on the corners of his mouth. But with every second that passed it grew perceptibly wider.

So it wasn't over! Dot was surprised by how much pleasure this realisation inspired.

There was something familiar about the smile too, although Dot couldn't place it at once. She thought first of a statuette an Indian colleague had given her many years earlier. Then, as the smile ripened, her thoughts turned to Rembrandt's self-portrait as Zeuxis laughing, that had so bewitched her when she came across it by chance while visiting Thomas in Cologne. It was both, and yet neither fully. There was something else. Something missing...

Then, from in between the Captain's withered, leathery buttocks, mooched the head of a stool. It was an inch and a half thick and the colour of ginger cake. Of course! The beatific smile belonged to no painting or statue. It was the smile that every new parent takes for the first expression of filial love... an instant before the stench hits. For several seconds the turd crept out of the Captain and across the grey lino until, at about eight inches, with a spit and a splutter, the tweaked tail emerged.

The Captain cranked his head up and looked at his composition. He smiled again – much more knowingly now. Fixing Tristan, he reached out and scooped up the stool in his left hand.

'Oh no! No, no, no! No you fucking don't!'

Ignoring Tristan's pleas, the Captain examined the dejecta on his outstretched palm. Holding it just in front of his pointed nose, and with deliberate movements, he started turning it over and about with his fingers, reworking its cigar-shaped form into a thick pat of paste. Tristan stood frozen, a look of unalloyed horror on his face. All that mattered to Dot now, futile as it ultimately was, was that the Captain was still evading him.

Using the index and middle fingers of his right hand as a kind of spatula, the Captain hooked up a kiss of the brown paste and, after shrugging off his Johnny-gown, smeared it down the length of his right arm. He paused for a moment, admiring his handiwork. Then, with swift movements, he likewise daubed his ribs, belly, legs and left arm.

Then, he rattled to his feet. Dot had never seen anything quite like this in all her life. Standing there naked, smeared in his own feculence, determined and battle-ready, he was at once noble and absurd, dignified and disgusting beyond all imagining. How much like a clown he looked! How much like a god!

In a final flourish, the Captain painted two lines on his cheeks and one stretching from the top of his forehead, between his eyes, right along the craggy bridge of his nose to its tip, before defiantly dropping his hand and letting what was left slop to the floor.

'For King George,' he said, creaking into a sprinter's squat. 'For Albion…' Clenching his fists. 'And for you,' he concluded, bringing the photo of his daughter to his lips, careful to avoid the gem of night-soil perched on the tip of his nose.

Then, unleashing a cry that echoed with all the pain, frustration and confusion ossified within him, the Captain zipped down the aisle towards the door, scooping up the colander as he passed it, flipping it over, and posing it jauntily on his head. His wheeling arm clipped Tristan, who was sent twisting onto Smithy's cot. Smithy grunted and kicked out, his foot crunching into Tristan's jaw. The Captain threw open the door and dashed out. Seconds later came the harsh shriek of the alarm. Dot smiled. He had breached the perimeter.

Pat helped Tristan to his feet. His mouth was gushing blood. They staggered out of the ward. Seconds later the sirens were disabled and the lights cut out. A different light, a yellow glow, remained. The Captain must have activated the security lamps outside. Dot turned over in her cot, lifted herself up by the headrest and peered through the barred window. At first she couldn't see anything except the rolling lawn and twin oak trees… Then, the naked Captain scudded past, just in front of her, followed moments later by Pat. The old boy showed no sign of tiring. A few more empty seconds passed before the security lamps died. Ward B was dark again.

Dot turned back over in her cot. The Captain would be caught, of course. There would be no car waiting for him, and the only border he risked crossing was the one-way frontier into the kingdom of the Doo-lally. But for the moment, anyway, he was free. For the moment he was in front, he was winning. And that still seemed important somehow.

Now that the excitement had passed, Dot realised she needed to pee. Since the door had been left unlocked, she decided to risk visiting the bathroom rather than struggling over the bedpan as they were supposed to do during the night. She smiled at herself, at her own petty rebellion. Perhaps the Captain wasn't as crazy as everyone thought. She sat up in her cot, swung her legs over the side, and dared a little hop to the ground.

As her feet stroked the lino she sensed instantly that something was wrong. Her bunionned soles didn't grip the floor, but slid out from under her. As the adrenalin swarmed through her body and events slowed down, she knew that, with her ankle twisted as it was and with her bulky frame, this wasn't going to end with only a few bruises.

Dot hit the ground with a slap.

'…'

In the cold clarity of mind that follows a trauma, Dot knew that there was no use screaming. Tristan would be tending to his own injuries and Pat was out rounding up the Captain. By the time they were done she would have long passed out with the pain.

She felt something wet and warm on her nightdress. She blushed. Had she added to her indignity by soiling herself? She dipped her fingers into the sap-like fluid and sniffed them. Vegetable oil.

Dot closed her eyes.

3

The small hole in the centre of the rosace was the still point about which the room and all its furnishings whipped and waltzed. Remembering Doctor Mountweasel, Raymond Cornish locked his gaze on it and prepared for deceleration. The hole had once held the fittings of a chandelier and was really, therefore, just another sign of the protracted fall from grace of the country manor, that had become an asylum, that had become Green Oaks. For Cornish, however, on the exit slope of his 'turn', the hole's story didn't matter. Nor did the fact that were he to probe it with a screwdriver or curious finger he'd likely have found nothing more than woodworm-riddled beams and wisps of fibreglass lagging. For him, prostrate on his desk, the hole in the rosace was nothing less than an escape into another world.

'If only… it was big enough… to crawl through.'

He was breathing bullets, barely giving the oxygen time to reach his lungs before expelling it through rock-hard lips. He slackened his jaw and held his breath for a three-count after each inhalation. The cold air drove a chill through his lungs.

The spinning let up and the rosace blossomed into focus. Decades of paint jobs had blunted the lines of the moulding, taking something formerly of distinction and fossilising it into a bland background feature.

'I know how you feel, old friend,' Cornish whispered. God, did he know.

The rosace always reminded him of the scores of mandalas he'd drawn, years earlier, as part of his therapy. Doctor Mountweasel, newly returned from a sabbatical in Zurich and drunk on Jung and Eastern mysticism, had insisted the young man depict his dream images in these brightly coloured medallions. The old zealot had been convinced they would guide him in his quest for personal completeness and 'at-one-ment' with the universe. He'd even given Cornish his own packet of wax crayons to draw with.

Not wanting to disappoint his doctor – disappointing anyone terrified him – or give him the impression of being backward, Cornish, who didn't dream in images but words – angry, accusatory words – had nevertheless tried his best. He still remembered the doctor's displeasure at the start of every session – the slow rotation of his head, the rabbity tut-tutting – but the scribblings had been the best that Cornish could manage. Faced with the blank page, Cornish had also worried about his increasingly itinerant mind. In its long periods of wool-gathering he was given to gnawing at the crayons. In the forty minutes allotted him, he was capable of chomping through two or three, paper wrapping and all.

The room stopped spinning: it was safe to get off. His forehead was slippery with sweat. He hopped down from the desk.

Crossing to the mirror above the condemned fireplace, he scrutinised himself. The turn had undone his hair. He righted it in three automatic gestures: re-establishing the zigzag parting, arcing the fringe and smoothing down the insolent pineapple at the crown, that flicked up again a moment later. He took a handkerchief from his pocket and dabbed at his forehead, marvelling at the grey hue of his skin. Harriet insisted he was imagining it, that his skin hadn't changed colour in all the twenty years they'd been married. But what did she know? How much did she even really look at him these days, except when she caught sight of his reflection in the television screen? If it was with anything like the rarity he looked at her, her opinion meant little. He was grey and getting greyer by the day. And from the inside out – a dull mould creeping about just below the surface. He tucked his paunch back into his trousers, fastened the collar of his shirt and straightened his tie, then tugged twice at his nose. There were discs of sweat under each of his arms, but his blazer would cover those. He also hadn't shaved since yesterday. Not that the Greys would notice.

The carpet was littered with debris, swiped from the desk as his 'turn' had taken hold. Plastic pens, the chipped mug in which they were kept, a photo frame, a blue calculator and a landslide of writing paper. All of these were his and their familiarity was reassuring. There were also, however, some alien presences – a collapsed stack of dog-eared pulp magazines, a vegetable-oil bottle and a dented metal colander. These he didn't recognise and their presence in his sanctuary set his teeth on edge.

He picked up the mug and scooped the pens into it. Everything was branded with sterile logos – for pharmaceutical companies, industrial caterers and the like. Droppings from the vultures forever circling above him, combing for scraps with their lifeless, dollar-shaped eyes. The pens were cheap and fragile. Useless for anything except signing carbon paper contracts, which was, indeed, all Cornish used them for. That and his penchant for gory doodles.

The themes of his sketches were as recurrent as they were terrifying. Hideous sex scenes in which faceless female mannequins were impaled on the members – saw-like, sword-like, hook-like, drill-like – of dead-eyed masculine outlines. The Frankenstein genitals were meticulously rendered, everything else just barely sketched. There were starscapes too, today. This was new. Swirling masses of suns and planets, gravitating around black holes drawn with such determination that the paper had crumpled and rent. Why this? Why today? He allowed himself a smile as he balled up the paper and dropped it in the bin. Who would have thought one imagination could house so much perversion, apparently without the world catching on?

He arranged several of the pens on his desk. Before, when he was still drawing for real, he'd put a lot of store in the pens he used: how heavy, how warm, how alive they felt in his hands. Still, there was something anti-artistic about these pens in particular. Something that forbade art. Even his signature came out twiggy and lifeless when he used them. Yet these were the weapons he had earned.

The photo frame contained the standard-issue family snap of Harriet and the boys. He had never wanted to introduce their presence to Green Oaks, but she'd wrongly interpreted this well-intentioned reluctance and insisted. The tragedy was that he remembered liking the photo the first time he'd seen it and indeed, as the photographer, felt he'd infused it with some of the love he wanted to feel for his family. But he'd seen so much of the photo now that it meant nothing to him. Every sweep his eyes made of the office glanced off it, burnishing away yet another layer of its glamour until, even when he looked at it closely, he could see nothing there, however hard he tried. It might as well have been a photo of three pinkish-beige eggs. Three pinkish-beige eggs with stupid haircuts.

He opened the bottom drawer of his desk and dropped the picture in, next to the reel of plastic hole reinforcers he'd forgotten all about.

'Teddy bears' bum-holes,' he said, allowing himself a smile.

Amongst the magazines, he noticed a couple of leaves of paper. One was on powder-blue Green Oaks stationery, most likely a note from one of the CareFriends. It was folded and he decided to leave it so. A CareFriend note was rarely good news. The other one was white, almost greaseproof, and striated with thin black lines. An order form for Phlegmolax, that new antipsychotic (or was it an anxiolytic… or a hypnotic?) currently being pushed hard by Big Pharma. Word was that it was effective. Cornish had no idea if this was true, although its nickname – 'the truncheon' – hadn't come from nowhere.

Next, he unfolded the powder-blue page. As he'd suspected, a note from the CareFriends. He vaguely remembered having seen it already. He read chunks of it again:

'*Mister Cornish… sending you this resident… Ward B… attempted escape… blah blah… theft of supplies… faecal matter… blah blah blah… severe delusions… World War Two… disruptive presence… injured ankle… possible accomplice… request transfer… in your hands… kindly.*'

'Kindly?' Cornish snorted. 'If there was a kindly bone in your body – you fucker – you'd have left me well alone this morning.'

He picked up the magazines: *Captain Combat. Sky Devils. World of Men. Air Souls!* 'What is this rubbish?'

On the back cover of *World of Men* was an advert Cornish knew well. There he stood: Beefcake clown Charles Atlas, flanked by his promises to make a new man of any weakling who practised fifteen minutes of his patented Dynamic Tension method each and every day.

Had there ever been a time when some shill wasn't hawking the idea of triumph over the world's sand-kicking bullies by determination alone? The natural order never allowed for such radical upheaval. Cornish knew the score: might was right and slick-tongued prophets like Atlas there would promise the world for the smallest handful of loose change.

It had been that way with West Church. They had swooped down and picked off Green Oaks when its original owner – a cousin of Harriet's mother – had retired to the Canary Islands, after Cornish had been in the job less than a year. West Church had kept him in place, promised him increased autonomy, but with the added security of being backed up by a company with a diverse range of interests: Care homes, school catering, waste disposal... the whole grim cycle of life. It hadn't taken long for the thumbscrews to be tightened, for fees to be raised and savings insisted upon.

He flipped the magazines onto his desk until just one remained in his hands: MEN TODAY. Four headlines were arranged about the masthead, each printed in a different block colour:

Exposed: Teenage Free Love Cults – their orgies and violence
Your Passion Analysed – Is it Normal?
Helpless Nudes for The Madman's Pit of Horror.
10 Sex Faults That Make You Repulsive to Women...

The cover was presided over by a lusty Amazon, cast from the Brigitte Bardot mould, her blouse and miniskirt strategically torn, exposing ample breast and leg to titillate, but not enough to turn the magazine into genuine top-shelf fodder. She was toting two guns: a shotgun that trailed at her side, and a revolver which she aimed out of the picture, straight at the reader, its barrel spitting a furious tongue of flame. Just behind her, a battle was raging for control of a timber shack, dressed with the Nazi foulard. A G.I., holding a machine gun, was cutting down four German soldiers whose acrobatic, almost enthusiastic, tumbling into their death throes had been frozen in mid-air by the wand-like paintbrush of the artist. A tank smouldered nearby. Cornish read the main headline aloud:

'*Vixen Assassins bring out the hostages of Hitler's death trap.*'

He tried to affect the disdain he thought it appropriate he grant this kind of trash, while knowing too that he would separate this magazine from the others and masturbate over the fictitious blonde later in the day.

Where was the harm, after all? Even the Greys were at it. He hadn't forgotten – would never forget! – when, caught short one evening on his way home, he'd crept into the residents' bathroom to piss and had stumbled on the Nigerian fatty giving a royal hand-shine to the shire-horse. In the fraction of a second it had taken him to volte-face and dash from the bathroom before he was seen, the image had scarred his brain forever. How the old bastard's mighty wang – twice the thickness of Cornish's own – had curled upwards through the dressing gown, an elephant's trunk through the flap of a big-top. How its plum-sized crown had pulsed. How his lips had foamed with spittle. How she'd liberated one of her orbs from that candy floss nightdress and was plucking at the nipple, tapping out a love-sonnet in Morse. And how both of them had grimaced with pained, forgetful ecstasy.

Cornish had rushed upstairs, unlocked his office door, thrown it shut behind him, flipped out his own wang and torn it to shreds, splurging, in less than twenty seconds, across the leather sous-main. For several days after that he'd been racked with fear that his indiscretion would be revealed. Perhaps he'd forgotten to close the door, or perhaps the window cleaner had caught him unawares. Neither of these, nor any of his other purgatorial fantasies, had born any fruit.

Now, when overcome with the boredom that afflicts many a captive chimp, he was capable of up to five onanistic frenzies before home-time. It had become so much a part of his routine that he no longer even bothered to check the door or hide the wadded tissues, dropping them in the bin with a smile. The cleaning lady be damned!

Opening the bottom drawer a second time, he dropped MEN TODAY on top of the photo, turning the toy key this time. His cock stirred and lifted its head in anticipation of a treat, before skulking back into hiding.

With a deep breath, Cornish leaned back in his chair and gazed at the rosace for a few more seconds.

4

Smithy was after something.

'Been out?' he half-barked, half-whispered, inches from Dot's ear. She jerked in the wheelchair, winced. For a man of his bulk he was unnaturally stealthy, able to slink up on his quarry with the furtive, silent scamper of a hungry crocodile.

'Smithy! You scared me.'

He perched his cartoon bulk on the windowsill and spent a few seconds unknotting himself beneath his dressing gown. Then, after kindling his pipe, he used it to indicate Dot's ankle.

'Broken your leg?'

She picked a chunk of plaster from her cast and flicked it at the window.

'You noticed? Ankle actually, but don't tell Lanyard. I'm hoping he won't spot it.'

Interesting. Why hadn't she told him it was only a sprain? Something had made her up the ante of the accident.

'What an embuggerance,' Smithy said. 'Bones don't knit so well at our age.'

'That's just what the doctor said,' Dot went on, consolidating the lie. 'Also that my pole-vaulting days are behind me.'

She wasn't sure why she was embellishing her injury, but could already feel its effect. It was paradoxical, but the broken ankle somehow completed Dot, affirmed her as a worthy resident of Green Oaks – *if she could do that kind of damage to herself in an old folks' home, imagine the hazards she'd face in the* real *world*. But the sense of completion didn't stop there. Ever since Leonard's illness, Dot had felt burdened with the awful guilt of being left more or less intact by the whole experience. Now with a part of her leg hidden beneath a plaster cast she felt, finally, as if she'd made an appropriate concession, offered up a part of herself in tribute to the man who had been almost entirely redacted from existence. Now she too had a battle-scar to be proud of.

And yet she also rather despised the doctors for patching her up so late in the game. For pretending her desiccated dumpling of a body was worth the plaster-of-Paris. How could they, who had been front-row spectators to life's macabre curtain call on hundreds of occasions, still maintain the charade that the end could and should be held off?

'How long have you been back?'

'An hour, I suppose. Maybe two. God, Smithy, I don't know. It's so difficult to tell with all these clouds. I can't see the sun at all.'

'The time-embargo,' Smithy said. 'Castorp's Curse, I call it.' Then, grunting suddenly, as if embarrassed by what he'd said, he turned away from Dot and cleared a small porthole on the steamed up window. Did he mean *Hans* Castorp? Surely Smithy hadn't read Thomas Mann...

'Have you been keeping lookout while the Captain's in the hole? Any enemy troop movements?'

'The hole again? Oh dear.' Dot said. Then, despite knowing Smithy had never expected an answer, she gave one anyway: 'There were a few teenagers – children, really – at the bus stop down the hill.'

She waited for the memories of her own adolescence that flared across her mind to die down. She looked at Smithy and guessed he was doing the same. Ageing had long made Dot feel like a caged animal. Those teenagers had their own cages, of course; and while they might be shrinking with every second, they were still so big they hardly noticed them. Hers and Smithy's were so small they could barely move.

'I just bumped into Hortense in the hallway,' he said.

'Hortense?' The name was new to Dot.

'Windsor's squeeze from Ward A? He think's she's a bit of alright.

I think she dresses kind of like an old-time prossie. Doesn't mix with us, but then the Preemies never do. Funny, she's never spoken to me before, but she just stopped me and asked me – as a *manually gifted person* – if I could answer her a question about wood.'

'Wood?'

'She wanted to know if knots could continue growing after the tree has been cut down. I told her I was pretty sure they couldn't. She didn't look too happy with the answer, either.'

'Strange,' Dot said. She was already losing interest. Why did nobody talk *about* anything here, only *around* it?

'Not really,' Smithy said, grinding his finger into his temple. 'That Phlegmolax could make a two-ton rhinoceros hallucinate.' He looked out through the porthole. 'I mean, do you ever find,' he said, 'that when you look out across the fields, beyond Green Oaks, everything just looks so flat, almost fuzzy, like a cheap postcard? Everything is in the right place, but there's just no… *depth*.'

Dot felt irascible suddenly, although she wasn't sure why.

'Was there something you wanted?'

Smithy leaned in even closer, enrobing her in his cloacal breath.

'They took you to the hospital, I suppose?'

'I think the ambulance men were torn between the hospital and the dump.' Dot wasn't sure that she was joking.

'Which did they pick?'

'I got lucky, I suppose.' Not sure again.

'Look,' he peered over Dot's shoulder to check they were alone. 'Do they still have a library there?'

Before Smithy had interrupted her, Dot had been trying to piece together the events between her passing out on the floor of Ward B the night before, and waking up in the Green Oaks Dayroom that morning. She remembered snatches of an ambulance ride, a procession of swinging doors, the nuclear thump of the X-Ray machine and the chalky high of the plaster room, but none of it with more clarity than an impressionist street scene. No… *depth*.

And now Smithy wanted to know if there was a library? Was he, then, a bookish man? She'd never, for a moment, imagined any of her ward mates, least of all this golem of knotted thews, to be readers.

'I was only in one night, Smithy. I didn't think to ask.'

His facial drapes crumpled as he digested her words.

'No. Well, I suppose it doesn't come naturally to everyone.'

Before she could protest he pulled a slim, pink hardback from his pocket, his gaze ticking between Dot and the door. 'Last time I was in, they had a trolley come round. The usual rubbish really, but I did find this.' He held out the book, but when she reached out to take it he kept a tight hold. She was just able to draw it close enough to make out the title.

'Shakespeare's Sonnets.'

Just the sibilance was enough to knot her throat. It felt like such a long time…

'So I stole it. Problem is, that was a year ago. The bastard old ticker has behaved since then, and now I know the whole thing back to front.' He released the book, letting Dot win the gentle tug-of-war she only then realised they had been fighting. 'Test me if you like.'

'I…'

'Test me!'

Dot opened the book at random and looked down at the page.

'Not that one!' The rejection forced itself out of her like acid reflux.

'Which one?' Dot swallowed:

'*When I do count the clock that tells the time…*'

'*And see the brave day sunk in hideous night,*' – Smithy picked up, breathlessly. '*When I behold the violet past prime…*'

'Please… Smithy!'

He tilted his head, as if trying to find the angle that best suited the new impression he had of her.

'You know it?'

Did she know it? Of course she bloody knew it.

All she said was:

'I taught literature.'

At that, Smithy inflated like a set of bellows and his eyes flared. Just for a moment Dot caught a glimpse of the man lost beneath the folds of decades. When he'd caught his breath he said: 'Then you brought some books in with you, of course.' It wasn't a question, rather a statement of the bleeding obvious from one initiate to another.

She *had* thought about it, and yet had still come to Green Oaks empty-handed. The best books stripped off the lies we swaddled ourselves in, shone a light into the dark reaches of the soul... and it was for quite the opposite reason that Dot was here. She had come to escape – from the world and from herself – to enter her final hibernation, to run down alongside Leonard. Her final few months outside had taught her enough about herself, about people, to last her the rest of this putrid, shabby life.

'No.' Smithy's disappointment was so acutely apparent that she lied again. 'I mean, the CareFriends took them off me when I arrived.'

'Bastards!' he hissed, slipping the sonnets back into his pocket.

'I... I'm sure they meant well. Perhaps if we asked...'

'No!' He'd started pacing, wringing his hands in time with his steps. 'The war always has two fronts, Dot. Hearts starve as well as bodies! Bread and roses, bread and roses!'

'The war? You're starting to sound like the Captain.'

Smithy stopped pacing and stared at Dot, his expression at once intense but inscrutable.

'You're right. Oh god, I knew it!'

He slumped back onto his windowsill perch.

'Knew what?' Dot asked. Smithy sighed.

'Look, I know we're not supposed to talk about things BGO, but...'

'BGO?'

'You know, Before Green Oaks... but when I was an apprentice machinist in the late forties, our factory had its own library, because our boss had got it into his head that no serious reader could ever be a fascist. Horseshit, if you ask me. But he insisted we take a book home every weekend and he'd quiz us on them Monday mornings. He'd read everything there. And after a few years I had too. So I joined the local lending library and took out three books a week. Politics mostly. I loved the big boys: Marx, Lenin, Trotsky...'

Smithy stood and turned to the misted window. Dot sensed that this speech had been maturing for months, perhaps years, awaiting a sympathetic ear. She was flattered he had chosen her. Anxious too – she knew the price of confidences.

He reached out his index finger and drew a rising arc on the window.

Dot shifted with discomfort as her mind ticked: *Exposition, complication, climax, resolution*. What the hell did he want with that?

'At first I thought this was the path I was on. Greater and greater knowledge. Everything made sense. Everything joined up. The dialectic. That was the big idea. Interdependence. The conflict of opposites. The march of history.' His finger retraced the line. 'It felt so scientific. I really believed that united we would change things. That revolution was inevitable. That I'd live to see it. And then...' He placed his finger back on the line's crest. He seemed to be hesitating, as if finally admitting something to himself.

'And then...?' Dot asked. Smithy's hand swiped downwards, drawing the mirror image.

Anti-climax, simplification, muddle...

As Dot focused on the small gap between Smithy's lines a memory bobbed to the surface – in hospital, cradling Thomas in her arms for the very first time as Leonard had clumsily unglued her matted fringe. For that moment she'd felt atoned, happy, unworried. At her pole. Unmoving. Her still point in the universe.

'Then one day I was talking with my grandfather. He was very old by then. He told me how after he'd come back from the Western Front he'd gone to the library and read back over all of the newspapers published in the days following Franz Ferdinand's assassination, to try and understand. Do you know what he found? None of them had predicted the horrors that were to follow. Not a single one. Nobody sniffed anything out. Nothing! And I suddenly understood the futility of trying to make sense of any of it. At that moment I lost faith that we could influence, or even understand, the march of history. To do so would require holding all of the world's knowledge in our minds at once. Because it's not just conscious intention that shapes things, it's unconscious intention as well. It's coincidence. It's madness. It's ghosts! The world is a haunted bloody house...'

'But you kept on reading?' Dot asked.

'Well, it kept me out of trouble. If I was reading, at least I wasn't meddling. But now I can just feel all that knowledge decaying. Snatches come back to me, but I don't know what to do with them. I'll be lying in bed and I'll remember that the planet earth is actually as smooth as a billiard ball, or that the very first thing to develop in the human embryo is the anus. But then what?'

'I had no idea,' Dot said.

'Why would you? And don't go spreading it around. I'm happy for people here to think I'm – what was it? – manually gifted.'

'I know it's not much,' Dot said. 'But the Captain keeps a couple of his magazines stuffed under his mattress. They could always tide you over for now.'

'Go through another man's things? I'm not sure. Betty would have my guts for garters if she found out.'

'Where is Betty by the way?'

Smithy shook his head:

'Confession.'

'With a priest? Here?' The news left Dot unsettled, as if the tectonic plates of Green Oaks had shifted beneath her. Just a little, but enough for her to feel giddy.

'Betty's the only one that bothers. Though I'm sure he'd be happy to see you too. If you're...'

'No,' Dot said. 'I'm not.'

Smithy chuckled.

'Ghosts not your thing, eh? Not mine either, really. Then again...'

And without completing the thought, Smithy turned and scuffed out of the dayroom.

5

Somewhere, a machine was pounding. It stammered, fluttered, stopped. A dishwasher? An air conditioner? A heart? Was that how it sounded, the music at the close?

A man huddled in the corner of a darkened room. Bunched body, stripped and concertinaed. Head pincered between knees. Peaking shoulder blades, the stumps of amputated wings. Spine, curved and combed. Loose muscles roping nautically about bones. Arms like knotted luggage straps, binding the composition tight. A flat-packed clotheshorse man prepped for transit to other realms.

Dead, then? Well, no. Not quite. Watch:

A big toe, gnarled like ginger root, flexed. Stopped. Flexed again. A calf muscle twitched – once, twice, three times. Intestines awoke, purled and whined as they eased out the night. Then silence and stillness again. And then…

The man sprung from his huddle – *Jack-in-the-box!* Limbs stretched, mouth gasped, a frog leaping from a lily pad, straining outward, upward, away. The man roared as he flew – a roar of affliction. Birth's roar.

But he was no frog, no Superman, and he crashed to the floor. Embraced his gut. Retched. Battery acid chunder. A thin smile. Not dead, then. Alive!

Fall in chaps.

Limbs: One, two, three… ah!… four.

Digits: Twenty.

Meat: One.

Veg: Two.

All present and correct enough. Intact. Unharmed. Battle ready.

On your feet, man! (*Hop, crack!*)

Reconnaissance: Empty room, seven paces long, four wide. Sour, armpit air. Fingers puckered on rubbered walls. Balloon taut. Like a lung. Like young flesh.

He squatted down.

As big as the room. As light as dust. A forgotten god coming out of hibernation. A not-quite-Buddha soul, not-quite reborn.

Patience soldier, you've been here before.

Solitary.

The inner sanctum.

The belly of the whale.

Home.

A bolt was thrown. An angle of daylight, then the flood. He covered his eyes.

'Captain,' a cautious voice said. 'Captain, show yourself.'

'Jesus, Captain,' a woman's voice this time. 'Is that vomit?'

He stood poker-straight, dropped his head back.

'You're not going to make this difficult for us, are you Captain? You'll be back in the ward soon enough, but the Director wants to have a little word with you first.'

'Nothing to worry about,' said the woman. 'Just a little chat.'

'Just a little chat.'

The two visitors edged into the room. The woman – a spring-loaded, albino gorgon – was holding a white towelling gown in her outstretched arms, like a Retiarius in the Coliseum. The closer they got, the more tentatively they moved.

'A little chat, that's all.' The words were a receptacle for their anxiety. A fortifying mantra. They reached their target, but still he did not move. The woman bundled him into the gown and tied the long belt into a bow.

'You know the Director already,' the man said. 'He's only looking out for your well-being.'

'Only wants what's good for you,' the gorgon said. 'Us, on the other hand… We've just become your worst nightmare.' And catching him off-guard, she twisted him into a painful half-nelson.

The triumvirate moved towards the door. Only then did the forgotten god speak, but so quietly that the man asked him to repeat himself. In a louder voice, defiant and determined, he complied:

'I care not a jot for Zeus. Let him do what he will.'

6

A knock at the door. Whoever it was sounded impatient. Was it possible they had knocked already and Cornish hadn't heard it until now?

He made to tidy his desk and discovered, to his bewilderment, a sketch, clearly the work of his hand. Its models were those two Ward B Greys rendered in the very mutual-masturbatory throes he'd spied them in all those months back. He was impressed by the detail of the sketch, especially as he'd drawn it from memory alone. There was no mistaking its two protagonists, or what they were up to.

The visitor knocked again.

'Yes?' Cornish said, folding the picture and tucking it under the leatherette sous-main. The knob rattled, but the door remained closed. After a short pause, it rattled a second time.

'What is it?' he called out. 'Is it urgent?'

'What do you think?'

Oh crap! It had to be her, didn't it? The girl CareFriend…whatever her name was. The only reason Cornish had kept her on during the previous month's purge was that he'd been terrified of her reaction if he hadn't. The old supervisor had been a brute, but a predictable one. This girl wasn't: she was lean and stringy in a way that only the dirt-poor seemed to be, and she had a feral look in her eyes. Atrocious… but unsackable. Thank god the door was locked.

'I suppose, yes,' he said, cowed. His weight heavily on the back foot. 'Care to enlighten me?'

'It's that resident you asked to see. He's here with me now.'

'Resident?' Cornish said to himself. 'The resident I asked to see?' After a 'turn', recovery of his thoughts was always like tidying up a house after an earthquake, struggling to remember what had once gone where. Had he asked to see a resident? Which one? That didn't sound much like something he would do. He feared the Greys' company and avoided it whenever he could. It was rare for one to make it as far as his office. He plucked at his nose.

'Well, best leave him there and get back to your... *rounds*? I'll only be a few minutes.'

'Right,' came the voice.

'Was there anything else?'

'Yeah. Tristan will be late in,' the girl said. 'Got a dentist appointment for his foot-and-mouth issues.'

'Foot-and-mouth issues?' Cornish frowned – wasn't that something to do with sheep?

'Smithy's foot, Tristan's mouth. Bloody mess it was, apparently.' The girl cackled. Her response begged a dozen questions, but Cornish knew better than to get mixed up in it.

'Okay, well thank you, um...?'

'Frankie.'

'Excuse me?'

'Francesca.'

'Oh right! Of course. Thank you, Francesca.' Cornish listened as her footsteps struck up, then faded away.

'Francesca,' He said, *sotto voce*, just in case. 'Stupid name.' He looked again at the debris – the magazines, the plastic bottle, the colander. A realisation breached. 'Oh fuck. Him again.'

He picked up the colander and turned it about in his hands.

'The plot thickens.' Noticing, suddenly, a small oblong of card hiding beneath the colander he added, with a bored sigh: 'And thickens still further.'

The card had been torn from the top of a cereal box. The reverse was marked up in ballpoint, with a crude imitation of an ID card. The 'photo' reminded him of the Cerne Abbas giant.

Crossing to the door, he took hold of the knob then stopped. Instead of opening it, he creaked onto his haunches, removed a crusty nugget of tack from the keyhole and peered out: Ruggles, Ward B's habitual rabble-rouser. It would have been easy to be deceived by the appearance of this thug into thinking him benign. Cornish had stumbled into that trap before. His scraggly frame, his small, pointed beard, jaunty whiskers and that permanent rheumy gleam in his eye lent him a rather Arcadian air. But his antics had been the cause of more turns these last months than anything else. Not that he did anything particularly serious – attempted escapes, theft of supplies, general disruption… all part of the Green Oaks grind. But the regularity of his escapes meant that Cornish was forced into contact with the residents much more frequently than he liked – and this acted as a catalyst for his turns.

Still unaware of the nearby voyeur, his shoulders curled inwards and his clasped hands resting in his lap, he did cut a rather vulnerable figure. For a moment, Cornish's heart flexed in sympathy.

But only for a moment. For there were procedures, exposited in the handbook he'd been issued after the buy-out… and procedures and handbooks existed for a reason. *No emotional involvement with residents* – that was the most important of the lot. Lose sight of the fact that these people had come to Green Oaks to die, and actually become friends with them, and the job would have quickly become intolerable. Life too. Much better to keep some distance, process the residents like paperwork, and let the families and chaplain cope with their pastoral concerns – when either bothered to visit.

Cornish glanced again at his reflection across the room, smoothed down the hair-pineapple and opened the door.

'You'd better come in.'

Ruggles said nothing, just stood and marched directly towards, directly *at*, Cornish, his wrists shackled by invisible handcuffs, thrust out in front of him. Cornish waited at the door, his hand stropped-dry and ready to shake. A noble sacrifice, he thought, considering that every physical interaction with a resident left him with a death-chill it could take a good half-day to shake. Ruggles ignored the gesture, striding into the office and plumping himself in what Cornish, with a grim irony, liked to call his 'guest chair'. Cornish walked around the desk to his own chair, the old nose-tugging tick, a hangover from his pre-therapy days, activated and in full swing, but didn't sit. Placing his hands flat on the desk, he leaned towards Ruggles:

'This has got to stop, you know,' he said, privately delighted by the masculine twang to his voice.

'*Entschuldigung, Herr Kommandant. Ich spreche kein Deutsch.*'

Cornish tugged so hard on his nose that his fingers snapped together.

'I'm not...' – a weariness had edged into his voice – '... speaking German.'

He walked across to the filing cabinet – just so he wouldn't fish-slap the old loon – and pulled out Ruggles' file. He scanned it for ammunition then crossed back to the desk:

'Try to see this from my point of view will you, Dylan. May I call you...?'

Ruggles didn't answer. Locking eyes with the stubborn Grey, Cornish groped for his chair and lowered himself into it. *Maintained eye contact consolidates authority* – another tip picked up from the handbook. From the handbook, or from Harriet's dog training manual.

'This is the sixth time you've tried to escape, the third time this month. I know you don't like it here Dylan, but where on earth do you think you'll go? Out there...' – pointing at the window – '...that's no world for an old man like you. Not any more. Hard. Dangerous. Uncaring. Here...' – prodding the desk now – '... here is where you belong. Surely you must understand? And yet you disturb the other residents, you steal expensive supplies and you make the attend...' Cornish paused, swallowed back his bile. 'You make the CareFriends' work ten times harder than it already is. What would you do if you were me?'

'I'm sorry...' Ruggles began.

'You're sorry? Well that's a start, I suppose. Very good.'

'I'm sorry,' Ruggles repeated. 'I don't understand German, *Herr Kommandant.*'

'I'm *not* speaking…' Cornish ventured again, before cutting himself off. 'Oh, what's the point?'

He stood up and walked over to the window. He spent a lot of time there, when alone, most of it calculating how much damage he would do to himself if he jumped. Sometimes he saw himself landing with the agility of a jackrabbit, haring off across the fields… Other times he imagined his balsa-wood tibias snapping, his broken body sprawling on the driveway, an abandoned marionette of a man.

'You know, your friend's ankle is in plaster this morning because of your shenanigans. You had heard that? She had to go to hospital, have X-rays. She'll be in a wheelchair for months, perhaps for the rest of her life.'

He discovered that he preferred talking with his back to Ruggles. It gave him more confidence, and that made him more loquacious. He turned to check he still had his audience. He did, just about. Ruggles was staring blankly at Cornish's chair.

'All because you had to have your fun. Show off. Play the clown. I'm also none too happy about the rumours you've been spreading about Ward C. There are some very sick people there. Very disturbed. The CareFriends do a good job. A really sterling job, in fact.'

He had no idea if this was true, although he doubted it. He hadn't visited the Feebies for a long time, not since the occasion of his first panic attack a couple of years earlier. Now, when he arrived in the morning and left at night, he preferred to walk past Ward C as if it wasn't there.

Outside, it was starting to spit. He picked up the small pair of theatre binoculars he kept on the windowsill, lifted them to his eyes and performed a sweep of the country vista before coming to rest on the bus stop at the end of the long driveway. A pack of teenagers, four boys and a girl, were sheltering there from the rain. Cornish recognised them. They were from Meanwell, but often hung out in the nearby fields. They made noise, but not trouble, although he always feared they would (and that he, in turn, would have no way of stopping them). The boys were all got up in dark, polyester tracksuits and caps, and the girl in a tracksuit top and pink miniskirt. She was sitting on a boy's lap. He had looped his arm around her and was lazily fondling one of her breasts, although the girl and the other boys seemed utterly indifferent to this. One of the boys was smoking, furtively concealing the butt in a duck-billed hand, and pacing back and forth under the shelter. The other two were looking at something on a mobile telephone and laughing.

Cornish's thoughts lit out, abandoning Ruggles for now, and he imagined himself addressing the teenagers from the window. In his reverie they wearily challenged him. Rather than retreating behind the net curtain, he opened the window and called back to them. He didn't know what they said to each other, but he made them laugh and won their respect.

The phantasm shifted and he found himself sitting with them at the bus stop. The girl was on his lap, her tightly-drawn ponytail dusting his face, his hands resting one on each of her bony thighs. Three boys were passing around a blue plastic bottle of something. When it was Cornish's turn to swig, he looked into the bottle and saw a snake, black and featureless, belt-like, thrashing about inside. He could just make out Green Oaks through the roping rain. The windows were glowing with an eerie white light. He brought the bottle to his lips and drank…

'Take that, Fritz! Right in the kisser!'

Ruggles' cry wrenched Cornish back from the bus stop into the subfusc reality of his office. During his brief absence, Ruggles had donned the colander as a kind of helmet, picked up the copy of *Air Souls!* and, knees hitched to chest, was gourmandising on it.

'*Ze Führer vill have ze last word, Shavings!* Ha! No he won't Jerry! No way!'

Ruggles' boyish ebullience made Cornish think of his youngest son, before he had morphed into the acned teenage gargoyle that now haunted his home, and for a second time his heart softened. Quickly, however, the affective needle swung back the other way, passing over the cheeses marked *Frustration* and *Irritation*, landing plumb in the one marked *Anger*.

'You're going to stop reading this trash, you hear?' he yelled, striding up to Ruggles, snatching the magazine from him and hurling it across the room. Ruggles gasped, winded, as a lose page eddied free of the ancient glue and fluttered to the carpet. Glaring at Ruggles, Cornish picked up the page, slid it into his cardboard file, then rolled the file into a baton.

Brandishing it:

'I've read your notes. I know your game. I wouldn't actually mind all this nonsense if you'd actually fought in the war, in *any* war. We could put it down to shell shock and move along. But you didn't, did you? Not a single day of active service in your whole sorry life. You're not a soldier! You're just a sad old man, determined to make things difficult for me...' – he checked himself – '... that is, for *everyone*. No wonder your daughter doesn't visit you any more.'

These final words hung in the close air of the office as, for a long time, neither man spoke.

'Torture me all you want, *Kommandant*,' Ruggles said, eventually, his voice childlike and small. 'I won't crack.'

Cornish sat down, ran his fingers through his hair and subjected his nose to a brutal tug.

'I don't want you to crack.' He was almost pleading now. 'Although it might be too late for that.'

The fury had subsided but the righteousness lingered. He couldn't bring himself to look at Ruggles. He reached for the blue calculator and slid it across the desktop with his fingertips. He keyed in a number – 58008 – and smiled. Clearing the screen, he keyed in another: 5318008.

'Look,' remembering Ruggles. 'You know what the CareFriends want? They want me to send you on a little trip. Where? Oh, not far. Just...' – he licked his lips – '... to Ward C.' He thought he saw Ruggles swallow back his fear.

'Yes. You understood that well enough. I'm not going to move you, though. Not just yet. But I will put your file up for review. Consider this your final warning.'

He rocked back in his chair, impressed by his own malign creativity. There was no review process for ward transfers. He had plucked that little flourish from thin air. For all their dictates and handbooks, West Church really cared very little about the day-to-day, as long as the bottom line stayed black. It sounded good though. Perhaps his artistic limb hadn't been fully amputated after all. And a stump was surely better than nothing.

Cornish had grown weary of Ruggles and, sensing their exchange had explored all its potential avenues, said:

'I think we've covered everything. You're free to go.'

Ruggles didn't budge.

'I said you're free to go. *Shoo!*' miming a broom with his fingers, hoping the gesture would sweep Ruggles out of the door, out of his day. Ruggles lifted himself slowly from the chair. Fully erect, he opened then refastened his gown, treating Cornish to a full-frontal exhibition of his repulsively withered frame. He straightened the colander on his head and began stuffing his deep flannel pockets with the magazines until no more would fit. The rest he wedged under his arms and clutched in his hands. Cornish considered objecting, considered insisting Ruggles leave the magazines and the colander with him, but he couldn't muster the will.

Cornish cleared the calculator screen and, after a moment of reflection, typed: 60436034. He grimaced. Less satisfying than the others. He hit AC again. As he searched for a more satisfying conclusion to his game, he realised that he was still not alone in the office. Ruggles had stopped by the door and was peeking under the sheet at the Green Oaks model.

Cornish had commissioned it early on his tenure, from Harriet's brother who, newly-graduated, was struggling to launch his own design studio. He'd excused the dubious use of funds firstly as a sop to his wife, and secondly as a way to lend the newly opened care home a certain, much-needed class. At the time Cornish had felt that nothing spoke more about the success of an institution, nothing showed more panache, than a model of its building in the lobby. It seemed unimportant that most similar models would have been constructed before the buildings themselves, that what they represented were the institutions' might, their ability not only to have a vision, but to make this vision a concrete-and-glass reality. These models carried with them the implication that whomsoever brought the finished building to fruition would be capable of looming over it in much the way that mere mortals could only loom over the model. It had been this very ability to loom over his own exercise in reverse-engineering that most appealed to Cornish. To loom over something implied control and detachment, implied power, sensations he'd struggled with then, and was struggling with still. He had specified that the model not be painted, that it be a pure, white, coldly schematised replica of the old manor house, enclosed within a glass vitrine to protect it from the wearying hand of time. He had hoped that when visitors inspected the model they would see the very essence of Green Oaks, divorced from the decay, the dirt, the temporality of the building and its residents.

For a while he'd convinced himself that this divorce had taken place. Every morning as he passed the model in the lower hallway, he would pause to admire the whiteness of the walls and dandle his fingers over the glass. The model's scientific coolness and apparent immutability had given him the strength to get through the day.

That was why when, one morning, several years later, he'd noticed that one corner of his Lilliputian sanctuary had warped – that the glue which before had bound the eastern and northern walls together had relinquished its hold on them, fanning open a fraction of an inch – he'd felt sick to the pit of his stomach. With the help of three attendants (as they were still known then) he'd had the model displaced to his office. After a closer examination of it had also revealed a mild discolouration of the white walls, he had thrown a sheet over it, under which it had remained for the last seventeen years. After a time it had become just another surface on which he could pile the mostly-pointless paraphernalia of his office. Cornish had never been sure whether the purpose of the sheet was to protect the model from further damage or to protect him from its continuing and inevitable decay. Either way, the fact that Ruggles had stopped, stooped, lifted the sheet and was peering under it, irritated him.

'Get out from under there!' he barked. When Ruggles didn't comply, Cornish stood and tossed a biro, which fell far short of its target and skittered to a halt at the old man's feet. 'Oy!'

Ruggles cast off the sheet and straightened up.

'Interesting,' he said, more to himself than to Cornish. 'Very detailed. Even the mills.'

At first, Cornish didn't understand, then realised, with a jolt of annoyance, that he was talking about the trees, the oaks themselves. These, for Cornish, had been the only dissatisfying element of the model, strangely stumpy and angular, the branches made up of nothing more than five or six overlapping strips of paper, pinned to the top of each trunk. He could see why Ruggles had taken them for windmills.

'I think you'll find,' he began, his pride bruised, 'that those are…' but before he could finish, Ruggles had left his office, closing the door behind him.

That last exchange aside, Cornish was pleased with how the interview had gone. He had lost his temper, but only once, and had managed to hold off another turn. That was something to be proud of. He tilted his head back, and focussed on the rosace for a few more seconds, counting his breaths in and out. Newly fortified, he considered getting down to some work. But what? There were most likely several competing bids that needed his attention, although with the scrapings Green Oaks received from West Church, he never faltered when making his choice: the cheapest won out every time.

There was also the riddle of the missing key. It wasn't of paramount importance, being only the key to the closet next to his office, but its absence from his keyring was perturbing nonetheless. When, exactly, it had gone missing, he had no idea. Even less who'd taken it. Although the chances of him actually mounting an investigation were slim. An investigation would mean conversations, contact, with the CareFriends, maybe even the Greys, and that would do him no good whatsoever. Give it time, he thought, and it would probably just show up again. Or he'd just forget about it. Either way, the problem would vanish.

Before anything, though, he had promised himself blissful release once the trauma of his meeting with Ruggles was over. Fingering the other smaller key from his pocket, he opened the drawer and took out MEN TODAY. He smiled flirtatiously at the Vixen Assassin, and imagined her smiling back as he started kneading his scrotum.

Nothing doing. Something had made him lose interest in this warrior slut... but what?

Not leaving his chair, Cornish pedalled to the window. He groped for his binoculars but couldn't lay his hand on them. No matter, he could just make out the girl. She was bending over, treating one of the boys to a protracted kiss, and Cornish to a view of her buttock-less arse, taloned by the curling fingers of her young lover. Cornish felt the blood course towards his groin and assumed the attack position abandoned at his desk moments before.

Leaning his face into the net curtain, he let the fabric form a damp caul over his mouth. He smiled to himself and shook his head. How old was she? Fourteen?

'**...t**hree... four... there! I moved it for you, Sir. What's the red? Piccadilly, is it? Give it to Windsor.'

'...'

Piccadilly *Circus*. Who's got it?'

'...'

'Hand it ov... Oh, Olive, wake up for heaven's...'

Dot hated Monopoly. Hated John Waddington Ltd for inventing it. Hated what it did to families. Hated what it taught. Hated how *real* losing felt.

'Olive, it's your... Shall I do the honours then?' – Lanyard rolled the dice – 'As usual. Nine! Nine! That's Marylebone Station. Marylebone, Olive. Does that interest you?'

Slumped in her armchair, a pendulum of drool dangling from her lip, Olive said nothing.

'Marylebone? Olive? Hum! Well let's just say, for argument, that it does, shall we? Smithy, it's your go.'

'...'

'Smithy!'

'Not now, old man!' Smithy barked, swatting off Lanyard's entreaty. He was lost in a labyrinth of thought... Dot could tell: it was drawn right there in his frown lines.

'Well, I'll do the honours. Again. Let's see. Six. Six. What are you Smithy? What token? *Smithy?*' Afraid that actual steam would soon start pirouetting from Smithy's ears, Dot leaned in.

'I'm Professor Plum, I think. Smithy's this thing. What is it? A warlord?'

'It's a *warrior*, Dot,' Lanyard snapped. 'An *alien* warrior. And you're not Professor Plum, dear.'

'Oh, I thought...'

'No, no. Windsor's *always* Professor Plum. You're *this*. The *Scrabble* piece. The Q.'

'Worth ten,' Windsor added, rising briefly from his own meditative fog. 'No small beans.'

Olive started awake, inhaled the drool.

'I thought I was the Q!'

'No, Olive. You're the X...'

'Worth eight,' Windsor again. 'Not so bad...'

'Quite right, Sir,' Lanyard said, dabbing his forehead with a hand-kerchief. 'So, *Dot's* the Q, *Smithy's* the alien warlord...'

'Warrior,' Dot said.

'Warrior! *Windsor's* Professor Plum. The *Captain's* the pound coin. And *Betty's* the shell.' The more agitated he became, the more Lanyard italicised his speech.

'Betty and the Cap aren't even here!'

'I'm *well* aware, Olive,' Lanyard said. 'But should they arrive at any time they'll be able to sooje into the game at...'

Smithy perked up, a hunting dog catching a spoor.

'To what, old boy?'

Lanyard hesitated.

'To... sooje. They'll be able to sooje into the game.'

Smithy leaned forward, elbows on the table, chin balanced on his clenched hands.

'To sooje? I'm sorry, Lanny, that's a new word to me. Would you be able to spell it out.'

Lanyard beamed his teacher's-pet smile.

'Sooje, Smithy. S-E-G-U-E. To sooje. Verb. An uninterrupted transition from one thing to another.'

'Sooje,' Smithy repeated, his face twitching with laughter. 'Well, I never…'

'May I?' Lanyard asked.

'By all means,' Smithy waved him on. 'Sooje away.'

'Thank you. As I was saying, as games time is compulsory, should Betty and the Captain arrive at any moment, they'll be able to sooje into…'

'Excuse me…' Smithy bolted to his feet. 'I'm sorry. I need a little… I'm just going to sooje over…'

Still trembling, he hurried across to the sash window, flung it open and stuck his head outside.

'Dot,' Lanyard said, unfazed. 'Your go.'

Dot looked at the board. Did she have to? She might not have minded too much if they were actually playing Monopoly, but since the set had been robbed of its money they had to make do with a bastardised version of the game. She wasn't sure any of them understood it. It was either genius or madness – probably both. Theirs was a world in which Professor Plum had left Tudor Hall for a life of hawkish property speculation in the capital. In which an alien warlord could win second prize in a beauty contest. In which barter and hock had replaced the money economy. And in which winning, even finishing, had lost all meaning.

All the other games were the same – old, and not a single one intact, with all the tokens jumbled together in a large plastic tub. Not long after her arrival Dot had tried to sift the pieces, but it had proven hopeless. The pack of cards was five cards short. Scrabble's vowels were missing. Someone had made off with the plastic visor from Mastermind and the five-hundred-piece jigsaw had no edges… not a single one.

'Must I?' she said, dropping her cards onto the board. 'I don't even understand the rules.'

'Director's orders, I'm afraid,' Lanyard said. 'It's good for our… what was it?'

'Cognition!' Windsor barked.

'Good too for keeping us out of trouble while the bastards sit in that room over there, plotting their next…'

'And she's off,' said Windsor, heaving a sigh and closing his eyes. Lanyard continued the game, playing for all seven of them, and commentating as he did so.

'Nasty business, your leg,' Olive said, trailing her fingernails along Dot's cast.

'It's just a small fracture,' Dot said, a slightly defiant edge to her voice.

'But bones don't... *gah*!' Olive blenched with a spasm that, had she been standing, would have set her limbs scattering.

'... Knit so well at our age? I know, Olive.' She wished everyone would stop going on about knitting. Olive shuffled in her chair so that she pressed close against Dot.

'They don't listen to me,' she said. 'But they should, you know.'

Dot knew it was wrong to indulge her, but her boredom pulled rank. 'I listen to you Olive. What's on your mind?'

'What's going on upstairs,' she said. 'Kalka. The human lab rat.'

'Olive!'

'What? Don't be so naive, Dotty!'

'Don't you be so ridiculous.'

'Can't you see it, Dot? This is all Mister Cornish's grand experiment. Look at the games!'

'I suppose you think the staff tampered with them?'

'Not just tampered with. *Creatively* tampered with. Made unplayable.'

'Things fall apart, Olive. Pieces get lost along the way.'

'Not like this! Not in such a neat way. And it's not just the games. It's the whole house.'

Dot puffed her incredulity.

'The clock. The chimes. They're purposely disorienting us. Why else did they take our watches?'

Dot swallowed hard. Olive's wittering was awakening her vertigo.

'Right,' Lanyard's voice winged in. 'I'll roll for the Captain too, I suppose.'

'And the wards, Dot,' Olive went on. 'Whoever heard of an old folks home with communal wards? He wants to *encourage* interaction...'

Olive clenched her hands, the long fingers twisted together like some fossilised arachnid. 'Everything's linked. Cornish plans everything. His meddling fingers are all over the place. We've still got some fight in us so they don't push things too far. That and the Captain. He holds them off for us. He's our lightning rod. It's the Feebies we should be worried about.'

'Ballerina special: double two!'

The vertigo ticked up a couple of gears.

'Where are the... Feebies?' Dot asked, pinching the bridge of her nose. 'I'd like to see for my...'

In the hallway, the grandfather clock chimed:

One... two...

'They'll never let you, Dot...'

'Three, four... Oh, Community Chest!'

'But don't tell me you didn't hear the noise they were making earlier?'

Five... six... seven...

'No...' A knitting needle jammed between the eyes. 'What noise?'

Eight...

'Go to jail...'

Nine... ten...

Dot's mind had hitched to a fairground waltzer now, snapping in violent loops.

'Panting and screaming, Dot... Whistling and whooping... The Derby, they call it... They chalk a track on the lino.'

'Go *directly* to jail...'

Eleven... twelve...

Fucking children and their fucking games!

Thirteen...

'Race them like seaside donkeys!'

'Do *not* pass Go...'

'Cracking... slapping... running... crying...'

Fourteen...

'Don't tell me you didn't hear it, Dot.'

'Do *not* collect two hundred pounds…'

Fifteen…

'It's the whole house!'

'Your turn, Dot!'

Sixteen…

'And you know what they say, Dot?'

'Dot!'

'The house always wins…'

'STOP IT!'

The seventeenth chime faltered and crunched to nothing. Everyone was staring at Dot. Dot was staring at the empty hallway, her hands trembling as they gripped the wheelchair's armrests. Her cheeks were lurid and pricked with sweat.

'There's… nobody…' she stammered, as the room stopped spinning. 'How…?'

'Something wrong with the mechanism, I'd imagine,' Lanyard said, apparently unaffected by her hellcat's roar. 'No machine runs perfectly forever. Something always gives. I should take a…'

Suddenly, the table and Lanyard were slipping away from Dot. It took her a moment to understand that Smithy had released the wheelchair's brakes and was rolling her backwards.

'Thought you could do with a little fresh air yourself,' he said, orienting her plastered leg towards the window.

'Thank you,' Dot said. 'I don't know what came over me.'

'No explanation needed.'

A breeze dandled across Dot's face. The birdsong outside was soothing.

'Was I very loud?'

Smithy laid a hand on her shoulder.

'You were… impressive.'

'Impressive?' Dot cracked a smile. 'Oh bugger. It was just too much all of a sudden. Olive in one ear, Leonard in the other.'

'Lanyard,' Smithy corrected her.

'What did I say?'

'Doesn't matter. Sounds like a perfect storm.'

'Why does he do it, though?'

'Why does who do what?'

'Lanyard. Why does he insist on playing that bloody pointless game? Hasn't he got anything better to do?'

'No,' Smithy said. The stony syllable killed her questions dead. He was right, of course. Games, bath time, feeding time – there was nothing else left. These were the perimeters of Lanyard's world. Of Dot's world too.

'I took your advice,' Smithy said, changing tack. 'I read a couple of the Cap's magazines. Complete trash, of course – that must be why they let him keep them, no danger – but I had forgotten how much I loved them when I was a nipper. I had forgotten how the stories never actually end. One *adventure* may end, but there's always the promise of more. There will always be a bigger villain for Dirk Shavings to fight next month. Or if not Dirk Shavings, then some other barrel-chested…'

Smithy paused to hawk something up into his handkerchief.

'*Air Souls!* That was my favourite. I haven't thought of that name in fifty years. I bought it every month for… I don't know how long, but it felt like years. Then, one day, I went to pick it up and the newsagent told me it was over. No more *Air Souls!* The publisher had gone bust. Kids weren't so interested in the war any more. And there was an obscenity trial too. Peddling filth to minors. It meant no more Dirk Shavings. Or Commander Desmond Putes, the French resistance fighter. A whole world of heroes – two-bit heroes, but heroes nonetheless – left hanging for eternity. Weren't they owed a proper ending at least?'

Dot turned to look at Lanyard. He was rifling through the property cards.

'Aren't we all?' she said. 'Though I've never seen a life end tidily yet. For my part, I'm sick to the back teeth of phoney resolutions.' She looked at the sparrows arcing from one bush to the next. 'They're not even for the birds.'

★

A few minutes later, when Dot and Smithy had rejoined the others at the card table, Betty came into the Dayroom. Smithy vacated his armchair for her at once. She occupied it without a word.

'How was Father Patterson?' Smithy said, pulling up a plastic chair for himself. When Betty didn't answer, his gaze made an anxious tour of the others before he tried again. 'How was he, Bets?'

'*Hmm?*' Betty said. 'Pardon?'

'Father Patterson,' Smithy insisted. 'Was he alright?'

'No,' Betty said slowly.

'No?'

'I'm sorry… I mean… I don't know. I didn't see him.'

'What happened?' Lanyard asked, his interest pricked. Without looking down at the board he hopped the alien warrior forward five squares.

'That CareFriend,' Betty said. 'The handsome one. What's his name, again?'

'I'm not sure any of them are really…'

'Tristan,' Dot said, interrupting Smithy.

'That's it,' Betty said. 'Tristan. One side of his face was swollen – all red and blue – and his lips were caked with blood.'

'Doesn't sound so handsome to me,' Smithy said.

'I didn't realise it was so bad,' Dot said. They all turned to look at her. 'Last night,' she said. 'During the Captain's escape. During the kerfuffle, I mean. Tristan fell onto Smithy's bed and… Well, you know how you're not the most peaceful of sleepers, Smithy.'

'Oh heavens!' Lanyard shrieked. 'What did he do?'

'It wasn't his fault, not really.'

'Spit it out woman!' Lanyard hissed.

'He kicked him,' Dot said. 'Square in the jaw.'

Olive squealed and clapped her hands, delighted. Smithy bit his lip, smiling nervously.

'You got him good,' Dot continued. 'I must admit I'd forgotten about it until Betty reminded me just then.'

'He looked so strange,' Betty said. 'I saw him before he saw me. On the upstairs landing, his forehead pressed against the closet door, muttering something. After a minute or two, he turned and I saw his face. The left side was completely untouched, but the right... It was just so swollen and disfigured. Monstrous! Then he grinned, winced, looked back at the closet one more time and swaggered down the stairs towards me.'

'And what did he say?' Smithy asked.

'Nothing at first, cocky little pig! But I couldn't help myself. I said: What have you got to be so damned pleased about?'

'And?' Lanyard interrupted.

Betty swallowed: 'I'm not really sure, but it sounded like... like *kalki*.'

The gasps of shock they had each earlier set aside for just this moment were loosed...then quickly smothered as the fog of general incomprehension settled.

'What's kalki?' Lanyard asked.

'Did he mean Kal*ka*?' Smithy said.

'Is *Kalka* in the closet?' Olive thrilled at the prospect.

'Don't be absurd,' Smithy bit back.

Dot laid her hand on Olive's knee and shook her head reassuringly. She didn't really know how absurd Olive's suggestion was, but as Kalka's usurper she was happy to play it down.

'I don't know what he meant,' Betty said. 'And to be honest I don't really care. The worst of it was the look in his eye when he told me he had cancelled Father Patterson's visits. The malice there was frightening.'

'But why cancel Patterson?' Smithy asked. 'Because of Kalka? It makes no sense.'

'It makes *perfect* sense,' Lanyard said. 'The Captain's recklessness is finally taking its toll on the rest of us. Punishment has no effect on him, so now they're coming after us. He'd be better off transferred. *We'd* be better off, anyway.'

'Don't be so sure,' Betty said. 'And besides, he didn't even mention the Captain. He just sneered and said he'd called Father Patterson and told him the mumbo-jumbo he was peddling was long past its sell-by date and no longer welcome at Green Oaks.'

'He has no right!' Smithy said.

'That's what I told him,' Betty said.

'And what did he say?'

'I don't know. After that he became very difficult to follow. He used the word paradigm quite a lot, though. And transcendence. It felt as if he was trying to explain an idea to himself as much as to me, but was having a difficult time doing so because it still hadn't really set in his mind. I felt like I was watching someone handling a meringue before it was done. If it wasn't so upsetting it might almost have been funny.'

'That'll be the painkillers talking,' Smithy said, pride inflecting his observation. 'For the fat face I gave him. They'll make scrambled eggs out of any human brain.'

'He wasn't completely scrambled, though,' Betty said. 'Sometimes he was far too lucid. Like when he…' She raised her hand to her chest and took several long deep breaths. An attempt, Dot was sure, to dispel the queasiness the memory evoked.

'Out with it!' Lanyard prompted.

'When he said, anyway, he knew exactly why I was so keen to see Father Patterson. And then…' Betty grimaced. 'He did this…' and she brought the V of her fingers to her lips and waggled her tongue between them. Dot winced – playground humour at its basest. 'What I don't understand,' Betty said. 'Is that of all of them, he used to be alright.'

Smithy was on his feet. He grabbed the back of his chair and his knuckles blanched at once.

'Little bastard!' he croaked. 'I'm going to bend his scrawny body backwards, stuff his head up his arse and dance the bloody hula-hula-hoop with him.'

'Smithy!' Betty said, but he didn't hear her. The chair was rattling beneath his grip.

'And I'm… I'm going to… flay him alive… and… use his balls as… as a…' Dot felt the charge drain from him suddenly. 'Use them as a…' He exhaled a monstrous sigh. 'No point, is there?' he asked nobody in particular. 'Nope. No bloody point.'

Betty took his hand.

'Sit down, love.'

Smithy looked at her, mouthed: *I'm sorry*. Betty shook her head and tried to smile.

'Let's change the subject,' she said. Lanyard nodded vigorously.

'Exactly, I'm sure it's just a misunderstanding. Whose go?'

Smithy reached forward and picked up the dice.

'No, I don't think it's…' Lanyard tried. 'Because you're the warrior, and the warrior just…'

After studying the dice in his palm for a moment, Smithy tilted his head back, dropped them onto his tongue and gulleted them.

'Ha!' Olive shrieked.

'Smithy! No…' Lanyard cried. 'They're the only… What have you…? It was Windsor's…'

'If Windsor's as concerned about the game as you are, old chap, he's welcome to accompany me to the crapper at…' – checking his watchless wrist – '… around nine o'clock this evening to see how he's done. Or you can come yourself. Though my guess it will be a Little Joe. That is, a pair of twos, or a hard four…'

Olive laughed again, slid off her chair and thumped to the floor. The noise stirred Windsor.

'What the devil?' he barked. Then: 'There! Do you smell it?'

'Don't worry, sir,' Lanyard said. 'It's just Smithy…'

'It's near! The crab!'

'Nonsense, sir,' Lanyard said. 'Try to rest.'

'Oh Dot,' Betty said. 'Your leg. I didn't even ask. I was so caught up in my own problems. Are you alright?'

'It's just my ankle,' Dot said. 'I'll be fine.'

'Break or sprain?' Betty asked.

'Break,' Lanyard jumped in. 'You wouldn't put a sprained ankle in plaster.'

'Wouldn't you?' Betty said.

'No. And it's terrible luck. Terrible! Bones don't...'

'... knit so well...' Olive chirped from the floor.

'... at our age. No they don't,' Betty said. Dot sensed Betty wanted to ask more but was holding back. Instead she reached into her pocket and pulled out a lumpy paper bag. She put it on the table and tore it open.

'Might as well,' she said, 'seeing as rules are being broken.'

Lanyard cast a furtive eye at the door, then smiled: 'Pear drops? Outside food!'

'My son slipped them to me last time he came down,' Betty said. 'I've been saving them for a time we needed perking up. He'll be back in a few weeks, so help yourselves.'

They took it in turns to finger a pear drop into their mouths, slurping on them like draining sinks.

'Windsor,' Betty said. 'You didn't take one.'

'Not hungry,' he said.

'It's a sweetie, old boy, not a Sunday roast. You don't need an appetite.'

'No, I said.'

After checking Windsor wasn't watching him, Lanyard searched out Betty's gaze and mouthed: '*Hortense.*'

'Oh,' Betty said.

Smithy gripped Windsor's forearm.

'Listen. You mustn't let your fancy lady's whims rob you of your appetite. A man could starve to death that way.' Windsor's tracheal tube gurgled his displeasure. He shook off Smithy's grip and snapped his fingers. Lanyard extracted a packet of cigarettes from Windsor's robe, plugged one into the tube's valve and lit it with a match.

'She's not my fancy lady,' Windsor said, a constant trickle of smoke escaping between his teeth. 'She promised me a *rendez-vous* and didn't keep her word, that's all.'

'Not Ward A again, Windsor?' Betty said.

'I'd expect such behaviour from *hoi polloi*...'

'He means us,' Smithy said with a smirk.

'Perhaps I do! I thought she was raised better than that.'

'We did wonder, though,' Lanyard said. 'If she might pull some strings.'

'There are no strings to pull,' Smithy said.

'Then how did Kalka get to spend a few nights there before...' Windsor stopped himself.

'What do you know?' Betty asked.

'Nothing!' Windsor said.

'Except?'

Windsor sighed out a lungful of smoke.

'Except... Kalka was there for a few nights after he disappeared, and then he wasn't. That's all. Hortense told me so last time we spoke. She was none too happy about it either.'

'Wrong caste, I suppose?' Smithy said. Betty nudged him, shook her head.

'Too sick!' Windsor said. 'It was a mistake and it seemed they fixed it, but it shows they can be flexible. When they want to be, anyway.'

'Go on, Windsor,' Betty said. 'Have a pear drop.'

'Bugger your pear drops!'

Smithy gripped his arm again.

'Remember,' he said. 'Every time we eat and shit that's another small victory against the universe.'

Dot looked at the Monopoly board. It wasn't the CareFriends that had tampered with the games, she understood suddenly, but a resident. Whoever it was had twigged. An interminable game might be enough to drive you mad, but how much worse it was when the game just ended.

'Well tell me this,' Windsor said, patting Smithy's hand. 'However many battles someone wins against the universe, have you ever known anyone to win the war?'

Smithy said nothing.

'Told you so,' Olive whispered into Dot's ear. 'The house always wins.'

25¢
NEW U.S MENACE: TEEN-AGERS IN BLACK LEATHER JACKETS
AIR SOULS!
INDIAN KNIGHTS
A CAPTAIN RUGGLES SHORT

INDIAN KNIGHTS

A CAPTAIN RUGGLES SHORT

*'Every stone in the Khyber has
been soaked in blood...' (George Molesworth)*

When most people think of The Great Game, they think of that epoch of strategic rivalry between our own empire and the Russians that petered to a dissatisfying truce with the Anglo-Russian Agreement in 1907. But with the invention of the Bolshevik state, the second round, the sequel, began, and after the signing of the Treaty of Rawalpindi, British presence in the Hindoo Kush was limited to our side – the Indian side – of the Khyber pass, whilst the Ruskies laid claim to Afghanistan. And like all sequels, it was bigger, brasher and dumber than the original.

The Kush is a queer place, the queerest I've ever known, and few cartographers have yet been intrepid enough to map its peaks and its passes in any detail. For there a battalion might advance barely a mile in a single week, and then in the following day cover a greater distance than might even seem possible on the flat. Great sheer rock faces, thousands of feet in height, rise unbidden out of nowhere, just as the heathen gods make merry in carving new and perilous valleys with their swords, where no pass existed before, stumping the native and foreigner alike and gifting the carcasses of many a lost traveller to the Griffon vultures that patrol the region from the skies. Treaties may be drawn up and borders sketched, yet the Kush remains indifferent to such human trifles.

I enrolled in His Majesty's armed forces at the age of sixteen, and on the ███████████████████████████████████ ████████████ my company was sent to serve in the Kush, at the ███████████████ Base, alongside recruits to a Gurkha regiment of the British Indian Army who stood as the first line of defence against any Russian incursions into our territory. They also protected the small teams of scientists from our great educational institutions, charged by the British government with the job of experimenting on and analysing the unparalleled atmospheric conditions of the region.

Our regiments, coffee and cream, served alongside each other, as brothers in arms, and it was in this way I came to know Bibek Karmacharya, both of us Privates at the time. I was young, and still somewhat oppressed by the restrictions military life had imposed upon my adolescent ebullience. For I grew up not quite in the countryside, not quite in the town, and during school holidays had always known the freedom of roaming as far and as wide as my feet would allow. I was drawn to this young Hindoo – who despite being of almost identical age, seemed to emanate the calm befitting a man decades older – not owing to our similarities, but our differences. I was following the advice of my father: stand closest to the man you most wish to emulate, and he will surely rub off on you.

Karmacharya was studious, though not on any student roll, his nose always poking into some book or other. He read when off-duty, while the rest of us played football or caroused as much as our isolated setting allowed. He was shy too, and would rarely start talking under his own impetus. Engage him in conversation, however, and by the time he was done your ears, and whatever grey matter you had in between, would burn as if set alight with a thousand candles.

The first time we spoke I was on my way back from the latrines – a plank suspended over the diciest of ledges – had taken a wrong turn, and found myself on a small plateau, beyond which a precipice yawned hundreds of feet downwards. It afforded one of the most striking views of the mountain range I had yet seen, but also one of the most terrifying. Karmacharya alerted me to his presence with a cough, loud enough to snare my attention, but not so loud as to send me hopping off the precipice in fright. I turned to discover him balanced on his head, his palms pegging him to the ground for support, and his legs folded above him. My first thought was that, thus inverted, he resembled an elaborately carved coffee table, the kind one might find in a Mayfair Gentlemen's club. My second was that I had blundered into his meditation practice.

I feared he would be angry, just as you, a Christian, might be were I to slap you across the chops during prayer.

'Magnificent, isn't it, the view?' he said in the English of his people, lilting with the sing-song babble of a mountain brook.

'It is,' I replied. 'So vast.'

'Vast, you think?' he said. 'Funny. I was thinking just the opposite. How small the peaks were.'

I expressed my incredulity with a swing of my jaw.

'Join me,' he said, patting the ground beside him. 'You'll see.'

Then, as now, my gymnastic skills were splendid, and I rolled into a perfect headstand beside him. How queer we must have looked together, balancing on our heads both, his legs folded, mine poker-straight above.

'See?' he said.

'They still look vast,' I answered.

'Keep looking.'

And he was right! As I fixed my gaze on the mountain peaks, something uncanny, something eerie occurred. My sense of perspective shifted. Whereas before the mountains had sprouted from the ground, immeasurable giants impeding our movements, now, they seemed to hang from the earth, like the stumpiest of stalactites in a cave, barely dipping a toenail into the true vastness of space that stretched onwards into this new below. Sensing that the shift he was expecting had taken place in me, he said:

'You are afraid of heights.'

Keen to preserve face I said: 'Not of heights, my good man. Of falling from them? Yes. Of the eventual impact? That too.'

Karmacharya only smiled. Anxious, as any Englishman is, to fill the awkward silence, I went on: 'You, I suppose, are not afraid?'

'It amuses, confuses, most Hindoos,' he said, 'how tightly you Christians cling on to your lives. Whereas the Bhagavad Gita tells us that just as a man discards worn out clothes and puts on new, so the soul discards a worn out body and wears a new one.'

'So,' I asked him again, lacing my voice with the dismissiveness I felt for his army of deities, 'you would not be afraid of falling, of the impact?'

'The impact, I confess, is not something that particularly appeals to me. Falling, on the other hand… You know,' he said excitedly, rolling out of his headstand, 'it is only when we are falling that we are truly still.'

I rolled out of my own headstand and, overcome with a sudden giddiness, almost toppled over the precipice. Karmacharya reached a hand out and steadied me.

'The Bhagavad Gita again?' I asked.

He grinned.

'Einstein.'

'What's an einstein?'

'Not what, my friend, who. He's a German physicist, perhaps the greatest genius our world has ever known. Albert Einstein? 1921 Nobel Prize for Physics? E equals M C squared?'

I nodded, with a non-committal air and said: 'Does he, does he? So it was this Einstein that claimed one is still when one is clearly plummeting towards earth? You're right, my man, he does sound like a genius. I'll stick with Isaac Newton, if you don't mind.'

'Newton?' He almost spat the name. 'Pah! Newton is finished, my friend. Look, Einstein proved that gravity and acceleration are equivalent, OK?'

'I'll take your word for that.'

'Do. Now as they are equivalent, if you feel gravity, you must be accelerating, correct?'

'Hmm.'

'And you feel the effects of gravity now of course, that's what is pinning you to the ground. Thus, you are accelerating. The only time you don't feel the effects of gravity… and I'm ignoring air resistance here, which I shouldn't do really, but you'll forgive me, I'm sure?' I nodded him on. 'The only time you don't feel the effects of gravity is when you are falling. Then you no longer feel gravity, you just feel as if you are floating. Just as you would up there,' he pointed, 'in space.'

He was on his feet. I joined him, and dropped an arm over his shoulder, ready to concede the point. 'Karmacharya,' I said, 'I see you have a lot to teach me.' He too put his arm on my shoulder.

'You, I'm certain have a lot to teach me too, Ruggles. And I'm looking forward to finding out exactly what!'

It was not uncommon for a single British soldier, or even a whole British fire team to fail to return from a patrol, having lost themselves in the mountains. When this happened the Gurkhas were dispatched, in pairs, to find them and escort them back to camp. On the occasion in question, the disappearance of Lance Corporal Groom, and through little but curiosity, I volunteered to accompany Karmacharya on the search. He was kind to accept. A British soldier was a liability in the mountains, and he knew he would not be able to count on any goat-like surefootedness on my part, or any ability to bear him back to our encampment should he be injured. His smiling acceptance of my company, demonstrated, I believe, the strength of the bond that had grown between us since our first conversation on that plateau.

It was a fine morning, and Karmacharya was excited to set out. It would, he said, give us the opportunity to visit a team of meteorologists, stationed several miles to the east, whom he had befriended on a previous expedition. They were visiting the region, he told me, to learn more about its particular climate. It seemed that Karmacharya had got to know the meteorologists so well that, whenever he visited, they gave him leave to inspect their equipment, all manner of barometers, anemometers, cloud atlases and weather balloons, lugged to their base camp by donkeys and Sherpas.

As we were scrambling down one of the thin passes that led to the camp, I marvelled at Karmacharya's confidence in this terrain. He hopped and sprang, while I wobbled and limped like some foolish geriatric.

'I suppose it should come as no surprise you feel so at home here,' I said, steadying myself by grabbing hold of a shard of outcropping rock. 'After all, this region is named for your people.' He stopped and turned to look at me. His expression that of the man who doesn't know whether to laugh at your stupidity or blast you for your ignorance.

'You have no idea what Kush means, do you Ruggles?' he said. I understood then I had made another *faux pas*. Fortunately Karmacharya was accustomed to these by now. I shook my head.

'Kush,' he said, giving the word what I assumed to be the correct pronunciation, 'comes from the Persian *Kushtar*, meaning slaughter or carnage. So, Hindoo Kush means Kills Hindoos, after the thousands of Hindoo slaves that died here while being transported to Central Asia. Thus, it was surely named more for your people than it was for mine.' His stern face cracked into a smile. 'It amazes me, Ruggles, how you can travel halfway around the world without doing even the skimpiest investigation about the place you are visiting.'

'It's the Englishman's greatest strength,' I said with a smile of my own, 'by being prepared for no foreign culture in particular, one is equally prepared for every foreign culture in general. The Englishman in India is equally at home as the Englishman in Africa, specifically by not being at home anywhere except in England herself! Come along.'

The pass opened out onto a plateau. Its eastern side was abutted by a huge sheer rock face, stretching hundreds of feet upwards, while its western edge opened out over a precipice of equal magnitude. We had approached from a pass at the southern side, but access was also granted by a thinner, narrower pass to the north.

'I won't be long,' Karmacharya said, indicating politely that he preferred to visit the scientists alone. 'You can wait on that rock there or, if you want,' he pointed to the pass at the northern edge of the clearing, 'a short climb in that direction will afford you one of the best views in the Kush. When the pass forks after a couple of minutes, keep left. I'll meet you up there when I'm done, and we can perform headstands together before continuing our search for Lance Corporal Groom.'

The view didn't interest me so much. In truth, after several months of mountain views I dearly longed for a glimpse of a desert plain, or the gently arcing horizon of an ocean vista. Still, I respected Karmacharya's desire to be rid of me. I was a dolt in matters scientific and if I were him I wouldn't have wanted me around either.

I set off alone on the thin pass. It wasn't long before the gravel gave way to a loose bed of scree and the rock walls began to close in so tightly that I was forced to crab. So narrow had the pass become that, while not touching the walls, my nose and the back of my head ached with the cold emanating from the mountain rock. It was a good quarter of an hour before I reached the fork of which Karmacharya had spoken and was relieved to see that the left fork fanned out gently towards a clearing whereas the right narrowed still further and twisted violently as it continued its steep ascent.

I was on the point of taking the left prong of the fork, when something caught my eye. There, amidst the scree of the prong to the right, I saw the single stripe of a British Lance Corporal. I squeezed along the pass to where the stripe lay and fished it from the scree. It had been well stitched, for it was still attached to the fabric of the greatcoat from which it had been torn. The options were few: Either there had been a struggle, a kidnapping, or, heaven forfend, a murder of this soldier, or so disoriented and lost was he in these mountains that when his stripe snagged on a shard of rock and was torn from his person, he had stumbled on, unwittingly, without them. Neither option boded well for Lance Corporal Groom, although I uttered a quick prayer for the second: as death by exposure in the mountains would be nothing compared to death by the Bolshevik's scimitar.

We had all heard the stories, and repeated them too often enough, of how the Russian battalions stationed here, cut off from their masters in Moscow for years at a time, had grown wild and rash, instituting their own laws, that bore closer resemblance to those of the kingdom of animals than of the kingdom of men. For the nasty, brutish and short life proscribed by this terrain required laws to match. They had, it was said, abandoned most of their uniforms in favour of yak hide and fur, while preserving their huge army-issue ushanka hats. What with their abundantly bearded faces, they were said to often be mistaken by the locals for the fabled Yeti, quite an advantage when their meagre rations were supplemented by sacking the mountain villages.

It was with these thoughts in mind that I continued along the ever-narrowing pass which, a hundred yards or so on from where I had chanced upon the lost stripe, took a sharp turn to the right. Imagine my surprise, my joy, my inexpressible relief when, upon turning in that rocky corridor, I saw the Lance Corporal perched on an isolated rock ledge some distance off. He had seen me too, I thought, because he was waving his arm in jerky, tired arcs. So overjoyed was I to have found him – and so secretly proud that it was I, not any of the others, not Karmacharya, who had done so – I twice called his name, vainly of course, for the wind dashed my words onto the rocks long before they reached his ear. I kept on advancing and Groom kept on waving, and with every step forward I felt like more and more of the hero I had always dreamed of being.

I must have been fifty yards from Groom when I realised something was awry. Forty when I understood that his posture was not that of a man at the peak of health, as he had been when he set off from the camp two days earlier, but was instead somehow crooked, somehow limp, somehow reminiscent of the scarecrows my friends and I had built for the local farmers in my youth. It was only when I was within thirty yards, however, that the Griffon vulture, the beast I had seen circling above but had paid little mind, swooped groundward, perched on Groom's shoulder, and with surgical precision plucked his eyeball from its socket, wrestled with it until the optic nerve snapped – and gulped it down.

The whole while Groom kept on waving. I withdrew my service revolver, aimed it at the bird and fired. I missed, but the clack of the gun's report was sufficient to frighten the scavenger into the air.

It took me a further few minutes to reach what I now knew to be Groom's cadaver, for the pass grew steeper and the bed of scree ever thicker. In that time, my mind conjured up all manner of grotesque fantasies about just what had happened to Groom, but none of them would compare to the true horror that awaited me as I pulled myself up onto that ledge.

His feet had been pinned to the ground by two heavy metal pegs driven in, judging by the encrusted blood and the writhing clump of insects, when Groom was still alive. His body, still clothed in his bloodstained uniform, was bound with wire to a makeshift crucifix, constructed from a pair of rusted tent poles, to which his now eyeless head had also been tied with piano wire. Indeed, only his right forearm had been spared the cruel spiral of wire. It had been elevated, but left loose at the end, so that, from a distance, I had mistaken its senseless flapping in the mountain wind as Groom signalling for help.

It dawned on me only then – as I'm sure it has already dawned on you – that the forearm had not been left free by accident but by design. So that from a distance an idiot soldier – an idiot soldier like myself – would mistake the jerking for a sign of life and hurry, his chest bursting with dumb pride, to the aid of his lost comrade. In short Groom, before he had even died, had been turned into bait, into a means of capturing more of his kind. And it had worked, for at that very moment, a pair of enormous arms held me in place as a club of some kind knocked me out.

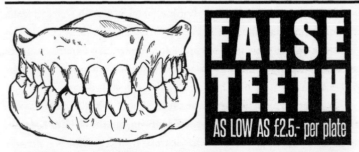

When I regained consciousness, the first thing I noticed, even before opening my eyes, was that I was vertical, that I too had been trussed by wire to a pole, although, as yet, my feet had been spared the metal pegs. Upon opening my eyes I saw the first blush of sunrise staining the sky behind the mountains, taunting me with this image of beauty. My head throbbed, but otherwise I was unharmed... not, I imagined, as a result of a sudden rush of human empathy in the hearts of my captors, but much more likely because they preferred their victims to be awake before they tortured and murdered them. Where, otherwise, was the fun? Some twenty yards to my right, I noticed as I turned my head, the wires slicing flirtatious lines in my cheeks, lay the Bolshevik camp. A cluster of five tents, each capable of sleeping up to four soldiers, huddled around an enormous brazier that still glowed from last night's fire. From one of the tent-poles the flag of the young Soviet state flapped lazily in the morning breeze. It looked old, although it had existed only for a handful of years. The mountain weather had drained it of most of its pigment, frayed its edges and, with that done, begun tearing it to shreds. On the same tent, something in Russian had been daubed in white paint. For now, the camp was still.

'Good morning, Rip Van Winkle.' It was Karmacharya's voice, coming from inside my head.

'I hear you, my friend.' I whispered, concentrating hard to ensure the telekinetic transmission of my words to wherever my mystic accomplice was holed up.

'Of course you can hear me, Ruggles, I'm tied up just behind you.'

Oh joy! But... Oh the despair! For Karmacharya to have been captured too, caused my heart intense distress. And yet, there was no other soldier whose presence in such a predicament I would value more than his. Good, honest, brave, loyal, smart Karmacharya.

'How did they capture you?' I asked him.

'Capture me? No, no, my friend, I let myself be taken in order to rescue you. The only pass to the camp is guarded, day and night. Alone, I would never have been able to overcome them, so I thought it prudent to let them do the work. As my objective was to breach the camp's defences, I believe we can consider it well attained.'

'But how did you know I was alive? You might have been killed.'

'I'll admit it was a risk, but it was a calculated one. Unlike the risk you took to recover Groom's body, that was indeed heroic.'

I didn't know whether to believe Karmacharya when he said he had let himself be captured in order to rescue me. He was indeed smart and brave, but could also be rather proud. Still, as he was offering me the benefit of the doubt concerning the reckless actions that led to my capture, I extended him the same courtesy.

'Your risk was heroic too, my friend,' I said.

'You are kind, but you are forgetting what I told you about us Hindoos. How can one be truly heroic when one believes in karma and reincarnation? You know, I have often found your Occidental culture rather absurd, although being tied up with you here this long night, I believe I came to a certain understanding of it. Heroism demands the potential for tragedy, and tragedy, almost by its very definition, requires the need for a single shot at life. How can a life be tragic if you've another one lined up just after it? Your beliefs, your culture, give you just one life, just one chance. One roll of the dice, nothing more. You are forever auditioning in front of your Heavenly Power before He rewards you with eternal bliss or condemns you to eternal torture. Of course you are nervous, timorous people… you're so terrified of getting it wrong! Of setting the bar too high and failing, or setting it too low and never reaching your potential. In truth, of course, the bar is always going to be either too high or too low, that's just the way things are, but that is also beside the point. For despite all of this, still, sometimes, not often, but often enough, you will risk your life, your one life, to rescue a person or defend a principle.' Karmacharya sighed, disappointed with how he was expressing himself. 'Look, I'm not saying I find it any less absurd than I did before, but for the first time I recognise that this absurdity is rather beautiful.'

Karmacharya stopped speaking for a moment and I could feel him writing against the pole to which we were both tied. After a minute or two he said: 'Rats! Tell me Ruggles, did the Bolshies take your wrist-watch too?' I shook my hands as much as the wires would allow to see if I could feel its weight. I could not.

'They did,' I said.

'In that case,' Karmacharya said. 'We'll have to judge our escape by the passage of the sun. Not ideal in the circumstances but…'

'Our escape?'

'You sound surprised, Ruggles. What did you have in mind? Waiting for the Ruskies to awaken and negotiating our freedom? That technique didn't work too well for Groom, did it?'

I had considered escape, briefly, but after taking stock of how tightly we were bound to the wooden post had determined it impossible, and any sign of an attempt as only likely to further anger our captors. And yet Karmacharya was right. Look at what had become of Groom. I understood then the queer paradox about Karmacharya and his people that had been needling me for some time: by not caring a jot for this life, by not clinging, desperately, onto it, not only do they somehow become much more adept at protecting it, but they also get more from it as a result. A desperate man will often act in panic. An indifferent man, on the other hand, will find it easier to keep a cool head.

'What have you got in mind, my friend?' I asked him. 'There'll be no escaping from this encampment unless we can shrug off these wires.'

'Quite true,' he said. 'But we must also be thankful for the tactical advantage these binds afford us.'

'How so?'

'Do you remember when we were performing headstands and looking at the mountains?'

'Of course.'

'How the mountains changed from being huge, almost insurmountable monoliths, to being mere baby toes dipped in the pool of infinite space?'

'Indeed I do.'

'However, we did not have time to talk about the effect the mountains had on the space itself. For space only exists in relation to the objects that fill it, the objects that shape it. Indeed, it is only with objects we can have space at all.'

'Einstein again? Or the Bhagavad Gita?'

Karmacharya expelled a rasping sigh.

'Why must it be anyone? Don't you believe a Hindoo capable of original thought?'

'I... I'm...'

Karmacharya gave my hand a friendly squeeze.

'I'm playing with you Ruggles,' he said. 'My point however, is a serious one. For it is only when we are tied up like this that we can get any real sense of the escape routes available to us. We are gifted a completely different view of the encampment than that of our captors, who, being able to move freely about, cannot see what we see.'

'And *what* can we see?'

'We see that they wrongly believe there to be only one route into or out of the camp, that being the pass to the east. All of their defences are arranged with this in mind. Sound planning, I'll admit, when your aim is to keep people out. Reckless when your aim is to keep them in. We shall use this oversight of theirs to our advantage.'

'I must confess,' I said, 'to being victim of exactly the same misapprehension. Apart from the pass to the east, there is only the peak to the west and north and the precipice to the south. If we climbed the peak we would be cornered, but to attempt to shin down that sheer rock face? That would mean certain death.'

'Certain, yes,' Karmacharya said, 'and yet...' He looked up at the sun. 'Now, Ruggles, enough chitchat, we are already behind schedule. We have to go.' With that Karmacharya began shifting his weight from one side to the other.

'You were going to ask, I suspect, how we would untie ourselves. Well, my friend, a demonstration will work as quickly as any explanation. My apologies if the wires smart somewhat.' What I only then noticed, but what Karmacharya had clearly observed some time before, was that the ends of the wire were pegged to the ground a yard and a half from the pole. Thus a tensile system had been constructed that would hold us firmly in place as long as the two static components, the peg and the pole, held firm. As Karmacharya rocked softly from side to side, and as the pole loosened in its berth of crumbly Kush soil, I felt the wires slowly begin to loosen, until the point where they could be shrugged off like a bathrobe. We stepped free of the wire and stretched out the night.

'Now what?' I asked. He checked the position of the sun.

'Now we wait.'

'Wait?'

'Calm down, Ruggles. Only for... two minutes.'

'We may not have two minutes, old boy,' I said, tilting my head towards one of the tents, from which a gargantuan bearded Russian had just emerged. He was wearing nothing but trousers, his monolithic torso trussed with enormous muscles. He staggered across to a small pool that had frozen overnight, crouched down onto his hands and knees and butted the ice, which rent with a mighty crack as his head disappeared into the glacial waters below. A few seconds later, refreshed, he flicked his head back, ran his hands through his hair, stood up and turned, to see Karmacharya and I staring at him with expressions of horror and awe.

'Get ready to run, Ruggles,' Karmacharya whispered out of the side of his mouth, before checking the sun once again.

'Run? Where to?'

'Just stick by me.'

The Russian wasted no time in lumbering towards us, bellowing something to his tented comrades. A rumble arose from within the canvas as Karmacharya jerked off in the direction of the precipice. We ran close to the edge, Karmacharya's head tilted downwards as if on the lookout for something.

'Drat!' he hissed as we skirted the precipice edge, the slavering shirtless Bolshevik galumphing just behind, crouched so low he might as well have been using the knuckles of his ham-like fists to drive himself forward.

Penned in by the edges of the plateau, Karmacharya yanked me off of our set course, and back in the direction of the Russian tents.

'Did you read what they have daubed on the side of their tent?' he asked me.

'It's in Russian,' I said.

'*Abandon hope all ye who enter here.*'

'Oh!'

'Dante,' he said. 'Just our luck to be captured by the most cliché villains in the Kush!' And on we ran.

More Russians, equally bearded, equally ursine, equally nude from the waist up, had, by now, quit their tents, and were approaching us from almost every direction, most of them unarmed, but a couple wielding rusted scimitars. Karmacharya, a childlike grin slapped across his face, was ducking and weaving between them. I followed blindly along, the back end of a pantomime horse.

'What's the plan, old boy,' I huffed. 'Just running from them until they drop, exhausted, to their knees?'

'Don't worry, Ruggles,' he answered, 'it's almost time.' Just as he said this, one of the Russians swiped at Karmacharya, scoring a diagonal flesh wound down the length of his back. My friend cried out, stumbled, perhaps slowed just a little, but didn't stop running, even as the wound began to gush with blood. With another yank of my arm, he set us on course for the precipice.

'Karmacharya,' I cried, 'you're touched.'

'I am,' he yelled back a mad grin on his face, 'but not mortally.'

'Are you in very much pain?'

We had reached the last few feet of ground before it plunged away to nothing.

'My friend, all life is but a waking dream. We have played the best game we could, but now it is Lakshmi's move.' He took hold of my hand. 'This could be the end of us Ruggles,' he said. 'Don't let go, let us fall together...'

And with that, the two of us, holding hands, ran off of the plateau and into the clutch of the abyss.

Falling is like dreaming. Or perhaps it's the other way around. Not quite real, somehow. The way in which one's surroundings move becomes distorted. Objects at a distance pass slowly across one's vision whereas those near at hand, like the sheer rock face beside which we fell, rush by in an impossible blur. Unless what is near to hand is falling too, of course, in which case it seems to float in front of you. Karmacharya floated in front of me. A moment after we had propelled ourselves off of the plateau, he clasped my other hand, forming a ring with our arms, and so we fell facing each other. His eyes were closed and his expression was calm.

I don't know if I felt completely still, as Karmacharya had promised, but I didn't feel afraid. When I remember that fall, remember all the thoughts, all the memories, when I catalogue each and every sensation my body was subjected to, from the icy wind burnishing my cheeks, to the arcing of my arm hair and the goosebumps on my neck, to the way in which every muscle, every organ in my body seemed to loosen, to slacken, when I would have expected them to tense... When I think of all that it seems almost impossible to believe we could have only been falling for a handful of seconds before...

Karmacharya opened his eyes.

'Look down,' he yelled above the roar of the wind. I heeded his instruction, just in time to see the monstrous white ball rush up towards us and envelope our bodies in the soft womb of rubber. For several seconds Karmacharya, myself and this mysterious ball spiralled into a rapid descent. Then we slowed, levelled out and just hung there at an altitude of several hundred feet.

'Weather balloons, Ruggles!' he cried, clearly reading the confusion on my face. 'The miracle of science! Put your fate in the hands of Lakshmi and she sends you weather balloons!'

So would begin Karmacharya's campaign to convince me he knew nothing of the launch. That we owed our continued earthly existence to the benevolence of the universe. It might seem a strange position for a scientific man to adopt, but not for a modest man who wished to remain so, and so I believe that Karmacharya's profession of ignorance was as much for his own sake as for mine. For my part, I was so grateful to him for saving us that I never felt it dignified to question his version of events.

The mountain wind bore us away from the precipice and out over the Kush, decidedly onto the friendly side of the Khyber Pass. We were losing altitude, but only slowly and, as unlikely as it sounds, were able to enjoy the vista as it swept along beneath us. It was the first time I had flown. I suspect the first time Karmacharya had too, and both of us were like children in our moon-eyed wonderment. Still holding hands, but lying comfortably now on the balloon's canopy, we took in the valleys, streams, caves and crevasses of this most magnificent of landscapes. From the ground the Kush can be forbidding, impervious to understanding, deceptive and cruel. A canker on the face of the earth. A part of the world that simply wasn't meant to be. Yet from the air... from the air, it just looked right.

A stream of warm air lifted us over a low peak and plunged us into a nearby valley.

'Look,' Karmacharya yelled, 'four o'clock.' I craned my neck in the direction he had indicated just in time to see a herd of Yeti, perhaps fifty or sixty in number, a-man-and-a-half in height, some carrying young ones on their backs, galloping along the dried out riverbed below us... And then, once again, the stream of air carried us on and away.

★

Captain Ruggles peered at the scraps of the Monopoly board. As he was concluding his story to his fellow prisoners, feigning an illustration, he had whipped the board out from beneath their noses, hammed a couple of circuits about the canteen, and whisked through the door to their patter of applause. As soon as he had assured he was alone, he tore it apart – first with his fingernails, then with his teeth, reducing it to tatters in a matter of minutes. The intelligence he had received that morning via ████ ████████ had proven erroneous. There were no maps, compasses or money concealed within the pulpy leaves of the board. No microfilms either, detailing orders or updating his intelligence with new and valuable information on the Nazi advances. Perhaps John Waddington Ltd had ballsed-up, sending the gimmicked board out to an evacuees charity and sending him this useless standard version. Or perhaps the company had crossed over to the Axis, and was furnishing them with information that should have come to him… Ruggles had no way of knowing.

Now, and so as not to raise suspicion, he would be obliged to eat the scraps of the board. An unpleasant task, but one he was more than trained for. He stripped the glossy film from a corner fragment, folded it in four and, taking a sip from the glass of water beside his cot, started chewing.

The taste was unpleasant, sure, but there was something in the motion of mastication that encouraged meditative thought – there was a reason, after all, that cows and their ilk were known as ruminants. The cud that Ruggles had to chew on, however, was rather bitter, and increasingly so as the days passed. Almost sixteen months had elapsed since he had parachuted into the Germans' clutches, and in that time, despite his best efforts, little had changed. His cellmates seemed unwilling to assist him in his escape attempts, or to resist the *Kommandant*'s dictates. They weren't a bad lot, but captivity had wrecked physical and mental havoc on them – and now even the new Private, who he had once been sure was the key to unlocking the impasse, had been crippled in action.

Ruggles swallowed, pressed a second flap of the Monopoly board onto his tongue, took another sip of water, and continued chewing. What was to be done? His faith in his ability to escape single-handedly had been dented so badly that he was quite sure he wouldn't attempt it again. He had also – through his recklessness – caused the injury of another soldier, and was finding it difficult to excuse himself for that. Still, in the theatre of war, injuries are commonplace, and one mustn't allow them to sap momentum, to crush the spirit... Where though, was the momentum supposed to come from now? Not from the missing Karmacharya, and not from his other cellmates either, that was for sure, and – it seemed – his own plentiful, but limited, fount just wouldn't suffice against these odds.

As much as Ruggles hated to admit it, might was proving to be right. He had to concede a grudging admiration for how the camp was run, how its systems and routines had been conceived to instil inertia in the captives, to strafe with bullets any head that dared lift itself above the trenches. There was a whole bushel of good apples here, he knew, but something in the barrel, some poison, was turning them rotten, one by one. When the rot had set in too far they were plucked out... And God only knew what happened to them after that.

Taking a well-earned pause between cardboard courses, Ruggles lit a *Gasper* and crossed over to the window of the Zellenblock to peer, as he liked often to do, through curtains of luxurious, healthful smoke, past the perimeter fence, across the war-torn moraine, towards England, towards freedom and, most importantly of all, towards Dulcie. Standing thus, the badly-sketched *dramatis personae* that was Captain Dylan Prometheus Ruggles, remembered how much, as a younger soldier, he had longed to be a hero, by saving the day, or rescuing somebody... anybody, from the evil clutches of the fashionable enemy of the hour. And yet he never had. Not once. Every one of his missions – from bringing back Lance Corporal Groom, to his escape attempt the previous night – had ended in failure. He hadn't lost faith that one day, when the moment was right, he would come good, that he would prove his worthiness to Dulcie. But as he watched the sun begin its descent – for what was almost the five hundredth occasion since his capture – he had to admit that time was running out...

CAPTAIN RUGGLES WILL SOON RETURN

IN A NEW THRILL-THRONGED ADVENTURE:

'WE'LL MEET AGAIN... WON'T WE?'

AIR SOULS!

On newstands the 5th of EVERY month.

Book Three

1

'**F**ucking savages.'

Tristan swabbed the mirror with the cuff of his overall. The wiped crescent, streaked with stubborn comets of encrusted toothpaste lather and dried saliva, at least afforded him a better view of his mouth. He pinched his chin and tilted it towards the mirror, shifting it from one side to the other until he awakened the gentle pang, the shadow of his former suffering.

The swelling had all but gone now. The punctured-football face he had been walking around with the past few weeks had faded, the bulbous, pulsing half-fucking-goitre had drained away. And yet, every time he opened his mouth, there it was. Nothing. Nothing where his tooth should have been...

It was only a tooth. That was what he kept telling himself: 'it's only a *fucking* tooth,' and other bromides like 'who wants to die without any scars'. But it was a canine he had lost, and that made it worse somehow. It would have been more bearable if it had been a molar. Not such a big deal. Why did it have to be a canine? One of his weapons. Without it he felt neutered, vulnerable... *de-dogged*.

'We'll see to that, son,' the redoubtable Afrikaner dentist had assured him, pulling a rack of porcelain studs from his pocket, each stained to mimic differing extents of abuse. 'You'll be good as new when I done with you. Nobody will notice the difference.'

Gud as nu? Nub'dy wool no'tice duh diffewence? Who was the dumb Boer trying to kid? Tristan felt the permanence of it the instant the tooth had sheered from its root. The intransigence of time's forward march. He was marked. The Reaper had been admitted to Tristan's party that night – and now he was making dull conversation, drinking other people's beer and criticising the music collection. A real fucking buzz-kill. He could never have got through it without Kalki's help.

He reached into his pocket, shifting aside the two halves of the rejection letter from Durham University, and fingered out a small, brown pill flask. He was almost out of the painkillers the doctor had prescribed him after the accident. Fuck the doctor and his miserly prescriptions. And fuck Durham. There were other universities. Other ways to escape this shit-hole...

He popped open the flask and tipped out the last pill. He had been saving it for this evening, but his fingers were already ahead of his thoughts, fiddling the chalky capsule onto his tongue. A taste now would help get him through the day. He chewed the pill, despite how sick the explosion of dust made him feel. It got to work quicker that way.

Gripping the edge of the sink, he swallowed the crumbs and waited...

Aaaaaaaaaaah!

Yes!

...

For a moment, Tristan was flying. Gravity had nothing on him. He had tapped into the life-force...

After a few minutes, the first rush peaked, and the long slow glide began. He opened his eyes and turned away from the mirror.

At the same moment, the door flew open and Frankie waddled in. The girl looked even crazier in civvies – leather bomber jacket, dreadlocks drumming on shoulder pads, baggy jeans she never stopped pulling up, and her thick-soled, fat-tongued para boots.

'*Trees-tonne!*' she trilled, mock-Jamaican. They sat down in opposite armchairs.

Why the fuck was she looking at him like that?

He kicked the coffee table.

'Shit, man!' Frankie said. 'You're still doping.'

Tristan scratched his face.

'Just a taste…'

'I fucking knew it. I could see it in your eyes. I told you to take it easy with that shit.'

'Don't worry about me,' Tristan said. 'Oh, and also – hypocrite.'

Frankie shook her head, smiled.

'We're not built the same, you and me,' she said. 'Never forget that.'

'Whatever,' Tristan said. 'Anyway, I'm out for now. I'm sure I'll have to beg the fucking doctor for one more round.'

'You could do that,' she said. 'Or…'

She fiddled inside her rucksack for a moment before pulling out a handful of OxyNyx. Several dozen of the tiny blue gemstones. Tristan leaned forward.

'I thought you said they were in short supply.'

Frankie lined up three of the spheres on the table and funnelled the rest into a ziplock baggie.

'Let's just say a reliable line opened up. Yours for a hundred and fifty.'

'Better not,' Tristan said, a tickle of regret in his gut.

'Suit yourself.'

'Got to keep a clear head. Got work to do.'

He shot out of the chair – unsure what exactly was propelling him – then scratched his scalp and walked over to the fridge. Perhaps the OxyNyx would sand his edge down a little.

'Work?' Frankie said. 'You serious?'

'Serious.'

'When did you become such a conscientious work-cunt?'

Tristan opened the fridge, looked inside, let the cool air enrobe his face, then closed the door again.

'Have you ever considered...' – biting off a hangnail on his left index finger – '... how strange it is that the Captain passed all the insanity tests?'

'The Captain again?' Frankie said. 'These last few weeks it's always the fucking Captain with you!'

'The AMTS, the MMSE, the 3MA, the CASI. He passed them all.'

'I guess he's in fine fucking fettle then, isn't he?'

'He's either *actually* off his rocker, which means we need new tests, or...'

Frankie sighed: 'Tell you what, mate. Why don't you invent a test of your own? He's bound to fail that.'

'Or...'

'Look, maybe you shouldn't take it so fucking personal. I get it – he's been the sand in your fanny crack ever since you lost your tooth...'

'Or he's putting it on. To spite me.'

The three OxyNyx crushed and cut into two lines, Frankie sank back into the couch.

'I should give *you* the AMTS, because you're fucking losing it mate. The Captain has been running that prison camp racket ever since his baptism. Fucker picked up the ball and legged it. To annoy you, bollocks!'

Tristan sat down again, determined to stay rooted this time. She wasn't going to need *both* lines, was she?

'Spite,' he said. 'Not annoy. And you can't deny the effect he's been having on the others recently. The Greys are getting restive. Remember how they destroyed the Monopoly board like a horde of nesting hamsters? That's why I asked Cornish to move the Captain to C. To wheedle the one bad apple out before it turns the others rotten. For all the good it did. Our grip has loosened these last weeks, Frank. We need something big to bring them back under our control.'

'Our grip?' Frankie said, licking her finger and swabbing up a line of the azure diamond dust. 'I thought our post-Ally working philosophy was very anti-grip. I mean... You've got to get a grip before you can lose it, homo.'

Perhaps Frankie was right about the Captain. Perhaps he should just let it go. But ever since that night last month when he had watched the emaciated old saboteur daub himself in his own faeces, Tristan had been unable to see him, even think about him, without being battered by fierce gusts of anger and revulsion. And he thought about him *all the time*. Before, he had just been bored by the Captain's antics. Now, it was the Captain's shit-streaked face that greeted him in the morning, contaminating his first waking thought, and the same soiled face sent him off to sleep at night.

'Where's Pat?' he said. 'We've got to prep for the families.'

Frankie pinched the bridge of her nose.

'Fuck,' she said. 'I totally forgot.'

Tristan smiled.

'What's going to become of you two when I leave?'

'Oh golly-gosh, I dread to think!' Frankie sneered, in what she, and only she, thought was her pitch-perfect Tristan. 'Any idea where you're headed yet?'

He fingered the envelope.

'Still no news.'

'Huh?' Frankie said. 'Weird.'

'What would you know?' Tristan snapped.

Frankie held up her hands in sarcastic surrender. Then she changed the subject, to one of her favourites: why they even bother pimping the place up every two weeks.

'Who do you think is paying for most of the Greys to be here?' Tristan said.

'So what? Fuck them!'

'Talk about biting the hand that feeds.'

'I mean it. I dare the cunts to come here and criticise the job we do. So it's not always spick-and-fucking-span, and we're not always Florence-fucking-Nightingale. But they sent them to this shit-hole – their own flesh – because they couldn't bear to fucking look at them any more. Well – newsflash! – you don't get a say in what happens to your garbage after you throw it out. It doesn't belong to you any more. Buyer's remorse doesn't apply here. Better to drink, smoke, drug and fuck yourself into an early grave like my folks did. Cheat life of its perverted fucking encore.'

'Jesus, Frankie.'

'To spend so much time, so close to death, day-in-day-fucking-out. It does your head in. If you ask me, we're fucking saints to do this job for the money they pay us. You know what I'm doing when I get off tonight?'

'After that outburst, I'll put my tenner on high-school massacre,' Tristan said. This at least raised a half-smile from Frankie.

'Not far off. This group – Vile Sphacelation – are playing The Queen Mum in town.'

'Traditional folk ballads?'

'Something like that. I'm going to bang my head off all fucking night. Maybe I'll come out of it halfway fucking human again.'

Tristan almost felt like telling Frankie about Kalki, about the incredible transformation that had come over him these last few weeks, about the conversations they'd had upstairs, about the seemingly endless depths to his wisdom. Perhaps it could even help her. But it was too soon. He would fudge the explanation and she wouldn't understand. He didn't even know if he understood it himself. That was what tonight was for, after all.

'Really, where the fuck is Pat?' he said instead. Frankie stood up, walked to the door and opened it. Pat was in the hallway, deep in conversation with Nurse Agnes, one fifth of the Three-Star CareTeam that coddled the Preemies in Ward A. Since hearing that the medical visits for B and C had been scaled back, she often came early to visit them as well.

'Bet you'd like to wreck that,' Frankie said, as Tristan joined her by the door. 'Take it down to the tool shed and bust it open on the pile of old tarpaulins?'

'You're a poet, Frank,' Tristan said, though he also felt himself getting hard beneath his smock. Agnes was actually quite pretty, in a homely kind of way. Reminded him a bit of Annie. Tristan sniffed, angry suddenly: 'But there's no way I'm touching Meatloaf's sloppy seconds.'

'Fuck knows what they've got to yak about,' Frankie said.

'Not bothering you, is he?' Tristan called out. 'We've been meaning to get him spayed, but we just don't have the heart.'

They both turned. Pat's eyes trained on him, a double-barrelled shotgun of disgust.

'He's a perfect gentleman,' Agnes called back. She laid a hand on Pat's forearm and whispered something. Pat smiled.

'Well, as much as I'd love to let you chat all day, we don't pay Casanova to keep the nurses entertained.'

Agnes smiled and rolled her eyes. She kissed Pat on the cheek, then said: 'He's all yours.'

Pat pushed past Tristan and Frankie into the staffroom, as the two of them watched Agnes climb the stairs. Suddenly Tristan felt Frankie's hand on his cock.

'Careful, girl,' she said. 'Your clit's showing.'

Tristan flushed. The Captain's shit-daubed face flared up in his mind like a Roman Candle. Fuck them all! They had no idea.

Frankie cackled and rushed Pat, jumping onto his back. The two of them play-wrestled for a moment until Pat shucked her onto the couch.

'What was the hurry, anyway?' he said, taking a clean smock from his locker.

'Families are coming,' Frankie said. 'Got to pimp the dayroom.'

'Oh shit,' Pat said. 'Sometimes I wonder if it wouldn't be less effort just to keep it nice like that the whole time.'

Frankie glared at him.

'That's why you ain't paid to think, Patrick.'

'And besides,' Tristan said, 'as you're on the four a.m. shift tomorrow you can go home right after.'

'I'm not on the graveyard shift,' Pat said, with an assurance Tristan found disconcerting.

'What?'

'I told you last week. It's my mum's birthday. We're going to that Italian where they sing for you. It's all booked.'

'Jesus,' Tristan said. 'Singing fucking Italians! What do they sing? Verdi? Puccini?'

'Nah,' Pat said. 'They sing Happy Birthday.'

'Well, you'll have to do it, Frankie,' Tristan said, turning to her.

'Fuck that. Vile Sphacelation, remember? I don't even plan on *seeing* tomorrow.'

'Well, I can't do it!' he snapped. 'I have the…'

Ceremony. He had almost let it slip. Pronouncing those four syllables would have made the whole thing feel weird – silly! – undermined it before the foundations had set, stirred up questions that he couldn't yet answer. It *was* weird – of course he knew that! But the choice wasn't his anymore.

Tristan looked at Pat and Frankie. They wouldn't understand, he was sure now. Nobody would. But at least ever since Kalki had started revealing himself, Tristan had a foil…

'You have the what?' Pat said.

Tristan licked his index finger, leaned forward and swabbed up the second line of OxyNyx. He inspected it closely for a few seconds before closing his eyes and sucking it off…

The effect was immediate, staggering, so much more intense than his first hit all those weeks back, so much less oblique. It was as if his mind had loosed itself from its cumbersome physical vessel, floated outwards, upwards, freed to take on its intended, expanded form.

'Holy Alexandrina!' he bellowed, unsure why.

An idea visited him, entering his thoughts like a benediction…

'Never mind,' he said, opening his eyes. 'Maybe I *can* do it…'

He started examining the idea for flaws at once. If it was as good as it looked, it might deal with the Captain and the night shift in a single blow. Restore his grip. He looked at the ceiling and tipped an invisible hat to Kalki, even if a part of him knew it was more thanks to the OxyNyx.

'Frankie,' he said, looking down again. 'What was that you were saying about old tarpaulins?'

2

It wasn't so much the legs, but the vision they stirred between them. The first thrust of adolescence had elongated the femurs and tibias, but the thickening that comes in the first lull of early adulthood had yet to settle in, so that the knobbly junctures of knees, ankles and hips made them seem far more fragile than they actually were. As did the translucent skin, traced with a faint map of veins, pimples and grazes. Skin that looked as if it would rive at the first touch, discharging its load of stringy muscles onto the office carpet. It wouldn't, of course. Youth was far more robust, far more supple, than it appeared. That was its secret and its cruel beauty. Vulnerable to scratches and tears, but almost mocking in the rapidity of its renewal, and totally deaf to the siren calls of the Reaper. He had spent too much time around the Greys, that was all. Their ailments had corrupted his understanding of how real life – by which he meant vigorous, young life – worked.

No, it wasn't the legs themselves that had set his mind alight, but the ghosts of the past that his mind's eye was projecting into that arch's frame. The turbulent waters of an oily-black sea, weighed upon by a sky of towering storm clouds and flocks of seagulls imprisoned in violently eddying pockets of air, tumbling and rolling at the caprice of the coastal wind. The moonlit ruins of a church or abbey, a garish set from a cheap horror film, placed atop a tumbledown cliff, lashed with rain.

Whitby. Cornish had visited the town only once in his life, on a family holiday to Yorkshire when he was nine or ten. He had always thought he had only two memories of that holiday. The first, his determined, but aborted, attempt to read *Dracula*, which he had begun upon learning from his mother that the town provided the backdrop to the Count's arrival in England. Parents, he had been discovering, were not much more than bulky children, stuck fast in thickets of personal disillusionment. They had little interest in the facts, but much more in consolidating and imposing their own worldviews, hard won consolation prizes of lives shoddily lived.

So, his mind engorged with hell hounds, poltergeists, Spring Heeled Jack and the Count, he had nagged his parents into a corner, from which their only escape had been to indulge their son in his quest for Stoker's claret-supping Romanian. As they had expected – and likely secretly hoped – the reality had disappointed him. The only trace of the Count in the town had been in the vulgar signage of guesthouses and pubs, or injection-moulded into souvenir key rings.

His second – and he had thought, last – memory of Whitby was of the arch perched on the west cliff, commemorating the town's history as a prosperous whaling station. It had been constructed from two enormous cetacean mandibles, linked at the apex by a weathervane, perpetually indecisive, even in the calmest weather. While his father had read aloud from a guidebook about how many of the town's houses had been constructed around whalebone frames, he had spent his time hopping back and forth across the arch's threshold, investing the full powers of his imagination in convincing himself that when crossed in the correct fashion, it marked the entryway to another, more vivid and, crucially, parentless realm.

It was this memory, he realised, that had muscled to the forefront of his mind, as his eyes traced the contours of the girl's legs. Although, apart from the obvious correlation of form, he couldn't imagine why they had sent his brain adventuring so. Surely there were hundreds, if not thousands, of more pertinent memories to dredge up than these. Why Whitby? Why Dracula? And why that gruesome arch? Could it be, he wondered, that those legs were, like the whale's jawbones, ever so gently cambered? Did people still get – what was it now? – rickets?

'Close the door,' he said, tugging at his nose.

The girl's obedience didn't increase his feeling of dominion. In fact, it somehow lessened it. The way in which she clunked the door into place, and jiggled the handle to check the catch had bitten, projected an assurance well beyond her years. It also seemed underwritten with the knowledge – correct, to his regret – that the door might be opened again at any moment she chose.

'Can I have the ten quid now?' she asked, scratching her neck as she cast her mildly revolted gaze about his office. Cornish felt at once judged and pitied.

'You can have the money when you've finished the work,' he said. The girl huffed through her nose, as much an assent to his conditions as her sense of entitlement allowed.

'Where do I start?'

Cornish eased his middle-aged bulk out of his office chair and walked over to the filing cabinet. He slapped it.

'You start here. I've been meaning to alphabetise the records for some time now, but things have been a bit hectic.' He was arrested by a queer doubt. 'You do know your alphabet, don't you?' The girl's eyes rolled languidly in their sockets. More annoyed than offended.

'Ay… Bee… See… Dee,' she demonstrated with brutal petulance. 'Etcetera.'

'Right,' Cornish said, his cheeks prickling. 'Well, I'd like you to apply your evidently capacious orthographical knowledge to bringing a bit of order to this filing cabinet. Alphabetise the residents' files by surname and then you can have your ten quid.' The girl crossed to the filing cabinet and opened and closed each of the three drawers, feigning scrutiny of their contents. From the look on her face, Cornish sensed a burgeoning negotiation.

'Give me fifteen,' she said, 'and I'll get it done by lunch time.'

On the storm-tossed cargo ship of their interaction, a felicitous swell had sent the wooden crates of advantage sliding back across the deck. It was both reassuring and mildly insulting that the girl suspected him of nothing more degenerate than tightfistedness.

'I *will* give you fifteen,' he said, affecting an air of benevolence. 'But take your time. As long as it's done by the end of the day.'

The girl lifted the ear buds that were hanging between her breasts.

'Alright?' she asked.

Cornish waved his consent.

It would have been quite wrong to refer to what was unrolling as Cornish's 'plan', for not a second of actual planning had gone into luring this girl from the bus stop to Green Oaks. More than a month had passed since he had masturbated over her from his crow's-nest office, a pornographic homage to Alfred Hitchcock, and since then she had slunk to the dark recesses of his mind, supplanted by a parade of real and imaginary women encountered in the meantime. And yet, reflecting on the chain of events, the happenstance, and his instinctive jockeying of it, he now saw the truth behind the Zen philosophy that once the self had been destroyed, the practitioner became at one with the practice. Another acquisition of his analysis. No matter that the destruction of his self had not been something he had set out to attain, but which had been visited upon him in a protracted three-way pincer strike involving his parents, his job and the natural injustice of the world. No matter either that the art he was practising – the corruption of a minor – was considerably less noble than archery, aikido or motorcycle maintenance. It was just refreshing to feel that he was doing something well for once. It had been such a long time.

After his bus had pulled up to the stop that morning, Cornish noticed the girl sitting in the same spot as some weeks earlier, alone this time. She looked exactly as he had embellished her during his onanistic flight: teenage, a little hungry, and with a glint in her eye for which the most fitting adjective was probably 'loose'. She was wearing the same tracksuit top, but a different miniskirt, denim this time, and a pair of grubby trainers.

'Mister,' she said as the bus coughed away towards the next village. Cornish had been the only passenger to get off the bus here – no doubt she'd meant him. He turned and expelled a queer little moan, composed of all the confusion, horror and exhilaration of that moment. Confusion, because a real interaction with this girl was the last thing he had expected; horror, because he had concluded – instantly, irrationally – that she somehow knew how he had debased his mental image of her, and was calling him out on it; and exhilaration, because even if nothing came of this interaction he would surely make masturbatory hay with it later, safely ensconced in his office.

'Gotaziggy,' she said.

'Excuse me?'

She frowned, as if he was the one bothering her.

'Got... A... Ciggy?' she enunciated, in much the way Cornish did when he spoke to the Greys. Cornish was torn. He doubted the propriety of giving a cigarette to this girl but also how 'square' – if that still meant anything – he might have seemed for admonishing her. It was then that the first thrust of Dharma genius rose up and out of him:

'Buy your own,' he said, winking at the girl. Where had the wink come from? Even though he hadn't seen it, he was sure it had been a good one. And had his riposte sounded as world-wearily debonair to her as it had to him? The girl shrugged and kicked at an invisible stone.

'No money.'

A more lascivious predator than Cornish would have pounced here and scared her off. But why would he have pounced? They were alone, nobody was expecting him, and she didn't look in much of a hurry. Roshi Cornish knew he had time, and he bode it.

'Too bad,' he said, making to walk off.

'Give us a quid then,' she called after him, 'if you won't give us a fag, I mean.'

'*Give* you a quid? Quite impossible, I'm afraid.'

'I can work,' she said after a moment, harvesting the idea Cornish had sown and assuredly crediting herself with it. 'I can push some of the old'uns about, or whatever.'

'Push them about? I think most of them are happy enough where they are.'

'Or whatever,' she said again, touching off a cluster bomb of sordid visions in his mind.

'I suppose you could… but we'd have to clear it with your parents.'

The girl dug a mobile telephone from her top, pressed and held a single button, then handed it to Cornish. He wobbled, for the first time in their exchange. How vilely connected everyone was these days, how terrifyingly tuned in. As far as new technology was concerned, Green Oaks was a haven. The Greys had no interest in using it, West Church no desire to invest in it, and the CareFriends no salaries generous enough for them to buy any of it. Outside it was different. You had to stand perpetually to attention, ready to converse, to engage, to convince, at the drop of a finger on a rubberised keypad. Cornish would have liked a solid five minutes of preparation, of slow-breathing, of rosace-fixing, before conversing with the girl's mother. Just to work up his lines.

It was her turn to wink.

'Mrs Biss,' she stage-whispered as a surprisingly well-spoken *Hullo!* crackled into Cornish's ear.

'Mrs Wha…?'

And yet he needn't have worried. If his handling of the girl had been deft, his *maniement* of the mother was masterful. Within a minute he had not only attained her permission, but had persuaded her that, despite all appearances, her daughter was an entrepreneur in the making. He wondered, for a moment, if it had all been too easy, but had put that down to the roll he knew himself to be on. As she took the phone from him, their fingers touched and she grinned. Breaking bread with an accomplice.

'Don't mention it,' Cornish had said, in response to nothing at all.

He looked at his desk, now. At the scribbled list of the day's tasks. It was written on one of the new pea-green carbon-paper forms he had ordered that day, last month, when Ruggles had made his unwelcome incursion into his sanctuary. The idea was that the CareFriends would, from then on, only communicate with him through these forms. He had sold it to them as a new directive, allowing Green Oaks to trace any and all communications involving the residents. Pure invention, of course. He had no idea how they'd managed it, but West Church had long ago redefined their activity sector so that, in the eyes of the law, they were exempt from any obligation to be inspected. Cornish was the only one who knew this, however, and intended on keeping it that way.

There were three items on his list:

Stationery order (binders for kids)

Keys?

Locate Indian!

In fact, it was only the stationery order that couldn't be put off until later. Thirty seconds of work and the rest of the day was his... was theirs.

'You know,' Cornish said, an uncharacteristic chattiness taking hold of him for a moment. 'Back when I was at school, if you saw someone wearing earphones, you bullied him for being cloth-eared. One boy in my class – Aiden, or Adrian, or something – used to wear – Aaron! – used to wear a hearing aid, a big fat boxy thing on his hip, and we made a lot of sport mouthing our words in silence to make him think it had broken.'

He stopped speaking, afraid suddenly that this confessional had only accentuated the generational yawn between them. He was about to backtrack when he realised, with a curious mix of relief and dismay, that she hadn't heard a single word he'd said.

The crossfire of sparrows was hypnotic. How they folded their wings against their lens-shaped bodies, and dipped like fat bullets from one side of the window to the other.

So beautiful, so tiny, so obscenely fragile, and yet so competent, so fearless in their pursuit of life's components. Tristan imagined snapping one of those matchstick legs. Taking it between finger and thumb and just splitting it in two with a determined flick. Or pulling a wing off. Wrenching it from the ball joint then taking both parts upstairs. An offering.

He tapped his other pocket, locating the baggie of OxyNyx and pulled the sash window closed.

The dayroom was ready for the families. Pat had left the windows open all morning to clear the lingering stench of decay. Just now, Tristan and Frankie had lugged in the couch from the staff room, rearranged the armchairs, and stretched the flower-scented covers over them all. Between visiting days, they kept the covers locked up with the other supplies. No point subjecting them to needless wear and tear.

Finally, and exceptionally, Tristan had filled a vase with wild flowers. That wasn't why he had picked them from the hedgerows, but when Frankie had caught him stuffing them into his locker, he'd had to find an excuse to deflect her questions. Thank god she hadn't seen the candles too.

As if summoned by his thoughts, Frankie joined him in the dayroom. She looked around, impressed:

'What a fucking crock!'

'Are they ready?' Tristan asked.

'Yeah, they're waiting in the wings.'

'And the Captain's in the rubber room?'

'Relax. Pat's dealing with it. We're more than ready.' She slapped Tristan on the back and turned to go.

'You're right, Frankie,' he called after her.

'About what?'

'It is a fucking crock.'

'Maybe,' she called back. 'But a fucking beautiful one!'

She had that way, Frankie, of nailing something with paradox. *A fucking beautiful crock*. A collocation like that was anathema to Tristan – and even though he had long known that their plains of existence, their moral topographies, were so wildly divergent, he was still often surprised by the way Frankie's mind associated ideas. While he liked to imagine that his own compass swung between the poles of 'good' and 'bad' – as any decent citizen's should – Frankie's seemed instead to be magnetised for the poles of 'boring' and 'fun'. And she lived her life accordingly, with a primal depth Tristan sometimes envied, sometimes feared, but which he always admired for its consistency…

That was likely how she had come up with the idea for the Ward C Derby. After all, if the Greys had to be exercised, what harm was there in chalking a race track on the lino, and running a book on the results? Most of them wouldn't understand what was happening, anyway. And those that did? Well, as she had said, who would believe their bat-shit ramblings?

And now with that thrown-away phrase – *a fucking beautiful crock* – she had just about nailed visiting day. Everyone knew it: staff, families, even the Greys. Everyone lied, and everyone knew they were being lied to, and yet lying and being lied to was preferable to the truth. Everyone played along. It was a fragile charade, a crockery-shy of hopes. They tried so hard to look human, the sorry old bastards, to still look as if they could be part of things out there. Perhaps in the hope that their families – or anyone, a benevolent stranger even – might pluck them out of this in-between world and give them one more shot at life. *I understand why the others are here, but you? No, no. You still have more to give…*

Pat was helping Windsor into the Dayroom, supporting him by the arm as he thumped the Zimmer forward. He hadn't been looking well these last weeks and was losing weight fast. Surely hospice-fodder before the year was out. It was almost as if Death was visiting him in the night, syringing the life-force from him drop by drop through that revolting tracheal tube, stained piss-yellow by the cigarettes he defiantly plugged there.

How much more the syringe suited the Reaper than the scythe. The scythe was swift, clean, almost merciful. But he scythed so rarely these days. Now he preferred the slow torture of Parkinson's, of senility, of the crab. These afflictions allowed the spirit to attend its own harvesting, to watch its vessel wither on the vine, to contemplate the void, to remain present, conscious, down to the very last drop of soul-marrow. Nobody escaped it.

Almost nobody.

As he thought again about his plans for tonight, the fur on his arms arced and waves of goose bumps rippled along his arms, advancing from his wrists to his shoulders, and meeting with a tingle at his spine.

Windsor had dressed up for the occasion, in his mustard cravat and threadbare smoking jacket. Tristan approached the hobbling couple.

'Thanks Pat, I'll take him from here.'

Windsor stared down at his slippers.

'You sure?' Pat said, releasing Windsor to Tristan's grasp.

'You go get the others,' Tristan said.

'I need a word,' Pat said. 'About tonight.'

Tristan eyeballed him.

'Later,' he said, indicating Windsor with a sideways nod. 'Go and make sure the Captain's in the lock up first.'

'It's been a while,' Tristan said to Windsor after Pat had left. Windsor glared out of the window, said nothing. 'It's a shame, you know, because

I've been doing my best with Mister Cornish, doing my best to get your transfer organised, and now I nearly have things in place, you…' – he gripped Windsor's hand, the old man was trembling – '… you dry up on me. How am I supposed to pre-empt the Captain without you as my eyes and ears.'

'I've told you before,' Windsor snapped, still fixing the window. 'He doesn't tell me anything.'

'Of course he doesn't. He may be crazy, but he's not stupid. That's why I need you to watch him, to listen to him. I need to know every move he makes. It's the only way I can stay one step ahead.'

Windsor turned to him, his eyes jellied with rheum:

'He's just a batty old man. He doesn't mean any harm.'

'Let me worry about that.' Tristan said. 'You just worry about how to keep your… privileges.'

Windsor stopped trembling, abruptly. For a moment Tristan wondered if his heart had given out.

'I need to move. Soon.'

'And you will. Soon.' Tristan released his hand and they edged forward.

'Today,' Windsor barked.

Tristan heard footsteps behind them. Pat again, this time carrying a plastic fern, fluorescent-green in a faux-terracotta pot. He set it down in a corner of the dayroom, rearranged the leaves and stepped back to admire his handiwork.

'Keep it down,' Tristan hissed. 'Today? No, no. How could you watch him if I move you to Ward A today? You'll transfer once the Captain does. Not before.'

'I may not have much longer,' Windsor said.

Tristan used his foot to hook out a chair, then eased the old man into it. Bending down:

'What are you talking about?'

'Look what happened to Kalka…'

'Who?'

'Kalka! The Hindu.'

Tristan stopped dead.

'Kal-*ki*,' he hissed. 'And what exactly do you think happened to him?'

'He bought it! Suddenly too. Although at least he got to spend a few days in Ward A before he was called up. I could… I just want… I don't *feel*…'

He was prattling now. Still, he had surprised Tristan with that nugget of intelligence. How had he found out about Kalki's movements? How much more did he know?

'Nonsense, nonsense,' Tristan said. 'I won't hear any more about it. You're a tough old dog, Windsor. You've got years left in you yet.'

He made to walk off, when Windsor croaked something behind him.

'What was that?'

'I said: It's not just down to you.'

Tristan crouched in front of Windsor so their eyes were level, their noses almost touching. For a second he wondered if Windsor knew that Ward A wasn't even part of his domain. West Church had contracted out care for the Preemies several years ago, to squads of bowl-cut nurses in black jumpsuits with grosgrain utility belts and a merciless adherence to hygiene. Since then it had been charging top whack for its 'Five Star' service, no doubt creaming off healthy profits. Not even Cornish had any real say over what happened in Ward A anymore. But that wasn't what he had in mind. He was thinking about Hortense.

'*Hmm*,' he said. 'That's right. Don't think I haven't noticed your… Plan B.'

He flicked the end of Windsor's cravat out of his smoking jacket.

'Careful, young 'un,' Windsor scowled.

'You didn't primp yourself up for your cheapskate family because you know as well as I do that they're not coming today. So who, I wonder, could you be making such an effort for?'

Windsor was burning up.

'And what,' Tristan went on, 'would *she* make of all that?'

'Who?'

He knew who. Tristan stooped and whispered a name into Windsor's ear. He blanched.

That'd teach the old fucker. Knowledge of the Greys' former lives, used sparingly, could be a real asset. A carefully trained word or two was enough to skewer them. Still, he was rattled. He hadn't anticipated Windsor's defiance.

Pat was back in the dayroom.

'How many today?' Tristan asked him.

'Just Olive's and Lanyard's for Ward B. And Hortense's lot too.'

'All this for three families?' Tristan said. 'And nobody for Black Betty? She will be disappointed. Have you told her?'

'I was just about to.'

'Leave it to me,' he said.

Betty had just waddled into the dayroom, her arm resting on Smithy's shoulder. Tristan had long suspected some revolting septuagenarian tryst between those two. He pulled a clownish grin at her. She responded with a reluctant nod. Smithy hung his head. Lanyard shuffled in quietly behind them and then...

'*Rrrrrrrrreeeeeee-rat-a-tat-tat-tat-tat!*'

... the Captain rolled in, riding on the back of the wheelchair. Dot was in the wheelchair itself, her expression stuck somewhere between terrified and exhilarated, and her plaster poking out before her like the mast of a storm-wrecked schooner. The Captain hopped off, yanking the chair to a halt. He tousled Dot's hair, then addressed them all:

'A 15 Crusader! Best tank I've ever driven... That's it, soldiers! Backs straight! Mustn't let the bastards think they've got to you!'

Tristan turned to Pat.

'I thought I told you to put him in the rubber room?'

Pat swallowed a smile.

'I didn't have the heart.'

'The heart? Didn't you?' Tristan spat. 'She's never going to fall for it, mate.'

'Who? Fall for what?'

'Come on! Agnes! Do you think we're all blind?'

Pat looked away. 'You don't know what you're talking about,' he said.

'Don't I?'

'No. And you can count me out of your little plan tonight too.'

Tristan stepped up to Pat, his voice dropping to a whisper: 'So I guess that means you're happy to do the graveyard shift after all? Because I can't, and I doubt either of us want to tell Frankie to cancel her date with Vile Sphincter... *a-thon*.'

'I told you already, I can't. But that doesn't mean I have to help you. It's cruel – plain and simple.'

Tristan closed his eyes.

'There's a word for people like you,' Pat said.

'Oh, yeah? What's that?'

'Bloody... loony!'

Before Tristan could answer, Windsor had exploded behind them. 'Red Cross? Intelligence? What are you on about, man?'

And now the Captain was hilt-deep in a new delirium. This was all Tristan needed. The afternoon was already sliding into chaos... and the families hadn't even arrived. As Betty tried to soothe Windsor, Smithy took the Captain by the arm:

'Rein it in, there's a good man. Don't want the Krauts getting wind of things, eh?'

'Don't fret, Corporal. These brutes haven't a word of English to rub together between them.' And with that, the Captain glared at Tristan and rasped his lips like an irascible stud horse.

'Don't you spoil this for everyone,' Windsor barked, just as the doorbell sounded.

'Here we go chaps! Positions! Fall in!'

Nobody was listening to the Captain anymore as they all craned to see whose number had come up first. Frankie opened the front door and the family shuffled in.

'Lanyard, look! You lucky thing.'

Betty's graciousness stemmed from the mistaken belief that her son would be here soon. He was normally the first to arrive, but she could surrender pole-position this once. Tristan would let her know soon enough, but couldn't resist the chance to watch the old bird's crest droop as she realised she wouldn't be seeing her boy today.

Lanyard vaulted from his chair and strode across to his brood. Remembering too late his long list of ailments, adding a limp and a cough for the benefit of the others. He ushered his visitors – two middle-aged women, a youngish man and three small children – to a table at the far corner of the room.

One of the women unpacked a tower of tupperware from her bag and popped several of them open, sending up mushroom clouds of steam. Tristan thought of intervening – 'outside' food was banned – but he was reluctant to engage with Lanyard's inscrutable gaggle today. There was no point encouraging the mayhem.

'Can't bloody bear the smell,' he heard Windsor gripe. 'Smithy, would you mind?'

Smithy stood and strained at one of the sash windows, until it flew open. A chill wind curled into the dayroom. Betty shivered theatrically, but was ignored.

Tristan's grip on the situation was definitely sliding now. Visiting day was always a nightmare – there were too many balls to keep in the air, any one of which could suddenly reveal itself as a primed hand-grenade. But today, with the ceremony, the preparation... with Pat not playing ball, and with Windsor... and with the Captain, on the loose and fractious... and the stitch in his gut that was tightening every second... Today was...

How many OxyNyx had he taken so far? How many was too many?

The doorbell rang again. Tristan clutched his side, caught his breath. Out of the corner of his eye he saw Betty smooth her crisp nightie and set her smile into an expectant crescent – which waned when she saw Olive's daughter and son-in-law slouch in. Tristan, bucked up a little by this, caught Betty's eye, mimed a phone with his hand and shook his head. The balloon-woman deflated before his eyes.

Olive's lot – if a measly two could really be thought of as a 'lot' – made little effort to disguise their awkwardness, their desire to be anywhere but here. The daughter searched out Tristan's gaze and rolled him a pair of complicit eyes. The son-in-law continued tickling the screen of his mobile telephone, panning for football scores, probably.

Christ, she resembled her mother! With their large, knobbish heads, they looked like a pair of ecclesiastical maces. The son-in-law was a ruddy pack of meat strung into a polo shirt. He had a stocky neckless body, a skinhead dictated by creeping baldness and a sheaf of keys beside the phone holster on his belt. The kind of couple that took long silent drives out to country pubs, for long silent lunches.

As Olive stood, she nodded at the Captain. He winked back.

'Mum,' the woman said, taking Olive in a stiff embrace.

'Mum,' the man echoed. 'How've you been?'

They sat at one of the tables. Olive laid her hands on the blistered plastic as an offering to her daughter, who patted them twice before burying her own hands in her lap.

'Andy,' the woman said tetchily. 'What did I say about making an effort?'

The son-in-law clucked his annoyance and holstered the phone.

'Happy?' he said. She wasn't, but nodded.

The Captain was fixing them with a determined stare. Tristan stepped forward, blocking his view.

'How're they treating you, Mum?' the man asked, already fingering his phone, ready to whip it out again at the first conversational lull.

'Well…' Olive began, an odd note of determination to her voice. 'My friend there, the Captain, he wants me to…'

The doorbell again. A bolt of electricity ran up Tristan's left side. He winced.

Even the families took an interest in new arrivals – for the chance it gave them to breathe. Pat opened the door to a wealthy-looking couple, flanked by two miniature versions of themselves. Original and Travel editions. The man and his homunculus were sporting identical moccasins, creased trousers, striped shirts, pullovers arranged meticulously on their shoulders and side-parted blonde hair, while the woman and her own pocket-sized accomplice were wearing summer dresses cut from the same fabric – a riotous chunder of flowers – buttoned up to the throat. Their angular bobs were held in place by wide, navy-blue headbands.

Hortense's tribe. She had already told the CareFriends that she would receive her family upstairs, but Windsor had no way of knowing this and was already struggling across to the door. When would he understand she wanted nothing to do with him? Tristan watched Pat escort the family to the stairwell, unlock the cage and usher them upstairs.

'Fucking butler,' he muttered.

Frankie was beside him in a flash, as if she had just popped into existence. She put her hand on his shoulder.

'Are you sure you're okay, mate?' she smiled. 'Going easy on the pills, I hope?'

'Why do you say that?'

'Well, for starters, your pupils are so dilated they've got their own event fucking horizons.'

Tristan sighed, heavily. What was her problem? All the characters in his 'faggot New York' novels – and, he assumed, all the writers who penned them – gobbled prescription painkillers and antidepressants as if they were candy. And the only side-effects, as far as Tristan could see, were a monolithic self-regard and fat-fingered inability to weave a plot that critics often mistook for genius.

'Look, I know you think you're some kind of badass and I'm a...'

'A little kitty cat stuffed into a sack with a couple of bricks, about to be thrown into the canal?'

Sand! It was all fucking sand between his fingers!

'Right. But I've got this.'

Frankie shook her head. 'You've got something alright.'

He turned his back on Frankie. Olive was halfway through stammering a complaint.

'… Lock the ward at night. So we can't go, even if…'

'I'm sure they have their reasons, Mum,' the daughter said. The son-in-law was back caressing his phone. Tristan stepped forward, ready to intervene, nip it in the bud. The son-in-law raised his eyes with an awkward but complicit look. *Hold your horses pal, I've got your back.*

'Come on, Mum,' he said. 'These folks have a hard job to do.'

Tristan could always count on the families. They weren't cruel, not really. It just made their lives easier if they believed the lies.

'And… they're all… on drugs!' Olive screeched. Tristan stiffened. 'The white pills, the pink pills…' – she went on, turning to Tristan, glaring at him – '… the *blue* pills. They're meant for us, but they keep them for themselves. Laughing it up in that room over there. Playing music. Buggering each other!'

The daughter looked appalled. This was new territory, thin ice, the outcome uncertain. The accusations were scattergun, barmy… but not *wholly* insane. The son-in-law nudged his wife:

'I wouldn't mind a few of those blue pills myself.'

'Andy!' she hissed, mock-scandalised. Then, turning back to Olive: 'You mustn't say such things, mum. It's not easy for us either. Seeing you here. You know we'd have you with us if we could, but—'

'We can't.' Tristan recognised Andy's tone.

'You understand, Mum?'

Olive's lips made the shape of a word but no sound came out.

'And it's not cheap, you know. We haven't had a holiday in…'

'Andy!'

'She should know…'

'She doesn't need to.'

'Listen, Mum…'

'*aaaaaaaggggghhHHHHHHH!*'

'*EEEEEEeeeeeeeeeee…*'

In his wired state, it would take Tristan a moment to settle on a coherent timeline for what had just happened, although no account could truly capture the events as he had lived them.

The first shot was fired by Windsor, who had scudded, *sans*-Zimmer, out of the dayroom, across the hallway, and through the gate, before collapsing halfway up the staircase, landing sprawled and spread-eagled as if he had been hurled from a Mangonel.

Simultaneously came Lanyard's scream. Or was it Betty's? Or the sash window thumping down? That must have been it: Lanyard – the thump – Betty...

She had been shivering in silence since Smithy had opened the window. Deciding she had suffered enough, she'd made her way over, intent on closing it. It wouldn't have been easy. The sashes were heavy. She would have had to hang on it, easing it out of the swollen frame, until it slammed shut...

So she had trapped her fingers? But that made no sense. She would have been gripping the top of the window, meaning her fingers would have been clear. So...?

The sparrow's cracked body had slumped from the windowsill by the time Tristan's mind had covered that ground. Its mangled left wing was bent, the whole body jerking like a broken clockwork toy, a wheezy, distress call whistling from its beak.

Tristan looked from the sparrow to Windsor on the staircase. He wasn't moving, just emitting a low-pitched, bestial rumble. Around him, the fingernail petals of a murdered chrysanthemum.

Everyone was watching... but nobody moved. The onus was on Tristan to act. But what could he do? Step on the bird? Grind it into the lino with his boot heel? All that *kindest-thing-to-do* bullshit. Who was it kind to, really? Not to Tristan, who'd have to live with that sensation of crushing the life out of it. Kind to the sparrow, perhaps? But who was he to decide that...? And still the spiteful little bastard lived, and jerked, and flapped...

And still Windsor moaned, and flapped, and lived...

The residents parted. Dot was on the move, wheeling herself towards the wrenching bird. She stopped inches from it, examined it for a moment, then continued forward, the wheelchair's tyre snapping the sparrow's neck, crushing its windpipe, stilling its agonies. Without looking back, Dot rolled past Tristan and out of the dayroom.

All of the Greys, all of the families, were staring at him. And he, in a strange way, was staring at himself too; watching himself – not moving, not speaking, not breathing…

Frankie appeared at his shoulder. She laughed.

'Fucking A!'

Short of breath, his chest tight and getting tighter, Tristan turned and strode from the room – it took all his effort not to run, not to drop down onto his knuckles and charge out of there like a spooked gorilla. He frisked himself for the OxyNyx… If he could feel the slingshot again, the weightlessness, then perhaps… perhaps…

Where was it?

No good. He had to see Kalki. Now.

He hurried up the stairs, ignoring Windsor's sprawled body. At the top, he fumbled a key from his pocket, opened the closet door and slammed it shut behind him.

ornish couldn't stop himself smiling. Nor could he see why he should. Smiles came so rarely, after all. That morning, he had been awake early and more depressed than usual. After an hour of fidgety sallies back and forth across sleep's threshold – earning him a couple of hardy toe-punts from Harriet – he'd risen, showered and electric-razed in darkness. He'd dressed from the airing cupboard, to avoid the bedroom, and had snatched a banana from the side as he bowled through the kitchen and out of the back door so that he wouldn't have to sit down to breakfast with his family. They had the habit of saying intolerably stupid things and he in turn of telling them so in that way of his that made them cry. By the time his bus was due he had been prepared to settle into another brain-fag day, life experienced as if swimming under water.

That was why, watching the girl work, his chair tucked tightly beneath his desk to hide the tent-pole erection, he allowed himself a smile. The mere presence of this girl in his office was so incongruous for a thousand different reasons, that it cast a glow of renewal over the room and everything in it.

It reminded him of falling in love. Of the early days of his relationship with the beautifulish young woman who would metamorphose into his wife.

His conscience nagged… but he was only looking, after all. And as far as he knew there was no law against that. Not yet, anyway. Objectively he was unimpeachable. Quite the reverse. What would they try him for? Soliciting filing from a minor after attaining her mother's consent? Hardly a crime, even in this pruriently puritanical age. That she was dressed like a little strumpet and rendered him so doggedly randy that his boner ached against the underside of the desk was purely circumstantial. That was the beauty of a mind capable of such lucid fantasies: looking was almost as good as touching. Almost.

So he looked. He looked as the girl – more industrious than he had expected – worked the files. As the stack reduced, she lowered herself to the floor and sat with her legs crossed. The sight of her skirt front straining open, rippling with tension, hauled his thoughts back to his groin. He could see no further than two or three inches above her knee, but in the shadow thrown by her skirt – that seemed, in fact, to writhe outwards, to be radiating from a core of vast energy buried somewhere deep within, the very source of the darkness, incomprehensible and eternally ponderous like a collapsed star – he saw in a flash, and with a convulsion of sickly hunger, the ordained and inevitable conclusion of their time together. Perhaps it wouldn't happen today, but it would happen, and he would end up in prison... or worse. He wasn't strong enough to stop it.

An almighty thump grounded Cornish and distracted the girl from her work. It seemed to be coming from the stairs. The girl was looking at him, a glimmer of concern in her enquiring eyes. Cornish held a finger to his lips.

A couple of screams rang out. This didn't sound good. The girl was still looking at him. He shook his head, mouthed 'wait'. A moment of silence, then a patter of footsteps up the stairs.

Cornish braced. This was it. They were coming for him. A rush of bovver-booted police officers were about to burst into his office, cart him off, lock him up with the prison bugger and throw away the key...

Except it wasn't his office door that opened, but the closet. Ever since he had mislaid the key he had tried that locked door every morning, and every morning it had refused to yield. But now it did... accompanied by a strange noise, a fierce rush of air, a giant's inverted snore, that lasted for a few seconds before cutting out as the door slammed shut.

He knew he ought to investigate, but...

'Cigarette,' he barked, standing abruptly, clipping the tip of his half-baked hard-on against the lip of the desk. She'd heard him say something, but not what, and grimaced at him to repeat.

'Cigarette?' he said again. She squinted at him for a few seconds before nodding.

He handed her a cigarette, struck a match and offered it to her. Cupping his hand in hers and pouting forward, so that the tip dipped into the shivering flame, she accepted. He felt a baptismal fervour, the dark ritual energy of initiation hanging over them. She took a long, slow drag, and then, rather than expelling the smoke, let it escape from her at its own rhythm, lazing out of her mouth in luxuriant arabesques. She looked as if she had been doing it a hundred times a day for the past half-century. When had teenagers become so damned sure of themselves? It was almost obscene how at ease they seemed in their skins. Wasn't adolescence supposed to be the time when one was humbled by the world? That was how it had been in his day – at least, how it had been for him. His stomach still turned when he thought back to the failures and humiliations of that time. They had begun with Lisa, his first love, who had spitefully rebuffed his request for a dance at the end of term disco the summer before Whitby...

'What's under there?' the girl asked, nodding at the sheet. Cornish pulled it back, revealing the model. As she stooped to examine it, her arm pressed against his hip.

'Funny,' she said. Cornish stooped too.

'What's funny?'

'That whoever made the model didn't take the time to finish it. Why would you paint patches of the walls and the roof like that, and not finish it off?'

She was right. There were painted patches. Painted, in fact, in quite splendid detail: sections of the brickwork pranked with lichen, a minuscule smother of bird shit on the roof tiles. How odd that he had forgotten...

'My house looks kind of like a model from here,' she said, crossing to the window and gesturing at Meanwell with her cigarette. 'Next to the church.' Cornish didn't want her to see him squinting, so he just nodded. 'My bedroom's in the roof.'

His heart flexed against his ribcage. She had mentioned her bedroom. He knew the code, but did she?

'What's your name?' he said, so as to put off the question he really wanted to ask, the question that could mean the difference between liberty and incarceration. She smiled.

'You're Raymond, right? Raymond Cornish.'

'Right,' Cornish said. 'How did you…?'

'Every kid in Meanwell knows your name.'

'They do? How?'

She hesitated, then mumbled something.

'What?' Cornish said. 'What was that?'

Her cheeks were burning.

'Raymond Cornish,' she said, clearer this time, though still shyly. 'King of the Crazies.'

Cornish lifted his cigarette to his lips and, after a long drag, left it hanging from his mouth, planting both hands on his hips. Was that what all these years of quiet service to the sick and dying earned you? Raymond Cornish, King of the Crazies – he could already hear the children chanting it as the refrain of some villainous playground game. And there was undoubtedly some vicious parental whispering that had led them to it. All those years of boring tie-sporting, invisible hat-doffing, sensible hair-wearing effort to be considered a beacon of normality, and this was how they thought of him in Meanwell: Raymond Cornish, King of the Crazies. How little one knew about the role one played in other people's stories. If he had been pushed, he might have guessed he was seen as a kind of Micawberish everyman. Or, at worst, a Walter Mitty. But it seemed Boo Radley would have been a safer bet. He would even have preferred Dracula.

'But in fact, you're not crazy, are you?' she said, turning to face him, letting a curtain of smoke rise from her mouth like some fantastic, inverted waterfall, and enwrap his face. He was about to agree, then stopped himself. Who was he to say? After all, none of the Greys – not even Ruggles – would have confessed to even the slightest lack of lucidity. Perhaps the first sign of madness was convincing oneself, unequivocally, that one wasn't mad. He swiped the cigarette from his lips, rocked back on his heels and laughed. How gloriously free her words had rendered him. As if, with that one revelation, that one quick slice of her tongue, she had amputated a hump that had been weighing on his shoulders for years. If the parents were determined to make a monster out of him, they shouldn't be surprised when he came for their children...

He reached out and ran his hand up her neck, into her hair, stopping when her quail's-egg inion rested in his palm. Under his touch he felt her tense at first, but she didn't pull away. Then, shifting her shoulders, she relaxed and just let her head be cupped.

'How old are you?' he asked, massaging her skull with his fingertips. She hadn't looked at him since he had taken hold of her head.

'Fifteen. Sixteen next month.'

An unparalleled joy coursed through his body.

'Let's celebrate your birthday together,' he said.

5

'Skulduggery!'

'Keep it down, you old bastard!'

'Skulduggery, I said!'

'What's wrong, Windsor?'

'I can't see a blasted,
buggering thing, Betty!'

'Night's always darkest
before the dawn, Sir.'

'Codswallop!'

'Lanyard! Smithy!
Let him speak.'

'It's half past eight in the morning.
Where's the bloody sunlight?'

'Blind!
Someone help me!
I'm blind!'

'Olive, *shhh*. It's alright…'

'Hold up, Windsor!
How do you know the time if…?'

'It's not alright, Dot.
I can't make out anything.'

'None of us can, woman!'

'Somebody throw the curtain!'

'Nothing.'

'We're all blind then.
They drugged the meat!
The little shits!'

'Olive, nobody drugged the food.'

'Naive, Dot. Naive!'

'Windsor, what makes you
say it's half past eight?'

'Body clock, Smithy.'

'Tick tock, Field Marshall.'

'I beg your pardon?'

'Timepieces are of the
essence, here.'

'You'd better shut your
bleeding trap, man!

'Both of you!
Shut your bleeding traps!'

'Easy, Bets.'

'He's right, though. I
know because…'

'Speak up!'   'Speak up!'

'My morning motion. It's starting.'

'Oh Jesus!'

'What was that?'

'*Eeeeeeeeeeee!*'

'Olive!'

'My lighter.
Whoever saw it can't be blind.'

'I saw it, Betty!'

'Which means I'm tempted
to second Windsor?'

'Second him, Bets?'

'I think he's right, Dot.
There's something wrong.'

'Now what?'

                                        'I suppose we should organise…'

'Form a…'

'Council of War?
Splendid idea, Soldiers.'

                                        'Oh, this won't end well!'

'*Atten'hut!* All those awake say aye!'

                                                        'Aye!'

'Aye!'

'Aye!'

                                                        'Uh huh!'

                                                        'Yup!'

'All present and correct,
Field Marshall.'

'Now… *huck! heurk!*
Excuse me… Heeeuurrrk!'

                                        'Are you *alright*, sir?'

'Fine, fine!
Now, it's ten to nine in the
morning, and none of us
can see a blasted thing.'

                        'Door's bolted too!'

'Thank you, Smithy.'

'And the windows.
There's nothing outside.'

'Blackout! This could be
the end game. Our boys
advancing over the tundra!'

'Nonsense, you cretin!'

'If anything this is a black-*in*.'

'With all due respect,
Field Marshall. *Watch*… it!'

'Stop your squabbling!
We need to organise!'

'Quite right, Bets!
I'm famished.'

'And Lanyard isn't the only
one with morning motions.'

'Enough with the potty talk!
Organise we must.
Being too unwell myself,
I nominate Ruggles.'

'Me, Field Marshall?'

'Sir? Are you sure that he…?
Of all people?'

'Desperate times, Lanyard.'

'But, Sir? *Him*?'

'Do you accept the charge, Colonel?'

                                        'Sir! I really must…'

'Captain!'

'Don't make me regret this.'

'I accept.'

'All those in favour?'

'Aye!'

                                                    'Aye!'

'Aye!'

                                                    '*Hmm!*'

'Carried with aplomb!
I humbly accept.'

'Now, if you'll excuse me,
I do feel rather un…'

                                        'Question!'

'What *now*… Smithy?'

                            'You still haven't told us
                        what makes you so damned
                            certain it's morning.'

'Surely that became moot the
moment we decided to organise.'

                                        'Moot?'

'Moot.'

'Moot, Smithy! Moot!'

'Shut it, Lanny. How is it moot?'

'Drop it, dear.'

'All I'm saying, Bet's, is
that it's hardly…'

'Can't we get on with…'

'… he said ten to nine. Ten to!
No body clock is that accurate.'

'Do… you… MIND?'

'Yes… I… DO!'

'Darling, please!'

'Field Marshall. Time to own
up wouldn't you say?'

'Own up?'

'About the watch?'

'What watch? Who's got a…'

'Smithy, *ssshhh!*'

'Bastard!
Nosy, bloody, buggering bastard!
After what I just did for you.'

                                                'He's got a *watch*?'

'After what you've been
doing these last months.'

'And what's that supposed to…'

'Delivering intelligence to the enemy.
For a few poxy home comforts.'

                                                'Windsor?'

'It's only a watch, for
goodness sake!
Shouldn't go nosing about other
people's things like that.'

'Shouldn't go around selling
out your own side to the
rat-faced Nazi…'

                                                'Captain!'

                                                'Easy Bets!'

                                                'Windsor?
Do you have a watch?'

'It was Sheila's.'

6

Beneath the plaster, Dot's leg had come alive. Twitching, fluttering, prickling with pain as if her body was conducting a series of experiments on itself. How alien that hidden limb had become to her these last weeks, without her even realising it. It was as if that part of her body had been erased, tippexed out. If she'd been told that beneath that plaster boot there was nothing but hot air and sawdust, bad breath and cobwebs, she would have had no trouble believing it... At least until now. Now it was pulsing into existence again. *Now you feel it, now you don't!* It could have gone either way – reappearing fully formed, or vanishing again, and for good this time.

The intrusion of an outsider's name into the ward was overwhelming. Olive howled, Smithy panted, even Betty whimpered. Dot felt sick to her stomach. It churned and clenched just as it had when, as a small girl, her father had told her that they – *all* of them, somehow, even though *she* hadn't done anything – were at war.

'Who is this Sheila?' Lanyard asked, with a tremor of jealousy.

'My wife,' Windsor said after a long pause. 'I had a wife and her name was Sheila.' It rang like a confession.

'And they let you keep her watch?' Betty asked. Dot couldn't tell if the noise Windsor made was a deep and pained sigh, or just the tracheal tube sabotaging his breath.

'After she went blind, the doctors gave her a Braille watch. This one. Sometimes she'd get so frustrated she would hurl the bloody thing against the wall. But it never broke. In the end...' – he sniffed back a balloon of snot – '…in the end she mastered it. After that, she never took it off. It kept her connected to the world. She could use her fingertips to see the sun rise and set again. See the moon too. After she… After, I would wear it myself, but then they banned watches. I wasn't going to let them take it, so I hid it…'

'Up your jacksy?' the Captain chirped.

Windsor wheezed with laughter. Dot had never heard him laugh before.

'No, Ruggles. I hid it under my pillow. But they found it, of course. That's when we came to our… agreement. I'm truly sorry about that.'

The Captain sniffed. As close to a conciliatory handshake as he could muster just then.

'This watch is all I've got left of our fifty-two years together. How could I let them take it? Once it's gone, she's gone. If I lose it, she vanishes. Without it, remembering her would be like grasping at a puff of smoke…'

Windsor paused again. His throat was acting like a blocked ballcock, stopping his words.

'Oh! It's no bloody fun getting old, is it? Living in a body held up by corns, by calcium deposits, by scars, gas, snot, by… by plastic body implements! That's the one advantage of the crab, I suppose. After it has you in its pincers it gets to work, transforming you, slowly, until, at one moment or another, you transcend all your other ailments and all that is left is the cancer…'

'Edward!'

Dot may have drifted off for a moment.

'Edward!' It was Betty. 'That was my husband's name.' And she laughed, a deep burble of exultation. 'How strange it feels to say it after all this time. Edward, Ed… ward. Eddy, too. Sometimes Eduardo, when I was feeling… Well, you know.'

The air in the ward was thick with transgression. Dot felt giddy with it. Afraid too. Afraid of what might be asked of her. Afraid of how they would react upon learning that her husband had been so close by these last three months and she hadn't seen him once. How could she explain that to them? She couldn't even explain it to herself.

'Vera!' It was Olive.

'Who's Vera, Ol'?' Betty called from across the ward.

'Who do you think?' she cried. 'Me! I'm Vera. You don't need to know my husband's name. Better off forgotten now, the miserable old bastard. But my name – mine! – is Vera.'

'Vera's a lovely name,' Dot said, puzzled. 'Why do you call yourself Olive?'

'Call *myself*?' she said. 'Call myself nothing! Why would I call myself Olive Oil? I'm Olive for the same reason he's Windsor and he's the Blacksmith. For the same reason you're Dorothy!'

'I... I don't...'

'The *baptism*,' Lanyard said.

'The what?' Her chest contracted, as if suddenly attempting to expel some parasitic kernel of knowledge. All around her the people she thought she knew were guttering like spent candles.

'Oh dear. You still don't remember, do you?'

'Remember what, Betty?'

'It happens... to the best.'

'Your baptism. The tin bath? The awful naming ceremony? That brute? How you *became* Dorothy?' She sung, softly: '*We're off to see the Wizard...*'

'I didn't become... I've always been...'

Had she? Of course she had. Hadn't she? Surely she would remember if she'd once been called... something else.

'I didn't remember mine either,' Olive said consolingly. 'Not at first. Not until I heard them doing yours, Bets. Then it all came rushing back.'

'And I got off lightly,' Betty said.

'The others I understand,' Lanyard said. 'I never got yours, Betty.'

It took Dot a moment to realise the sound she could hear was Smithy's rough, butcher's hands against his bare chest. Then – '*Looky*

looky yonder... Looky looky yonder... Looky looky yonder... Where the sun done gone' – Perfectly imitating the drawl of a Mississippi bluesman. *'Wooah Oh! Black Betty!'*

'Bam-a-lam!'

The chorus of voices startled Dot. Olive's, was it? And Lanyard's? Betty's too?

'Wooah Oh! Black Betty!'

'Bam-a-lam!'

'Black Betty had a baby.'

'Bam-a-lam!'

'Black Betty had a baby.'

'Bam-a-lam!'

'Damn thing gone crazy.'

'Bam-a-lam!'

'Damn thing gone crazy...'

The chorus scattered into giggles.

'Oh, it does you good to sing,' Olive said after catching her breath. 'Music does you good.'

'Yes, I got off lightly,' Betty said again. 'Probably because they couldn't have lifted me into that bath even if they had wanted to. I was Patricia, by the way.'

'I've always thought it was a dumb move, the way they named Bets,' Smithy said.

'Why?' Olive asked.

'Because they took a normal, unwell old woman and they made...' he paused. 'I'm sorry to put it like this, love, but they made a Magic Negro out of you.'

'Easy on the Negro, Whitey!'

'I'm sorry, but you know what I mean! They turned you into something foreign, something inscrutable. Something... hoodoo. They don't mess with you in the same way they do with Olive and Lanyard. The baptism is a way of asserting their control, but it didn't work that way with Betty. She ended up with control over them.'

'Control's over-egging it a bit,' Betty said.

'Okay, but the casting gave you something. Just like the Captain's did. The only difference being that you had enough wits about you not to lose yourself in the part. The CareFriends are too dumb, and too young, to have any notion what the seeds they plant will flower into.'

'Nobody can ever know that,' Betty said.

In that horrible soupy darkness, Dot felt she didn't know any of them. They had been torn to shreds in front of her and then reconstructed as real people. Bafflingly, terrifyingly unknowable.

Every story we tell ourselves has to exclude something, almost everything in fact, Dot realised now. All that mind-time, that can fill a fraction of a second with a hundred different thoughts and emotions. It's like dark matter, a particle of it is heavier than the sun. So we pare down, eliminate, discriminate, ignore. We smooth the sharp edges, lop off appendages, hollow out... until we're left with something of a size that can be packaged, presented, maintained, held in the hand and examined like a trinket. And then, when we realise how little we're left with, we invent, we project, we rebuild others in our own image.

But it can't be sustained, not forever. It's only in books, those self-contained units of infinite smallness, those exercises in sculpting, in inclusion and exclusion, incision and excision, those closed universes subject to the despotic will of a single mind, that any attempt can even be made at a concise and coherent portrayal of character... and still there was no guarantee it would hold together. For when one person sculpts another, the result is riven with all the fault lines, all the unexplored plains, all the submerged abysses of its creator. Show me a realistic portrayal of a person on a page, Dot thought, even in Tolstoy, and I'll show you a million little sacrifices, a million little compromises, a million little lies.

She was as guilty of it as anyone. How easily she too had accepted Betty as the Magic Negro, from her very first morning here. She had immediately sought a dose of Earth Mother comfort, antediluvian succour, in her foreignness. And she hadn't paused to question this feeling, not once, despite all the signs Betty had given that she was more complicated than that, the episodes of soreness, of jealousy... How Dot had mistreated her! How she must have mistreated the others too. All of them.

'Oy,' she stage-whispered. 'Captain!'

'F... falling in!' he gasped, jolted awake. 'Present and correct.'

'Captain, did you hear any of that?'

'Every word, Private. We're establishing a council. The Field Marshall appointed me, we're...'

'No. About the names? About the baptisms?'

'...'

'Captain?'

'Present and correct, Private!'

Dot wanted to throttle him.

'What's your name?'

'Captain Dylan Prometheus Ruggles,' he said. 'British Army First Airborne Division. I'm surprised, Private, that after all this time you didn't... Are you feeling ever so slightly less than chipper?'

'Please,' Dot begged. 'Just hang up this nonsense for a minute. Please Ruggles, I...'

'Dotty,' Betty said. 'It's no good. He won't.'

'He has to...'

'You mustn't ask him to. It's not fair.'

'Not fair, Betty? What about what's fair for me?'

'He doesn't want to know,' Betty said.

'What about the rest of you, though? Why do you put up with it?' Dot felt so desperately alone.

'I suppose it served us all in different ways,' Betty said. 'At first, anyway.'

'Are you sure you don't remember, Dot?' Olive asked. They wouldn't listen to her. They couldn't. Knowing that one amongst them had been spared the indignity of having her name stripped from her would make their own loss all the harder to bear.

'There's nothing to remember.'

'If not your name, then surely there's something you want to share. A husband, a child…'

She thought of Leonard and Thomas, their long, happily uneventful lives together.

And then it came: the sadness, the humiliation, the awful crippling guilt. For what she had done and what she hadn't. She knew, now, why she hadn't seen Leonard. It had nothing to do with discretion, with not wanting to cause a fuss. She had been grateful for the anonymity of Green Oaks, had liked the way it stripped them down to hoary clichés, made of them all the kind of characters one met only in the most torrid train-station novels. It was horrible, of course, but only in principle. And principles were only for when the pain was mild enough to bear. She hadn't seen Leonard for one very simple reason: she hadn't wanted to. Seeing him would have just made it all too real.

'No, Betty,' she said. 'Nothing.'

A moment later, Dot started as a groping hand settled on her forehead, but recognising its contours she relaxed at once. The Captain. Neither of them said anything as his fingers sought out her scalp and ran through her hair. A few seconds later a whiskery contraband kiss landed on the tip of her nose. She reached for the hand, took hold of it and squeezed. The hand squeezed back.

'Private Dot's quite right,' the Captain said. 'Now is not the time for idle chit-chat. If we're going to make it out of this mysterious blindness, there's work to be done.'

He set to it at once, giving orders, organising squads… but he asked nothing of Dot. As she lay there, the thoughts she had been fighting off for so long rained down upon her. The man she had reduced to a word, an incantation, a symbol for all that had been lost in the flood… Leonard. There he was, a pinprick of light at the eye of the black hole, at the centre of the vortex. She peered at him, transfixed. The more she stared, the larger and clearer he became, the more detail her mind rendered onto him… until he was almost there with her.

There was his soft, bear-cub build, arsier than a man had any right being. And there were his gardening Wellingtons, those old grey corduroys – his 'elephant slacks' – tucked in and blooming like pantaloons. There were his bamboo canes, held crossed in his left hand like a pair of duelling pistols. There was his swollen paunch ('if it was good enough for Buddha…'), his gorsey cardigan, his one remaining tuft of hair.

And there were his eyes, as dark as coals. Eyes that had refused to dim as the face that framed them had dried out and shrivelled up, blistered with liver spots and coarsened after decades of clumsy shaving. Those eyes. Looking right at her. Smiling.

And then, very slowly, he held out a hand, beckoning her in. When she didn't come at once, he turned the hand at the wrist and offered it to her. It was too much. She reached out, took hold of the hand and let him pull her down into the gyre.

7

She had finally admitted that something was wrong the day Leonard hurled his book into the fire.

'They're laughing at me, you know,' he said, glaring with rage at the hearthrug. 'They used to be good, but they're not now. They're buggers!'

'Who's that, Tubby?' Dot asked, keeping an eye on the smouldering leaves, in case one should eddy free.

'Who do you think, you silly woman?' he said, turning his wrathful gaze on her now. 'The Puzzle People.'

'Oh,' Dot said. 'The Puzzle People' was their marital shorthand for the anonymous team of riddlers that compiled the collection of crosswords and conundrums she bought for him every week. For her, the sobriquet conjured an image of balding boffins, with leather patches on the elbows of their tweeds, beavering away in an oak-panelled, smoke-filled, study somewhere – Cambridge most likely – sharing their flights of inspiration on an old chalkboard, striated with the faint memories of bygone puzzles posed and solved. It was their way of humanising what they knew was probably the rather dry process that week-in-week-out produced this digest of fifty-two pulpy pages, bound with a single staple and wrapped in a glossy sheath. For all the attention she paid them, they might have been using the same pool of puzzles in a random rotation, but they were not meant for her. They had been a way to keep Leonard, a proud non-reader, occupied as he rode the bus to work. Even though he had declared them a frivolous waste of money, he took to them with such enthusiasm and aptitude that she continued buying them even after he had retired.

So he would come out with things like, 'The Puzzle People have pulled out the big guns this week, Peachy-buns,' when he was struggling, or 'The Puzzle People are getting sloppy bollocks' when he wasn't, and she would smile back at him, content not so much with what he was saying but with what the manner in which he said it repeatedly confirmed – that during their long lives together they had forged an offshoot of the language that was theirs alone. Dot had never imagined he could twist this language to make it sound so menacing.

'You'd think people would complain, but no one does. No one cares.'

'Complain about what?'

'The puzzles. They used to have solutions, but they don't anymore.'

The pages of the burning book curled in on themselves, constructing a black and grey chrysanthemum at the heart of the fire, before evaporating out of existence. Dot turned to him and lowered her reading glasses.

'What do you mean? Of course they have solutions. What would be the point if...'

'They don't,' he interrupted, 'and they're laughing at me, and that's the way things go, and that's the way things are.'

She had heard that a few times recently – *and that's the way things go, and that's the way things are*. Sometimes it didn't seem out of place as a way to close down the conversation, to insist that his judgement not be questioned. At other times, however, when she had offered him tea, or when she had pressed him to explain why he had emptied the kitchen cupboards and left their contents scattered over the worktops, this refrain – *and that's the way things go, and that's the way things are* – rang like a conditioned response gone awry, reason's needle skipping and jamming in the wrong groove of the brain. Until then, she had acquiesced in this conversation halter, unwilling to probe too deeply, a faint intuition whispering that she may not like what she found. On this day, however, the words escaped before she could catch them by their tail.

'Nobody's laughing at you. Don't be silly.'

'Don't be silly. Don't be silly,' he parroted, meanly. 'It doesn't matter what you say, anyway. I'm leaving soon. I just have to wait for them to come and get me. Take me home.'

'Wait for who? Take you where? This is your home, you stupid bugger.' She felt there was something cruel in what she was saying, but she couldn't stop herself.

'IT... IS... NOT!' he raged, picking up one of his walking canes and heaving it across the room. The curled end hooked the matryoshka doll from the mantelpiece and sent it tumbling to the hearth, splitting the outer doll open and sending the inner one rolling out.

'Well,' she said, her voice creaking. 'Let's say no more about it, then.'

She took the remote control and aimed it at the television. The box blossomed to gaudy life. The programme was about gardening, the presenter one of those interchangeable robots that seemed to front everything now, carved from resin and lacking all semblance of character. Even though she could hear the show perfectly, she pressed the volume button, constructing the on-screen staircase step by step. She didn't listen to what the presenter was saying, she didn't care. She just closed her eyes and let the sound crash into her.

A week or so later, Dot awoke in the middle of the night to an empty bed. She reached across to Leonard's shallow trough in the mattress. It was still warm. The bathroom door, which led directly onto the bedroom, was closed, but the tell-tale slither of light that advertised its occupancy was absent.

'Darling?' she croaked. She cleared her throat and tried again. 'Are you there, Tubby?'

Nothing.

She waited for several minutes, raising an army of explanations for his absence: He's in the bathroom but, not wanting to wake me, didn't turn on the light. He couldn't sleep and went to fix himself some hot milk and honey. He had always loved honey. He heard a noise and went to investigate, and would discover that it was nothing any moment now, and come back to bed…

However much she tried though, a part of her wouldn't be fooled. She sat up and swung her legs off the side of the bed. She filled with a queasy understanding, not so much in her brain as in her bones, that were she to slide on her slippers, pull on her gown, and go in search of her husband, there would be no turning back from the horrible reality of things.

She hesitated. Perhaps, after all, it would be better if she were to just close her eyes, attempt to hijack sleep. Chances were he would be back in bed by morning, and then life could just go on. That was all she wanted. She wasn't greedy for change – that was an ailment of the young. All she asked for was stasis, the old routine left unmolested, for them to go on treading the same happy patch of water forever. She was asking for so little, really, and yet she knew too that it couldn't be that way. The one thing she was asking for was the one thing that could never be granted. In every life, something eventually had to give. And after one thing gives, then comes the deluge. Dot wriggled her toes into her slippers and, bracing herself against the bed head, rocked forwards onto her feet.

She heard the water running in the kitchen as soon as she opened the bedroom door. The air in the hallway was humid and a film of dew sparkled on the photos of Thomas and his family that tiled the walls – charting their genesis from newlyweds to a vigorous five-strong Germanic brood. The kitchen was dark, and the door only slightly ajar. Steadying herself against the wall as she walked, Dot shuffled along the hallway. She wondered if she should knock before entering and was struck by the strangeness of the idea. As if either he or she was a guest in the bungalow they had shared for almost twenty years. She took hold of the handle and inched the door open.

Clouds of steam were rising from the sink as Leonard hunched almost double over it. Forgetting her hesitation, Dot rushed towards her husband and threw herself onto him. Over his shoulder, she saw how he was trolling his hands under the jet of water surging from the hot tap. He was muttering something. His hands were as red as tenderised meat. She reached for the tap and shut off the water. For a moment they held still in their embrace, and then Leonard's body heaved with an almighty sob.

'It won't... It won't go away,' he whispered, heaving again. Dot took hold of his hips and turned him around gently.

'What, my darling? What won't go away?'

Seeming to notice her for the first time, he held his hands up in front of his face and rotated them first one way, then the other. The skin was badly scalded. She wanted to take hold of those hands, press them close to her chest, kiss them, lick them, anything to soothe the awful pain he must somewhere be feeling.

'It won't go away,' he said again. 'The stuff.'

'What stuff? What stuff, darling?'

'The *stuff*,' he said, scratching at the back of his left hand, scoring white hot lines in the skin. 'And that's the way things go, and that's the way things are.'

'*Shh... shush*,' she begged. Not that sentence again, not right now. 'There's no stuff, my love. That's just your skin.'

He looked into her eyes for the first time since she had come into the kitchen.

'That's. Not. My. Skin,' he said, a hostile determination punctuating his sentence. 'That skin. Is old.'

Something inside Dot cracked. A single fat tear escaped from her eye. She smiled.

'You are... *we* are old, my darling. You're seventy-six.'

He squinted at her, and smiled in the way he used to at modern art, a smile that said he might not understand, but he refused to be fooled.

'You don't know what you're talking about,' he said, pushing her roughly aside and walking out of the kitchen towards the bedroom. 'Fucking trollop.'

The following day the doctor came to bandage Leonard's hands. Perhaps it was the presence of an outsider, but throughout her visit he was lucid, witty even.

'That'll teach me for not testing the water before doing the washing up,' he said when asked how he had burnt himself.

'The washing up?' the doctor said, raising her eyebrows and smiling with complicity at Dot. 'Aren't you Mister Domesticated?'

Leonard reached out and took her hands between his bandaged bulbs, from which only the thumbs protruded.

'She doesn't appreciate me,' he said, a flirtatious grin lighting up his face as he nodded in Dot's direction. 'What do you say you and I elope together, right now. There's life in the old dog yet, you know.'

With a delighted girlish squeal, the doctor rocked back in her chair. How old was she? Fourteen?

'I'm sure there is. But I'm afraid I've got appointments all day today. Another time, perhaps.'

Leonard released the doctor's hands and turned to face Dot. He was elated with his performance. Dot just smiled. She used to hate Leonard's flirting, and still felt the old jealousies stirring – but more than that she was happy to have her husband back. She dreaded the moment the doctor would have to leave.

When Dot was showing her out, she pulled the living room door shut and asked for a moment more of her time.

'Your husband's quite a character, isn't he?' the doctor said, buttoning her jacket.

'He is, but…' Dot stopped. She felt as if she was on the point of an awful betrayal.

'But?'

'But recently he's been acting strangely.' The doctor's expression, which until that moment had been fixed in a practised rictus of joviality, straightened.

'Strangely how?'

Dot explained, in time with the doctor's bobbing head, about the burning of the puzzle book, the queer repetitive turns of phrase and how Leonard had really injured his hands.

'And I'm not sure, but I think he called me,' she lowered her voice further, 'a fucking trollop. He has never used language like that before. Not towards me, anyway. Never.' She didn't like the look she thought she saw fleet across the doctor's face. It was a look that seemed somehow to side with Leonard's judgment over her sense of grievance. Dot closed ranks. 'But I'm sure it's nothing. I suppose we are all becoming a little doddery. It'll pass, won't it?'

The doctor's face made Dot think of an unlettered tombstone.

'Listen,' she said, 'we'll keep an eye on him, okay? It could be nothing, it could be something. But we're here to help you, if you need us. If you really can't cope, there are institutions that can.'

Dot bristled.

'I didn't say I couldn't cope.'

The jovial grimace returned.

'Of course you didn't. But there's no shame in admitting when you need a little help, that's all. Sometimes it can help to play with them, to calm them down.'

Dot opened the front door.

'Them?'

The doctor chose not to answer her question.

'You know, tell stories, invent worlds. It can take them out of themselves for a while. It can really help.'

'Them?' Dot insisted, but the doctor didn't bend.

'So you have my number. Call me if you need me. Otherwise I'll be back in a week to change the bandages.'

Back in the living room, Leonard had put on the television but didn't appear to be watching it. He was holding his bandaged hands in front of his face, scrutinising their new attire.

'The doctor will be back in a week,' Dot said, taking her seat next to his.

'What are you talking about? That wasn't a doctor. That was my wife.' He turned in his chair to face her and stretched out his hands, wriggling his thumbs. 'Now will you get rid of these two things, or won't you?'

★

For several weeks, little change. No improvement, but no deterioration either. The doctor replaced the bandages once a week until, about a month after the incident in the kitchen, they were removed altogether. During the time his hands were bandaged, Leonard had taken to rubbing his thumbs together as if trying to kindle a fire. At first Dot had tried to stop him, but he would always pick it up again moments later, and it seemed to calm him down. As did the television, which he could watch for hours at a time, showing no preference for one channel or programme over any other. He no longer looked at the puzzle books, but for whatever reason Dot couldn't stop buying them.

It still upset her when he'd erupt with a barrage of non-sequiturs, or when she'd discover something freakishly out of place – a paperback in the washing machine, a handful of gravel in his coat pocket – but if this was to be the extent of the illness, whatever it was, then she was determined to learn to live with it and, if only to spite the doctor, to 'cope'.

A fortnight after the bandages were removed, the centre announced a visit to the forest for a picnic and Dot signed them both up. Her hand, clutching the pencil, had hovered over the form as she weighed her decision. On the one hand, she felt protective towards Leonard. It would break her heart if he made a fool of himself during the trip and – although she winced as she admitted it to herself – embarrass her too. On the other hand, he had so far behaved with impeccable restraint in public, and it was the only time Dot felt she could let her guard down a little and relax, just enjoy her husband. The clincher, though, was the buried hope that someone in the group might recognise his symptoms and speak with Dot about them. It would only take a word, perhaps just a look, any indication that it was really him with the problem and not her. He called her 'silly' and 'mad' so often these days that she sometimes wondered if he was right, if it was her losing the grip on things instead of him. She pushed the graphite point into the paper and scribbled their names on the list.

When the day came, aside from having to help him lace up his shoes ('They've changed the system. Why doesn't anyone tell you these things?'), Leonard was cooperative and seemed pleased at the idea of visiting the forest.

'You'll be able to show off what you know about the trees,' she said to him as she tied his shoes. 'All those Latin names you learnt!'

'Yes,' he said. 'I had a book about it once.'

'Yes, you did!' Dot sobbed with joy. Not only had this memory bitten but he had landed it.

'But they came and they took it away. And that's the way things go, and that's the way things are.'

Dot tugged hard on the laces and felt Leonard wince.

'Come along,' she said. 'Let's go outside and wait for our lift.'

It was late spring and the weather was perfect. In the back of the minibus, Leonard sat with his eyes closed, sunning himself like an old crow. He had taken off his glasses and wore a gentle smile on his face: the smile of a very small child who has yet to discover that all is not well with the world. He looked healthier than he had done for years, and happier too. Leonard was the only man on the trip – most of the women came to the Centre for some time away from their husbands (those that still had them) – but for now he sat oblivious to any and every attempt by the ladies to corral his attention, and when a question to him went unanswered, Dot preferred just to shrug a proprietary apology at the asker.

When they arrived, Leonard opened his eyes and the small smile blossomed into a broad grin. They had stopped in a secluded glade. At its centre was a large, reed-webbed pond, the water dark and primordially green. On the far side of the pond was a small shed, so long abandoned that the forest had started the process of reclaiming it as its own, slowly composting the wood, and covering the slate roof with a thick coat of verdurous moss. On the near side of the pond were four picnic benches, scattered randomly on the patch of grass, and an information board pasted with a yellowing, wrinkled map. Also on the grass, a wild pony and her foal, feeding calmly, unperturbed by the group's arrival.

They disembarked and gathered on the grass to ease out the stiffness after more than an hour in the minibus. There was something reassuring for Dot to be out here with Leonard, away from the hardness, the coldness of suburbia and closer to nature. It was so difficult to imagine somewhere as beautiful as this disturbing him in the way the very angular existence of the town seemed increasingly to do.

As the group dispersed – towards the picnic benches, or to pet the ponies – one of the ladies, Edna Savage, a well-preserved widow of about Dot's age and a recent arrival at the Centre, approached Leonard and asked if he would accompany her on a walk around the pond. Her legs, she said, were not what they used to be, and she would value the arm of a strong man to hang on to should she lose her footing. That Leonard walked with two canes seemed not to dissuade her. And why should it? Dot knew from her own experience that while the outer woman may atrophy early, the inner woman and her machinations live on far beyond the moment biology demands. Leonard looked to Dot for her approval and, pleased he had done so, she nodded. What harm could it do? Edna looped her arm around Leonard's and the two of them set off slowly along the track. After they had shuffled a few yards Dot called out.

'Leonard!' The promenading couple stopped and turned back to her. 'Perhaps you can show Edna how much you know about trees?'

Leonard smiled, but Dot felt ashamed the instant the sentence was out. It had not come from a desire to show her husband off, but rather to show him up. She doubted whether he could even tell a tree from a shrub anymore, let alone distinguish one tree from another. It was also her jealousy at work again, wanting to ward this widow off by unveiling the extent of Leonard's decay.

After they had gone a good quarter of the way around the pond, Dot, feeling somewhat conspicuous in her immobile solitude, set off around the path herself. She was hardier than them, and had to monitor her pace so that she didn't come too close and risk being called out on her jealousy. So at intervals, when she had almost caught them up, she would stop and pretend to smell a flower or to have discovered something of interest in the gravel until they had the chance to pull away from her again. As they progressed, she caught stray snatches of their conversation on the breeze, and was again astonished by how well her husband was able to disguise his symptoms.

'What about that tall, thick one, over there, with the funny pattern?' Edna said at a moment, pointing to a twisted old plane tree on the far side of the pond, near where the minibus was parked.

'That?' Leonard said with an assurance Dot found almost frightening. 'I believe that's called Glenda.' Edna laughed and they moved on. Dot knew that Leonard had been unable to recognise the tree, but his quick-wittedness, his deviousness, in response was astounding. At first she was annoyed at how he had managed to elude the question and keep his problem hidden. Yet it also demonstrated that at a certain level Leonard understood something was awry, and the very fact that he felt the need to pretend broke Dot's heart. She'd spent so much time worrying about how his problems were inconveniencing her, she had given little consideration as to how it must feel for him. To sense that something is wrong, but to not know what. To realise that your brain is no longer working as it should, is letting you down, letting you go. It must be terrifying. She stopped walking and let them advance.

That side of the pond, just in front of the shed, was in shadow, except for a single spot of rogue sunlight that sliced through the dense canopy of leaves overhead. Dot positioned herself in the glare and, closing her eyes, looked upwards. Her face warmed up at once and her vision flooded with an intense orange light. At first the light seemed uniform, but as her eyes grew accustomed to its glow, she saw that it teemed with detail, scratches and motes, slicks and eddies, drifting across the internal panorama. Perhaps it was a result of her recently diagnosed glaucoma, or perhaps this detail was always there and we just looked through it, distracted by the grander things underway further out in the world.

Feeling the need to check up on Leonard, she dipped her head, opened her eyes. He and Edna had made the full circuit of the pond and were busy petting the larger pony. Edna stood beside it, rubbing the distended belly, while Leonard stood in front, smiling, scratching both sides of the long equine face and muttering something with a curious intensity. He looked almost as if he was making a declaration of his love and would, at any moment, kiss the beast square on its leathery, lecherous mouth.

Dot closed her eyes again. She understood now why Leonard had looked so peaceful on the journey out. How efficient sunlight was at scouring everything away – one's ailments, one's worries, one's life, one's regrets. Of course there was a part of you that remained anchored to this world, but it didn't take a great leap to imagine how it must feel for the anchor to be weighed and to float off on the sea of pure existence. Perhaps what she was experiencing now was a taster of what she could expect at the end.

She hoped and, in her irreligious way, prayed that what had befallen Leonard was also in some manner comparable to this. That if his brain was disintegrating – and how could she believe it wasn't? – the space left behind would be filled with this serene, all embracing light. She hoped and she prayed it was so, but she just couldn't believe it. There was nothing light about what was happening to him. No. When she thought of his condition, of how his brain must look, and about how he must feel inhabiting it, she couldn't rid herself of the visions of war ravaged European cities that had filled the newspapers of her childhood. The apocalyptic landscapes of ruins, of rubble and of the occasional building thrusting upwards, miraculously, though indiscriminately, unscathed. There was an inescapable darkness to all of those photos, even though most had been taken during the daytime. A darkness that, even as a child, had always filled her with despair. She knew that, much as she hoped otherwise, when he had been bathed in sunlight in the minibus, that was all it had really been; a rare sunny day in Dresden.

The scream came as a shock, without somehow being a surprise. As it rang out, she knew that the day was rising to its preordained climax. It was only natural that at a moment the stress of disguising his condition would become too much for Leonard, that the deep running fissures, which had already made rubble of the foundations, would rise to the surface. In a way, that was what Dot had counted on happening all along, what she had wanted even, as a palliative for her loneliness. What she hadn't expected was that, just like a boiler in an old cartoon, the extraordinary build up of pressure could only lead to an explosion of comparable proportions. She opened her eyes.

Where before Leonard had stood alone with Edna, an arc of traumatised, gaping biddies had now formed, Leonard's strolling partner reabsorbed into their number. The group's collective attention, and choral cry for pity, was directed several yards in front, where a blurry Leonard still stood beside the pony. Dot raised her spectacles and the whole scene sharpened by several degrees.

All of a sudden, she couldn't breathe. Beyond the arc of old ladies, she could make out her husband now, seeming devilishly powerful despite the geriatric diminution of his frame, holding the cowering pony by its drooping, sock-like ear and landing punch after heavy, closed-fisted punch right between the poor animal's eyes.

8

Tristan closed the closet door and turned the key. The landing wasn't well lit, but after almost eighteen hours of candlelight it took his eyes a while to readjust. He flicked open the pill flask and tipped out three OxyNyx pills and the small writhing creature onto his palm. He felt grounded again, after his wobble with the sparrow.

'Thank you,' he whispered, not for the first time.

What could it signify, this boon? Every move Kalki had so far made, every gesture, every riddle he had posed, had been pregnant with some meaning or other, some message, some lesson. But this? This was altogether new. Never, in the weeks since their friendship had begun, had Kalki offered Tristan something physical. And not just physical, but alive!

Never.

Until now.

Fingering the small creature to one side of his palm, and the OxyNyx to the other, he pinched up one of the pills and placed it on his tongue. Then he tipped the other pills and the creature, back into the flask and closed the lid.

It was a message, but one he was currently unable to decipher. That would come, though, with time. The very fact Kalki was sending Tristan messages at all was extraordinary. If he hadn't seen it, if he hadn't *held* it, he wouldn't have believed it himself.

Setting off down the stairs, Tristan felt as if he could take on all comers. He checked his watch. Four o'clock. Almost the end of his shift.

As he approached Ward B, he intentionally softened his step, careful not to make a sound. After taking one last look at the small grub writhing about in the pill flask, he dropped it in the chest pocket of his smock. Then, pressing his ear to the door, he listened…

Silence.

The tarpaulin had been trickier to attach than he'd expected. Indeed, considering the darkness, Tristan was impressed it had stayed up at all. It had been slapstick worthy of Laurel and Hardy as he had fallen from the stepladder, got twisted in climbing plants and head-butted the wall in the darkness. And he had stirred up a racket too, as the barking of gaffer-tape and the rasp of Stanley-knifed tarpaulin was only amplified in the calm of the night. Still, after a little less than an hour, all four windows of Ward B were covered.

He was happy to be discovering the fruits of the exercise alone. Pat, once so biddable, had changed of late, his eyes often pregnant with a judgement Tristan felt he had no right to make. As for Frankie, she would no doubt miss the point, and would just be sent into raptures by the orgy of shit and misery.

The point? It had only occurred to him in the early hours of the morning, as he sat in communion with Kalki, that this undertaking had any other point than keeping the Greys contained for longer than they were used to. But by now this secondary purpose had blossomed in his mind to such an extent that it had almost displaced the original aim.

If things had gone as he hoped, the Ward B Greys would have spent the last eight hours or so in a state of such confusion and distress that the moment he opened the door he would become the saviour, the light-giver, the embodiment of a new dawn. Just as when a gosling hatches and its brain is imprinted with the first face it sees, adopts that face as its parent, loves it and would die to defend it, so he hoped the Greys would respond to him, and the recent insubordinate mood would be nixed once and for all.

And surely it was only right, now Kalki had chosen Tristan as his messenger, that the messenger should have a flock.

He slid the key into the lock and turned it as quietly as he could. Then, gripping the knob, he swung the door open. He couldn't resist.

'Let there be light.'

And there was.

'*Guten morgen!*' The Captain pivoted on his heels and glared at Tristan. The old bastard was impeccable in his pyjamas, the dented colander screwed down on his skull, a pugnacious grin deforming his face. Under his arm was a metal rod plied from one of the cots, clearly intended as some kind of baton. 'We had a little problem with the lighting here. Though I'm pretty sure you'll find everything in order.'

Everything in order? Tristan rushed into the ward, then gagged as he inhaled the lavatorial fug. *Everything in order you barmy old cunt?* His head fluttered, left to right, as he took in the scene…

In the twenty hours since he had locked them in for the night, the ward had transformed. Not, as he had hoped, however, into an outward manifestation of their collective despair. No, this was something quite different.

In the far corner, where Olive's cot had once stood, was a makeshift latrine. A rudimentary construction, just a bedpan perched on Dot's wheelchair, but someone had tacked a sheet to the ceiling to separate it – if only symbolically – from the rest of the ward. Windsor's cologne had been uncorked and placed on the windowsill beside it, clearly intended to stifle the stench. It was just a gesture, and a useless one, but the fact they'd had time enough for gestures angered Tristan even more.

One of the Captain's magazines lay flopped open over the wheelchair's backrest. Tristan yanked it up. Empty! Its pages torn out, one by one, and used for…

Christ! Tristan was boiling over. The Captain sidled up behind him.

'Thank goodness King George trains his army for all eventualities, wouldn't you say, *Unteroffizier?*'

'What?' Tristan spat.

'Textbook stuff, really. Ever since your boys played dirty with mustard gas during the Great War, all British units have been trained to operate sightlessly in an emergency.'

Tristan fixed Ruggles. Eye-fucked him. The old goat's folded lids hung heavy, but the eyes themselves were sparkling. As bright and as blue as OxyNyx. Why hadn't he thought to lock him up?

Tristan caught himself: *His training*? Ruggles wasn't a soldier. Never had been. But he had used his 'training'? He was delusional, off his fucking nut, and yet... it had worked!

He knew. That was all Tristan could think. He knew where he was, who he was. He knew what was going on here... on some level at least. He knew... and he was taking the piss.

'Organisation, camaraderie, discipline...' Ruggles was still speaking. 'A common enemy helps, of course.'

And they had eaten too. The corner opposite the latrine had been converted into a tip – biscuit wrappers, crisp packets, plastic tubs, empty save for the slug-tracks of sauce. All that contraband!

Tristan had lost his hold over Ward B now, that was certain. Although at least he had been spared being so brutally undermined in front of his staff. If they had seen the Captain get this one over on him he would have called it quits there and then. Given up his wages for these final two months and just not come back. Perhaps he'd do that anyway.

He fingered the pill flask through the fabric of his smock.

But that wasn't going to happen. That couldn't happen. Not now. If it wasn't personal before, the Captain had just made it so. If the old bastard wanted a war, then he could have one. And with Kalki on Tristan's side, he couldn't lose.

'I was scared at first...' Olive butted his train of thought off the rails. He turned to her. She was grubby, mussed up and ragged and, from the way she was blinking, her eyes hadn't yet fully adjusted to the light. But the expression on her face...

'What?' Tristan snapped.

'It reminded me of when I was a little girl,' she said. 'Of the Blitz, of the war. It was fun, in a way, the war. Thank heavens for the Captain, though.'

'Thank heavens!' Betty chipped in.

'Shut up!' Tristan turned to face her. She was in Smithy's cot. The two of them were lying there, their titanic bodies berthed side by side on a mattress barely big enough for one of them. 'And get back in your own bed... Jesus! What do you think this is, some kind of flop house?'

'I won't stand your blasphemy, boy,' Betty scolded him, her voice calm but firm.

'You... Won't you?'

He scanned the other faces. There had to be one upon whom his plan had worked. One, surely?

Smithy? Nope! The brute certainly looked put upon, but not overly so, not any more than usual. Lanyard then, or Dot? Both looked a little stunned, but otherwise practically indifferent.

Windsor? He sought out his mole in the reordered ward. Surely he had thundered, lamented, beaten his chest, scorned the Captain and his follies... Hadn't he?

His eyes alit on Windsor at the same moment Olive's did, and because of the violence of her scream, there was no chance of Betty chastising him for blasphemy a second time when he uttered:

'Oh Jesus... *fucking*... Christ!'

Book Four

1

Tristan hurried into the empty staff room, the enormous duffel bag slumping over his shoulder like a dismembered human torso. He closed the door behind him, let the bag fall to the ground and perched on the old leather armchair.

Six o'clock. Two hours until the night shift ended and the day shift began. Two hours to mull over the promise of this, his big day. Two hours to luxuriate in the denouement of a story that really should have been closed down weeks ago.

Then again, if he had closed it down earlier, how drab and unsatisfying an ending it would have been. In being forced to bide his time, his imagination had been given the occasion to range, to dream, to concoct. No, not to concoct… to *compose*. For there was something almost poetic about his plan.

But that was for tonight. After his shift was over, after the Greys had been put to bed, and after Cornish, the unwitting old numbnuts was long gone. He hoped to make it upstairs too, to see Kalki, for confidence and consolation, but that would depend on what else the day threw at him.

He unzipped the duffel bag and took three letters and a parcel from it, as well as the baggie of OxyNyx. He was down to his last half dozen pills, and didn't know yet where the next stash would come from. He had tried the pot dealers that hung out under Meanwell Pier, but none of them had heard of it. He had also dropped the name into conversation with his doctor, but the squint and sneer it had won him suggested that avenue would prove fruitless too. And he couldn't ask Frankie again – she had pegged him for an addict months ago and asking her for more now would feel like admitting defeat. Particularly as he *wasn't* addicted. He may have had a habit, and a mild one, but nothing he couldn't break. He thought of the habit like a Pomeranian – yapping, demanding, insistent, constantly in need of care… but it would also be easy enough to snap its neck and drop in the dustbin whenever he chose.

After fingering two OxyNyx into his mouth, he picked up the parcel and began scratching at the tape. He already knew what it was, the size and heft were achingly familiar to him, despite the fact that five or six years had passed since he'd last held it in his hands. It had arrived this morning. After three days of empty-handedness, three days of recriminatory mutterings directed his way, the postman had looked relieved to be able to present Tristan something substantial. He had already taken the parcel out of his pannier and was waving it triumphantly long before Tristan met him at the gatepost. The postman had released it, and the other letters, into Tristan's hand, as if feeding a half-starved street mongrel, muttered '*I hope it's what you've been waiting for*' without making eye contact, and strode quickly on to the next house.

Two of the three letters were for Tristan's father. The other one, addressed to him, would have to wait. His nail caught on a seam of the tape and it squeaked apart. He lifted a flap of brown paper along one of the shorter edges, and slid the book out.

It was just as he remembered it. The blue block lettering of the title, the vivid acrylic illustration on the cover, the *Other titles in this series* panel on the back. And the publisher's logo, a black and white line-drawing of the world, superimposed with a solid black Latin cross.

Tristan had been given his copy of the *Bumper Book of the Blessed* as a gift to mark his first communion, and had thrown it away about a year later, after deciding to cleanse his life of religion. He had taken the decision following a schoolmate's descent from a solid beta to a pathetic delta in the class hierarchy, after revealing the depth and breadth of his family's religious practice during an R.E. lesson. If those were the kind of problems religion caused, Tristan could do without it, and the boy's social resurrection after his selection for the rugby first fifteen a few months later had done little to convince him otherwise. It had also proven so easy for him to shuck off the vestments of religious belief that he could only assume they had long grown threadbare anyway and were about to disintegrate of their own accord. Neither had his mother cared. Her own faith had long lapsed and she had only insisted he take catechism classes to outdo her sister in the eyes of their parents. Indeed, Tristan's maternal grandparents were the only devout people he knew, and he remembered pitying them their daft ideas long before it was appropriate for a grandson to do so.

He had been thinking about this book a lot in the last few weeks. It was a clumsily written *Who's Who* of the beatified. Aimed at children, three hundred pages thick, with postage-stamp portraits of its subjects and, in the case of the more illustrious – the Saints and Martyrs, as opposed to the mere Blessed and Venerable – full page illustrations depicting the holy ones either muscularly enacting their miracles or being slowly tortured to death. Nobody could accuse the Catholic Church of sparing its children from the horrors of the world.

He flipped through the book, from front to back, then from back to front again. He wasn't sure exactly what he was looking for, but knew he would recognise it once he saw it. When this refused to yield the expected blossoming of comprehension, he set it down on the coffee table and began turning the pages one by one.

On page two hundred twenty-seven, he stopped dead. There it was. There *she* was. He read the entry aloud to himself in a breathless whisper:

"Alexandrina de Balazar. 1904–1955. Nationality: Portuguese. Status: Blessed. As a young girl Alexandrina bled spontaneously from her brow, as if a crown of thorns had been placed upon her head. Afterwards, Jesus came to her and gave her the name Alexandrina of the Sorrows. Aged fourteen, she was paralysed after jumping from her bedroom window to escape intruders. Confined to her bed, Alexandrina experienced numerous mystical visions, including further visitations from Jesus. From March 1942 until her death, Alexandrina took no food except

the Holy Eucharist. Medical doctors have been unable to offer any explanation other than the divine…"

'You're back?'

He almost leapt from the armchair, almost choked on the half-dissolved OxyNyx that were still rattling about his mouth. He chewed them up, swallowed.

'Shit, Frankie! Where the fuck did you spring from?'

'I was taking a piss,' she said, sinking into the couch. 'And I thought you were signed off for another week. Fucking limp-dick convalescent.'

'Nah,' Tristan said, the syllable jagged on exit. 'Doc said three weeks was already too much. Don't know why he insisted on so long in the first place.'

'Dunno,' Frankie said. 'Could've had something to do with the fact that Pat had to scrape your gibbering, shit-filled panties off the bathroom floor the day Windsor died.'

He jammed his eyes shut. He was still waiting for the frictionless ascent. The effect of the OxyNyx had dulled these last weeks. Now it was less about the rush, more about just feeling normal… but he'd take anything right now.

'That wasn't what happened…'

That *wasn't* what had happened. Tristan had been overdoing things for months, he understood that now. Ever since Cornish had halved the size of the team, and put him in charge. *That* had been what caused his fall. Physical exhaustion. If the locum doctor hadn't been passing, chances were he would have lifted himself up, brushed himself down and just got on with his work day… while promising himself a few good nights of sleep, and a few days off the 'Nyx. But the locum had been passing and, for whatever reason, had decided to make a fucking show out of the whole affair, prescribing Tristan four weeks of home rest on the spot. It was excessive, *abusive*… which was why he felt absolutely no guilt in returning to work today without the doctor's say-so.

'Whatever,' Frankie said. 'You've got something blue on your teeth, by the way.'

Studiously avoiding the hole left by the missing canine, Tristan ran the tip of his tongue over the front of both rows of teeth. It tingled as it swabbed up the leftover drug-dust.

'Say that it didn't happen that way,' he said, his eyes springing open.

'What?' Frankie had never looked at him like that before. Not fear, exactly, but there was definitely an uptick of caution to her gaze.

'I want you to take back what you said,' he repeated, slower this time.

'Which bit?'

Tristan pursed his lips.

'Gibbering shit-filled panties,' he said.

'I only know what Pat told me,' Frankie said.

'Pat's a fucking liar.'

Tristan was on his feet suddenly. Aware of how this might look, he walked to the fridge, opened it, pretended to examine what was inside, then closed it again and returned to the armchair.

Fridge, armchair, mirror. Mirror, armchair, fridge. Armchair, mirror, fridge. Fridge, mirror, armchair...

'Whatever,' Frankie said again. 'It'll be good to have you back. Agnes's been helping out how she can, but I'm fucking knackered covering for you. Pat too.'

'I've noticed what a state the place is in.'

Tristan had watched the decline of Green Oaks in his absence with a certain satisfaction. For despite not working these last weeks, he had come to the old manor house several times, letting himself in when he was sure he would not be seen, before hurrying upstairs to Kalki.

Windsor's death had shaken him. It didn't make sense given... everything. He had gone to Kalki with questions, with concerns, with demands for explanations, for concrete demonstrations of the truths he had learnt. That was when they'd had their conversation about the Captain. And that was when he had delivered the other eleven apostles.

'Maggots!' his mother had shrieked when she'd found them in the jam jar. And: 'Don't let your father see what filth you're bringing in with you. He already thinks you're a fruitcake.' Tristan had snatched the jar from her hands and curled up around it on the bed. The bitch had no idea.

'*Consider it all joy when you encounter various trials, my brother…*'

'… not the physical side to the work.' Frankie was talking. Had she heard him? Had he spoken out loud? Bent forward, an elbow on each knee, Frankie's forearms, wrists and hands made a small plinth for her head. Her tilting, tired, miserable-looking head. 'I mean, I totally understand why you crack… I mean, why you needed some time off. It's all this fucking pretending to be good, all the fucking time. It's so fucking oppressive that I sometimes just have to do something…' – she paused, savouring the word on her tongue – '… bad. Just to relieve the pressure a little.'

'Do you think she *shat*?' Tristan said, surprising himself as he pushed the book across the table towards Frankie.

'*This one here, he hasn't taken a shit in three weeks…*' Pat's words from all those months back pin-balled about his skull.

'What?' Frankie said, sitting back. Her posture was straight, suddenly. Defensive.

'… *Nothing going in, nothing coming out…*'

'That one there,' he said, planting his finger in the middle of Blessed Alexandrina's face. 'She didn't eat for thirteen years. But it doesn't say if she shat?'

'… *I don't understand how he's still with us…*'

'Mate,' Frankie said, slowly. 'That's a children's book.'

Of course Pat hadn't understood. How could he have?

'But don't *you* think it's important?'

He threatens no sanctions. He doesn't judge. He only absolves.

'I honestly don't know what to think…' Frankie said.

Tristan didn't like her look. It was how they'd all been looking at him these last weeks. As if they were watching him defuse a bomb with his teeth… and didn't think he had it in him. But he had to keep her onside. He needed her help.

'Forget it,' he said, swiping at the air. 'How's your girly handwriting?'

'How'd you mean?' she asked, a note of resignation to her voice.

'I mean: Can I assume you spent your early years ostensibly as a girl?' He felt Frankie relax. She rolled her eyes, smirked.

'Ostensibly, you can, yeah.'

'Before you transformed into... into...' – waving his hand at her as if conducting an orchestra – '... into whatever *that* is.'

'Watch it, peanut-dick.'

'And can I assume you picked up the necessary techniques to replicate that repulsive, bubbly cursive, so beloved of young girls?'

'You mean did I heart my i's, kiss my t's and biro-fuck my o's so hard they all looked like capital fucking q's when I was done with them? I was once known to, yeah.'

Tristan shook his head, stunned.

'I think we're on the same page, then.'

He plucked a blank index card, a note in his own scribbled hand and his mother's pilfered fountain pen one by one from his bag. 'If you would be so kind I need you to copy that...' – indicating the note – 'onto that...' – the card. Frankie read the note, then looked at Tristan. Her eyes were stretched wide and her mouth cocked into an impressed sneer.

'Something bad?' she said. 'Count me fucking in.'

While Frankie copied the note, Tristan opened the brown window envelope. He recognised the university admission board's logo at once. What with everything these past months, he had almost forgotten about his applications, his escape plan. He was no longer even sure if wanted to go. Going to university would mean leaving Kalki behind...

The stakes of the situation weighed down upon him, tightening his chest and shortening his breath. One of them was bound to make him an offer – he had set his sights low enough – and he was bound to accept. He wasn't yet brave enough to refuse. Not on his own. And then everything they had talked about, everything he had promised would...

He unfolded the letter. There was the familiar logo, and there the familiar grid. He read the left column first:

Exeter.

Warwick.

Southampton.

All except Birmingham. His gaze travelled to the right hand column. Unsuccessful.

There's another way.

Unsuccessful.

A way for this to continue.

Unsuccessful.

A way for you to stay.

'*Ha!*' Tristan threw his head back. Kalki had thought of everything. Of course he had. Upstairs in that room of his. That shrine. Not eating. Not shitting. Rising above all that was base. All that was earthly. All that could perish...

'*Ha... ha... ha... ha!*'

That look was back on Frankie's face.

'I'm done,' she said, with a flick of her wrist sending the card spinning towards Tristan's face. He snatched it from the air, examined it for a moment, then nodded.

'Perfect,' he said. 'Now, if you'll excuse me, I've just got to pay a little visit to the Captain.'

2

'**O**h, no, it's nothing. Really.'
'Really, it's nothing. I mean…'
'It's just a little something…'
'It's nothing!'
You're nothing! Really!
'Sweet sixteen. You know what they say…'
When chickens are plump…
'They say…'
They're ready for plucking…
'Not that!'
When girls are sixteen…
'No, I said!'
They're ready…
'Stop it!'
…
'What *do* they say, though? *Ach!*'

The small box, wrapped in red crêpe, tumbled to the carpet, the right hand finally losing its catch-catch rally with the left. As Cornish bent, his sciatic nerve caught and twanged him straight, just as his fingers grazed the box. Massaging the back of his thigh, he looked at himself in the mirror:

'You broken old bastard,' he said, flattening the pineapple with his left hand as his right continued working the thigh. 'Whatever made you think…?'

He punted the small box with his toe, regretting it at once, worried he had undone the jeweller's handiwork. He shuffled across to the gift and, more carefully this time, his right leg kossacked in front of him, squatted to retrieve it.

Ever since he and Lisa had agreed to spend her birthday together, Cornish had thought of little else. What should he buy her? What would he wear? And she? Where should they go? How would he…? Would he, even? And would she? What would it *feel* like?

Harriet must have noticed the change in him, but she wouldn't let on. Not for a while yet. Their relationship was founded on its capacity for attrition: modifications in the other's behaviour ignored in the hope that, should they butt for long enough against a resistant surface, they would eventually butt themselves out. She was a jealous woman, but only for show. The rare times other women had circled Cornish – smacking their wolvish lips – she had always ruthlessly defended her mate. A catty remark here, a proprietary peck there – enough to fend off the pack, and to crush any ideas he may have had of straying.

She would never have believed him capable of something like this. Wouldn't have credited him with the – what was that word she'd picked up from that American TV show? The one with all the wives? – the… *cojones*? '*Who, Raymond*?' – he imagined her confiding to her friends over the taste-holocaust of a calorie-controlled cheesecake – '*he'd have to find his cojones again first,*' before tapping her butch handbag. There was just too much stacked against him: his cowardice, his middle-aged girth, his ashen pallor.

And he shared Harriet's doubts. Even now – checking his watch – four hours before Lisa's scheduled arrival, he wasn't sure if he could really go through with it. What was done could never be undone. What was broken could never be fixed, not really. Was he truly ready to jeopardise everything? Until that moment it had felt little more than a game, a flirtation with another world – more intense, but more dangerous too. A dark pool into which he had only dipped his toe, vicariously enjoying its deeper, more shadowy pleasures, but also one from which he might quite easily withdraw, turn away, forget… eventually. Would he be able to plunge?

Although perhaps it wasn't that way at all. Perhaps the sensation of forever teetering over Humiliation Canyon, over Shame Gorge, of viewing himself as a ham-footed funambulist destined to lose his footing… Perhaps *that* was the illusion. If he could muster the confidence to stray from the narrow wire, maybe he would just keep on moving forward, and the drop itself would prove to be the illusion, a *trompe l'oeil* chalked on a solid pavement by some dickhead from Bath.

'Perhaps.'

Perhaps not.

He fingered the small pot of blusher from his pocket. Harriet wouldn't miss it. The drawers of her dressing table were overflowing with this injection-moulded scree. And this one in particular, its chemical cake disintegrated and cracked, couldn't be one of her favourites. Turning it over in his hands, he read the sticker on the back: *Daring Damask*.

He flipped open the lid and kneaded his thumb into the dusty surface. Then, tentatively, he smeared the make-up onto his right cheek, before looking in the mirror again. The smudge stood out welt-like on his face. After working it into his skin a little more, smoothing off its edges, he repeated with the other cheek.

Harder than it looked, making up. No wonder girls started practising young. No wonder so many were so bad at it. The first attempt had left him glaring through the looking-glass at some clapped-out Rococo bum-boy. Absurd. Idiotic. Although marginally less grey than before. It was unlikely the girl would be fooled. If he looked like that when she arrived he'd frighten her off, and those weeks of anticipatory onanism would have been for nothing.

He took a small packet of cleansing wipes from the same pocket and coyly massaged his cheeks with one until they were clean. Grey, but clean. The second attempt with the Daring Damask was no more deft than the first, although left him rather more Battered-Husband than Georgian-Queen this time.

A second wipe removed the faux bruises.

'One more go,' compressing his thumb onto the blusher then onto his cheek, before describing wide circles on his razor-scuffed skin. It was better this time. More natural. Almost real. He attempted to repeat the gesture precisely for the other cheek and succeeded, more or less. At least he thought so. This far down the line it was impossible to tell. The third attempt was certainly *better* than the other two, but was it *good*? What exactly does a well made up man even look like?

'Shit!' he hissed. 'Hopeless!' – banishing the third sally with another cleansing wipe. They had a tart, chemical odour that picked at the nose. It was unpleasant, but at least it gave him a little respite from…

It was almost a week now since he had noticed the smell, almost a week since he had persuaded himself that it was best ignored, that no good could come of investigating it and that, most likely, it would vanish as inexplicably as it had arrived. Most problems vanished of their own accord, given time. Ignore them long enough and they went away… or else some bigger problem came along that pitched the earlier contender for hand-wringing into a new light, or into the long grasses of forgetfulness. So he had waited for the smell to fade, waited for the bigger problem to arrive. But it hadn't faded, it had intensified.

It was vinegary, at first, spiced – like Sauerkraut or Kimchi – but with an underlying sweetness too. Unlike anything he had smelled before. And after all his years at Green Oaks, he thought he had smelled everything. A day or so later it had matured into something distinctly… well, distinctly meaty.

And then this morning, when he had almost gagged as he unlocked his office, he had understood for the first time that the funk he had assumed to come from without, was actually coming from within. His office was not downwind of anything. His office, or its environs, was the very source of the funk, the malodorous pit itself.

It made sense to Cornish, just as his grey skin made sense: *literarily*. The metaphor of stagnation, of decay, of festering, maggot-addled putridity as applied to his life was one he indulged in repeatedly. And while he had never accepted Harriet's denial of his wanness, he had admitted to himself that it just might be the result of some kind of somatisation… although no less real as a result. But the smell? How much credit should one give to the body's voodoo, anyway?

This interpretation had also offered the path of least resistance, so Cornish had opened the window and, once the smell had cleared enough for his mind to wander, had crossed over to the mirror and begun practising for Lisa's arrival.

'But there's the rub…' he said, as he and his doppelgänger gestured anxiously at each other through the glass. 'She's coming in – what? – three and three quarter hours. And even with the window open… the pong… *ach! ach!*' and he rasped his throat to clear the itch.

It wasn't going anywhere, he knew that now. Not unless he tracked down the source and excised it. He closed the window and waited. It didn't take long for the miasma to settle, for his eyes to prick and dampen, for his gag reflex to start its warm-up stretches. Worse and worse!

Crouching, the intensity increased. He manoeuvred himself onto all-fours, doggy-style. Jutting his nose out, he sniffed for the spoor.

'Not built for this, are we?' he said, disappointed to discover his nose was incapable of dowsing any particular direction of travel. He shuffled a couple of feet backwards, then forwards again, then rotated his head first left, then right. No good.

This must have been the first time in almost twenty years that he had crawled about in his office. There was no reason for him to have done so, and yet… The carpet caught his interest first. He was so accustomed to the pattern – rust-red fleurs-de-lys on a scarlet background – that he was almost blind to it. But the weft – the woof? the weave? – how it followed a separate pattern, an independent design, serving not the motif of the carpet but its internal workings; that was something he had never noticed before. Likewise how chipped the legs of his desk were, after years of being rammed by the splayed limbs of his office chair. Likewise the old-fashioned plug socket in the skirting board, with its three rounded pins, obviously overlooked during one of the periodic re-wirings of the old building. Likewise the slim air vent, almost invisible in the condemned fireplace…

Cornish scooted across the room on his knees. There! Under layers of matte black paint, the relief of a metal vent was still visible. Some of the diamond holes were even unblocked. And the smell… yes, the smell was stronger here than by the window. Gripping the fireguard he leaned deep into the chimney, his body straining as he edged as close as possible to the vent. He held his breath, a part of him determined, if this was the source of the smell, for his discovery to be incontestable from the very first inhalation. With his nose almost touching the vent, Cornish closed his eyes and inhaled.

…

… !

       The gravel in the driveway kaleidoscoped in his vision for a moment before the cataract of falling vomit touched down. The chill of the pure country air stabbed at his lungs, his body yowling: *This! This is what you need to be breathing! This! Air! Got that, you dumb bastard?* Everything was sharp, magnified, the world around him presented in exquisite, almost sarcastic detail.

The memory of his flight from the fireplace to the window, on the other hand, was far from clear. That was driven by pure instinct. His head poking out the window now, he even had difficulty remembering just what it was he had smelled. His mind had locked that memory down, quarantined it, and every time he tried to access it, it just tickled his stomach as if to say: *forget the smell, just remember the consequences.*

In truth, since the moment the smell had appeared – as a hint, a suggestion, almost a lacuna – he knew it could only be one thing. Knowledge of this particular perfume was hardwired. Cornish had done his best to ignore it, to deny it, to attribute it to anything but that. Now as the carousel of vomit-strewn gravel slowed to a stop, he was unable to deny it any longer.

'Death,' he said, hoping in pronouncing the word he could exert some kind of dominion over it. 'Decomposition'.

Although whose?

Or rather, what's? A mouse?

Or a resident?

He straightened up, still not releasing his grip on the windowsill.

Chance'd be a fine thing.

'Or residents, even. Plural. Maybe they've all popped their clogs.' He smiled to himself. 'The CareFriends too. Something in the soup did them all in. Something in the water.' The idea cheered him, and his mind riffed on the vaguely comic sequence of events that could have led not only to the coordinated deaths of the residents, but also of the CareFriends, and his remarkable failure to notice. Now he had noticed, how long might this charade be maintained? How long could he go on exacting payment from the families and the state for care of nineteen... eighteen... no, nineteen expired residents? Years probably, if he planned it well.

Turning back to the office, high on lungfuls of fresh air, he had almost forgotten what made him hang his head out of the window in the first place. But it wasn't the kind of stench that was forgotten for long, and the elaborate caper was muscled out of his thoughts by the image of the rotting carcass of a mouse lodged somewhere in the building. Or perhaps it was a rat? Or a stray cat? It was difficult, after all, to imagine a puny cadaver giving off such a potent and enduring pong. The other question, of course, was where exactly it was lodged. Although Cornish was ahead of the game on this one.

After lifting the sheet he carefully slid the glass from the top of the vitrine, leant it against the wall, then reached in, gripped the edges of the roof and eased it from the model. It had been built so that it could be displayed open or closed, with the roof and two of the side walls detachable from the main structure. He set the roof down in front of the glass and as he did so, something caught his eye. How detailed the rendering was.

He had never really noticed it before. Every clay roof tile was painted in meticulous detail, each with its own pattern of moss or lichen, a crack here, an irregularity there. Several were missing in just the spot above his office where, last winter, his ceiling had sprung a leak. He looked from the model roof to the blistered patch of ceiling.

'Extraordinary.'

But he couldn't get distracted. He had the corpse of a mouse to locate and dispose of before Lisa arrived in – his watch again – three hours and twenty minutes. Peering down into his office, it took him a few seconds to orient himself. If the window was against that wall, the fireplace must be – he changed sides – here! Which meant the vent led to – of course! – Ward A, the long, L-shaped room which, along with his office, his private toilet and the upstairs bathroom, completed the list of rooms on the first floor.

Completed it? But what about…? He turned from the model, strode to the door and flung it open, before peering about the empty landing. He counted the doors – one, two, three, four… and his made five. Looming over the model again, he counted the rooms. One, two, three, four… The closet hadn't been included in the model.

Its absence baffled him. Harriet's brother had been meticulous in his measurements, and Cornish had given him full access to the house. He had even included the nook under the stairs… So why then omit a whole room? It must have been a mistake, the closet overlooked owing to its unimportance, the fact it was used for…

…?

What *was* it used for? For the life of him, Cornish couldn't remember ever having gone into that room. His interest in it had been briefly piqued a couple of months ago when the key went missing, but even that enigma had been quickly swept aside by… well, by *events*, probably. Now, though, he felt a baying need to get in there.

'Supplies, supplies…' he muttered, opening the desk drawer. A penlight. Just the ticket for any crannies that needed probing and… and? … he inverted the drawer onto the desktop. Yes, perfect, Cajeput oil: also plundered from Harriet's stash of tinctures and potions last winter when he had been gunged up by a persistent cold. He liberated another drawer from its runners and inverted that too. There! The roll of yellow, clinical-waste bin liners, pilfered years ago. He jammed the roll in one jacket pocket, and dropped the penlight and cajeput oil in the other. Ready!

As you'll ever be…

He walked out to the landing and glanced into the stairwell to check he was alone. The house was quiet. The door to Ward A was ajar and at the far end of the room, draped over her chaise-longue, as if arranged by a window dresser with a flair for baroque absurdism, was Hortense, her affenpinscher keeping lion-couchant guard at her feet. Impossible to know if she was asleep or not. The scrotal eyelids of old folk could be duplicitous. He stood in the threshold and lifted an invisible hat in acknowledgement. Nothing. Emboldened, he performed a sarcastic bow-and-scrape, his right hand whisking circles in the air, before crowning it with a muted raspberry. At this, the affenpinscher emitted a low growl, but Hortense still didn't move. Cornish retreated, pulling the door to.

Sidling up to the closet, he rattled the knob, but the door didn't budge. He remembered now, on the day he'd met Lisa, someone rattling the same knob and finding it more cooperative. The fleetness with which his mind constructed the scenario of that stranger's unfortunate demise in the closet, impressed even him…

A second rattle proved just as unsuccessful. He stepped back and examined the door. The knot really was impressive, although he didn't remember it always having been so. It was the size of a dinner plate and almost unnaturally dark against the surrounding wood. Its grain twisted in a loose spiral, as if being sucked inwards towards its centre which, even after all these years, and despite the varnish, was still bleeding, a halfpenny bubble of sap sitting defiantly at its core. There was something hypnotic about its sinuous grain so that, should he fix it for long enough, he suspected it might start turning, drawing him in towards the nipple…

He snapped his lips shut, wiped the drool from his chin: 'Concentrate!'

Taking hold of the knob again, he butted his shoulder, weakly, against the door. It shuddered, but nothing gave.

Pathetic, Raymond.

A second, harder butt caused the door to flex against the lock, a chuff of toxic air confirming his suspicion that the something dead lay behind that door.

'Third time lucky!' backing up...

His charge was rewarded with the keening of torn wood as the door flew open, tumbling Cornish into the closet and onto his knees. In the panic of the fall, he kicked out, catching the door and sending it closed behind him.

Christ, the smell!

Get us out of here!

He fuddled the cajeput oil from his pocket, soaked the handkerchief with it, and pressed it to his nose. Its protection was limited, its defences pathetic, worse than futile. This kind of reek was physical, embodied, solidifying into a fetid incubus, that scratched at the eyes and poked its fingers down the throat, tickling for the gag. His stomach kicked, making a break for freedom. He pressed his back against the door as he fumbled the penlight from his pocket and twisted it on.

The beam was puny, contained, and the first panicked sweep revealed nothing. Using the torch as a kind of dragnet, he angled the diluted light at his feet, then started brushing the floor with it – left, right, left, right, left, right – inching forward, afraid suddenly of what he might find. The floor was maculate with old stains, tumbleweeds of dust and hair, a vast tundra over which the smaller beasts – the ants, the spider, the house-fly – were terrorised by their larger brethren, the – *ach!* – cockroach and the mouse (deceased).

The weak beam collided with a vertical surface several feet in front of him. A cushion? No, too wide. A mattress then? Yes. An old one. Probably stashed in here when the cots were changed five, six... however many years ago. As the beam climbed it picked out something wholly unfamiliar. Two somethings, in fact. Their surfaces gnarled and twisted – bonsai trees, he wondered. No. Too symmetrical. Almost mirror images of each other. Five regular branches spindling from a stumpy bric-a-brac trunk, tapering to points after one, two, three articulations…

Say it, coward!

'No!'

Say it!

'Feet.'

Bingo!

His stomach bucked so violently this time it almost knocked him over. Reaching for the wall, his hand landed on a light switch and inadvertently tickled it on. The naked bulb pinged – a scoffingly meek cymbal crash for this particular curtain-raising. Cornish dropped the penlight.

Whoever it was – whoever it *had been* – had been dead for some time. The body, covered from ribs to knees with a white sheet, had attained a stage of for-earthworms'-eyes-only decomposition: a warty, blistered wraith, withered and mildewed, the skin, where skin remained, dappled with puddles of fermenting, prismatically ribboned gloop. It was taut and tanned – the skin of a peat bog corpse – bucking the arms and legs and twisting the face into a mask of animal terror. Its jellied black eyes stared at nothing and everything at once – holding miniature reflections of Cornish imprisoned, ensorcelled, within – and between the legs, concealed in part by the sheet, rested an elephantine avalanche of shit.

Cornish's adrenalin flooded mind observed all of this, and more besides, in the split-second before he turned around and fled the closet, closing the door even before the penlight had finished rattling on the floor.

'The Indian. It has to be,' slamming his back against the closet door. 'The poor, bastard Indian!'

These last few months – ever since the Indian's name had dropped from the official resident register but his family's contributions had continued nonetheless – Cornish's stomach had been periodically visited by flights of phantom butterflies, foretelling that this anomaly would come back to bite him on the arse. But since the anomaly seemed to be working in his favour, the heady fog produced by the fact that, for once, he was actually winning, had snuffed his fears out before they could force him to act. A shame really, because now the anomaly was back, and it had its curling canines sunk hilt-deep in Cornish's gluteals.

He slid down the door until he was able to wrap his arms around his legs, parcel himself up. So many questions! Riddles! Who had put him there? Why? When? Had he snuffed it in that room, or was he moved there after his death? And what were the candles for? There must have been a good dozen of them – fat and votive – arranged around the mattress, glued to the floor by pools of their own wax. The scattered flower petals too, some browned and withered, others fresh… Who was behind these perverse twists? It was utterly mystifying.

Any remotely feasible explanation eluded him, and yet an explanation was exactly what he would need: for the family, for the doctors, for the police… Fuck, even West Church weren't lax enough to let this one slide! He'd be fired, replaced. Cast out. A pariah. Although not for any perceived culpability – they'd believe him when he told them he had nothing to do with this… *just look at him, how could he have? Pathetic! He doesn't have it in him!* – but for his blindness, his stupidity… which in a way was even worse! How, Raymond – they'd ask – how could this happen right under your eyes, under your nose, without you realising, *ferchrissake?* Mister Kramercher… Karmararach… That Indian gentleman was merrily liquefying barely yards from your desk! Not in a hidden cranny of the house, or in the garden shed, but right next door to your office. Really, didn't you at least *smell* something?

And he would have to play the penitent, the hangdog, explain how terribly, awfully deeply, sorry he was, how he just couldn't understand it himself (true enough!), how, of course, procedures would be introduced, the family compensated, the guilty identified and punished… If he had been richer, better known, then a week or two of publicised rehab would probably have sufficed as penance…but how is a nobody supposed to shuck off disgrace?

And Harriet! Shit, shit, shit! She would never let him forget it, the harridan! Oh how she would revel in her disappointment, how she would delight in her embarrassment at the whispering in supermarket aisles, how she would wallow in the shame this brought crashing down on their family, ruining them for generations. And how she would make him pay, over the years, with interest! And he would take it because, after all – after all this! – who else would have him?

'No!' His surprise refusal echoed about the landing.

No?

'No!'

Go on…

'Lisa!'

The girl was, in a way, all he had left now. In a little less than three hours she'd walk right into a swamp of recrimination, of finger-pointing, of martinets and mirthless laughter… if she could get past the police tape, of course.

'Shitting, shitty, shit!'

She deserved – *they* deserved – better. But what was he going to do? Call it off? Ring her up and cancel? Blasphemy! This was his only chance with her. Call it off and one or the other of them would get cold feet, back out before another date could be arranged. She was a teenager, after all, and a girl – did any more capricious creature even exist? Just because he had enticed her onto his domain didn't mean he had secured the rights to any kind of *Droit de Seigneur.*

It was a lamentable bind. Either he cancelled, and risked losing her, or he let her come, walk into this, and lost her for certain… Or…

Or?

'Or.'

His fingers plucked at the roll of clinical waste bags jutting from his jacket pocket.

'No. No, no, no, no, no…' pacing away from the door he performed an about turn at the top of the stairs, steadying himself on the chairlift rail. He cocked his head and stared at the door, right into the knot's hypnotic swirl. 'I mean. It wouldn't be possible, would it? Someone would… I'd be…' – swiping the idea away – 'No, no, no!'

The plan had already hatched, however, and was now frantically beating its stunned wings as it ran lunatic circles around the inside of his skull. Building up momentum, edging closer and closer to escape velocity...

He ran backwards through the details: The clinical waste truck passed on Wednesday, transporting the bags, unopened, unexamined, directly to the incinerator. With today being Monday, the bags would need to sit undiscovered in the yellow wheelie-bin for a paltry forty-eight hours.

How many bags? He unrolled one and read the small print:

'Twenty litres. He was never a large man, seventy kilos at most. Let's say, for argument, one kilo of body and a litre of bag space are roughly equivalent, that would mean...' – he paused to calculate – '... the whole lot should fit comfortably in four bags. If, of course, the bones are brittle enough to be snap...'

He caught himself, used his sleeve to burnish the film of sweat from his face. Was he really thinking of doing this? Did his immediate future hold the prospect of snapping human femurs, tibias and ribs to make sure they fit comfortably in bin bags? Really?

'I should wrap them in towels. I don't want one of them catching and tearing the bag open.'

He was then, it seemed. His mind's bureaucracy had taken the decision, stamped its approval, without consulting Legal and Ethics. It was probably the kindest thing to do, anyway. The family shouldn't have to be put through the trauma of a post-mortem, an inquest, a trial. He would wait a few weeks and then telephone the children and explain how their father had left in the night. How he had made his bed, how he had written a note, how they had found footprints in the flowerbed and a scrap of his nightgown on the garden fencepost. Just like in a bad novel.

In many ways he would be the unsung hero in all this... like Judas in the Easter story. He was the one who would have to brave the smell, the maggots, the malevolent gloop, who would have to twist the head from the spinal column, being careful not to spill any brain.

And the truth? Fucking hell! According to that oh-so-meticulously crafted model, this room didn't even exist! Didn't that make it, in some way, immune from the truth, outside of its dominion, outside of the rules? Just as a crack in the floorboards was both part of the floor and nothing at all, all at once, so this room, and whatever came to pass inside it, could be seen as in some way exempt, an exception, a zen koan, a quantic fallacy. Right, Dr Mountweasel?

Right. See you around, Raymond.

He shrugged. Probably. It would do as an explanation... for now. He took a dozen small towels from the airing cupboard, then checked his watch one more time.

3

'**A**ll I'm saying is – and I *know* they have a lot of work to do – but all I'm saying is… Oh heavens, Dot, I clipped you on the jamb… Are you alr… is that they could have made a little effort for the service…'

Betty had a point. The hallway was cluttered with empty cardboard boxes, refuse sacks, appendages of broken cots, bedpans and other apparatus that Dot didn't recognise but which was clearly designed to stand in for one burnt-out bodily process or another. The decline had started slowly, in the few days after Windsor's death, but had quickly accelerated. Green Oaks had always been rough around the edges, but now it was starting to look like a slum.

Betty parked Dot in the middle of the dayroom. Despite the mess, Dot had never known her so lively. Or so Nigerian. Her long-buried accent – rich in syllables, blunt on consonants – had started oozing through the cracks shortly after that long, blind night. Now there was almost nothing but the accent left.

'Lanyard seems to be taking things hard,' Dot said.

'Old Greyfriars Bobby?' Betty said, pulling up a plastic seat next to Dot. 'I keep expecting to find him curled up at the end of Windsor's deathbed one morning. But he's a leech… and I don't mean that cruelly. As long as he can find someone else to latch onto before it's too late, I'm sure he'll be fine.' Pausing, she looked around. 'Where *is* everybody?'

As if on cue, Olive was through the door, striding towards them.

'Ladies,' she said, unfolding her own plastic seat, and perching on the edge.

'I didn't know you were coming,' Betty said.

'Oh, of course. I wouldn't miss it. Why?' – her eyes narrowed – 'is someone not?'

'Well, Alain… Smithy, he says he'll remember Windsor well enough without the instruction of some geezer in a frock who didn't know him from Adam…'

'And the Captain?' Olive asked. Betty grimaced.

'I don't know. He seemed preoccupied with something this morning. I couldn't get more than a *Hmm* out of him.'

'How are you, Olive,' Dot asked, 'with all this?'

Olive craned her neck over her shoulder, as if surveying the hallway for eavesdroppers, then lowered her voice to a whisper.

'Fine, actually, strange as it sounds.' She bit her lip. 'Good even. Windsor, poor old bastard, of course, but… Something has changed since that night. Don't tell me you haven't felt it.'

Dot and Betty exchanged glances. One thing that had certainly changed was Olive – Dot couldn't remember the last time she had collapsed. It was as if someone had reached down her throat and tinkered with her workings, realigned her gears.

'Changed how?' Betty asked.

'I don't know, but something cracked. Cracked *open*, I mean. I realised, all of a sudden, how stupid and small everything here is. How brittle the machine is. How…' – another glance over her shoulder – '… how *fake* it all is! Like one of those soap operas. Tell me you haven't noticed!'

Dot couldn't. She knew what Olive meant… and yet she couldn't get as excited about it. What had cracked open in her that night was the vault of memories, of her life before, her life with Leonard, all packed away so tightly until then. One of the cases she had come here with – the one stuffed full of memories – she had punted under the bed the day she arrived, and tried to forget about. She had never truly forgotten, but had somehow managed to turn the volume down, flatten the tone, so that it had just murmured in the background, like the distant thrum of a city long left behind, or like tinnitus – live with it long enough and you learn, for the most part, to ignore it.

For, ashamed as she was, ignoring Leonard's illness was the only real way Dot had found of coping. The people from the Centre had reacted in much the same way after the forest visit. When they had called – once each, as if a roster had been drawn up – nobody had mentioned Leonard by name. It had quickly become clear that her husband's head, and everything that was wrong inside it, was the price Dot would have to pay if she ever wanted to return herself.

She had never returned. Leonard had transgressed one taboo too many for her to go back. There was something unacceptable, almost vulgar about his struggle – for the Centre, but for Dot too. Cancer, or heart disease, were upfront illnesses that everyone could understand, that Lanyard could categorise, that whip-rounds could be organised for, chocolates and flowers bought to soothe. There was no soothing what Leonard had. His error had not been flaunting his illness and ruining an otherwise splendid outing, but being overwhelmed by a condition which was not only little understood, but which also gave everyone the willies.

Which, Dot realised, had also been why her efforts to locate Ward C had petered out almost before they had begun. And why two months after she had sprained her ankle she still wore the plaster boot, mouldering and yellow now, and beginning to stink. Being able to walk again would mean being able to explore, to track down, to locate. And being able to locate would mean being forced to see, to accept. And Dot – foolish old coward! – just wasn't ready for that.

Although at least she had the silent collaboration of her unconscious. For while she could remember everything about their life together up to and including that trip to the forest – at times in detail too lurid for her to bear – what had occurred between then and her arrival at Green Oaks had been locked down, quarantined behind thickly frosted glass, reduced to little more than churning blotches of colour and emotion. It was for the best, she supposed, but it left her with an ache of bereavement, of separation, as if Leonard now existed on a different plane. A plane to which Dot couldn't find the bridge across.

Betty was tugging at her cardigan.

'Where's Olive?' Dot said, coming to.

'Gone!' Betty said with a frown. 'Said to come and get her if anything happened.' Dot's eyes traced the fixtures and fittings of the dayroom, foraging for any suggestions that today was different, that something, against all expectations, had been done right.

'Do you think they might have forgotten Windsor's service?' Dot said. 'They have been somewhat understaffed of late.'

'Not anymore they're not,' Betty bit back. 'The boy – Tristan – I saw him just this morning. He was looking a little rough around the edges, but he was here. Father Patterson must be running late.'

Dot didn't understand why Betty had pressed so hard for this memorial service, but suspected it had more to do with an attempt to reinstate the religious visits than with any special affection she harboured for Windsor. Her insistence irritated Dot. That after a clean, irrefutable death, Betty should fight for Windsor to have a clean, irrefutable memorial service too, however pathetic. Some people had it all! What about those whose departures from this world were more... ambiguous? What did they get?

Lanyard was the next to materialise at the door. Dot heard the whisper of his slippers a good five seconds before he koala'd his head and arm around the doorjamb. He cut a sorry figure – sorrier than usual. Slack grey skin, hunched shoulders, pyjamas that had fit him right enough a month earlier now clownishly oversized. Perhaps Betty had been right about him being a parasite, shrivelling up without his host.

'Afternoon, Mister,' Betty bellowed.

'*Hmm?*' Lanyard lifted his head, squinted as if through a fog. Betty twice snapped her fat fingers.

'Hey, Mister. Over here. I said: Afternoon.'

'Oh, yes. Sorry Betty. Afternoon,' Lanyard said, tugging at the cord of his pyjama bottoms.

'Are you not coming in?'

'Oh, what's the point?' Betty turned to Dot, rolled her eyes so violently her whole face got drawn into the arc.

'I thought Windsor was your friend,' she said. Lanyard sighed, a deep yogic exhalation which, if it had been any more intense, would have turned him inside out.

'Which is exactly why,' he said, 'I refuse to have anything to do with this… this… *washout!*'

Betty turned to Dot again. This time, though, her eyes didn't roll. They were fizzing with pique. Dot shrugged.

'Nonsense,' Betty said. 'To both of you! Father Patterson will be here any minute.'

'With the greatest respect, I think you're the last person here to believe that, Betty,' Lanyard said. Then, uncurling himself from the doorframe, he shuffled off in the direction of the bathroom.

'What do you think is wrong with the Captain?' Dot asked Betty. This wasn't an attempt to nudge the conversation onto less controversial ground – at least, not just that. She had also noticed the Captain's despondent mood this morning, and it worried her to see him like that. For several days after the long night, he had seemed quieter, almost fulfilled. Dot had even wondered whether all this time he had just needed to win against them. Just once. To send that snotty little brat packing. But it hadn't been enough. At least, not for long.

'Today or in general?' Betty asked.

'A bit of both, I suppose.'

Betty thought for a moment, adjusting the folds and flaps of her abundant flesh as she did so.

'I don't know anything about who he was before he came here, but to me the Captain has always felt like a hero who never got the call. He was ready for greatness, hungry for it, but his phone never rang. Nobody wanted him. Nobody needed him. Perhaps we all feel that way to a certain extent, but we come to terms with it, we have to. There's more to life than greatness, thank the Lord. Perhaps the Captain's tragedy is that he has refused to come to terms with it. And it's far too late in the day for him to be a hero now.'

'I think you're right,' Dot said, surprised by a sudden updraught of spite. For the Captain; for Betty, the messenger; and for herself, the gullible, indulgent fool. 'He never came to terms with it, because he never grew up. He's a child.'

'Then again,' Betty said, a noticeable palliative edge to her voice. 'At least the Cap' does *something*! Not like my Alain. You wouldn't know it to look at him, but he's a thinker. Thinks himself into knots. The problem is, think too much and you leave taking action to those who don't think enough. One day, you've got to learn when to stop thinking, stop moping, and jump!'

'Only a bloody idiot jumps on the strength of a fantasy,' Dot could hear herself snarling. Too bad. 'Just because your mind dreams up meteorologists, it doesn't mean there's actually weather balloons.'

Betty squinted at Dot. Perhaps she didn't remember the Captain's story about the Kush, no doubt pilfered from one of his magazines. In truth, Dot had been surprised herself by the force with which that ridiculous *deus ex machina* had muscled its way to the front row of her thoughts. The two women sat in silence for a long minute, their gazes locked.

'Are you a praying woman?' Betty asked, finally. Dot gritted her teeth – if Betty really thought now was the time to reel her in, she was in for an enormous disappointment.

'You know I'm not a believer, Bet,' Dot said.

'That's not what I asked. I don't care if you believe. I asked if you prayed. You don't have to believe there's anyone up there to ask for His help from time to time… or to curse Him.' Dot was destabilised by the line of attack.

'Put that way,' she said, 'I suppose I can be.'

'I'm going to let you in on something,' Betty said. 'Once, not long after arriving here, I was praying before bed, and it suddenly all felt so… ridiculous. I knew those words wouldn't make a damned bit of difference. That none of them had ever made any difference, except to me. All those

Bible stories, the miracles too – the *silliness* of it hit me. How manmade it all was. How cardboard. I felt stripped, naked. As if a light had gone on and I was standing there exposed. I had stopped believing God was Love, that Jesus was His son, that the Bible was the divine word. And all that preaching!' Her hands flew up, as if beseeching the very heavens she had just that second declared fictive. 'The missionary position! I don't want to convert anyone, Dot. People are people and I like them as they are. With every single one of their faults.'

'But you read the Bible all the time.'

'Well that's just the thing, you see,' Betty said, leaning in conspiratorially. 'The only person I could speak to about it was Father Patterson. I told him how ridiculous it all seemed. All the miracles, the saints, the rules. And he just sat there, nodding silently. When I had finished, he reached out and took my hand, and he didn't speak, but his eyes seemed to be saying: *Welcome home, Betty* and *What took you so long?* It was wonderful.'

'I don't understand,' Dot said. 'What does all this have to do with the Captain?'

'I'd been looking at it all wrong, Dot. Religion isn't a destination, it's a journey. To accepting the unknowable, the yawning chasm that everyone has to run into sooner or later. Life's nothing but a giant riddle, an enormous, endless parlour game that we're all expected to play, whether we like it or not. Except there's no rulebook, so we have to play with the tools, with the vocabulary, we have. And that's terrifying. Horrible! But that's also the beauty of it. Because as far as I can see, when it comes to the riddle, one vocabulary can be as good as any other as a means to solving it. So I stuck with mine.' Betty grinned broadly, then winked at Dot. 'Mostly because – as you'll soon see – Father Patterson is quite a dish.'

An hour or so later, even Betty was starting to have her doubts.

'I hope nothing has happened to him on the drive up here...' She looked across the dayroom and out the window. 'The roads can be... *treacherous.*'

'Not just the roads,' Lanyard said. Despite his complaints, he had joined Dot and Betty again after his visit to the bathroom. 'Oh, how that harlot treated him! I'll carry the sense of betrayal to my grave.'

'He never gave up though, did he?' Olive, back too, chipped in. 'Windsor and I never really got on, but the way he tried to charge up those stairs to Ward A. I found it rather magnificent. So... *manly*.'

'I think he knew,' Dot said, 'that it was almost over for him.'

'Oh, the *injustice*,' Lanyard whinnied. 'Why did it have to be him and not... Well, I don't mean any of *you*. But why him?'

'Oh Sir!' Smithy – who had strolled in, dressing gown flapping, during Lanyard's lament – clapped him hard on the back. 'The good die first. And we whose hearts are as dry as summer dust, burn to the socket.'

'Is that supposed to be droll, Smithy?' Lanyard said.

'Don't know,' Smithy said. He sought out Dot's gaze and winked. 'Ask Wordsworth.'

'You're the worst kind of rotter!'

'Easy, Lanny,' Olive said. 'Without this rotter, Windsor would've died right there on the stairs. Smithy was magnificent that day too.'

Everyone turned to Smithy, who was smouldering with embarrassment. The memory of how he had marched up to Windsor's splayed body and – with stupefying ease – plucked him from the stairs and carried him, not over his shoulder, but under his arm, like a rag doll or a rugby ball, back to the ward, still burned brightly in Dot's mind.

'*Well*,' Smithy throated. '... I mean... I take it we're done here, are we? Old Black Frock came, worked his Semitic juju, then – *puff!* – turned into a bat and flew off out the window?'

'No,' Betty said.

'You mean he's still here?' Smithy gazed up at the ceiling. 'I'm quite sure Green Oaks doesn't have a belfry, which can only mean...'

'I mean no, he didn't come,' Betty said.

'Oh,' Smithy said, and before he could say any more, their attention was snared by a noise from the hallway. A middle-aged man Dot had never seen before was hefting a bright yellow bin bag, stretched to bursting with jutting refuse, down the stairs. He was wearing a CareFriend smock, which was crisp and clean, but his trousers were flecked with something red and brown... and were his bare feet glistening?

'Who...?' Dot began.

'Mister Cornish,' Olive whispered, with the measured cadence of the twitcher. 'A rare sighting, indeed.'

'What's he...?' Dot tried again, before being hushed by a flock of flapping hands and a chorus of restrained shushing. Mister Cornish, giving no indication that he knew he was being watched, crossed the hallway and went out the front door. He left it open for the twenty seconds or so it took him to dispose of the refuse, after which, unburdened, he closed the door, careful not make any noise, and scurried back up the stairs.

'Can anyone smell bleach?' Olive asked, when it seemed the director would not be reappearing any time soon.

'Chance would be a fine thing,' Lanyard said. 'They haven't cleaned in weeks.'

'What could he have been doing?' Dot asked.

'And what was in that bag?' Olive joined. 'Nothing good, that's certain.'

Smithy grinned, picked at something in his teeth.

'Probably one of the Preemies snuffed it in the night...'

Smithy, through force of habit, turned to Betty for her gentle chastisement, but none came. Betty hadn't been listening. Whereas all the others had turned their attention from the hall, hers was still fixed there. Except it wasn't Mister Cornish this time, but Tristan, swaggering towards the staffroom. Dot hadn't seen him for more than three weeks. Not since he had fled from their ward after finding Windsor's corpse.

'Boy!'

Tristan stopped.

'Bets,' Smithy tried, but she was already on her feet.

'Yes, you boy!'

Tristan turned.

It only lasted an instant but what Dot saw in his face frightened her. The smile was broad but flat, a knife-wound rictus that seemed to cup the glazed shark's eyes above it. It was a zealot's look, the look of the high-school pupil on his way to massacre his classmates, the look of the terrorist *before* the atrocity, the look of the toddler as he throws himself on his mother's newly pregnant belly...

He strode towards Betty. They met on the threshold.

'Where is he?' she said.

Tristan mocked a frown.

'Where is *who*?'

'You know who.'

Tristan looked over Betty's shoulder at the others.

'Well,' he said, 'I doubt you're talking about the Captain, and you can't be talking about Lover Boy, because he's here,' with which he made a V of his fingers, brought it too his mouth and waggled his tongue between them. Dot looked at Smithy. He was gripping the plastic arms of his chair. His hands, normally lobster-red, had blanched with the strain.

'Father Patterson,' Betty said.

Tristan looked surprised.

'The old priest? I told you months ago that we were exorcising Green Oaks of his particular brand of ooga-booga. This is now a haven of rational, humanist thought...' He turned his head to the side and spat a wad of phlegm onto the floor. After scrutinising it for a moment he looked back at Betty and said. 'It's actually rather beautiful.'

'He was supposed to come...' Betty said, the fight leaving her. 'For Windsor's memorial service. The girl said she would arrange it.'

Tristan's brow crumpled. He looked at Betty, then over her shoulder at the others again. Then back at Betty. Then he laughed, just a single *ha!*, barely more than a cough. He took a baby step towards Betty then leaned forward so their noses were almost touching.

'I've *genuinely* no idea what you're talking about.'

Before Betty could answer, Tristan spun on his heels and was heading back across the hall.

'Don't turn your back on me, boy!' Betty said, as the staffroom door clacked shut.

For a moment, Betty didn't move. Then, she turned and walked directly up to Smithy.

'Not so chipper now, are you,' she hissed at him. 'Not so bloody talkative now!'

Smithy flew out of his chair, sending it cartwheeling behind him. His fists were still clenched. He glared at Betty, then at the others.

'Damn your eyes!' he cried at nobody in particular before striding out of the dayroom. He was going after the boy! After all these months, the boiler was finally fit to explode. If the raw power with which he had manhandled Windsor was in evidence, this was going to be some show...

Smithy collided with the bathroom door. It creaked shut behind him.

Betty smoothed her nightdress.

'He'll be alright once he cries it out,' she said, lowering herself onto her chair. 'Blubbering twit.'

Dot laid a hand on Betty's thigh. It was as hard as granite. A great throbbing hippo of a vein surfaced on her neck, wallowed a while, then descended.

'It's alright, Bet,' she tried. 'Perhaps Father Patterson really was just... indisposed.'

'He's retired,' Betty snapped back, her eyes not leaving the staff room door. 'He lives in Meanwell. This was his only appointment. He's not indisposed.'

Dot bit her tongue. A second possibility hung so obviously in the air between them that Betty responded to it.

'And he hasn't' – aggressively air-quoting – 'gone to Ward C. You never saw him Dot, he was as vigorous as a young buck. He's been forced out. For raising concerns.'

'Concerns?' Olive leaned in, interested.

Dot felt the early stirrings of vertigo. *What did Betty just say?*

'You lot didn't think the Captain was the only one with a plan, did you?' Betty went on. 'Father Patterson and I had been building up a file on Green Oaks for months before his visits were cancelled. We were only weeks away from submitting it to the appropriate authorities.' She cupped her face in her hands. 'But now... Now that's all over.'

'Perhaps he'll still submit it,' Olive said. 'He'll know they've forced him out, and he'll submit it, and the inspectors will come... Oh Betty!'

'Even if he does, Olive, don't you see? They're not frightened of an inspection,' Betty said, looking up at Olive. She wasn't going to let herself cry, but her eyes were red. 'And I've just understood why.'

Olive looked stunned; the defiance, etched on her round face for as long as Dot had known her, had vanished. Canute at the moment he realised the waves could not be held back. Her voice was reed thin as she finished Betty's thought.

'Because the inspectors don't exist.'

Dot hated to see Betty like this. She had always been the standing stone of the group, about whom the other residents danced. Although now Dot knew why: Betty had had a secret. Betty had had a plan. Unlike Dot, she hadn't been waiting for the earth just to swallow her up. She may have lost her faith but she hadn't lost her fight. Betty had been up to something, all along. She had been going somewhere. At least until now.

Betty had a plan. The Captain had a plan. Windsor – he'd had a plan too, of sorts. How many of the others were plotting something? Olive? Smithy? Surely not Lanyard? All of them, probably! All this time she had thought she had their measure, and all this time she had been wrong. If the Long Night had loosened the labels she'd tied to each of them on her first day here, the last few minutes had yanked them off, torn them up and scattered them like confetti to the wind.

Bastards! Dot was incensed. Incensed and embarrassed. How dare they? She had come to Green Oaks to step back, to wind down, to expire. She had imagined the others all wanted the same thing. That it would be some kind of group effort. Idiot! Not a bit of it! The bloody, bloody nerve! She was almost pleased Betty's plan had failed. Almost...

But it wasn't just anger that was whipping up her vertigo. There was something else too. Something she wasn't now even sure she'd heard right...

But if she had?

The dayroom fragmented in Dot's vision. Then she passed out.

4

'**M**ucky business,' Cornish said, exhaling a dense lungful of cigarette smoke. 'Mucky, mucky business.' The last wisp expelled, his face contorted into a half-smile of something like – but not quite – satisfaction.

He was flecked from head to toe with blood, faeces and other less identifiable bodily fluids. His hair was caked and matted with the same cocktail, touched off with a fine splinter of bone, of indiscernible provenance – although it was gently cambered, so may once have formed part of a rib. More than mucky, the work had been hard, and cleanliness (to say nothing of godliness) had been the first norm sacrificed. He'd removed his jacket early on, tucked his tie inside his shirt and rolled up his sleeves. A little later, after almost losing his balance to a puddle of gut-gunk, he'd kicked off his shoes, pulled off his socks, and completed the operation barefoot. After half an hour, he'd even shed the mask and its cajeput stuffing – his body, bucking expectation, not only getting accustomed to the smell, but positively high on it. It was a rich tapestry of odours: cured meat, hundred-year-egg, stagnant water, rusting metal. And not only that, but it was actually *embodied*, almost granular. With every inhalation a miniature sandstorm erupted in his nostrils and the back of his throat.

Bits of the Indian had got between his toes, under his fingernails, in his eyebrows and ears, up his nose, on his lips and even inside his arse-crack… although that might have just been particularly viscous beads of sweat. His clothes, of course, were ruined. Luckily he had brought a change – sharp shirt, jazzy tie – in anticipation of Lisa's visit.

Now, once again, he sat sprawled in his office chair, the image of a dissolute, louche and murderous renaissance Prince – Raymond Borgia! – one leg dangling, the big toe tickling arcs on the floor like Foucault's pendulum, the other thrown goadingly, belligerently, over the armrest.

He couldn't say the whole process had confounded his expectations, having never possessed any such thing on the subject of cadaver dismemberment. Still, had he, he is sure it would have. Specifically the ease with which some parts had rent and snapped, whilst others had proved surprisingly springy and resistant. The limbs, for instance. Before detaching them, he had readied himself for the same clumsy twisting and tearing of cartilage, the dislocation of ball joints, required to separate a chicken leg from its carcass. In full anticipation of this, when he had taken hold of the left arm, he had anchored his foot in the armpit, so as to increase purchase. Unnecessary! On the count of a futile three, the left arm had snapped from the shoulder with such ease that Cornish was thrown into the closet wall, splattered, moments later, with a cannonade of putrid human deliquescence. The ligaments… or tendons… or whatever – biology had never been his forte – having decomposed to such an extent that they had torn from their moorings as if made of jelly. Which perhaps, by that point, they were.

And yet the bones themselves had proved stubborn buggers. To fit the femurs into the waste bags, they had not only to be removed from the hips, but also snapped in two. You would have thought – *he* had thought – that the bones of a man as old as the Indian, hollowed out over the years by a kind of skeletal speleogenesis, would have snapped as easily as honeycomb. Wrong! A real boner there! He had first tried to strong-arm them in half with his bare hands. When that failed, he'd tried using his own femur as a fulcrum but, perhaps through some filial solidarity, his bone refused to collaborate. Indeed, judging from the crashing pain of the impact, if either of the two femurs had come close to snapping, it was most likely his own. Next, wielding it clubbishly, and feeling every bit the Cro-Magnon, he'd struck the wall with it once, twice, three times… but only succeeded in chipping the ball-joint that had formerly anchored it to the hip.

He'd begun to despair. If he couldn't break this bone in two, his plan was doomed. And if he'd thought if would be difficult to explain away the intact body… Shit! By ripping the arms and legs from the torso, and detaching the hands and feet, he had graduated from a mere know-nothing rube to a full-on participant in this garish cabaret. He had no choice but to break these bones to bits… but they just wouldn't cooperate.

'What a shame you weren't a woman,' he had said, kicking the Indian in the ribs, his big toe penetrating, with a squelch, to its hilt. 'Osteoporosis would have made this a breeze. Just look at the fat old grey in Ward B. Her ankle gave way under…'

Of course! Idiot! It was all about the angle, all about the weight brought to bear. So, he'd anchored the bone in the corner of the closet, taken a step backwards, then brought his foot crashing down halfway along its length. It had hurt like hell… but it worked! With a sound unlike any he'd ever heard – a kind of mournful pop, a mineral death – the femur had given way. It was a clean break, right in the middle of the bone. The perfect size to be wrapped in a towel and bagged. On a roll, he'd picked up a second femur and holding it above the gaping mouth of a waste bag, shucked off the crisped skin and jellied muscle mass. This second hadn't broken so cleanly. As he rushed it, he skidded on a lump of something – a hunk of kidney? – struck it askew, lost his balance, spun a full one-eighty, and pitched forward, square on top of the Indian. The tableau-*half*-vivant might easily have been taken for a necrophilic sixty-niner.

At that moment of utter debasement, Cornish had understood, in a flash of crystalline cognisance, the nature of the change that was being visited upon him. For as he had panicked, yelped, leapt up rushing, tearful and disgusted from the room… he had also watched himself do so. He had watched himself find a rosace to fix, watched himself feel his skin, feel his breath and employ a volley of other life-banishing techniques Doctor Mountweasel had taught him. He had watched all this from his position on top of the Indian, his lip resting on the violet and tangy prepuce. Then, as the vision had run off the spool, he'd lifted his head in a slow, measured arc, and only so that he might catch his breath. After considering how it would look – his pasty, puffy, ogreish body apparently in the act of forcing oral sexual congress upon the dead body of an old Indian man, well along the road to decomposition, and missing both legs already – he had erupted into a lusty and prolonged fit of laughter…

After it had subsided, he'd stood, given himself a futile brush down, and got back to work. The rest of the operation had proceeded without a hitch. His gestures had been measured, fluid, every one of them a success – a Zen master again, just as he had been when he met Lisa at the bus stop. The flesh had slipped from bone to bag in easy, perfect cascades. The bones had snapped just where he wanted them to. The gloopy clods of flesh had held together just long enough to be bundled up in towels and deposited in the waste bags – not a single one of which had split. Not as he filled them, not as he puckered their mouths and closed them with cable-ties, not as he dumped them in the corner of the room, ready for their descent to the yellow-topped bins. He'd been right, earlier, to think of the closet as a zen koan. *This* was the sound of one hand clapping. Roshi Cornish was back.

The offal was the final hurdle. After almost all of the bones, muscles and flesh had been cleared away – except for a section of spine, eight or nine vertebrates long, which he'd been unable to reach – he was left staring at a blancmange of tripe, a delicate coagulation of innards, a kaleidoscope of blush-reds, speckled-purples, waxen-pinks. He had recognised some of them – the lungs, the liver, the heart… all the big boys – but had been astonished by how much there was he didn't really know – something brown and leafy, something else yellow and twiggy, a hairy purple ball…

The intestine had impressed him most, given him the longest pause. If ever given cause to list the internal organs, he would most likely have begun – in descending order of importance – with the brain, the heart, then the liver, the lungs, the kidneys, and maybe even the spleen, before finally deigning to honour the intestine, the stomach or the oesophagus with a mention. Perhaps because they seemed in some way predicated not so much on what they did, but on what was done to them and, specifically, what passed through them. They generated nothing. They were pipes, tubes, nothing more... hardly organs at all.

But looking at the decomposed (and now mostly deconstructed) body of the Indian, no organ looked more integral to the man, no organ seemed more to define what this creature was than the tube that ran, circuitously, from mouth to anus. Not the heart – a vulgar pump, no more. Not the lungs – just a clumsy set of bellows, really. Not even the brain! He had bagged that early on with barely a second thought for all the memories, experiences and, indeed, second thoughts it had once held.

At first there had seemed something of the parasite about this tube, as if the body had been taken over, colonised, by an extra-terrestrial worm, that had been set to grow ever stronger, ever fatter in the belly before, one day, bursting free to live its own, independent existence. But no, it wasn't that way at all, in fact. This tube was the essence of the body. It wasn't that the organ itself was a pipe, a tube, nothing more, but that we – the most vainglorious of creatures – were nothing more than tubes, than pipes ourselves. Strip away all the accoutrements, all of the meaningless guff, and what were you left with? A tube. A tube that takes in energy at one end, burns what it can use, and excretes what it can't. On and on, without meaning, without purpose, for four score years – barely a blink in cosmic-time – before the tube shrivelled up and died. The worm was *already* living its own independent existence. And the other organs? Slaves, the lot of them! Existing only to better serve the tube! The poor, old brain – so self-satisfied, so proud! Not Yorrick, no! Polonius! Good for nothing except tracking down food, keeping the tube happy, and then distracting itself with sound and fury while the tube digested its quarry.

We take ourselves for gods, but all we are is...

'Bumholes,' Cornish had whispered. 'Nothing but bumholes.'

No wonder we fled at the first sight of shit. No wonder we recoiled from farts. No wonder the WC and what went on therein was such a taboo. It reminded us all of our true nature, of our futile tubular existence… A turd reminded us – as brutally as we could be reminded – that despite all the frills, life was just a race to the bottom – literally! – that one day, our tube-selves would wear out, stop wriggling, shrivel and die. And no amount of religion, no amount of love, no amount of romance, and no amount of art would make a damned bit of difference.

His parents had been right to nip his artistic ambitions in the bud, he could see that now. It was just they had been so wrong about everything else. They had been right to say his paintings were worthless, it was just they had forgotten to tell him that everything else was worthless too… Everything! And their tepid, self-satisfied, bourgeois-humanist, 'isn't everything beautiful and remarkable if only you step back and look' *diarrhoea* couldn't change that.

His mind crackling with these thoughts, Cornish had stooped, reached into the blancmange and started pulling out the intestine. It was strikingly intact when compared to the rest of the body, admirably muscular and firm. But then, why shouldn't it be? As the very essence of a man, of course it would take longer to break down. He had tugged and tugged, as the rest of the blancmange gave way around it, pulling it loose, hanging it over his shoulders, draping it across his chest, wrapping himself up in it, dancing himself into it.

'What long worms we are!' he had cried, almost sung. 'Yards and yards and yards of us… Yards and yards! Whoever would have thought it?'

Toga-ed in the intestine, and resembling a majestic old tree with a snake coiled about it, Cornish had felt something he could never recall having felt before: Light. Unburdened. And – he had almost dared not think it – free! He had felt a glimmer of something similar last month when cupping the girl's head in his hand – but had taken it for the simple thrill of transgression. But it wasn't that… At least, it wasn't *just* that. This, he realised, was what he had been running from all those years. This was what he had been denying. The worm! The utter meaninglessness of the worm, the utter futility. All his life he had been desperately hunting for meaning – or at least running from meaninglessness, which surely amounted to the same thing. But the quest had crippled him, had got to his knees. He was arthritic with the weight of it! The terrible responsibility… For if there was a single meaning to be found, there was also an enormous – alarming! – room for error. How terrifying it was, the thought of getting it wrong. Of putting your money on the wrong horse. And there were no spread bets on this race, no each-way wagers, and certainly no accumulators, regardless of what the Buddhists claimed. You had to pick your horse without even seeing the form sheet! What chance had he, Raymond Cornish, of getting it right? What chance had he of winning? Of merrily stumbling upon the solution to the riddle when so many great minds before his had failed. It was absurd, ridiculous. Unthinkable!

Now, though. Now he had invited the worm in, embraced him, called him a brother. Now he had accepted that his life – *all* life – was meaningless… It was a trite observation, perhaps, but one that so few people ever really accept with their gut… *by* accepting the gut. Now there was nothing for him to get wrong. Nothing to get right, either. Everything was equal. Everything just was. And everything was permitted too, in service of the worm. Or not. Even the worm was of no real consequence. All crimes, no matter how heinous, would be forgotten eventually. What use was forgiveness, repentance, redemption, when forgetfulness was assured?

Cornish had shucked off the intestine, letting it splatter to the floor, and with renewed energy had got back to the job of dismantling the Indian, whistling while he worked.

Now, draped across his office chair, he admitted to himself that he had got somewhat caught up in the moment. It was difficult not to when wrapped in another man's intestine. At that moment he had felt capable of anything, of raining down any horror on the world he wished. As if, indeed, the world itself had lain on his open palm, waiting to be crushed or spared at his whim… or else as the result of an involuntary spasming of his fingers. It was hard, though, to maintain nihilism at that pitch – the brain just wasn't suited to it, he supposed. And yet the overwhelming sensation of liberty, of lightness, had not entirely faded.

It was still journeying around his mind, infecting, like a plague victim, every thought it came into contact with. Perhaps it would fade away to nothing. Or perhaps it wouldn't. Perhaps he'd find himself permanently changed. Or perhaps he wouldn't. Either way, he now felt more suited than ever to the role that had been ascribed to him without his asking, ready now to assume its implications, to play it with such conviction that it would no longer be uttered in jest, but in fear – for themselves… for their children! – or at the very least, fearful respect…

He was Raymond Cornish, King of the Crazies.

Still, his decaying fervour had made him reckless, briefly, undisciplined – and the problem with lack of discipline is that sooner or later somebody will come along to discipline you. In Cornish's case, the disciplinarian hadn't been a someone, but a something: the squint-eyed little Affenpinscher that lived in Ward A.

He had cleared three of the four bags without being spotted. He'd been cautious, at first, donning a spare CareFriend smock to cover the worst of the damage to his clothes, checking the landing was clear, closing the closet door behind him, rattling the knob to be sure the busted catch had bitten, leaving the bag at the foot of the stairs as he scoped the hallway for any potentially awkward encounters. By the third trip, however, he'd grown sloppy. As he reached the landing, stretching out his shoulders in readiness for hauling the final bag, he'd almost collided with Hortense who was standing at the top of the stairs, her eyes fixed on the closet door – ajar, Cornish had winced to notice – and squawking in that rattly fashion especial to old biddies:

'Sebastien!'

His mind had whirled, searching for the explanation that might spare him. Then, a smudge of black in the periphery of his vision had caught his eye.

'There you are!' she had crooned at her sidekick. 'What has the naughty little monkey-dog found?'

What *had* it found? Cornish turned his head as slowly as he could.

'A bone!'

A bone? Oh shit… The keystone had been pulled. And so soon!

'A bone,' Cornish had echoed through a clenched-tooth smile. 'I can't imagine where…'

Hortense – demonstrating an inbred authority – had shoved at the air to silence him, then creaked into a squat and taken hold of the dog's leathery black cheeks.

'Who's the cleverest? Who is? Who? Who?' Cornish had hoped she wasn't really expecting an answer… they could be there some time. The dog shook its face free of her blue-liquorice hands, turned its head towards Cornish and dropped the bone at his feet. It – at least – knew.

'Ha!' Cornish had exclaimed, unable to contain himself. 'Ha ha! Ha ha… ha ha!' Then, under his breath: 'How would the naughty little monkey like my big toe wedged four inches deep up his fundament?' Audibly adding: '*A-booga-booga-booga-boo*!'

Taking this as her cue, Hortense cranked herself straight again.

'He obviously likes you Mister Cornish. Look, he's brought you a present.'

'So… he… has!'

As he crouched to retrieve it, the dog loosed a low pitched rumble, making Cornish think better of it.

'It's a bone.'

The intonation she'd put on that final incriminating word was so desperately hard to read.

'So… it… is. I wonder…'

'It's terrible, Mister Cornish. He could find a bone anywhere this one.'

Then, she had reached out and taken his wrist.

Was the old hag flirting with him? She still had a tight hold and was peering upwards with rheumy blue eyes, their pupils wildly dilated.

'Even in a eunuch's Y fronts.'

'Aha!' – he'd flustered – 'Ahem… Aha ha ha!'

She *was* flirting with him, and he… he had responded. What had happened to him? Time was – and not long ago – when the mere touch of a resident would have given him tremors for weeks, plaguing his sleep with all-too-literal Night Mares. And now one of them had turned him on? Insanity!

She had moved on to stroking his wrist, crystallising her intentions. In truth, when she was young, Hortense had probably been a bit of alright… And even now. Sure, she was time-ravaged but made an effort at least – to paint over the blue-liquorice veins on her cheek, to clip her Monroe wig firmly into place, to truss up her melted-wax tits, bum, belly and kneecaps into something resembling a human form. He was even certain she pulled forward her knicker elastic once a day, in order to spritz perfume onto her…

Cornish had caught himself. Lisa! He couldn't forget her.

Gently, courteously, through insistently, he had detached Hortense's hand from his wrist.

'Well,' clearing his throat, 'well, well.' Then, crouching again and, in defiance of the dog's growls, he had picked up the bone. 'I'll get rid of this. Most likely one of the CareFriends dropped it in there during lunch. The girl, probably… voracious appetite, that one. Unless…' He'd paused, enjoying how his impeding recklessness tickled his prostate. 'Unless you think Sebastien would like…'

'Keep your bone,' she'd snapped. 'Although rest assured I'll be bringing it up with the nurses. It's nothing against you, Mister Cornish, it's a question of hygiene. You understand.'

Squinting at the spurned biddy, he'd made a mental note to speak with the nurses himself about how disruptive she had lately become, how her paranoid episodes had increased in regularity and intensity, and how perhaps a higher does of Phlegmolax would probably be the appropriate course of action.

Forgetfulness was assured.

'Oh I understand my dear. I understand, very well.'

Although by the time the sentence was out, Hortense was back in Ward A, negotiating her descent onto the chaise-longue.

★

Cornish picked at his teeth with the bone once again. Now that he had disposed of the body, stashed the mattress behind the tool shed, for burning later on, and scrubbed the floor of the closet with bleach, the whole mucky business seemed a strange, and strangely distant, memory. Once he stripped, showered and changed his clothes, perhaps, outwardly, it would seem as if nothing unusual had taken place at Green Oaks that day. He certainly hoped that was how Lisa would find things when she arrived. And yet the idea that his dark-afternoon-of-the-soul might fade away into the background of his own memory saddened him. If an experience of that intensity could leave him unchanged, what hope was there for him, really? If – after the initial rush – it merely dented the hard casing of his spirit, not penetrating any deeper than the surface, mildly perverting what lay within but fundamentally transforming nothing… what would have been the point of any of it?

The bone, he decided, he would keep. It was the only outward and visible sign of the inward invisible grace he had experienced in that closet. It would be his fetish, his talisman, his hero's amulet. He might even polish it up, make a small hole in one end, string it onto a leather thong and wear it around his neck. If anyone asked – not that anyone would, except maybe Harriet – he would tell them he had bought it from that hippy stand in Meanwell market, the one with all the blankets and joss sticks. The idea that this little splinter of bone might be recognised for what it was, and they might get found out, was simply ludicrous. He couldn't imagine the chain of events that could bring it about.

They might get found out. He insisted on thinking in the plural, because he mustn't allow himself to forget that, despite it all, he had only really acted as the cleaner of somebody else's mess, somebody else's transgression. Whose mess, though? Whose transgression? The whole thing was baffling. At first he had thought it ambiguous whether the Indian had died in that room, or had been transported there after his death. On reflection, however, he had grown increasingly convinced it was the former. Whether that scree of turd was lain before his death, or whether it had been the result of the well documented insult-to-injury voiding that takes place moments after expiration, both led inevitably to the conclusion that the Indian had spent his last waking moments locked in the darkness of that room. But why? And what was the meaning of all those votive candles, all those rotten flowers? Who was mad enough to…

A vibration in his pocket confused him momentarily before he remembered the mobile telephone he had bought to allow the exchange of clandestine messages with Lisa. He never took it home, locking it in his office drawer at night, but slipping it into his pocket first thing in the morning and keeping it close to him throughout the day. There was only one name in the directory: hers. And she was the only person to whom he had given the number – so any vibration contained both promise and fear. The promise of a summons, the fear of a rejection. His fingers tingled as he pulled out the phone. The monochrome screen told him he had '1 MSG'. A further clumsy manipulation revealed it:

THX RAY! CAN'T B BOVD 2 CUM 2 GO. HOUSE EMPTY. CUM 2 ME? XX

A summons! Oh rapture! And not only that, but the message was positively littered with porno. Two CUMs and three Xs, two of them clearly – explicitly! – kisses. And he would go to her home, to her adolescent attic bedroom, and lay her down on her single bed and… And maybe it was a honey trap, and he was a dumb bear, but so what! She was sixteen. Today. The law couldn't touch him… not with this message as evidence!

Another thought, a realisation, suddenly flooded his mind, and with an incredulous laugh he tossed the phone onto the sous-main. It scudded across the leather before turning to a halt on the very edge of the desk.

'Pointless,' he muttered, shaking his head with disbelief, before picking up the bone and examining it. He laughed again. 'The whole thing was pointless.' Addressing the bone, he went on: 'I could have just left you where you were… Do you understand that? I could have just let someone else deal with you…'

Cornish stood, opened the drawer and dropped the bone inside. He reached across the desk for his phone, the overhang of his belly dislodging the sous-main an inch, exposing the corner of a folded sheet of notepaper beneath.

Unaware of this, Cornish turned, picked up the towel he had set aside for his shower, and the carrier bag with his change of clothes and headed out onto the landing of the upstairs bathroom. Passing in front of the closet door again he paused, took hold of the knob and threw open the door. Apart from the smell of bleach... nothing! He really had done a grand job, and once he himself was cleansed there would be no evidence left of what had transpired there today.

It really was a mucky business being King of the Crazies, he thought. But nobody else wanted his job, at least there was that. It was his for life. And, as it seemed, it was his job, indisputably so, then he was just going to have to live up to it.

Good for you, Raymond!

Cornish closed the door and made his way to the shower, too pleased with himself to pay attention to the low pitched rumble that seemed, against all logic, to be coming from behind the closet door, or to see the black knot begin rolling in the grain of the wood, churning around the spot of sap at its centre, that resembled nothing more closely than a pitch black rendering of a human eye, blinking.

5

Something *extraordinary had happened...*

Tristan couldn't sit still. He was pacing back and forth in the staff room as if with the regular beating of his footfall, the rhythmic lurching of his body, his logic might, somehow, be brought into step. Might make sense. That he might understand...

But it *defied* understanding! His thoughts roamed and twisted... so that just when he felt he had a hold on them, they eluded his grasp again.

Kalki. He had...

Vanished?

Departed?

Evanesced?

It was ridiculous, unthinkable, idiotic and yet... *real!*

It was as if he never was, never had been.

Panic had born down on him when he had entered the closet, surging across the plains of consciousness like a tsunami. This was it! He... *they*... had been discovered. Someone had discovered Kalki and had been too thick-headed to understand. Had been unable to see him for what he was. Had taken him for a what... a *cadaver*? Heresy!

But how could anyone else have got it? Nobody else had been there from the start. Nobody else had seen what he had seen. Nobody else had watched him *transcend* life after several weeks in the dark. And to think, Tristan had only moved him there that day because he didn't know what else to do with him.

The tsunami had hit, but instead of carrying Tristan off, its waters had passed over him, with barely a splash. Then they had subsided, tickling his ankles as they drained away. For a simple truth had dawned – if, as he assumed, Kalki had been discovered, where was the scandal? Where were the recriminations? Where the sanctions? Where the revenge?

Tristan stopped pacing, looked at the last four OxyNyx pills in his cupped palm, where they had been sweating for some time now. He gulleted them in one.

But if he hadn't been discovered, then what…?

Could Kalki have stood up, dusted himself down, and left of his own free will? Set off to walk the earth, a god errant destined to roll into rural villages at times of great distress or strife, healing ills, righting wrongs, sparing harvests? But he had been blind for as long as Tristan could remember and besides, he wasn't that kind of prophet. He wasn't a *mover* – quite the opposite! Moving was anathema to him… He stood for stillness, for immutability, divorced from the universe of births and deaths, of grotesque, bloody beginnings and shoddy ends… That was his message.

Which left just one logical conclusion:

Ascension!

But why?

He thought back to their final conversation a few days earlier. Kalki had never moved his lips when he talked to Tristan, had never indulged in any of the imbecilic tongue-flapping that more mundane creatures relied upon to communicate. Tristan would lay hands on him and the conversation would flow back and forth between them like an alternating electric current.

You're distressed, that final conversation had begun.

'I'm distressed,' Tristan confirmed aloud.

Why?

He felt ashamed, but there was no use lying. His probe was already planted deep in Tristan's brain – penetrating to its reptilian core.

'Everything's falling apart.'

Everything?

'Well no, not everything, of course. Not you.'

So let's start there.

'I don't understand.'

A long moment passed without either of them speaking. Then:

You're afraid you'll never leave.

Tristan hung his head, as if in confession.

There's another way.

'Another way to... what?'

A way for this to continue. A way for you to stay.

'No!' – regretting his impetuous tone at once. 'No. I couldn't face it. There's no way.'

There is a way. There is a way you can win.

'How?'

Another silence. This was how their conversations had often ended; abruptly. Tristan would drop a question and, like a radio running out of juice, Kalki would fade away, leaving the question hanging...

Not this time.

Tristan lifted his hands from his calf and rubbed them together, as if in doing so the connection might be regenerated. Instead of replacing them on the leg, though, he shuffled a couple of feet to the left, and rested them on the balloon-taut skin of Kalki's belly. He had never touched it before, and was surprised how tight, how springy it was. Still, though, Kalki refused to answer. Without really knowing why Tristan's fingers then sought out the navel. After circling it several times, the hand straightened and with a firm jab punctured the stretched skin, plunging into the cavity of his gut.

An efflux of fluid forced itself out, past his wrist, and spattered to the floor. It was warm inside. Warm and... alive! His hand moving on full instinctive autopilot now, he frisked until his fingers looped around a section of intestine. His quarry cornered, he pinched it, softly at first, then...

Slay the Hydra.

Tristan almost laughed. He had come back! He knew at once, too, who the Hydra was. Every time you lopped off the Captain's head, a new one grew back... a stronger, madder one. And yet, eventually, the Hydra had been slain. By Hercules.

Tristan wasn't Hercules.

'Impossible' he said, still pinching the section of Kalki's gut.

It is possible.

'I've tried and failed before.'

Try again. But succeed.

'How?'

Whatever one has created, one has the power to destroy.

'Created? I didn't...'

Once again he tuned out. And however much Tristan pinched or squeezed, this time he wouldn't be woken. Whatever one has created? That was unfair. *He* hadn't baptised the Captain, after all... His hand set to roving again until the thumb and index came to rest over the *linea dentata*, the dividing line between the rectum and the anus. He pinched it hard.

He stands for everything you do not.

He pinched it again.

Accepts everything you cannot.

Again.

Accepts everything I am not.

And again...

Destroy him!

Tristan jerked his hand from the belly, bringing with it a spout of warm body-juice. In his upturned palm sat the eleven squirming apostles.

'How?'

Silence.

'How?'

But those had been the last words they would share.

Now, several days later, he thought he understood – what the Captain stood for, what he accepted... and why he must be destroyed. What Kalki had taught Tristan was how to refuse the mechanical world, the world of processes, of induction, of action and reaction, of death. Rather his was a world of permanence, of meaning, of categoricals, of full sets of teeth... of everlasting life. And it wasn't that the Captain had made the other choice – a lot of people did, the world would always need warriors as well as monks – but that he refused to choose at all. He stood with one foot in each world, thumbing his nose at both. He mixed the two worlds... Separate, they were chemically inert. When mixed, they became perilously volatile. He was a Warrior-Monk, the very worst kind! That was how he could use his shit as war paint. That was how he could throw himself, smirking, into the free-fall of life. And that was how Tristan knew that Kalki was right. He had to complete the cycle and destroy what he had created. Otherwise his creation would destroy them both. Destroy them all.

And yet there was some doubt. For, so embodied, did Kalki not also straddle these two worlds? Was his existence not, in a certain sense, even more volatile than the Captain's? Should he not also be destroyed? He had posed these questions that morning in the closet, squeezing the *linea dentata* as he did so. But Kalki hadn't responded.

Standing, Tristan had pocketed the apostles and before leaving the closet had begged.

'Give me a sign...'

And he had. Today.

Kalki had destroyed himself.

...

Tristan swiped a sealed envelope from the coffee table and headed for the door.

He emerged into the hallway at the very moment the OxyNyx bit, and had to reach for the wall and glare at his feet for a few seconds just to steady himself. When he looked up again, he saw that he wasn't alone. At the far end of the hall, a woman was hanging from the grandfather clock. Her arms were flung around the clock's body while her legs slumped uselessly below. A rejiggered mock-up of that famous silent movie scene, the scales absurdly askew.

It was the one they called Olive Oil. Of all the pet names they had for the residents, this one was perhaps his favourite. For not only did she bear an almost perverse resemblance to the paramour of the most famous muscular dystrophy victim to ever sail the seven seas, but her catalepsy meant her feet would often shoot out from under her as if the floor had been greased with...

But what was she doing on the loose? This one had always been fractious and foul-mouthed, was always trying to upset the Green Oaks applecart with an outrageous accusation about something or other. Outrageous? Most of the time, yes... although poke your finger often enough, randomly enough, and it sometimes risks landing on something true. She might have been dangerous if anyone took her remotely seriously, even for a second. Yes she was paranoid, but yes, they were *actually* plotting against her...

Olive, unaware she was being observed, looked extremely cross with herself. Some months earlier, Ally and Frankie had whipped up a storm in Ward B about the trails of fingerprints the residents left on the clock case as they skirted the hallway. They had threatened them with a parade of ghoulish punishments, the violence of which had increased as gutsy one-upmanship had nosed its way into proceedings. The fingerprints – which they had never cared about one way or the other – had disappeared the very next day.

He wondered if it was this memory that was worrying Olive. She was experimenting with releasing the grip of one arm, so that she could massage her legs back to life. But every time she tried, her body would rattle and shake. After three failed attempts, her features rearranged themselves into an expression of stony obstinacy. She released her grip and thumped to the floor.

'*Meeeee-ow!*' Tristan wailed, as much to his own surprise as hers, lancing the silence of the hallway. The old woman went as rigid as a corpse.

Tristan swaggered towards his victim.

'Hickory, Dickory, Dock…' he intoned with a sneer. He was so at ease in the CareFriend smock, and the personality he had constructed around it, that even the most inspired of his taunts now rose out of him unbidden. As if he was a spectator to proceedings, to the unstaunchable flow of his own malign genius, he doffed an invisible hat to the artfulness of the goad.

'… A mouse has *touched* the clock…'

He was impending over her sprawled body now. After all this time he was still surprised by the elfin proportions of most of the residents. Even the old fatty he had earlier squared up to possessed an underlying smallness that could not truly be appreciated until physically confronted with the fact. It was almost like coming face to face with another species, similar to his own in many ways, but genetically distinct, like the hobbit creatures turned up periodically by archaeologists on far-flung Pacific islands. He could hardly imagine how he must look to them.

Olive was trying to say something, but her voice, at once reedy and croaking, was not cooperating. Tristan abandoned his improvised nursery rhyme without regret, knowing it would struggle to maintain its previous heights, and crouched to look her in the face.

'What was that?' he asked.

'Toi-let,' she managed, her thin lips pushing and curling outwards from her haggard face, a kind of enormous peach stone.

'And I always thought you pissed yourself on purpose because you liked Frankie sponging you… down there.'

Her eyes puckered. Their black marbles glared up at him.

'Can't. Wait,' she said, more in control of her voice now. Tristan crouched and took hold of her left wrist.

'Less mouthy when there's nobody in the cheap seats, aren't you?'

He dragged her upright as if landing a fish, then leaned her against the wall. When it was clear she wouldn't collapse again – not immediately at least – he turned his gaze to the clock's casing and the small cluster of fingerprints Olive had left. Shaking his head:

'We make such an effort to keep Green Oaks nice for you lot. And this is how you see fit to repay us? If we can't trust you to go about the place without this kind of... kind of...' he rifled his mind for the word, and when he landed upon it had to suppress a smile. 'Kind of... vandalism! Then we'll have to start locking the ward again until you learn.'

'Please,' she squeaked, apparently alarmed at the thought of being the origin of a group punishment.

'Perhaps...' Tristan said, feigning being struck only now by a notion that came to him the moment he had seen her in the hallway. 'What if...? But no, I'm not sure you're really up to it.'

Olive made a heroic attempt to puff herself up.

'I'm sure I can manage,' she said.

'Alright,' he said. 'There's one little thing you might do for me, to make up for the time I'll have to spend polishing away the damage.' He brandished the envelope that contained his request, his insistence, that after recent events – recent events not due to happen until this evening – the Captain be transferred to Ward C. Olive flinched.

'I was on my way to deliver this to Mister Cornish, but thanks to your high-jinks I'm not sure I'll have the time now. Do you think you could...'

'Go upstairs?'

Tristan wasn't sure if she was excited or terrified by the prospect. They both looked down at her legs, jiving beneath her as if possessed by the spirit of Elvis. Maybe she'd make it, maybe she wouldn't. It didn't really matter either way. The wheels had already long been set in motion.

'And deliver this to Mister Cornish, yes.'

'I've never been upstairs.'

Tristan, astonished, dropped his guard:

'Never?'

Olive shook her head.

'How long have you been here?'

She attempted a shrug.

'Well this is your lucky day, isn't it?' He creased the envelope length-wise and tucked it into the pocket of her ratty nightie.

'How shall I know where to find Mister Cornish?'

'You won't need to find him, he's already left for the day. Just kick it under his door.'

'How shall I know which door is his?'

Tristan smiled.

'It's just at the top of the stairs. The one that says Do Not Disturb.'

'And the toilet?' she asked.

'After,' he insisted. 'If you can hold on, that is?'

Olive nodded without much conviction.

'Splendid! Hurry along then…'

And with that Tristan straightened up, clapped and rubbed his hands in cartoon triumph, and walked back in the direction of the staff room.

'A doddle,' he said to himself. 'Child's play.'

6

Dot's eyes flickered open…

She *had* said it. *Betty* had said it.

It was the dead of night and Leonard was missing again. It wasn't the first time. Every night, for weeks now, as soon as she turned off the light he would start shifting beside her, his incessant whispered monologue increasing in tempo, more jagged and menacing than it was during the daytime:

Stupid, stupid, shit! he would spit into the darkness, or *The bitch thinks she's won. But she'll see… she'll see…*

Then he would fling back the blanket, snatch his canes from the bed head and stagger out of the room banging the door after him. At first, she had followed close behind, hoping that she might be able to soothe him, convince him to return to bed. But it had been as if she wasn't there. If she was standing in the doorway, he would swat her out of the way with his arm or cane as he trundled past, possessed with a strength that he'd never had before and that made his canes, upon which he had been so dependent these last five years, look little more than theatrical props, badly wielded.

So instead of following him, she had taken to securing the house before retiring each night – locking the doors and windows, hiding the fragile ornaments – and then clearing up his wreckage in the morning.

Dot reached to her left, to be sure Leonard's space was really empty. Her arm fell into the void.

'Oh,' she muttered, groping at the cot's metal frame and blinking into the darkness. 'Green Oaks.'

This wasn't the first time Dot had woken in the night and forgotten where she was, forgotten that she wasn't at home anymore. Forgotten that home wasn't, anymore. But it was different this time. Her memories – of the mind, but of the body too – were draped over the fixtures of Green Oaks like past-painted dustsheets.

And Betty *had* said it. About Father Patterson:

'He hasn't *gone to Ward C*. You never saw him Dot…'

What could she have meant except…

Rex has 'gone to live with the neighbours'.

Old Peg 'has moved to the country', 'to live with Auntie Vi'.

How dare she take Ward C and turn it into… into what? A *euphemism*? Tommyrot!

She had to find Leonard.

Dot's arms trembled as they took the strain. The chrome tubing of the Zimmer was greasy, and warmer than she had expected. Could it be, through some quirk of science, that the last trace of Windsor's life force had been preserved on these oily handles?

The Zimmer was too tall for Dot, forcing her arms to jut out either side like a pair of stunted wings. All of her weight currently rested on her right leg, with the plaster boot suspended an inch or two from the floor. But she was too old to hop, even with the Zimmer for support. If she wanted to advance, if she wanted to find Leonard, she would need to call upon both of her legs.

She touched the ball of her left foot to the lino… then withdrew it at once, images of split saplings glistering in her mind. She took several deep breaths then tried again. Less of a surprise the second time, the pain was more bearable, and she was able to take a small step. Her first in months. She shuffled the frame forward as quietly as she could. Then stopped, and looked around, straining her eyes to check she hadn't disturbed any of the others, but they were all sleeping soundly…

All? No. She started as she realised the Captain was gone. First Leonard, now the Captain. What was happening? She remembered talk of his strange humour earlier that day, of an uncharacteristic despondency... and now he had gone. And not with his habitual crash, bang, wallop, but with the silence of ghost...

To Ward C?

Dot pressed the big toe of her left foot against the floor. The pain helped her focus, grounded her. So the Captain had gone? So what? He couldn't have gone far... he never did. She should be relieved that this time, at least, he hadn't inveigled her into his shenanigans. And yet...

She looked again at the empty bed...

No. The Captain would have to wait until morning.

As she continued her tremulous advance, Dot thought about how something had hardened in her since Leonard had become ill. His increasingly erratic existence had done its work on her. Living so close to that vicious disease had stripped her of so many comforting illusions. That nature was essentially benign. That senility was a good way to go. That love conquered all. That tenderness and compassion would defuse almost any situation. That good things happen to good people... These platitudes had shrivelled one by one, poisoned by their own absurdity in the face of what she was witnessing. She had stood by, impassively, as they had detached themselves from her and fluttered off like autumn leaves. Now deep in the winter of her own life, she couldn't regret their loss. Indeed, in some way she was proud of the grizzled, leafless trunk she had become. As a younger woman she had always pitied the soldiers who, on returning from battle, had seemed drained of human empathy. Not any more. Now she understood.

For how well, really, did she know the man with whom she had lived for almost fifty years? The man who – *only... when was it... yesterday?* – had forced her up against a kitchen cupboard and screamed, *Let me out of here, you cunt! Stop fucking keeping me here!* All of the nastiness, the cruelty, was being pumped out of Leonard, not pumped into him. How long had it been festering away in his brain, held back by the flimsy scaffold of social convention? Not only was he a stranger now, perhaps he had actually been a stranger all those years. This was Leonard. The real, unfettered Leonard. And she had just been too blinkered to see it.

She was almost at the door now, and could see that it had been left open a crack. She smiled thinly – at least she could thank the Captain for something. She felt hot, all of a sudden, but was unable to tell if the heat was coming from within or without. Leaning all of her weight onto her right leg, she released the Zimmer and rolled up the sleeves of her cardigan.

Her red cardigan.

Dot looked down at her torso. There it was. The red, rib knit cardigan, buttoned up to the neck. Always one of her favourites, until… But, how queer. She hadn't brought it with her to Green Oaks. She was sure she hadn't. Yet here it was, so… what did she know?

Five more steps and she was at the door. Leaning the Zimmer back on its rear legs, she butted the door with the front two. It eased open.

Darkness lengthened the hallway. All five of the doors were ajar. Dot liked to leave them that way, to avoid the mustiness that quickly descended upon a small closed room. She regretted the caprice now, regretted not adapting it to the new reality of Leonard's illness. How she hated her bungalow at night. How dreary and inhospitable it looked in the bluish gloom…

She pressed her left foot hard into the floor. Knitting-needle pain. *Not* her bungalow. Green Oaks. For a moment the bungalow's hallway pulsed out of existence and that other hallway, with its grandfather clock, piles of rubbish bags and white cage at the foot of the stairs, hanging open now, replaced it. But only for a moment. It soon all came rushing back – the floral-print wallpaper, the photos of Thomas and the children, as real as it ever had been.

So this was a dream, then? Dot hadn't climbed out of bed, hadn't set off on the Zimmer, hadn't gone in search of Leonard? And yet it *felt* so real. But what other possibility was there? Sleepwalking? Hallucination? Could the house itself be…

She pressed her left foot into the floor again. The electric jolt sharpened her thoughts a scratch. Whatever it was, she knew had no choice but to keep moving forward, no choice but to face it, no choice but to find Leonard. And that was what terrified her most. For the moment she was to step out of the ward, out of Green Oaks, and into the hallway, *her* hallway, *her* bungalow, the stakes would be drastically altered. For Leonard wouldn't be in Ward C any more, whatever that meant. Leonard would be on the loose.

… there was no light in the bungalow, nor a single discernible sound except for the persistent, low-pitched humming of the old refrigerator…

She inched out into the hallway, but was held back by a light tugging on her left arm. Turning, she discovered that her cardigan had snagged on the head of a bent nail. A frayed strand of wool had unravelled until halted by the seam. As she stared at it, a story bobbed to the surface of her mind. Theseus and the Minotaur. How neat! The ball of wool, the labyrinth, the Minotaur. Her snagged cardigan, Leonard's louring evasiveness in the tiny bungalow. Very bloody artful.

And very bloody callous too, of her brain, reminding her of that story then. For Theseus had been a gallant, virile warrior. What was she in comparison? Ariadne's wool too, marking the route for the return of the conquering hero. For Dot there could be no such return. Whatever happened tonight, whatever became of Leonard, her own story was nearly complete. She had seen ten times as many sunsets, at least, ten times as many dawns as she would ever see again. It was just plain mean of life to demand heroism of her at this stage. What had become of the denouement, the happily-ever-after? She took hold of the snagged wool and yanked it free.

It was cooler in the hallway than in the ward, and a draught of air exited the pearls of sweat that had sprouted along her calves. She inched forward. After several steps she felt a knot tightening in her chest. She had forgotten to breathe. The Zimmer, she noticed, was gone. The plaster boot – gone too.

She was in the middle of the hallway now. The dead centre of the bungalow. Somewhere nearby, Leonard was lurking. Perhaps asleep, perhaps ready to attack. One was as likely as the other. It didn't really matter a great deal where he was, or what he was doing. So much had their lives been subsumed by his illness, and so much had it poisoned the air of the bungalow, that it was difficult for her at times to identify just where Leonard ended and where the bungalow began. It was a crazy thought, and a part of her knew it. But still she couldn't rid herself of the feeling.

Just as she reached the kitchen at the end of the hallway, she felt a presence close behind her and, spinning about, caught sight of Leonard's bony heel disappearing into the study. Her determination to confront him had departed and had been replaced now by simple, distilled fear. She wished she had never left the bed. Not just tonight, but that first night months before when Leonard had burnt his hands. Perhaps if she hadn't interfered, things never would have turned so bad. Perhaps by shining a light on his problems she had just made things worse. She cursed her mulish nosiness.

Trembling violently, Dot reached out for the wall to steady herself.

The bungalow was quiet again, and still. She had seen Leonard go into the study, but the proliferation of doorways meant that he might, once again, be anywhere. Back in the living room, or even upstairs... How dastardly the bungalow's elaborate floor plan, that had once so delighted her, now seemed. She slipped into the study.

Empty.

As her eyes roamed about the windowless room she saw that the door leading onto the kitchen was closed, whereas the one that opened onto the spare bedroom was ajar, perhaps even swinging slightly, or perhaps not, the darkness made it so difficult to tell. She decided to check the spare bedroom first.

A feeling of awful fatality burgeoned within her as she pushed open the door and saw her husband lying, straight as a rule, on the single bed. His eyes were closed and the muscles in his face were still. He looked at peace. Could this really be how it ended? Not with a bang, but a whimper? An odd emotion, which it took Dot a moment to identify as happiness, so incongruous was it, broke over her. It was finished, then. For her, but much more importantly, for him.

Now that he was gone, she welled up with all of the sympathy that the horror of dealing with his condition had prevented her from feeling. Poor, sweet Leonard. How nightmarish it must have been for him to see his existence constructed and deconstructed constantly. She sat down on the bed, beside her husband's body and stroked his forehead. Still warm...

The force with which the body threw her backwards and the agility with which it pounced from the bed and pinned her to the wall with a cane would have astonished her even had she not thought she was caressing a lifeless sack of flesh. As it was, the terror prevented her from screaming, channelling itself downwards through her bladder onto the front of her nightdress and collecting as a pool about her feet.

Dot jabbed at the floor with her left foot. Once, twice, three, four times... Nothing! She had seen enough, she wanted out, longed to escape from the bungalow, to return to Green Oaks. She remembered everything now.

'Bitch! I'll show you...' he said, his voice transformed into a malevolent gargle. He leant harder on the cane, which flexed against her neck, pinching her windpipe and obstructing all but the reediest passage of air.

'P... Plea...' Dot attempted, but the words wedged beneath the bamboo.

'I'll show you a thing or two.' His face was pressed up against hers. His eyes, although bulging with intent, seemed to be looking right through her. There was something childish about his expression – although not childish innocence, childish malevolence. The kind of stone cold, amoral visage that descends on a small boy as he sits pulling the wings off a fly.

'And that's the way things go, and that's the way things are...'

'No!' Dot screamed. The force of her cry surprised him, and she used the split second of respite to wriggle from his grasp and rush into the hallway, slamming the door behind her. She skidded to a halt. Where could she go? None of the rooms had locks, and with the horrible strength he had shown, maybe no lock would hold him anyway.

Leonard hobbled out of the study.

'Shut up, cunt!' he barked, lunging for Dot, the curl of his cane cracking into her collarbone. Dot staggered forward, reaching the staircase just before Leonard launched himself at her ankle. He yanked it out from under her, and Dot collapsed on the stairs. In a flash, Leonard was on top of her, his ham-like left forearm, pressing down on the back of her neck, crushing her throat.

She could feel the whole of his weight bearing down on her. A swarm of flies burst across her vision. With his right hand Leonard began fumbling inside his pyjama trousers, frotting his hand and its flaccid charge against Dot's outer thigh. She closed her eyes, spreading their twin load of tears before they could overflow.

'A thing or two, cunt,' he said. 'I'll show you. And that's the way things go…'

Is that the way things go? – Dot thought – Is that really, after all, the way things go? Leonard had wrestled his penis out of his pyjamas now and was squashing it hard against Dot's furry inner thigh, itself tacky from her earlier accident. It was still soft – a baby-sock filled with Jelly, but Dot could hardly feel it anymore. For want of oxygen her thoughts were wandering, erratically, dredging another, much older memory from the depths.

Dorset. A family summer holiday. One of the last. She and May had broken free from their parents for an afternoon and found themselves beside a small brook, presided over by a sheer cliff face of pearly-grey Purbeck stone, about forty feet high. May, always quickly bored, had challenged Dot to climb the rock face, and when she had refused, called her a chicken and a scaredy-cat, and scaled it herself. So easy had her sister made it look, and so much had her taunts stung, that Dot had stood up, brushed herself down and approached the rocks.

For the first twenty five feet or so, everything had gone well, the procession of outcrops and divots seeming to have been laid up the wall almost with the intention of permitting the swift, vertical passage of someone of her precise build. Then, just as dramatically, they had vanished. Clinging onto the cliff with hands gnarled into tight talons, she scanned the rock above her. Nothing. A wall of pristine stone stretched above. May was calling to her.

'What?' Dot screamed.

'Don't stop!' her sister cried a second time.

'Too late,' she shouted back, fear cleaving her voice.

'That's not the way I went. Go back.'

Dot looked down. Far below her on the boulders she could see their sandals and their two packs, so small, and yet so homely and familiar, so comfortable, chiding her for her recklessness. She could clearly see the footholds and handholds she had used to get this far, but as if the cliff were some sarcastic metaphor for time itself, the old cliché of looking-before-you-leap writ horribly physical, she could also see how they only permitted progression in a single direction.

'I can't,' she said. No longer shouting, speaking more to herself than to May now. 'I just can't.'

Her hands were beginning to cramp and her arms tremble. May was still shouting, but Dot could no longer hear what she was saying. She looked again at the smooth rock. Perhaps it wasn't as smooth as she had first thought. Perhaps there were some cracks, some small knots of rock that she might be able to make use of. If only she could...

But who was she trying to fool? She was no climber. Her brutish pride had got her this far, and into this bloody fix, and now it had let her down with the job only half done. The cramp spread all across her body, splayed and twisted across the rock, as if she had been fired straight at it from a circus cannon. She didn't know how much longer she could hold on like this. Certainly not long enough for May to get help. She was already twitching with pain. Minute spasms were coursing through her muscles, easing her from the rock and into the plunge.

What would it be like, she wondered, just to let go? There would be the impact, of course, but that just didn't seem real right then. Much stronger was the anticipation of blissful release she would feel as her fingers straightened out, as she kicked her contorted feet from the two divots, as she gave herself up to gravity's cradle, to the soothing caress of the air as it whorled about her floating body. She would die, most probably, but death seemed so abstract just then, an element of the equation so unquantifiable as to be almost negligible. How easy letting go would be…

But that wasn't the only force at work within her. Beneath the ruins of her self-belief, beneath the ashes of her hope, something else was smouldering. The desire, the necessity, the obligation to live. She closed her eyes and took three deep breaths. The air seared her throat and lungs.

'Climb!' a voice in her head ordered.

(*A voice which she recognised for the first time as her voice, her voice now, as an old lady, as a resident of Green Oaks, speaking back through the decades, ordering herself to climb. But how could time's arrow be ridiculed like that?*)

Dot climbed.

With an almighty flat-handed shove she cast Leonard off. He landed in the hallway on his feet, then, like a Japanese Daruma doll, he rocked before finally tipping backwards, cracking his head on the hard floor. Dot watched him for several minutes, but he didn't move. Suddenly, the whole building trembled beneath the sound of an ear-splitting animal roar. But Leonard's mouth had remained closed.

When she came to, the scene was just as she remembered it. Leonard unconscious in the hallway. Except the hallway itself had changed. Not quite her bungalow, yet not quite Green Oaks either. An uncanny hybrid of the two – her wallpaper, photos and carpet, Green Oaks' mouldings, floor plan and rubbish pile. The haunted old house, its show over, was reorganising itself before Dot's eyes… But she was too tired to be surprised. She thought she knew how a soldier must feel upon waking the morning after a murderous battle. Bruised, perhaps, but basically unscathed and with a certain sentiment of hard won invincibility. There was a bitter odour in the air, and it took her several seconds to realise it was coming from her. There was a dark patch on the carpet. Clearly her bladder had emptied itself once again while she was out. This discovery didn't upset her, though. In fact, some part of her took pleasure from the realisation, revelled in the stench. What was it, after all, if not a sign that, despite everything that had happened, her old body was still functioning?

Leonard's breath was sawing in and out of him, and his right hand was twitching, setting off an army of invisible spinning tops. All Dot could think of was what had happened earlier. Not how he had attacked her, tried to rape her with that broken-down old member of his. But how, seconds before that, he had looked so much at peace. Although she had entertained the thought on several occasions, it was only now that it seemed not only a real possibility, but also the right thing to do. For both of them...

Careful not to make a sound, she crossed over to the pile of trash and fished an old pillow from one of the bags. Without hesitation she laid it across Leonard's face. Moving both of her hands to the middle of the pillow she was surprised for a moment to be able to feel his features through the down. The ridges of his cheeks, the crest of his splendid nose, the brick-like angles of his jaw. Maybe it was the layer of stuffing, she couldn't be sure, but her fingertips reported a striking resurgence of youth, of vitality, and she imagined that her husband's face had transformed once again into that queer, youthful assemblage she had fallen so deeply in love with. She wanted more than anything to feel that face again, to go on exploring it forever if she could.

She pressed down harder on the pillow, but Leonard was already gone.

0 REASONS WHY YOU
VILL DIE YOUNG
AIR SOULS!
25¢
Daddy,
We're coming for you.
There'll be a car
aiting in the copse
t midnight.
Come alone.
Private Dulcie
Ruggles
WE'LL MEET AGAIN... WON'T WE?
A CAPTAIN RUGGLES STORY

WE'LL MEET AGAIN... WON'T WE?

A CAPTAIN RUGGLES STORY

I

In only fifteen minutes...

'Hey Skinny! Yer ribs are showing.'

Ruggles peered at the skeletal chassis atop which his stately noggin teetered. The jibe was well trained. For even beneath his pectoral muscles – two flaccid, fried eggs barely worthy of the name – it was his ribcage that gave form to his torso; a fragile vase of ripples, so pronounced that those above cast those below into shadow.

The rest of his body followed the same ignoble pattern. A sunken abdomen, spared its full helping of shame by his red bathing shorts, worn high at the waist. Denied any quadriceps to give them form, the shorts flared skirtishly at his hips. Humiliated, Ruggles curled his toes into the hot sand. He wouldn't look up. He couldn't.

... A New Man ...

There was a second pair of feet beside his own on the sand. Shod in black mules, they shuffled, an outlet for the embarrassment inflicted upon his female companion. Junoesque and sporting an elegant two-piece bathing suit and a perfect bell of straw-blonde hair, she was a portrait of loveliness; outwardly modern, but with a traditional core. The exquisitely balanced, because chemically inert, cocktail of sex and mother. The Grail of every adolescent boy's crusading fantasies. What did she see in him?

'Watch what you say, fella...' Ruggles said, because after such a long silence he had to say something. He summoned his courage, lifted his gaze and glared at his tormentor.

... What's my secret?

The figure that stood before him, a cock-mouthed sneer deforming his features, was a brute – a handsome, well-groomed brute, as gristly as a prize bullock. His blue shorts bulged liked a well stuffed haggis. Ruggles knew the face, had seen it before, although he couldn't quite place it.

'Shut up, you bag of bones!' the brute said, as he jabbed at Ruggles' jaw.

'Don't let him hit you, Dylan...'

Too late. The fist, as large and as hard as a strung ham, connected. Ruggles reeled. A sharp pain coursed down his left side. Once, twice, three times his body spun before dropping, without a sound, to the sand.

An endless room of electric blue. A voice.

Take an honest look at yourself. Are you proud to go through life being half the man you could be?

A smiling colossus was impending over him. A shiny helmet of slicked-back hair, chalk-white teeth, a pair of leopard print trunks, straining at the seams. Tarzan?

Believe me, Ruggles. I know how you feel. I was once a scrawny, ninety-seven-pound, half-alive weakling, just like you.

The colossus plucked him from the ground and set him on his feet.

I was ashamed to strip for sports or the beach. Shy of girls. Afraid of healthy competition.

Ruggles rubbed his chin. Where he expected to feel pain he felt... nothing.

But one day I discovered a secret, a magic formula. It took a mouse and made a man of him. A real He-Man from head to toe. A man who stands out in any crowd. A man, covered with a brand new suit of beautiful, rock-hard, solid muscle. And now I'm passing that secret on to you, Dylan...

The colossus stooped and, closing his eyes, kissed him gently, the tip of his tongue flickering between their pressed lips. With that kiss the colossus inhaled a burning seed into his belly and Ruggles filled with an extraordinary heat. His muscles tensed and relaxed, tensed and relaxed... worked by a dynamism not of his own making. The waistband of his shorts tightened, then rent, as his whole body blossomed with Atlantean thews, filled with an almost titanic power. He was a beast transformed.

The colossus looked at him with deep, almost paternal, satisfaction. He was dissolving into the blue, becoming first a silhouette of black polka-dots which, as he disintegrated further, flared with colour – magenta, cyan, yellow. Bewildered, but energised, Ruggles found his voice at last:

'Who are you?' he stammered. What was left of the apparition smiled again and winked. As he disappeared, the voice rang out one final time.

I'm the world's most perfectly developed man…

Ruggles sprang from the sand. The brute, with his back turned, was blind to this Phoenix-like renaissance. Ruggles rolled his prodigious new shoulders, twitched his pectorals in quick, masterly, succession, learning the ropes of his overhauled frame. He stepped forward and prodded the brute between the shoulders.

'Here's a love tap from that bag of bones. Remember?'

Before the brute had time to react, Ruggles lunged at him, planting a heavy uppercut on his chin. So hard and so clean was the punch that a shower of sparks and stars rained from the point of contact. The seaside air shuddered with communal esteem.

'What a man!'

'And he used to be so skinny.'

His squeeze in green, all signs of her former humiliation banished, hooked her slender arm through the puckered eye of his biceps.

'Oh Dylan,' she husked, demolished by her love and simpering admiration. 'You are a real He-Man after all.'

II

What Captain Ruggles took, upon waking, to be the granular sensation of sand in his mouth turned out, after investigation, to instead be a leaf of coarse paper tacked to his tongue by the gum of sleep. He had stayed awake late the previous evening, swotting up on combat techniques from one of the warfare manuals he normally kept hidden beneath the mattress. But he had been careless, unaware perhaps of the extent of his own weariness, and had fallen asleep while reading. And for all the time he had been asleep, the manual had lain exposed, a kind of Lilliputian tent propped open upon his Gulliver-sized features.

He was appalled at his own sloppiness. These manuals were contraband of the highest order and their discovery risked exposing the convoluted supply chain – from ████████ to ████████, then from ████████ to ████████ and ████████, before finally handing them to ████████, who handed them to Ruggles – that kept him in patchy contact with HQ. How many plans, how many lives, would have been in jeopardy had one of the guards stumbled upon it on his rounds. He dared not even imagine.

Had one of his subordinates been guilty of such negligence, he would have recommended… well, if not court-martial, then at least a damned thorough dressing down. Under the circumstances, as the highest-ranking officer in the camp after the unfortunate demise of the Field Marshall, he resolved to devise his own punishment. On the vast mental chalkboard tacked to the inside of his skull, which he returned to whenever something needed to be planned, to be mapped out or – as in this case – to be remembered, he marked up a double exercise drill for this afternoon, and a halving of his rations for the day, the leftovers to be shared between his fellow detainees as a symbol of his contrition.

With the manual secreted, his thoughts returned to his dream. It was a queer one, and no mistake. It was unusual for Ruggles to remember his dreams, and when he did they were rarely so vivid. There had been a recent one in which he was a radio technician, and another in which he was an apprentice carpenter, but he struggled now to recall any more than these sketchiest of details. More common were the single subject dreams in which a theme clanged about his skull like a pinball. *Stomach Ulcers!* the crisp voice might trill. *Asthma!* or *Piles!* sometimes with enough force to cast him clean back across Nod's frontier.

Yet while he knew it was the very nature of the dream-beast to be uncanny, what aggrieved him about this newest one was its hangover. The ghastly feeling that, tangled up in the events of the reverie, there was also a lesson, a message, waiting to be unpicked. It hovered just out of his reach, however, like a forgotten birthday or bill, or the intuition of a looming catastrophe. The kind of presentiment that dodged any attempt made at landing it, right up to the very moment its knowledge became useless, at which point it burst across consciousness, horribly, maliciously limpid.

If his brain so desperately wanted to tell him something, why all the gratuitous accoutrements? Whose team was it batting for anyway? Perhaps its message was a simple one: Don't stand for others pushing you around, Ruggles! Meet violence with violence! Or something along similar lines. But trying on each of these explanations in turn, none of them fit. Who was the girl? Who the brute? And who that brawny seraph, the world's (self-anointed) most perfectly developed man?

He guessed he had a little less than ten minutes before the siren would sound, rousing the other detainees. Just enough time for his ritual. He slipped his arm under the knotted pillow and, locating the picture of Dulcie, closed his fingers about it. He didn't need to look at the photo, it had been seared onto his retinas the very instant he first saw it, as if he had looked directly into the sun. Its importance for him was less as a tool for memory now and more as a kind of fetish; as if Dulcie herself was confined within its white border, cut off not only from the war and all its horrors, but also from the ravaging effects of time itself.

If he wasn't vigilant, Ruggles could be prone to the fantasy that, upon his return, the Dulcie he found would be unchanged from the Dulcie in the picture, so a part of his ritual consisted in constructing an image of his daughter how she could look now these two... or three... or however many years it had been... later. He knew that he would put himself at risk to protect the photo. But while emotional attachment was a dangerous path for any soldier to tread, it could also be his greatest motivating force. What were entreaties to fight for 'King and Country' after all, if not appeals to the basest instinct of tribal attachment?

But for Ruggles, King, country and the conquest of Teutonic evil were all just happy side effects of his principle campaign. He was under no illusions that he was fighting for Dulcie alone. For her future, of course, her safe progression into adulthood; but even that was a difficult idea to release from the abstract realm. He was fighting, above all, for the moment when she threw open the door of their cottage, saw her father, battered and war-wrecked, standing on the front porch, and collapsed into his hungry embrace.

So with this totem sitting in the palm of his hand he began, as he did every morning, to reconstruct the image in meticulous detail. The cloudless, argentine sky. The old cooking apple tree, black moss at its base, pranked with white lichen and hatted with leaves quivered into a grey haze by the summer breeze. Suspended from a wayward, low-hanging bough, a wooden swing of his own construction. On the ashen grass a little way in front of the swing, the wreckage of a teddy bears' tea party, the largest of the two guests – Blue Bear his mind astonished him in recollecting, even though he was a dashing silver in the photo – listed to one side, while the smaller, a beady eyed astonished looking creature, of which he had no memory beyond the photo, looked on with a lively, fearful regard. The hostess, called upon to pose for her portrait, was standing beside the swing. Her spotted tabard projected from her tiny frame with an almost geometric uniformity. Her delicate limbs spoked out from the polygon of fabric, while her legs tapered to bare feet, partially hidden in the grass, and her arms were planted upon her hips like amphora handles. Her dazzling white hair was twisted into a single thick plait, which lazed across her shoulder. She was smiling, a black smudge of emptiness holding the fort where her front teeth had once been.

There was a remoteness to the scene, imposed by time, of course, but also by the washed-out greys and the liquid chemical haze, the faint shadows of the photographic fixer in which the image had first been born. Where the photo had been folded and unfolded, a hundred, a thousand times, a line, woven like barbed wire, further barred their access to each other.

But as his hands toyed with the photo beneath his pillow he realised, with a twinge of foreboding, that something was different. Something was wrong. The lacquered texture of the card, against which his finger ridges normally tugged as he fiddled, was absent. The texture was coarser too, and as though he was suddenly hyper-sensitised he added the thickness and the dimensions of the photo to the list of things that had changed.

He whipped his arm out from under the pillow and held the… the… the *thing*, before his eyes. This was not his photo. This was not even *a* photo. Just a folded index card. He spun about in bed and, tossing the pillow to the floor, scanned the sheets for his picture. It wasn't there. Neither was it on the floor at the side of the bed, under the mattress or in any of the pockets of his fatigues, which he searched then slung aside in his frenzy. He riffled the combat manuals, no longer caring if he was caught, hoping that perhaps he had unthinkingly turned to it when in need of a bookmark.

Nothing.

Ruggles felt the need to roar, to rampage, to scream bloody kidnap! To turn the whole cell-block, the whole prison camp, upside down, until his photo was returned to him. Only a fist jammed into his mouth prevented him from doing so. He gnawed at it with a fury until he tasted blood. How could this have happened? Where could it have gone? It didn't make any sense. It had been there last night. He remembered unfolding it and kissing it and returning it to its rightful place. But it had vanished, fallen through a slit in the fabric of reality.

His darting eyes landed on the index card – the vile imposter! – that had tumbled to the floor as he'd dervished about on his cot. What was that? He couldn't recall ever having seen it before. He dangled from the cot and scooped up the card. Something was written on it.

As he read, the desolation was displaced by something else. It had been so long since Ruggles had been subject to this compound emotion that it took him some time to identify it. There was disbelief, and perhaps fear and happiness too, but these sensations were all just dressing, really. It wasn't until he had read the card a fifth time that he was able to identify the thickest, most potent strand of all. Hope.

III

A Heinkel bomber sharked across the mottled sky, the drone of its engines, muffled by the distance, was almost indistinguishable from the murmuring of flies feasting upon the nearby latrine.

Captain Ruggles, alone at the open window of the cell-block, plucked a *Gasper* from the band of his helmet and, striking a match against the sole of his boot, lit it and took an unhurried, meditative drag.

The elevated position of the camp afforded him a dramatic view of the grounds and the surrounding countryside. As it tumbled past the ruins of the smock mills and skidded beneath the perimeter fence, before beginning to level out as it reached the small coppice just beyond. For the past seventeen months, that fence had marked the extent of his world, the focus of his intelligence gathering, the object of his resistance, the framework for his campaigns. It was difficult for him to believe that within a few hours his arena would expand to take in everything that lay beyond. Difficult and strange. And, he admitted to himself, frightening too.

The land beyond the fence – the rightful sovereignty of which he had never definitively established – was pockmarked with bomb-sites and dug-outs, enclosed, as far as he could make out, by uniformly built barricades of sandbags and razor wire. A cruel inversion of the tumescent hedge-scored

English landscape, which his mind didn't so much as remember anymore as emotionalise, in bold hues and unadorned arcs, and which held at its centre, as in his every vision of England (as though she were the very lynchpin about which the country turned) the image of Dulcie, carved it seemed, after the lost photo, from the pure substance of light itself.

Beyond the horizon he noticed a dense plume of smoke chuff skyward. Fifteen seconds later the air cracked with the explosion's report.

'That's it boys,' he said. 'Closer every day.'

The *Gasper* singed his fingertips. He had forgotten about it and it had burnt down unattended. The mysterious arrival of the note, slipped under his pillow while he slept, had made a whirligig of his mind. He had hoped that the isolation of the empty yard and the honing effect of tobacco on the brain might help. He lit a second *Gasper* and plucked the index card from his waistband.

The authenticity of the note couldn't be established beyond doubt. When he had last seen Dulcie, her handwriting was the spidery scrawl of one to whom the pencil was still an unfamiliar and complex tool. There remained something spidery about this looping cursive... but could it really be his daughter's hand? To believe it so was a risk... but not so much of a risk as to believe it otherwise. What if this was his best – and his last – chance of escape? It would be reckless not to seize the opportunity, however flimsy, not to make the leap of faith.

The sound of a door's catch tripping yanked his attention back to the cell. He tucked the note in his waistband and, feigning nonchalance as best he could, looked over his shoulder. False alarm. It was only Lieutenant ▓▓▓▓, the prodigious representative of the 1st (West Africa) Infantry Brigade. Although she was walking straight towards him, pitching to and fro as she shifted her bulk from one elephantine leg to the other, her eyes were fixed past Ruggles, and out the window. She stopped beside him.

'Do you mind if I join you?' she said. Ruggles' head twitched its assent. For a minute they stood, side by side, looking, for all the world, like a silent-era slapstick double act. Then:

'Count me in.' Her words thrummed into Ruggles' eardrum like a well-trained arrow.

'In?'

'Yes, *in*. In whatever mindless schemes you've got tucked away up your sleeve, Captain. You can count me in from now on.'

Ruggles turned to face her.

'It could be dangerous,' he said.

'I don't care. I've had enough.'

'Thank you, Lieutenant,' Ruggles said. 'Do you mind me asking what…?'

'You can't fight madness with reason, can you?' she said, addressing the question as much to herself as to him. 'I mean, I always knew they were a bunch of bastards, but I trusted they could be kept in check. By the director, by ███████████, by…' She stopped speaking. The third name on her list was the hardest of all for her to admit. 'By Father Patterson. We had something up our sleeve too, you know. He wanted to help us. He spoke to people. I thought that if people only knew then somebody would intervene. That was what I thought the problem was – that people didn't know. But it's not. It's not that people don't know. They know well enough. It's just they don't *want* to know. You're right about one thing, Ruggles: There is a war on, and we're forced to fight in it every single day…'

'Every single day,' Ruggles echoed. He felt the weight of his quandary more than ever now. After months of trying to rouse his fellow detainees, it seemed the seeds of rebellion had finally started to bud. With ████████ on board to convince the others, they might just be able to mount a successful escape, maybe even a tunnelling out. However, with the gifted Private's obduracy seemingly insurmountable, and her leg still in plaster, it would be a significant gamble. On the other hand, there was the note and its promise of freedom, but freedom for him alone. How could he justify leaving his troops at the very moment they were beginning to rally behind him?

'I won't let you down, Lieutenant,' he said.

For the first time since she arrived, the Lieutenant turned to look at Ruggles. Her eyes were narrowed, barely visible in the crack between her heavy eyelids. She was trying desperately to scrutinise the inscrutable. Then she shook her head slowly, exhaled a long slow draught from her nose and began lurching back towards the door.

Once she was gone, Ruggles dug out the index card one more time and read the message aloud.

'*Daddy. We're coming for you. There'll be a car waiting in the copse at midnight. Come alone. Private Dulcie Ruggles.*'

IV

Ruggles was packing. He had already stripped his pillow, hidden it below his cot and was now jamming one or another of his essential possessions into the emptied pillowcase. His change of uniform, his tin helmet and his stash of cutlery, pilfered, over a period of weeks, from the canteen. His two most prized possessions, however, he was keeping about his person, knowing that if he was chased he might be obliged to jettison his payload to increase the speed of his flight. First there was the index card, which since this morning had become a surrogate for his lost photo of Dulcie, and which was tucked in the waistband of his trousers. Second, and of much more practical importance, was the cluster of keys filched several weeks earlier, which he kept hung around his neck on an old, knotted bootlace. If all went to plan this evening, the keys would be of little use to him anymore, but he knew that he couldn't take the risk of confiding them to any one of his comrades. For if they were turned up by a guard during a search of the Zellenblock it would mean curtains for whoever he had given them to, and he refused to have that on his conscience.

Since their exchange of that morning, the Lieutenant had been carping about the perimeter of his thoughts. Ruggles knew that to leave her now would be interpreted at best as a rejection and at worst as a betrayal. That was why he had written a note of his own that he intended to hide beneath the pillow of the loyal Private, just as Dulcie's note had been hidden beneath his own last night. In it he explained, employing the most unequivocal language, that their Captain had not abandoned anybody, that they would just need to sit tight a while longer, and that he would be back to rescue them as soon as circumstances allowed.

It was with immense chagrin that he thought of his failure to enrol the Private in the rebels' ranks. He knew, from the first day of her internment, that she was of exceptional character, that indeed it was only with her support that any escape attempt might succeed. She also detested the regime in the camp as much as any of the others, and made no secret of it. And yet there was something holding her back, which Ruggles had been unable to fathom, but which had soured her to the world, or at least to the possibility of her future within it.

Where will you go? What will you do? Who will take you in? Her barbed questions wounded him all the more because of his own lack of answers to them. Why could she not see that none of that mattered? What mattered was escaping, building up the speed and busting out. If they could manage that, they could achieve just about anything else through sheer carried-over momentum.

What about the others? She would also challenge him with a peculiar ferocity. *What about the poor buggers in C? Who will break them out?* The fate of the unfortunate victims of those profligate Nazi medics troubled Ruggles too, but surely they were much less use to them cooped up here than on the outside, where they might be able to launch a rescue mission. Although, at least the Private didn't deny the very existence of Zellenblock C, as some of the others did. Ruggles could understand that it wasn't pleasant to think about the horrors that took place therein, but surely to think it out of existence was even worse.

As much as he had bombarded the Private with arguments, her redoubtable defences had held. Maybe it was the war that had done for her, or maybe it was just life. Maybe it didn't matter one way or the other. For so many, Ruggles knew, the only difference between life and war is how quickly someone else's decisions – someone else's grubby, selfish, cynical priorities – get a man (or a woman, or a child) killed. Whatever the outcome of a war, there were always winners and losers on both sides, winners and losers made up of precisely the people who were winning and losing before the great firework show began.

A part of him did understand why the private had lost her fighting spirit. What suddenly seemed a lot more difficult to understand, in fact, was why he still hadn't lost his.

With a glance at the doorway, to confirm he had the all-clear, Ruggles squatted on his mattress and then, channelling the frog on the lily pad, he loosed the coiled spring of his body and leapt across to the Private's cot. He slipped the note under her pillow, with only the slightest physical effort, hopped back across to his own.

V

'Helmet?'

Check!

'Compass?'

Check!

'*Gaspers?*' Ruggles' index finger wound a tight slalom over the top of the open carton of cigarettes in his shirt pocket. Four. Eight. Twelve. Sixteen. Eighteen.

All present and correct, Captain!

'In that case,' he smiled, 'you can move off when you're ready.'

Very good, Captain.

'One more thing, though, before you go…'

Yes, sir?

'It has been a privilege fighting so closely alongside you… I just wanted you to know that.'

The feeling's mutual, Cap.

'You bet it is!'

Ruggles loosed a broad grin. As emotional farewells with brothers-in-arms went, indulging in one with yourself was, he knew, pretty low. Still, he'd had the urge to tick that box knowing, somehow, that things wouldn't have felt quite complete without it and, owing to the top secret nature of his shenanigans tonight, that was his only choice.

His only choice? Perhaps not quite. There was always the Private… She would certainly have read his note by now. All evening he had tried to catch her regard, to establish whether she 'knew' or not, and all evening – he felt, although he couldn't say for sure – she had avoided his eye.

He had underestimated the thickness of the crust that had formed about her, locking her in, pinioning her when she should have flown! Life had wounded her, as it wounds everyone… but those wounds that don't kill you, while they may scab at first, eventually they heal. The Private's wounds hadn't healed though, not yet. They had only scabbed, thicker and thicker, weighing her down how a docked ship is weighed down by the incrustation of barnacles on its hull. And unless something happened to crack those barnacles, to jemmy them off, they would eventually drag her under. Ruggles had seen all of this from the beginning and had determined to help her. What he hadn't seen, what he hadn't been modest enough to see, was that he just wasn't the man for the job… But if not him, then who else in this hellhole?

The Private was sleeping now, as was everyone else in the Zellenblock. Her breathing was so deep that each exhalation susurrated like a regretful sigh. Part of him, the cowardly part, felt relieved to have been spared the goodbyes. For a goodbye it was to be, perhaps an *adieu*, but certainly not an *au revoir*. He would have liked to believe otherwise, but sometimes war required you to face up to things with cold blood, to glare into the barrel of the gun. None of them had shown any interest in breaking out, in busting free. Not really. His cellmates' hearts just weren't much into life anymore. There was a resignation about them that Ruggles just couldn't understand. They had clearly long ago decided that there was only one way out of the Stalag. Lie down for enough of each day, taunt gravity, and perhaps the earth would just open up and swallow them. More than anything – more, even, than his reunion with Dulcie – that was what tonight meant to him. He may have been leaving without them, abandoning them all, but it had to be this way… It was up to him to show them that there was another way than death, than *disparition*, *dissipation*, than giving in to decay... Death was one option, but so too was...

Glory? No. He no longer believed in that. Death had been lowering over him for so long that he was almost used to the rancid old fishwife. And what happened when you had to live for almost two years in death's slurry rather than being surprised by it on the battlefield? First, Glory quickly revealed herself for the harlot she was, with her empty promises of eternal life. She had *cha-cha*'ed off even before Ruggles had left solitary for the first time... and she had never come back. And with that weed pulled, the other flowers in life's garden – the small ones, the hidden, insignificant, inglorious ones – got a chance to breathe, to blossom. It was those small flowers he believed in now – the kisses, the smiles of children, the first gust of summer wind, the last... all those bloody silly clichés! He'd ended up believing in every single one!

Ruggles smoothed over the bed sheet for the final time and checked his cabinet and the floor around the cot for anything that might incriminate his cellmates. He had disposed of the manuals this afternoon, tearing them into shreds, balling and dropping them into the latrine, pleading dysentery to the guards to excuse his repeated trips outside his cell. He had felt a twinge of regret as he destroyed them. They had given him succour during his time here, but he didn't need them now. He had ingested every sentence, every technique, every anecdote, every image... As if they were some kind of convoluted mantra, his whole being now resonated with their words. Their frequency had become his frequency, their advice had become his knowledge. Their matter-of-fact tone had become his insurmountable confidence. After so much time spent poring over those manuals Ruggles felt almost as if he had become a chimera, part man, part book. Another species, a new one: *Homo Libris*.

The door had been left unlocked. He had listened out for the bite of the latch, the turn of the key, but it had never come. He hadn't given the guards much trouble these past weeks. They were getting sloppy.

After fingering his shirt pocket for Dulcie's note, he surveyed the cell one final time, tipped his helmet at his sleeping comrades, opened the door and stole out.

VI

How close the stars seemed tonight. How coddling the slither of moonlight winking through a slit in the clouds. How forgiving the damp sod on the calluses of his bare feet. How fortifying the cool air...

Half a dozen steps out of the cell-block he stopped, felt himself into this new world. A world of liberty looming. Breathing it in was as exhilarating as tonguing an ice-cold bowie blade. Captivity pinned a man into life's most sordid stratum... The corporeal stratum, the hunger stratum, the piss-and-shit stratum, the kill-or-be-killed stratum. He had forgotten the tart scent of freedom. How it tickled the nose, how it set the teeth on edge, how it knotted the bowels... How terrifying it was and yet how the body, unbidden, would fight for it to the last.

But it wasn't his. Not yet.

There had been no guards patrolling the Zellenblock, and there were none outside either. He wasn't so drunk on the thrill of the escape that this didn't give him pause for thought. He knew it could be a trap, but then couldn't everything one way or another? The guards might be onto the escape – probably were! – lying in wait so that they could not only round him up, but Dulcie and her comrades as well. A calculated risk. On his part and theirs. He'd get himself killed before he let them take her, fight them like a cornered mongrel, let their bullets sieve his body if only it would allow his daughter to escape...

Down the hill, a little to the left, a torchlight blinked once. A dark cloud shuffled in front of the moon, snuffing it out. Ruggles hucked the cigarette lighter from his pocket, struck it twice in response. A moment passed and the torch blinked again. He pivoted towards it, setting his course, then pocketed the lighter. With the moon obscured, he couldn't see a thing. The next stage in his journey would have to be undertaken blind. A slow, groping trudge towards the memory of the light. He scrunched his toes into the grass and set off.

Darkness: the staunch ally of visions. Under its cover they rolled on like fog off the ocean. Without the raw material of light to work with the brain picks up the slack, building mirages in the soupy black from husks of recollections and echoes of dreams. His recollections? His dreams? They had to be, and yet... They resonated, throbbed with a queer intimacy. But how could they have come from him, telling as they did of a life not lived... at least not this time around, not by him.

As an opening, the dream matter constructed a church. A priest, marrying a man in a suit to... a coffin. The congregation, a swamp of black, weeping and wailing. The coffin thumped and shuddered, bleeding from the sap-scabbed knots in its wood.

'Til dust us do part...

Ruggles shook his head, dissolving the scene and stepped out of this hallucination across the darkness and into another...

An office, vast as an aircraft hangar, populated by dapper, striding giants. A desk, large as a house. A stool on legs, tall as giant redwoods. And him, Ruggles, perched on top, a midget, a sparrow on a telegraph pole. His hand resting on a rubber stamp, the size, the weight of an ironmonger's anvil... He lifted the stamp, thumped it down, then lifted it again. in black block capitals...

A mountaintop. A man. Endless plains below crackled and flared, popped and ruptured, the acne blossom of a distant war. A harsh wind rose, scattering the man like a heap of autumn leaves...

Ruggles' foot caught on something in the grass and he tumbled forward, onto his hands and knees. He decided it safest to ramp forward on all fours. Yet the fog lower down was thicker still…

A doctor's surgery. ███████████████████████████████

███████████████████████████ A leather topped desk.

██

███████████████████████████ A bald spectacled physician, crowned with a pair of spiralling goat's horns, shoulders iced with military epaulettes. Telling someone, a gangly adolescent not to weep, that there's really no shame in being born with a weak heart and one leg two inches longer than the other, it's just no use to the British ███████████████████
██

A father's slipper. A young boy's soft, pink buttocks. An accusation of day-dreaminess, of good-for-nothinghood. The slap. The sting.

██
██
██

████████████████████

A storybook. A hero. Lantern jaw. A fan of pages, endlessly turning, unstuck at the spine, forming a pulpy inviting vulva. A new centre of gravity, dragging him in…

██
██
██
██
██
██
████████████████████████

An old hollow-eyed figure in a hospital cot. A young woman, abdomen gently hummocked with child, the burial mound's beautiful counterpoint.

I don't need this! Not now... A scraped-blackboard voice. A siren in his skull. A song. *I need my daddy back... Forget it! Forget me! Especially now...* Hollow-eyes smiled dimly, faded out. ███████████████████

██

... His forearm plunked into a puddle as the ground evened out in front of him. The odour of damp leaves, of bracken. He was close now. He fumbled for the lighter, struck it. Once. Twice. Waited.

Nothing. He was still punch-drunk from the visions... The ghosts they had woken, while faded now, still danced a diaphanous ring-a-rosy about his head, pricking the pitch darkness with phosphorescent flashes. Was it possible they had disturbed him so much that he had veered off course? He squirmed forward several more feet and tried the lighter again. For a second time, nothing.

Perhaps Dulcie had gone to ground, or been forced to retreat, spooked by the Stalag guards conducting a reccy that he, in his distraction, hadn't noticed.

He waited. He could lie there all night if need be... although in this darkness even time shed its linear, downward flow. Rebelling against its channel, becoming fluid, curvaceous, rippling and eddying back on itself, playing. Dragging himself forward a few more feet, onto a drier and flatter patch of turf, Ruggles made a cradle of his arms and nestled his head into it. He was tired, and struggled to fight off sleep. How strange it was that, in this near-total absence of light, sleep's frontier seemed a lot blurrier than usual, as if he could stand with one foot planted either side and not really notice it at all.

He scrunched his toes until they cramped, this little electric jolt the only corroboration he could think of that he hadn't yet fully crossed over...

The flash of light arrived as suddenly as the cloudburst of an electric storm... but didn't fade. He saw it first on the grass, fenced in by his arms, an extra-terrestrial, effulgent green, almost as if the light wasn't shining onto the blades, but shining out of them. He lifted his head, squinted, but the glare was too harsh. Was that, perhaps, the scratched silhouettes of trees, black lines, fissuring the brilliant white plane? He couldn't be sure. He looked again, forcing himself to hold it longer this time. Yes, there were trees, but also figures... Three humanoid forms: two stumpy homunculi, with round heads and digitless limbs, and the third... a woman... a girl, sitting, rocking, swinging...

Dulcie!

He pushed himself up onto straightened arms, padded forward. The scene, still burning in furious light, was familiar... That scene he had pored over a hundred thousand times, in monochrome reproduction, had been wizard to life before his eyes. The girl, the swing, the teddy bears, the tea party. How could it be so, unless lying there he had... Was this the light they always spoke about then? When life runs out on you, like film flapping its last through a projector, leaving nothing on screen but the bulb's naked glare...

Had his body, worn and battered by captivity, just, quite literally, given up its ghost? Or had he fallen asleep there, been surprised by a guard, a pistol lodged gently against his skull, the trigger pulled? He still *felt* alive... but then what did he know of how it felt to be... to be... otherwise?

The urgency of these questions was nothing, however, compared to the urgency to approach the scene, to beg its acceptance, to become one with it. He inched forward some more. His body no longer felt tired, no longer felt anything, except a profound, giddy weightlessness.

He sprang to his feet, squinted again, and again the scene sharpened. He was behind her, he realised. All the better for surprising her, scooping her up in his arms, nuzzling her neck as she whistled through her broken teeth, chattering in his ear about her afternoon playing teatime with Blue Bear...

Blue Bear? His eyes were accustomed enough to the night now to see that neither of the stuffed toys was blue. The revelation jabbed him in the gut, winded him. *Wrong!* The bear was the wrong colour. The girl... he took two more steps forward... the *girl* was the wrong colour, the wrong shape, too tall, too broad. The hair too, no fine blonde gossamer, but cord-like, snake-like. The albino gorgon…

He remembered the daemon of Dulcie that had tormented him those first few days in solitary. Had it come back to haunt him now? His hands fisted, his lips retreated, baring his clenched teeth. He was running, suddenly, arms a-windmill… His body had made the decision, without him, to go into battle…

A face poked out from behind one of the trees. Not *a* face… *that* face! The brute from the beach, the one that had assaulted him in his dream. Its mouth opened and its foghorn voice blasted:

'Now!'

The figure in the swing turned, leered, rode up then rushed forward, her boots thumping into Ruggles' chest, crumpling his ribs like a tin can. He reeled backwards, his balance lost, just as from behind him a thick sack was pulled over his head.

He dropped to his knees and roared into the darkness.

Book Five

1

'**D**otty!'

'*Ghn... Hmm?*' She was being dragged from sleep by a hand on her good ankle.

'Dot!'

'Olive?'

'It's marvellous! You have to see it, Dot.'

'Marvellous?' Dot massaged her eyes with the balls of her hands. 'What wonder could possibly await me? Honey in the porridge? The face of the Christ child on a pee-stained bed sheet...' She paused. Her voice was suddenly less sure. 'The Captain's come back?'

Olive, long inoculated against sarcasm, failed to detect the switch to sincerity.

'None of the above, Dotty. Not even close. Now hurry, before it's over.'

Dot opened her eyes in time to see Smithy's grapple-loader arms descending to scoop her up. She feared hers would be the fate of the fairground teddy bear – targeted, grabbed, lifted, then dropped and bounced on her head by a predictable slackening of the arms. But it didn't happen. Smithy, she'd forgotten, was as strong as he looked. The faintest flame of desire – not for Smithy, exactly, but for brute, masculine strength – flickered in Dot's gut. She finally understood why Betty had chosen him. What other man here could have handled her?

Loaded and propped in the wheelchair, she took in the ward. The others were all lined up at the window.

'The light…' she said, forgetting her crotchetiness as Smithy wheeled her forward into the blood-orange blush. 'I don't know how long it's been since…'

'Beautiful, isn't it?' Smithy said, leaning over her shoulder. Then stooping, he whispered for her alone: 'Dazzling and tremendous how quick the sunrise would kill me, if I could not now always send the sunrise out of me.'

Dot didn't know the line, although she knew enough to know that a line it was.

'"The World as I Found It?"' she tried.

'Wrong continent.'

'Whitman, then?'

'Bingo. "Song of Myself."' Smithy straightened up. 'Come on folks, make room for a small one.'

As the gathering parted and Smithy parked Dot close to the window she felt even more of a fraud than usual. She hadn't told any of them about how she had stood up and walked that night last month. What would she say? That from one hour to the next – and in the dead of night, no less – she had felt the urge to stand, the urge to walk, at first with Windsor's Zimmer and then entirely unaided, hunting the shade of her husband through the hallways and rooms of a Green Oaks transformed? They'd peg her as crazier than the Captain!

And perhaps they would be right to. Dot was still struggling to under-stand what had happened that evening. When she had woken the following day, her first thought was that it had all been a dream, but the moment she had shifted in bed, her aching, sullied body informed her otherwise.

A hallucination, then? It was possible, likely even, that this was the solution to the riddle. That in some liminal state of consciousness Dot had staggered from her bed, and pitched and rolled about the hallway and up the stairs, that to any observer she would have looked as confused and lost as any Bedlam inmate.

But there was a third option too, which Dot had repeatedly tried to prevent her mind entertaining, but which kept bobbing to the surface, like a bloated corpse in the slate-black waters of a mountain lake. That this was neither dream, nor hallucination, but real. That the transformation visited upon Green Oaks was not coming from within, but from without. That there was something – some force, she could say no more than that – manipulating elements of the building like the pieces in a sliding block puzzle. That the house had, through some evolutionary hiccough perhaps, become… and she felt deranged for even thinking it… *conscious?*

Dot had never believed in ghosts, but neither was she one of those tawdry little materialists, who limited life by limiting their vocabularies to dull, *reasonable* words. She had long felt the limitations of our meat-and-bone machines, first instinctively, then through bitter experience. But neither could she accept that the whole universe was a soulless, purposeless machine, just grinding away. Who was she to deny this house some form of agency beyond her understanding?

They were all staring at her, awaiting a reaction. She looked out the window. The cloud blockade had been breached. Its seemingly impenetrable ranks had busted and scattered, sculpted in cones, conches, and cornices, daubed in gaudy pinks and purples. Behind this vaporous glypotheca the morning sky was in the full throes of the most glorious blending exercise, transitioning from gold at the horizon to a pearly blue at its zenith.

'It must have happened during the night,' Betty said. 'The sun woke me early. It was such an unfamiliar feeling. I almost forgot where I was for a second.'

'It has been a few weeks coming,' Smithy said. 'I first noticed something while you lot were waiting for Windsor's memorial. Then it was just a shaft of light that made it through, and just for a moment.'

'And you didn't think to tell us this before?' Lanyard said.

'What was there to tell? Shouldn't it be the most natural thing to see the sun breaking through the clouds?'

'It was a sign!' Lanyard almost belched. 'For Windsor.'

Smithy scoffed. Dot felt privately embarrassed. Did her reflections moments earlier mean she was forced to align herself with this kind of lunacy? Her internal jury was determinedly out.

'Yes!' Olive said, rubbing her hands together. 'A sign! Just like…'

'Oh, to you everything's a sign,' Dot snapped. 'It's weather. Nothing more. We've had a grey spell and now that's over.' Was she trying too hard?

'Out of interest, Ol,' – Betty laid a calming hand on Dot's shoulder – 'If the first shaft of light was a sign of Windsor, what would you say this morning is a sign of?'

Olive stepped closer to the window and took hold of the metal bars. She set to examining the sky for an answer or an omen.

'Don't!' Dot said. She knew what was coming. Since the Captain had disappeared, any mention of him was enough to set her on edge. Even though the note he had left stopped her from believing the very worst, she still missed her friend terribly.

'An ending,' Olive said. 'Or a beginning. I don't know. A change, anyway. Movement. That's why I have something to…'

'Things certainly have changed,' Betty said. Olive, despite long accustomed to being interrupted, glared at Betty. 'What with Windsor leaving us, then the Captain.'

'The Captain hasn't…' Dot began, that feeling rising up again. She couldn't blame Betty, or the others for thinking it. Particularly as none of them knew about the note. 'I mean, we don't know if he's…'

'We don't know what's happened to him,' Betty said. 'But either way, he's not here anymore, and we are. We can no longer count on him to resist on our behalves.'

'Exactly,' Olive attempted. 'Which is why…'

'On our behalves?' Smithy said. 'I loved the old fruitcake as much as anyone, but to say he was resisting on our behalves? Come on Bets…'

'Say what you want, but think on this. How many times have you been locked in the rubber room? How many times have you been strapped to your bed? You can go on thinking that this will all stop now he's gone, but I know that things tend to find their own level. The CareFriends never treated us well before, but they left us alone because they were busy with the Captain. Take away the lightning rod and everything is liable to be struck.'

'I suppose he wore a crown of thorns too?' Lanyard sneered. 'I suppose he died so that we might live?'

'He's not...' Dot almost screamed it. 'Stop speaking about him as if he's gone.'

'He is gone, Dot,' Betty said, firmly. 'Whatever happened to him, he is gone. I hate it as much as you do. I miss him as much as you do. But there's no point pretending he's still here. And now Father Patterson is definitively out of the equation, we only have each other.'

'You're wrong, Betty,' Lanyard said, a spiteful scowl puckering his face. 'He didn't shield us from anything. He wasn't a lightning rod. He was the bloody lightning. Any trouble we had was because of him, not in spite of him.'

'We'll see,' Betty said.

'We've already *seen*,' Lanyard spat. 'And as we're speaking frankly, Betty, I'm going to say what we've all been thinking. Without the Captain's idiotic and selfish actions, Windsor would still be with us. Your lightning rod ran my friend right through the heart. You'll never make me believe he didn't.'

'Shut up!' Olive slammed her hand against the windowpane. 'Shut up! Shut up! Shut up!' She waited for the echo of her cries to die away. 'Why do you have to ruin this? All of you? Why isn't a beautiful sunrise enough for you, if only for now? Why does it have to be just another opportunity to squabble about Windsor or the Captain? Why don't you...'

Betty reached out a hand to calm her, but Olive batted it away.

'No, Betty. No! I've spent my whole life being interrupted, being ignored. Nobody has ever taken me seriously. First with my father, then with my husband, then with my daughter and that useless pack of meat she married. And now with you lot. And just as I was standing there, feeling the sun for the first time in goodness knows how long, I had decided... I thought I had decided... to speak up, to show you all something important. Something I found.'

Lanyard sniffed:

'Somewhere in the golden triangle between here, the bathroom and the dayroom?'

'Lanyard!'

'Come on, Betty. What could she have possibly found that nobody else did?'

Olive took one last look at the sky before turning her back to them all.

'I went upstairs,' she said, an icy calm to her voice. 'I went upstairs and I found something. And I was going to show it to you, but I just can't be bothered now. Not because you don't deserve it – although you don't. But because I know it's important, and the way you all are today you'd just squander it anyway.'

They all watched in silence as Olive strode back to her cot and slithered between the sheets. So stunned were they by her outburst that nobody noticed the sun wink behind a cloud again, one that was darker than the others and the shape, almost, of a fox's head.

2

'**D**id you see how quiet he was today?' Tristan said, snapping off his rubber gloves.

'No surprise with all the meds you're feeding him,' Frankie said. 'I'd be surprised if he even knew his name. So, yeah, he was quiet. So what?'

Tristan slumped onto the couch, kicked his feet onto the table.

'Could be,' he said, biting at a hangnail. 'Could be the meds. Could also mean he's planning something. The calm before the storm...'

Frankie snorted.

'Planning something? Right now he couldn't plan to wipe his own arse after taking a shit. Triple dose of Phlegmolax will do that to you.'

'*Hmm*,' Tristan said, unconvinced. Frankie popped open the first few buttons of her smock, exposing her yellowing sports bra, and walked over to the fridge.

'Brewski?'

Tristan had been avoiding substances since packing in the OxyNyx. It had been a difficult few weeks, but his unwillingness to cave in front of Frankie had carried him through. Social embarrassment, he had discovered, can be a powerful motivating force. Still, a beer would be unwise.

'It's only just midday,' he said.

'I didn't ask you the time, pretty boy.'

A can came twisting across the room. Tristan caught it and set it down.

'You know your problem?' Frankie said, dropping into the armchair opposite him. 'You miss the old cunt.'

'Bullshit.'

'Thanks for giving that the thought it deserved. Truth is, you've been bored out of your tiny mind ever since we moved him to C. A whiny little bitch too, if you must know. The Captain was the only grey you considered a worthy opponent.'

'Opponent?' Tristan thumped his feet to the floor, leaned forward on the couch. 'Jesus, Frankie. These people aren't my opponents.'

Frankie peeled open her beer, took a long draught.

'What are they, then?'

'They're... They're my...'

'Fuck, you really are as dumb as Pat looks.'

Tristan stood up and walked over to the hand basin. Turning on the tap, he cupped his hands under it and plunged his face into the cold water. He glared at his newly-glistening features in the mirror.

It wasn't supposed to feel like this. It was over. He had slain the Hydra. He had won – that night three weeks ago he had actually *fucking* won. So why did he feel like such a loser?

Maybe Frankie was onto something. Maybe the fight had just been too satisfying, too much fun, and now he'd just have to live with that feeling of hollowness until his batteries recharged. Or perhaps the dis-orientation, the despair, and the existential loneliness were just part of laying an old obsession to rest.

That day, and for the first time in his life, he had felt as if his gears were meshing with the world's. As if, against all odds, he finally understood. He had experienced all the satisfaction, all the inner-com-pleteness of the denouement. And then... well, then life had gone on. Hollywood never prepared you for that. For the aftermath. Hollywood always ended with the kiss of reunited lovers, with the planet rescued from alien conquest. It never bothered with the tedium of habit-ual love-making or the interminable bureaucracy of a full planetary clean-up.

Whatever Tristan had felt that day, he had expected it to endure. It had not. Like everything else, it had faded. Even the lessons Kalki had taught him were wearing away in the war of attrition that everything pure must engage in with life...

Pure? No. Now that it was over, now that he had vanished and showed no sign of returning, and now that his own mind had been purged of OxyNyx, there were even times when Tristan felt that everything that had gone on upstairs, could seem, if he was honest, somewhat... silly. He understood now why people evangelise. It's less about convincing others than about convincing themselves anew. But how could he talk about it? They'd lock him up!

And as the force of his conviction had faded and he had got clean, something else had forced its way in. Lying in bed at night, all he could see was the Captain's face just before the sack was pulled over his head and they had carried his suddenly limp, suddenly light body back up the hill to Green Oaks. In those few seconds he had snarled, bared his teeth, bitten his lip, barked like a dog, roared... but his eyes had shown none of that fight. They had just sat buried there in his face, shimmering pebbles of despair. Now that Tristan had won, definitively, now the old man was lying in a chemical coma in that room across the hall, much of the animosity had drained out of him. Had he misjudged everything so badly?

'I don't know why you get so uptight,' Frankie said. 'So what if he was your opponent?' She opened her bag, took out a plastic tub and set it down on the coffee table. Reaching in the bag again she pulled out half a sliced loaf.

'What the fuck's that?'

'Lunch,' she said, popping the lid. It was full to the brim with a soupy red liquid, its surface tainted with the ribboning of blood and animal fat. She took two slices of bread, folded them, and dipped them in the liquid, hooking out a stringy lump of meat which she slipped into her mouth.

'Jesus! Are you eating that cold?'

'All the same to me,' she said, smacking her lips as an act of aggression. 'And the subject's not my fucking lunch. So I'll say it again: Big fucking whoop if he was your opponent...'

Tristan dropped back onto the couch.

'Can't you hear how disgusting that sounds?'

'Just because it's disgusting, doesn't mean it ain't true.' She plunged the bread in the sauce again, this time salvaging a soggy hunk of some nameless vegetable and the bone of a small animal that she let tumble back into the tub, before gulping the bread and veg as one. 'And again… what's the big deal? You had some fun with the old cunt. He was a royal pain in the arse. You didn't kill anyone. It's like they say in the movies: you neutralised the threat.'

More bread, more meat.

'It's not a fucking war, Frankie.'

'For him it was. And he was right too, if you ask me. It's *always* a fucking war. With everyone, over everything.'

'Optimistic outlook you've got there.'

The tub emptied of solids she picked it up with both hands and, funnelling one of the corners between her lips, sluiced it down.

'I don't know. Serves me alright. But I ain't got nobody to bail me out like you do. Just a whole load of people waiting to shit on me from a really great fucking height. You can put on the overall because you know that one day soon you're going to step out of it and into something better.'

Tristan twitched. *One day soon…* He wondered, now, if he had been reckless not replying to the acceptance letter Birmingham University had sent him a few days after Kalki's disappearance. Not only the not replying, in fact, but the tearing it up, the burning of it in an ashtray on the floor of the closet. He had seen it as both an offering and a sacrifice, as well as a testament to the strength of his faith. Had. Now it looked kind of like the recklessness of an opioid junkie.

'About that…'

'No. I haven't finished. I ain't got the luxury of leaving. This is my life. If I'm lucky. You get that? If. I'm. Fucking. Lucky. CareFriending's a fucking holiday compared to what I could have ended up doing – even with the cutbacks and double shifts. I learned really young that I'd have to fight. Took me a few more years to learn that I wasn't ever going to win. That people like me just have to fight for the right to keep on fighting. So I figured, might as well enjoy it. Fuck up or get fucked up...'

'Mark Twain?'

'Fuck you, College Boy. You're not as smart as you think, and all that half-hearted learning has just acted like a freaky magnet on your morals, screwing them all over the joint. I don't know what it is you're so fucking terrified of, but unless you do a lot of work on yourself, I'd bet you'll be just as terrified after three years in college. Look, why do you think Pat didn't show the night we shafted the Captain?'

The mention of his former henchman – so mutely loyal in the past – irritated Tristan.

'Because he's a fucking coward.'

Frankie shook her head.

'Would've been much more cowardly if he'd showed.'

'Then enlighten me.'

'Because he thought about it and decided it was a cuntish thing to do and that he wanted no part of it. That's how minds work when they're not smeared with shit like yours is. Dumb man, dumb morals. But they work for him.'

'So why did you show up?'

'Me? Because. I. Don't. Give. A. Fuck. Never pretended otherwise. Surprised you haven't noticed. I thought it would be a giggle. I was right, too. The look on his face was fucking priceless.'

Frankie dumped the emptied tub in her bag.

'Where the fuck is Pat, anyway?'

'Jesus. Chill the fuck out. Look, how about we go have some fun with B. Fuck with them a little. Surprise inspection or something.'

'Not in the mood, Frankie.'

'Come on, it'll cheer you up.'

'You really think that's what I need?'

Frankie finished her beer, crumpled the can and lobbed it in the vague direction of Tristan's head.

'As a matter of fact, yeah, I think that's exactly what you need.' Frankie pulled a plastic sandwich bag from her jeans. Tristan's gut bucked. How he'd missed those gorgeous blue spheres... Frankie threw a fistful of them into her mouth and started chewing.

'What the fuck?' Tristan said. Frankie squinted.

'What? A girl can't eat dessert in peace no more?' she said.

'Dessert? You take OxyNyx for dessert now?'

'Oxy...?' It took a moment for the memory to surface. 'Jesus! You didn't actually believe... These are *Canonballs*, you dumb bitch. Sweeties. Fifty pee a packet. I was fucking with you.'

Tristan was across the coffee table and on top of Frankie before he could stop himself, gripping her neck, burying his thumbs in her windpipe...

'You ripped me off, you cunt! I paid you a hundred and...'

But it wasn't the money. A hundred and fifty quid was nothing, a drop in the ocean, a big weekend on the town... What had made him launch himself at Frankie, murder on his mind, was that she had just lifted the curtain. And showed Tristan he was wanting. For if he couldn't blame the OxyNyx, what could he blame? The sugar crash? He'd be laughed out of court! There were only two paths remaining to him, that he could see. And neither of them were palatable. Either he was genuinely insane, or he was a pathetic, biddable arsehole.

He looked down at Frankie. Her face had turned purple. Though not because he was suffocating her, snuffing her out – he couldn't even get that right! She was purple from laughing too hard. And in her eyes he saw that, again, he had been wrong. There weren't just two paths, but three. Or, not three exactly, but not two either. Because the other option, the one he hadn't considered, and the one Frankie had long ago pegged him as, was not an either-or, but a both...

He released Frankie's neck and closed his eyes.

Insane. Biddable. Arsehole.

A few minutes later Pat pushed open the door.

'The wanderer returns!' Frankie chirruped. 'What kept you, P-Man?'

'Hey Frank,' Pat said. He pulled his smock over his head and turned to Tristan, who was back in his chair now. 'Hey Tristan.'

Anger like that doesn't subside, it needs to be drained.

'Hear something, Frankie?' Tristan said. 'Could swear we've got mice, sometimes. Keep hearing this spineless little squeaking about the place.'

'Jesus, Tristan,' Pat said, towelling the sweat from his pot-belly.

'Yup... yup! There it is. Pathetic, lily-livered, chicken-shit squeaking. Remind me to lay down the poison before I knock off tonight.'

Pat opened his locker, tumbled the dirty smock in and took out a pressed and folded replacement. He pulled it on and turned to face them.

'Guys,' he said, pausing to be sure they were listening. 'I'm done here.'

The fragile patch-up job Tristan had done on himself these last weeks since getting clean... since *thinking* he had got clean, gave way. He floated from the couch and was bearing in on Pat. It was strange, he felt light, empty, the inside of his skull felt raw, scraped clean of thoughts the way flesh is stripped from a coconut shell. Everything was externalised now.

'Think again, Tubby.' They were a couple of metres from each other but their postures were squaring up. 'It's double shifts all round, remember?'

'No,' Pat said, looking away from Tristan and out the window. 'I mean, I'm done, here. With this job. With Green Oaks. I'm telling Cornish at the end of my shift.'

'You?' Tristan spat. He was watching himself, from a corner by the ceiling. Watching himself become a foaming, rasping fool... but unable to stop. 'You're leaving? For what? Who'd take you?'

Pat turned away.

'I've got something lined up.'

Tristan watched himself grab Pat's arm, spin him around.

'Something? What? What the... the fuck can you do? Emptying bins? Humping bricks? Digging graves?'

Pat stared Tristan's empty body down. Then, half-smiling at the sentence he was about to loose:

'I'm going back to school,' he said. 'To be a nurse. Agnes helped me apply.'

The two Tristans thumped back together.

'Ha!' Frankie squealed. 'And there we were thinking you were just trying to get into Agnes' panties. A nurse? When did you decide this?'

'A few months back. The night the Captain smeared himself in his own shit. It really got to me, you know. Right inside my head. Surely there were better ways to spend my energy than chasing down and rugby tackling an unhappy old man.'

'Fuck, Pat,' Frankie said. 'Good for fucking you!'

'Cheers, Frankie.' Pat said.

Tristan turned.

'Good for him? Are you serious? A fucking nurse? I can't wait to see you swishing about in your little fucking pinny.'

Pat stood menhir-still, looking at Tristan.

'Say what you like, I couldn't care less anymore. And besides, what's it to you. You're leaving too.'

'Yeah!' Frankie said, with a cocked grin. 'It's poor orphan Frankie you should be worried about.'

'Of *course* I'm leaving!' Tristan spat. 'And in five years time I'm going to be a fucking psychologist. I'm just worried that it'll be me who has to take care of all the poor fucks unlucky enough to encounter this incompetent bozo on the wards.'

'Enough!' Pat yelled. 'Enough. It's over Tristan. All of your stupid shit, all of the games, all your bullying... all *our* bullying. It's over.'

'Amen,' Frankie said.

'Put all that crazy shit down to overwork, or whatever, and just move on. I've done it... At least, I'm trying to do it. And that goes for whatever you were up to in that closet too. It's all over now.'

How dare he mention Kalki? How dare he? If only he knew... Tristan closed his eyes and took several deep breaths.

'Frankie?' he said. 'Are you still up for that surprise inspection?'

'Hell yeah,' Frankie said, though her voice was empty of its earlier enthusiasm. 'Course I am.'

'Right' – Tristan said, stepping back from Pat, ostentatiously cracking his knuckles – 'let's go then.'

Frankie hopped to her feet and made for the door. Before she left, Tristan watched her as she turned and looked at Pat. Second thoughts? Pat shook his head slowly, mouthed: *No*. With a thin-lipped smile and a shrug, perhaps meant as an apology for the grim inevitability of what was to follow, Frankie left the staff room.

Tristan turned to Pat. At first he thought he wanted to say something, but in the end he just smirked, blew a meaty raspberry, and followed Frankie into the hall.

3

'**Y**ou like that, don't you, you filthy little bitch?'

  '*Gnnrrguh!*'

'Oh yeah? And what about that?'

'*Aarglefupft!*'

'I know, baby, I know.'

'*Furgle…*'

There was no getting around it, Raymond Cornish was a lost soul. Anything – everything! – turned him on. Barely a month had passed since he and the girl had first fucked, but since then his life had changed beyond recognition. It was as if a meteorite had struck and shifted the axis of his world, razing all priorities, all moralities, all idols, and thrusting new ones – darker and more twisted – up through the mutilated lithosphere of his skull to spawn. Cornish was at once both astonished and appalled by the phantasms that flowed out, and by what could cause that old mutt in his pants to lift its head and play at being the frisky young puppy.

That he had thought she was a virgin, that she had turned out not to be; the way her veins webbed across her milky skin; when her blonde hair was tied back and when it hung down to her shoulders in filmy, flypaper tongues; when he caught sight of her from the front and from the back; her cultivated glottal stops, hiding the fact that her family was rather good; the vinegary fetor of her armpits; the tart taste of her arse-hole; her lazy eye; the tincture of toy-perfume on her neck and breasts; when she tickled him with her blunt fingernails; when she nibbled at his eyebrows; the way she worked his scrotum until he almost puked… the most insignificant gesture from his pubescent lover could render Cornish a raging dervish of desire.

And when they were apart, he still traced his route through the world by tuning into the arcane throb of the ley-lines of lechery. A sniffer hound, he latched onto the spoor of sex that ribboned through the air all about him in an endless and monstrous tangle, a pheromonal Spaghetti Junction writ billionfold. And just like the sniffer, when he did trap the scent he was now genetically incapable of relinquishing it. In a certain way he felt blessed, as though given access to a previously hidden, parallel world. In another more vital way, though, he was exhausted, frayed about the edges, a lone commando several weeks into a do-or-die mission – jaded to the extreme, but fully aware that retreat, even repose, would not be possible. Single-minded, dogged advance was the only option he had… and the hell with the rug burns that bloodied the shaft of his penis.

So even when they weren't barricaded in his office together – when she was off doing homework or playing video games or whatever it was she filled the rest of her time with (he didn't ask… he didn't care!) – Cornish's spastic libido gave him no rest. It may have been Nurse Agnes' looping signature that touched him off, or the way flesh muffined from the pumps of the fat lady that boarded the bus at his stop every morning: a spark is a spark, and one was as good as any other. He had even started fucking Harriet again, sometimes twice a night – something that hadn't happened for years.

But what was most electrifying was that nobody, not even Harriet – languorous and shagged-out atop her new, plushly downed mare's nest – suspected him of anything. Was it this way, then, with every deviant of more than a little brain. Was it only the clumsy ones that got rooted out, tarred, feathered, and splashed across the front pages of the tabloids?

The girl brought down her hand and paddled his face one more time.

'*Hchwoor,*' he yowled through the ball-gag.

She smiled.

'You really are King of the Crazies, aren't you darling?'

I really, *really* am, he thought. And proud of it too. Time was when the thought would have upset him that people could regard him with contempt or sadness, when their jokes about the mad harlequin king, trapped in his castle on the hill would have felt... well... unkind. Ha! Time was.

'*Ahyammaqueem,*' he attempted.

'What did you say?' She loosed the leather strap at the nape of his neck and he worked the rubber ball through his teeth before spitting it out.

'And you're my queen.' She shook her head and laughed.

'You say such silly things, Raymond.' She picked up the cigarettes from the desk, pulled out the last two, crumpled the packet and dropped it to the floor. She plugged one in his mouth, lit it for him, then walked across to the window and, leaning against the frame, lit her own.

She had arrived after lunch in a trench coat instead of her usual tracksuit top, and carrying a brown suede travelling bag Cornish hadn't seen before. The trench she had filched from her mother's wardrobe, he was certain. The shoulders were too broad for her frame, and the skirt reached down to her ankles. It gave her the air of an orphan or refugee, and gave Cornish, in turn, a blistering hard-on.

He had taken the bag from her and, surprised by its, weight, hefted it onto the desk. Something inside had jangled. Before Cornish could enquire after its contents – smitten suddenly with the fear that she might have packed up her things and come to him 'for good' – she had whip-cracked open the belt of the coat letting it slide from her shoulders onto the floor.

Cornish had gawked. Then he had gaped. What had he done to deserve such a bounty? Beneath the trench Lisa was dressed – if that verb could be applied to such flimsy accoutrements – in a bastard hybrid of lingerie and bondage wear: black silk panties and a lacy bodice, knotted to a pair of thigh-high black boots that drooped from her pencil legs like fisherman's waders. These too, there was little doubt, she had pilfered from her mother's closet and Cornish felt his mind wander, conjuring up sordid images of the mysterious Mrs Biss, the founder of his recent bout of feasting. He visualised a middle-aged woman, in many ways much like her daughter, but with a fuller, doughier body, shimmering with cellulite, wearing the effects of years of tugging gravity like a stained glass window in a medieval church – that's to say by an almost imperceptible thickening at the base. It wasn't the prettiest of apparitions, but it had tickled a nerve in Cornish and he began imagining ways in which he might arrange to meet and seduce this cocotte.

How queer it was that the very things that repulsed him about his own wife – the pale dimpled skin, the chicken drumstick legs and buttocks, the drooping saddlebags of flesh, the tigerish stretch marks – were just the things that thrilled him when he pictured Mrs Biss. But he had grown too accustomed to his own perversions these last weeks to be surprised by his contradiction.

The bag, it had turned out, contained a dungeon-load of sexual gizmos – further plunder from the Biss bedchamber. They must, Cornish reasoned, constitute Mrs Biss's arsenal in the quest to capture a replacement for Mr Biss, absent for more than a year now, so the girl said. (Indeed, that first time he had visited her at home, the fugitive *pater familias* had been almost all she wanted to talk about – how he had stolen off in the night without saying goodbye; how her mother had hired a private-I to track him down; how he had finally been located, barely ten miles away, living in a council flat with a woman not much older than her. It had taken the greatest of Cornish's efforts not to lose momentum in the face of this tedious kitchen-sink slapstick…)

In addition to the ball-gag there were several cats-o'-nine-tails, of varying size, some thick leather belts, a studded paddle about the size of a child's cricket bat, four dildos of varying form and calibre, and a twelve-foot length of heavy iron chain. Cornish would never before have confessed a penchant for the kind of sex-play these instruments implied, would never, in fact, have believed it possible that he might permit himself to be trussed up and clobbered. It was humiliating – and what possible fun could there be in humiliation? But as Lisa had unpacked the bag, arranging the demeaning devices one by one on his desk, with all the calm, torturous intent of a Stasi officer – though also, Cornish had noticed, with a tremble of shock, suggesting that she too had not been aware of the full extent of the bag's payload – he understood that the impending plunder of his dignity had perhaps been all he had ever wanted.

Why else had he spent so much of his life rowing against his inclinations? His renunciation of poetry, his loveless marriage, his tedious, hateful job, even the desperate sally that had lured this girl to his lair: every choice he had made in his adult life could be read – in the icy light of self knowledge – as just another crack at achieving the total degradation of his being. He was quite sure he would never again stoop as low as he had during the few hours he'd spent disposing of the Indian. This was a strange, and strangely comforting realisation. Now the topsoil of his life had been stripped away, now he had hit rock bottom and walked barefoot on its bed, now he had felt its cold throb underfoot… Well, wasn't rock bottom just a little bit overrated? So much of life was spent avoiding degeneracy, despising it, fearing it… and therein lay its strength. Most people would get themselves killed if it meant avoiding rock bottom. In the end, though, like most bogeymen, it could only be overcome by getting to know it. Getting to know it stripped it of its power. The only question he had left was: *Where can I possibly go from here?*

His mind afire now, his thoughts were dragged back once again to Whitby and to Bram Stoker's masterpiece. Several years after that holiday Cornish had again tried to read Dracula, and this time had made short work of the book, finishing it in only two days. As Van Helsing's net had closed around the Count, the adolescent Cornish found himself increasingly sympathetic towards the harried vampire, and increasingly sickened by the actions of his eventual slayers. Their goodness, their self-righteousness, revolted him, and while he had never dared hope for any outcome other than what the narrative rulebook dictated, when the denouement eventually came, when Dracula's throat was sheared and his heart run through with a Bowie knife, and when he metamorphosed into a pillar of dust, a great wave of sentiment had risen up within Cornish, and he had wept. Not because the Count would no longer be able to terrorise the world – *au contraire!* He had wept because the world would no longer be able to terrorise the Count. His main crime, as Cornish saw it, was to have been a beast who had acted in accordance with his nature. A nature the capricious world he found himself in rejected. Another place, another time, maybe… who could tell to what heights he could have risen?

Earlier, as Lisa had lifted the chain from the desk and started encircling Cornish in its embrace, under his arms, over his shoulders and between his legs, binding him to his chair and securing him in place with the very same cable-ties he had used to fasten the bags of Indian, it was just that pillar of dust – at the brief moment it hung, evanescent in the air, waiting for gravity to get to work – that Cornish realised he had been shooting for, unconsciously, all these years. Even the game of dress-up he had played with the Indian's intestine had been little more than a means to this end…

Now, after more than an hour of rapturous abuse at the hands of his lover, with her play-smoking at the window, her tawdry costume ruffled and rent by her own exertions, spying on her friends at the bus stop – he imagined, despite the dark night, goaded on by a love of meretricious narrative symmetry – just as he had spied on her that four-month-lifetime ago. Now, the moment had come for her to finish him off, to draw a line between the world and Raymond Cornish, to make of him a pillar of ash, from which someone else – whom, he knew not – would arise, Phoenix-like, and start living the life for which he had been made…

In the garden, an owl hooted. Seconds later, a chorus of other hoots replied.

The cigarette, he noticed, was in desperate need of attention.

'*Gnnrgh!*' he groaned. The girl turned.

'What is it, lover?' the awkward affectation of that last word sent a further rush of blood to his heavily-engorged member. His hands useless behind his back, he shifted his hips, trying to use the unruly organ as a pointer to indicate his distress.

Instead of coming to his aid, Lisa picked up her mobile telephone from the desk and pressed one of its buttons, awakening the demon within. Then, smiling as she did so, she pressed another button, but instead of holding it to her ear, peered at Cornish, a smile of delicious anticipation pinching her mouth.

Such was the extent of new and strange discomforts visited upon his person in the past hour, Cornish had momentarily forgotten that the ponderous pebble in his anus was, in fact, the lumpy plastic phone. The tickle as it detected her call, and then the full-scale, enthusiastic vibration, not to mention its murderous rendition of Greensleeves, provided him a three-pronged reminder.

But why now?

The answer was at the end of his nose. The tube of ash, still coalishly hot, trembled as his body reacted to the gizmo vibrating against his prostate. He counted the rings. Three so far... the call would go to answerphone after eight.

She was grinning now as she watched him engage in stony combat with gravity. Four rings, five... The cigarette was shedding tiny flakes of ash but, for the moment, its body was holding. Lisa leaned in close and his penis, independent, batted for her.

Six, seven... He was in control now. He was going to beat it.

Eight!

The vibration cut off. Relieved, transcendent, and worked up into a sexual fury the like of which he had never known, Cornish shuddered, the ash dropped, and the thrill of the burn, its pinpricks on the fluffy globe of his belly, kicked off the preliminary contractions of climax. Noticing this, Lisa pulled a cable tie from her boot and – with an obscene deftness – fastened it around the base of his cock.

'We're not done yet,' she said, as his contractions receded, leaving a profound queasiness behind.

Since the very start, Cornish had never asked her for anything outright, and yet at every step she had perfectly intuited what he needed. Now that the acme of their affair was near – and now she had made a living, if ersatz, Priapus of him – he had no doubt that she would once again know how to pilot him through the moments leading up to his exalted release. She was the archer now, and he the arrow, and in becoming one with the other they would presently find their target.

Her gaze was drifting from the desk to Cornish and back from him to the desk as she selected the instrument with which she would orchestrate his escape. For a moment, her hand hovered over the largest of the dildos – a rupturingly broad, double-headed, crescent-moon, royal-blue atrocity, with its own battery pack and power lead – before settling, to Cornish's regret, on one of the leather belts. She picked it up, doubled it over and slapped it against her boots.

'Ready?' she asked.

'Ready,' he said.

As she strode towards him, Cornish saw, or imagined he saw, an odd expression fleet across her face. It was difficult for him to pin down exactly what that expression meant –there were strands of self-doubt woven into it, and of an effort being made, of a desire, perhaps even more, of a *need* for attention, for approval, for reassurance. And for love…

Leaning over him, so that his cock twitched like a fish on a line, attempting with all its might to butt against her, Lisa looped the belt behind the headrest of his chair and fastened it so that the buckle pressed down firmly against his Adam's apple. Taking a few steps back, she propped herself against the desk and admired her handiwork.

'Fucking hell, Raymond,' she said. 'You really are a sight.'

Her words caught him off guard. He had spent so much energy ingesting every detail of her that he hadn't paused for a moment to consider that she too had been observing him. Indeed, that he was a presence to be observed at all was almost too odd for him to countenance. In some way, these last weeks, he had been living almost as if disembodied, some kind of spectre of sex, as though, should he choose, he might pass through walls, into locked rooms, and latch, leech-like, onto the back of one or other of a rutting couple, and feed off them unnoticed. Almost – the thought swept over him, leaving in its wake the potent emotional cocktail of one part joy, two parts nauseating dread – like the Count himself.

Forced to consider it now, he supposed a 'sight' was just what he was. First there was his gut – spheroid, scored and furry – the gravitational centre of his being from which everything else – his rickety legs, his unimpressive torso – jutted. Mountain flotsam from a giant cartoon snowball. Then there was his ashen skin, less visible now than before, but still prominent about his eyes, elbows and the backs of his knees. And then his thinning, though still rebellious hair, his archipelagic eczema, and his slumping jowls. And finally, of course, there was his uncircumcised member, plug-ugly as a mollusc from the off, and already mangled from years of maltreatment, now newly punch-drunk. It made him think of a circus boxer who, through misplaced hubris, had resurrected his career for one last fight, and lost. Add to all of this the tightly wound chains, the leather choker and the cable ties, and Lisa's choice of words seemed at worst diplomatic and at best positively adoring.

'Pull it tighter,' he said, indicating the belt with his chin. She squinted.

'Are you sure?'

'Pull it tighter,' he said again.

The first wrench of the belt launched a shower of stars across Cornish's vision, which receded again as the prong eased itself into its hole. His windpipe pinched, restricting, though not obstructing the flow of air to his lungs, Cornish felt hyper sensitised, as if nerves all across his body were awakening from a period of extended hibernation. Despite a mild giddiness he tingled from head to foot and most intensely about his genitals, which were quivering as if on the verge of a once-in-a-life-time blossoming.

Cornish remained both very much there, chained to his chair, with Lisa… and at once blissfully absent. The burgeoning hypoxia had loosened the bounds between his mind and body, so that before he knew what was happening…

… he was hovering over Green Oaks. There was the lichen-pranked roof-tiling, there the bird's nest in the chimney pot, there the length of half-fallen guttering. Green Oaks or the model? He couldn't tell anymore. Such detail…

From this new vantage point, he felt a sudden, and peculiar, stirring of affection for the place. There had been much to despise about his lot, but at least he'd been autonomous, the manager of his own distant trading post, three weeks down the river... Raymond Kurtz of Green Oaks! And now he had found Lisa again, all those years after she rejected him at the disco, finally – finally! – the king would have his queen and everyone in the kingdom would rejoice!

But what about his subjects, the Greys? He knew – as he had probably always known – that there was something very wrong about people living out their final days like this. Yet, from this new outpost, bodiless and behind the veil, with a backstage view of life's tragicomedy, the ethical realm seemed very distant, very low. Unable to pity and unable to judge. Those capacities had been stripped from him like harlequin's rags.

And that, Cornish realised, was why it had to end now. Why he had to end now. Why it was time for him to clock out on life. Nobody should be able to see what he had seen, to do what he had done, to think what he had thought... and then live. The universe, putting up its front of thuggish indifference, might be able to tolerate it... But he, Raymond Cornish, the human being – at least what was left of him – would not. He had to rebel. Give two fingers to the cosmos. For if he came back from this, was allowed to breathe, allowed to live, he would unleash a monster from within. Nobody would be able to stop him. He wouldn't even be able to stop himself. He would do such things, what they were he knew not, but they would be... etcetera, etcetera!

When had he taken the fork in the road that made this turn of events inevitable? Perhaps it was only recently, or perhaps it had been many years earlier. Why, he wondered, hadn't anybody warned him? And yet – for what might have been the first time in his life – Raymond Cornish had no complaints.

All endings were arbitrary, in the scheme of things.

His only fear now was that it might not be an ending at all. That he might be stranded in this hazy in-between world, this limbo for... well... ever. A harrowing thought. Not eternity itself. Not the part that would see Green Oaks crumble, dancing away as dust in the wind – that, he imagined, he would rather enjoy. Nor the cold, dead, tundra – nuclear, probably – the dribbling past of empty millennia as the planet began its slow spiral into an expanding sun. Nor sitting out the rest of time until entropy was achieved and the universe exploded or collapsed itself out of existence. No, those parts didn't bother him at all. It was just the first, however many – five, ten, perhaps twenty? – years. When he'd be forced to watch Green Oaks plodding blindly on, the same awful carousel, throwing some people off, accepting new people on, but never really changing, regardless of who replaced him. The rise and fall of the horses determined not by their own legs, but by the poles they were skewered on. That he just couldn't bear to watch.

'Come on, Raymond. That's it, baby…'

Although he also knew he wouldn't have to. Irony may be the universe's stock-in-trade, but even that had its limits. And besides, irony, like tragedy, demands an ending, otherwise it loses all meaning. And what could be worse than meaninglessness?

'My crazy king…'

'Do it, for me. Let it go…'

A strange sound and a queer sensation, centred around his crotch, reeled his spirit back to where the action was, scattering the hallucination like particles in a rain cloud. His body must have squirmed itself back to life.

Lisa, primordially attuned to Cornish's basest desires, had reached behind her and picked up a handful of Green Oaks notepaper, and was kneading it into him. Maybe her ambition was purely sensual – hoping the sharpness of the balled-up paper against his naked flesh would elevate him to plains previously unvisited. But he knew, even if she didn't, that there was far more to it than that. For what had made this whole adventure at once so depraved – and so delicious! – was not just that he had lured Lisa to his office and permitted her to debase him, but also that it was being carried out at the specific expense, the reckless neglect of a whole house of dotards. The absolute dereliction of duties he had never asked for and had always resented, but had passively fulfilled for the past twenty years – in deference to his own, abominable pursuit of rapture.

'*Hooooooo! Hoo! Hoo!*' Cornish howled.

There it was… the monster! Waking from its slumber the instant he caught his breath. Cornish couldn't allow it to live. He had to take them both down. Leaning forward, he jammed his windpipe against the belt. With a sudden snap, his oxygen intake again abandoned its resistance. The gates to the abysses of his unconscious flew open and the outflow of the long imprisoned creatures of the deep now began in earnest.

One by one, the twisted fragments of his psyche populated his office. Those he knew – friends of his parents, whose names he had forgotten, his primary school teacher whose petticoat hem he had been punished for noticing, the first girl he had loved and also the first who had rejected him – appeared as mutilated grotesque chimeras, that mingled freely, the separating lines between them fluid, amalgamating one with the other, then dividing again. There were others, far too deformed for him to attach any memory to, creatures unsuited to all but the darkest of fantasies; hundred-pawed phalli, vertical flesh wounds carved into the air, out of which shiny cockroach armies marched…

'Lisa,' he said.

The girl lifted her head, a strange look in her eyes.

'My name's Caroline.'

Caroline? Who then was…?

'Pull it tighter,' he said.

She obliged. He had tunnel vision now. Furry, black tunnel vision, pulsing with a diabolical geometry. His gaze centred on the model of the house which, as he fixed it, began to unfold wall by wall, shedding its paint, until it was a single white sheet, with Cornish rotating at its centre. His mouth hung open. The contractions of orgasm began again. Lazy, slow, rolling… this was going to be a long one. Now even the collapsed model disappeared. Everything started churning, spinning, being sucked into the very centre of his vision, crushed to… nothing.

'Tighter,' he gasped.

'Are you sure?' her voice was so distant now.

'Tighter,' he repeated.

She tugged again on the belt.

RUGGLES TO THE RESCUE!

A WARTIME FACT STORY

'Let's have the map, old boy.'

  'The map, Sir?'

  'Of the camp, L.C.'

  'Sir?'

  'You didn't bring the map?'

  'Um. No, Sir.'

  'And the intelligence reports?'

  '…'

  'And the orders from HQ?'

  '…'

Captain Ruggles, until then spread-eagled on the damp grass, rolled onto his left flank, propped his head on his hands, and glared at Lance Corporal Knot. The Lance Corporal, his pudgy, currant-bun face camouflaged with fingered streaks of mud, shook his head and looked away from the Captain, dejected. Ruggles laid a reassuring hand on his second's shoulder.

  'Not to worry, old chap. I took the initiative of memorising everything before we set off. At least now, should we be taken in by Jerry, you've saved us the job of having to devour the evidence. Good work, L.C. Microfiche tastes so bloody bitter.' Knot smiled shyly.

  'Thank you, Sir.'

  'Although I'm relieved, I must confess,' Ruggles said, 'that I didn't charge you with remembering our secret weapon.'

Since the night he was ambushed and transferred to Zellenblock C, Captain Ruggles had been scouting out a substitute for the valiant Private whose ankle had splintered during their escape attempt. It hadn't been easy. Not only was the Private a rare breed but his new cellmates were in a much worse state than Ruggles had imagined possible. Before leaving England he had read the usual intelligence reports concerning the Nazis' forays into human vivisection, but these had grotesquely, almost wantonly he felt, underestimated the extent of the enemy's villainy. Most of the detainees in Zellenblock C, through the use of chemicals and the implementation of ghastly surgical procedures, were maintained in a state somewhere on the threshold between life and death, only dimly aware, if aware at all, of where they were or what was happening to them.

The guards had tried to inflict the same fate upon Ruggles, but he had been ready for them. They may have force-fed him pills and capsules, held his nose until he swallowed, and digitally inspected his mouth to ensure nothing was secreted in his cheeks or under his tongue, but they had not reckoned upon the sheer sedulousness with which Ruggles had trained his body in general, and his intestinal tract in particular. Drawing inspiration from the animal kingdom, Ruggles had long ago mastered the regurgitative techniques of both ruminants such as the dairy cow and practitioners of trophallaxis, such as *Canis lupus*, the grey wolf. This had permitted him to bring all the vile medicine up from his stomach before it could have too much of an effect upon him, and to keep a clear head as he hunted for his second.

It was early on that Ruggles identified Lance Corporal Knot as the block's only possible candidate for the role. Aside from the Captain, he was the least incapacitated, and the only one with whom Ruggles had succeeded in engaging in anything resembling a conversation. Knot's physical condition had remained a concern for him, however. During his time in the camp the guards had fattened him up so that, as he sat on his cot, rubbing his thumbs together in the compulsive way that seemed to be his wont, he reminded Ruggles of a marmot he had once observed while on an undercover mission in the Alps. Just like the marmot, which had rocked with indifference on its fat haunches, working its teeth around a nut or a grub as the soldiers constructed their camp nearby, Knot spent most of his time sitting up in bed, manipulating his thumbs, lost in the warrens of his mind. It also appeared that some procedure had been carried out on his legs, so that when he did walk it was with difficulty, and only with the aid of two curling bamboo canes that flexed impossibly in turn as he shifted his advancing bulk from one foot to the next. Knot also had significant trouble recollecting his past, and Ruggles had been obliged to fill him in with the details of the war in general and the camp in particular, details the Lance Corporal had resisted at first, but after significant persuasion had, grudgingly, accepted. Still, he was the fittest contender for the role and had responded well to the kindness and camaraderie the Captain had shown him. Though Ruggles maintained his reservations, and had vowed only to deploy Knot if circumstances absolutely demanded it.

After two weeks, circumstances had issued their clamorous demand.

'Let's go over the plan once more. Just to check we're singing from the same score,' Ruggles whispered into Knot's ear.

'Right you are, Sir.'

'Some days ago, I received intelligence, through channels I cannot reveal, that a particular soldier of the British Empire – one Warrant Officer Karmacharya – was being held in isolation somewhere in the camp.'

'Karma… charya,' Knot repeated, uprooting a tuft of grass. The name was distantly familiar to him. 'A Hindoo, Sir?'

'Quite right, L.C. But also quite irrelevant. I trained alongside Karmacharya in the Kush. You couldn't hope for a more loyal and ferocious soldier to back you up than him. Try to stay focussed.'

The Lance Corporal nodded.

'Now, according to the reports I received, Karmacharya is proving of particular interest to the Nazis. When he was captured, he was already severely injured – seventy per cent burns and delirious, so the intelligence has it. By all estimations, whether he had been captured, rescued or killed on the battlefield, the war was all but over for Karmacharya. At first they installed him in Zellenblock B. Is this causing any bells to chime within that cavernous cranium of yours, Knot?'

'Distant bells, perhaps, Captain,' said Knot. 'Although I'd be lying if I said I could name their tune.'

Ruggles kneaded the doleful Lance Corporal's back with his knuckles.

'Not to worry, L.C. Never have I come across an imagined weakness in a man that hasn't later proven itself to be a strength. As I was saying, the Nazis saw in Karmacharya the perfect lab rat – a passive and incognisant vessel for the most dehumanising, the most brutal, of their experiments. What they did to you and the other internees would look like a Sunday School picnic compared to what they were to do to dear old Karmacharya. We do not have all of the details, of course, but intelligence suggests he had been subjected to freezing temperatures, blasts of mustard gas, surgery without anaesthetic, and forced to subsist for periods on sea water alone.'

'Oh! The humani—' Knot yelped, before Ruggles could thrust the loose clod of earth he had been fingering deep inside the Lance Corporal's mouth.

'For heaven's sake, L.C. Don't forget where you are. Though I agree that it's horrific enough to make any man want to howl with rage, we cannot currently permit ourselves such an indulgence. Later, when this mission is over, I swear to you, we'll strip to our waists and roar a chorus at the moon, but for now we must retain our composure. Do you understand?'

'Perfectly, Sir,' Knot lisped, hawking the remains of the clod into the undergrowth. 'My apologies.'

'Think nothing of it, soldier,' Ruggles said. 'You're an affective fellow and, truth be told, that's why I like you. Just try to muffle your trumpet a little next time.'

'Count on it, Sir,' Knot said.

'Now, if they had stopped there with Karmacharya, he may have been just another unfortunate casualty of the criminal Reich. However, your Nazi is an avaricious beast, L.C., his hunger for brutality rarely satiated. After they had pushed Karmacharya's body to the brink of expiration, they saw one territory as yet unconquered.' Ruggles planted his index finger in the thick crease bisecting Knot's well-upholstered brow. 'The *mind* of the unfortunate Warrant Officer.'

Anticipating the barbarity he was soon to be made privy to, Knot clenched his fist and sandwiched it between his rickety dentures.

'Go on,' he mumbled through the knobbly gag.

'Our boys in intelligence have long heard murmurings of attempts by the Nazis to develop medicines that might be used to augment the performance of their soldiers on the battlefield. You surely read in dispatches of the occasion when the mighty Dirk Shavings...'

'Dirk who, Sir?' At this, Captain Ruggles lost all mastery of his facial muscles so that his jaw dangled helplessly; a porch lantern in a hurricane.

'Dirk Who, Lance Corporal? Can it really be that the exploits of our American brethren's foremost defender of liberty and scientific verity has so utterly passed you by?'

'Do you mean Superman?' Knot said, helpfully he hoped.

'If, Lance Corporal,' Ruggles said, struggling to maintain the measured cantor of speech that was appropriate to a soldier of his rank. 'That is, if and when we make it back to Blighty, I will issue the unprecedented order of enforcing upon you a whole week's leave simply for you to familiarise yourself with the example set by Dirk Shavings Jr. It beggars credulity that our Field Marshals would see fit to send a man to the front line without first acquainting him with such an undiluted paradigm of soldierly virtue. But these are, I suppose, desperate times. For now, Lance Corporal, and for the integrity of this mission, try to forget our digression down this blind alley.'

'No sooner said than done, Sir.'

'Attaboy! What did I say about a man's weaknesses becoming his strengths?'

'Don't ask me, Captain,' grinned a complicit Knot. Ruggles clapped his hand on Knot's shoulder.

'As you are aware, L.C. The clean living Tommy needs little more than a snort of Scotch and a generous pinch of rough shag to stiffen his sinews for battle, so British research in the area of chemical enhancement was considered futile. Jerry, however – craven and limp-wristed to a man – has rather stolen the march on this one. Their research has centred upon extracts from two plants, the southern European Jimson Weed and the Central American Peyote cactus. We know little, thus far, of their results, except that they have been rather unexpected, particularly so in the case of Warrant Officer Karmacharya. It has come to our attention that… Lance Corporal? May I ask…?'

While holding forth, Ruggles had kept his gaze locked on the central Zellenblock, some fifty yards across the lawn and the target for this expedition. So engrossed had he been in counting the seconds that elapsed between each sweep of the watchman's binoculars, he had failed to notice the Lance Corporal hoist himself into a cross-legged posture and pop open the lid of the honey bucket that he had gone to some dangerous lengths acquiring. At the moment he turned to face Knot, the Lance Corporal plunged the four fingers of his left hand into the bucket and was hurriedly attempting to manoeuvre a pat of the viscid golden gum into his mouth. Feeling the Captain's eyes on him, he froze.

'May I ask,' the Captain repeated. 'Exactly what you think you're doing?' Still petrified, the honey percolating between his fingers and lazing back into the bucket, Lance Corporal Knot said nothing, but his lower lip began darting about in every direction, apparently in the hope that it might pluck an explicatory word or two from the ether. Ruggles took hold of Knot's wrist and stropped his fingers against the sharp edge of the honey bucket, before holding them up to his face.

'Lick,' he commanded. The Lance Corporal obeyed with vigour, working his tongue over the crannies and carbuncles of his hand. Ruggles released his wrist, picked up the lid and snapped it back into position, but it refused to bite, smirking open at the opposite side to wherever Ruggles pressed.

'Broken,' he said sharply. 'In your haste to satisfy your deviant appetite, Lance Corporal, you have enacted full bloody mischief on the lid of this bucket.'

'Perhaps if you were to...' said the panicked Knot, rocking forward onto his knees and reaching for the lid. '... just to turn it a wee bit here and...' He worked the thin lid about in jerks. Ruggles watched him in silence. '... just find the position when it holds and... press a little here and...' He flipped the lid onto the grass and slumped back onto his haunches. 'Broken,' he concurred at length.

'And already infested,' said Ruggles, using the lid to swipe an advancing queue of ants from the bucket's edge. 'We can't leave something as delectable as honey open even for a minute on terrain like this, Lance Corporal. Gaia is a duplicitous mistress; offering a boon with one hand while whipping it away with the other. Now that the lid won't hold on its own account, one of us – specifically you, Lance Corporal – shall have to make sure it stays closed. I beg you to take a seat.' Ruggles tapped the repositioned lid and Knot, fearing further chastisement should he refuse, nestled on top of it.

'What role – if you don't mind me asking, Captain – does the honey have in all...' Knot waved his hand vaguely, '... all this?' Ruggles permitted himself an uncaptainly groan.

'I see that, once again, you have forgotten a crucial element of our mission. So let me, once again, reiterate. Lance Corporal, honey... I mean, rather, honey, Lance Corporal, is one of the most versatile of foodstuffs. For a soldier it serves a minimum of four functions – it is, if you wish, the *couteau Suisse* of comestibles. The first, of course, and the function you were so eagerly demonstrating just then, is sustenance. My only complaint is that you set about sustaining yourself a little too early on in the mission. The second and third functions employ the extraordinary adhesive powers of this aliment. Heaven forfend we have any walls to scale tonight, but if we do, a good frontal coating of honey, with extra lashings applied to cheeks, hands, feet and knees, and the assent becomes markedly easier, just as Dirk Shavings proved in the... But of course, forget it! The third function is as a sealant. When we reach Karmacharya, we will need several minutes to interrogate him. If we have to bust open the door, crippling the lock, a good coating of honey about the doorframe, gluing it shut, as well as a generous sluice in the corridor, could buy us the extra minute or two we need to extract the crucial information. So, you see...'

'And the fourth,' cried Knot, forgetting the Captain's entreaty for quiet in his joy at being able to demonstrate that this time he had been paying attention. 'You said there were four uses and you have outlined only three.' Ruggles nodded, satisfied with this irregular display of discipline on the part of the Lance Corporal.

'Ah, yes! The fourth,' nodding still. 'The fourth function is the most important of all. Use X.' The Captain crossed his index fingers an inch in front of Knot's nose, by way of elucidation.

'X,' Knot read aloud from the Captain's hands. 'Wha...'

'Use X. The unknown function. The unexpected function. The fortuitous function. The serendipitous function. It's the use that could mean the difference between success and failure, the use that could save your life.'

'But more specifically, Captain?'

'Impossible to be more specific, L.C. That's the secret of Use X. It is the offspring of the once-in-a-blue-moon coupling of Kairos and Tyche. No one knows what it resembles until it arrives, and then it shimmers before you with its sheer bloody obviousness.'

Ruggles straightened his tin helmet, which in the excitement had slipped down one side of his head and was threatening to fall. To secure it against further slippage, he took hold of two tufts of hair sprouting through the bullet holes, and tied them into a double bow. Knot made one final tour of his hands with the tip of his tongue.

'But none of that explains why Karmachawawa is of *particular* interest to us, Sir.'

'I was coming to that before your insolence forced me off track, Lance Corporal. Now if you'll permit me?' Knot drew an invisible zipper across his lips with his finger, gritty and still glistening, catching it with a flick of his tongue on the off-chance there was any honey remaining.

'Much obliged, soldier. Quite simply,' Ruggles said, his own voice cracking with emotion now, 'a long time ago Karmacharya saved my life. I owe everything to that dear Hindoo officer. I must tell you the story, one of these days.'

'Roger that,' Knot sniffed.

'Now. As you can see, we have a good fifty yards of open terrain to cross between here and the Zellenblock.' Ruggles traced a line in the grass with his finger. 'Our objective is to get ourselves, the bucket of honey and the length of rope to the west entrance of the Zellenblock without being seen.' Upon *west entrance* Ruggles prodded the end of the line of flattened grass. 'Easy, you might think? Not so. We face two principle obstacles. The first is the security light. It's triggered by motion sensors and its range reaches from the Zellenblock to approximately that smock mill there. One person can pass beneath it unnoticed, but if two or more people are caught within its net then the whole terrain will light up as if someone has pulled a flare. To be sure, even before we reach that smock mill, progression will be made one soldier at a time.'

'Which smock mill?' Knot said, lifting his spectacles from his nose and buffing them on his shirtfront before repositioning them in front of his scrunched up eyes.

'Who… Wha…' essayed the Captain, rendered dumb with incredulity. 'Why Lance Corporal,' he said, finally reining in his tongue, 'what else would you call that towering black edifice, that shears our view of the block?' The remainder of Knot's face was drawn into the scrunch as he tried with all of his might to make out the mill that his Captain was indicating. To little avail.

'Why, unless I'm much mistaken, Sir, I'd say that was a rather fine example of the sessile oak. Is the smock mill you speak of perhaps located *behind* the tree?' Despairing, Ruggles brought both of his hands to his helmet and began fingering a drum solo upon it.

'Okay, Lance Corporal,' he said after a while. 'It is of little importance whether you recognise the mill as a mill or whether, for whatever reason I cannot fathom, your embattled brain prefers to see it as an oak tree. What matters, in the end, is that you can see it at all.'

'I see it, Sir, although I must confess, however hard I try to see it as a smock mill, it remains an oak to me.'

Ruggles looked away from Knot.

'Damn those Nazi wizards!' he muttered between clenched teeth, into the darkness. 'Damn them for making yet another buffoon of a fine British soldier.' Turning back to Knot: 'As I was saying, L.C., it is important only that you see it, because it marks the range of the security lights. It also provides us with valuable cover from the second obstacle; the regard of the night watchman. Every minute throughout the night, the watchman comes to the central of the first storey windows and scans the grounds with a pair of binoculars. Can you make out the window I'm talking about?' Knot had given up trying to see what the Captain was indicating. He felt himself in safe hands and had decided that was enough for him to give his assent.

'I do, Sir.'

'And do you see... wait for it... there! The glint of the moonlight on the lenses of the binoculars?'

'Very clearly, Sir. Impossible to miss that.'

'Bravo, soldier. Bravo!' said Ruggles, greatly cheered. 'Now, in two minutes time, just after his next passage, we wait five seconds to make sure the watchman has moved on, then we have precisely fifty five seconds to gather up the rope and the honey and make it to the shelter of the smock mill. As it is the most unwieldy of the two, I will take the rope. Do you think you can manage the bucket of honey?'

'I... It's...' said Knot, a burp of emotion stymieing the exit of his sentence.

'What is it this time?' Ruggles asked, a curt edge to his voice. Knot picked up one of his walking canes and swiped the air with it.

'My sticks. I can't get anywhere without my sticks. But with my sticks, I can't carry a thing.' Ruggles brought his right hand to his forehead then dragged it slowly down his face, as if trying to forcibly draw the solution from his brain.

'Your sticks. Of course. Your sticks. Then there is no other solution but for me to make several trips. After the binoculars glint, I shall take the rope, cross over to the mill, wait for the next glint, rush back to you, pick up the honey, wait for the...' Ruggles stopped, assailed by a thought. 'Lance Corporal, forgive the effrontery, but what are the odds that as soon as my back is turned you will once again lay four-fingered siege on the honey pot?'

Knot hung his head, but kept his chastened eyes on Ruggles.

'Rather tasty odds, I fear, Sir.'

'Much as I thought, Lance Corporal. I respect your honesty, if not your sense of discipline. Alright. Let's start over. After the binoculars glint, I take the honey, cross over to the mill, wait for the next glint, rush back, pick up the rope, wait for the...' Knot was waving his index finger in the air, a timid child angling for his teacher's attention. 'Yes, Lance Corporal?'

'Forgive me, Sir. What about the ants?'

'The ants?'

'You said yourself, Sir, that the ants would be all over the honey in a minute. If my calculations are correct, there will be at least two minutes between when you leave the honey at the tree... I mean, the mill... and when you return with the rope.'

'While I confess, Lance Corporal, that I shed my usual precision before and used the generalised expression *in a minute* rather sloppily, your point remains valid. Abandoned for more than a minute and the honey will surely be overrun. So let's start over, once again. What if, old boy, first we send you over to the mill... empty handed of course. I wait for the next glint, rush over with the honey, wait again, rush back...'

'Leaving me alone with the honey, Sir?,' a doubtful Knot interrupted.

'Quite right, quite right!' bristled Ruggles. 'I need to think.' He rolled onto his back and peered up into the clear night sky, swirling with stars. 'You cannot carry anything except your canes. I cannot carry both the rope and the honey at once. I cannot leave you with the honey, that is certain. I cannot leave the honey alone... for more than a minute. The watchman makes his rounds every minute...'

'What if... what if...' yelped Knot, all of a sudden, eyeballing Ruggles for permission to go on.

'Proceed, Lance Corporal,' Ruggles said, unable to banish a weariness from his voice.

'What if, sir, you wait for the glint, take the honey half of the distance, leave it in the grass, rush back, pick up the rope, wait for the glint, rush to the honey, exchange the honey for the rope, rush to the mill, wait for the glint, rush halfway back and then pick up the rope and return to the mill.' Breathless, Knot thumped the ground in triumph. Ruggles stayed quiet, letting the Lance Corporal's idea sink in. After a minute he said:

'Extraordinary work, L.C. You have excelled yourself, truly you have. There is one minor element you have forgotten, however. Your good self. How and when will you make the crossing?'

Knot picked up his thumb rubbing again as he thought aloud.

'Well, I cannot go before you, Sir, because that would mean leaving me alone with the honey again. So I suppose I shall have to go after you.'

'Quite right, but that means you having to know exactly when the right time is to cross without being seen. Are you sure you are able to make out the glint of the binoculars?' Regretting his earlier acquiescence, Knot admitted:

'I must confess, Sir, that I'm not.'

'Then what if I find a way to alert you, without crossing back over. I cannot call out to you, of course...'

'And I couldn't guarantee I would hear you if you did.'

'Indeed, you couldn't. I do, however, have in my repertoire a rather convincing female tawny owl.' Ruggles constructed an elaborate cup with his hands and conjured from it an otherworldly screech. Seconds later, and from all about them, a barrage of similar hoots arose.

'Drat,' Ruggles swore, 'male owls. Trust them to scotch a plan. The last thing I need is to get dive bombed by an amorous strigiform.'

'And besides, I shouldn't know if it was you hooting or one of your feathered suitors.'

'Oh, Lance Corporal Knot, your Christian name wouldn't happen to be Gordius, would it?' Ruggles said as he rolled onto his front, throwing an arm over his dejected second.'

'Forget-me!' the Lance Corporal exclaimed, to both of their surprise. A pained expression fleeted across the Captain's face.

'I beg your pardon, L.C.?'

'Forget-me-not!'

The Captain squinted at him.

'Forget-me, Forget-me-not? She-loves-me, she-loves-me-not? Oh Lance Corporal, now isn't the time for infantile games. All I meant to suggest was that I fear we've got ourselves into a rather inextricable tangle.'

'Inextricable,' Knot echoed by way of giving his assent.

'If only there was…' Ruggles began again, before letting the tail of his sentence escape unspoken.

'Inextricable,' Knot said again, a sudden note of doubt inflecting his sentence.

Ruggles hung his head, lost in thought. Suddenly Knot's head flicked ___ he said, his ___ ing into a grin. 'W___ ___ ere to take

huddled in the dark recess beneath a dilapidated wooden staircase in the Zellenblock.

'All clear, Lance Corporal?'

'All clear, Captain.'

'Well, I have to confess, Lance Corporal, I wasn't sure you had it in you.'

'*It*, Sir?'

'Indeed, Lance Corporal. If I had known you were capable of such astonishing flights of strategic genius, I should have involved you earlier on in the planning stages. The manner in which you got us inside by... But no, now is not the moment for pointless recapitulation or complacency. There'll be plenty of time for self-congratulatory anecdotage over sherry and cigars back in the Officers' Mess when this whole sorry struggle is won. Until then, we can only permit ourselves to look forward.'

The sound of a door slamming overhead reminded the soldiers of exactly where they were and what they were supposed to be doing. Ruggles brought his finger back to his lips and thrust his free arm out in front of Knot, in case the Lance Corporal should panic and bolt from their hiding place like a spooked grouse.

The echo of the slamming door was joined by the clicking of determined, metal-heeled footsteps, and the sound of something heavy being dragged. Vigilant about the potential for his body to pop and whiny if overly solicited, Ruggles rocked forward onto his knees and steadying himself against Knot's trig-point bulk, unfurled slowly into a standing posture. The stairs were made of old, worm-riddled wood, overlaid up the centre with a worn tongue of red carpet. The riser of the eighth stair, however had warped over time and shed a knot at its left hand side, forming a perfect spy hole, into which Ruggles screwed his bulbous right eye.

The footsteps reached the edge of the landing just above them, then stopped. A moment later, their cubby filled with a terrible din and something whirled past the hole, clumping down the stairs, before thudding into the floorboards at the bottom. Knot tugged at Ruggles' shirttail.

'What do you see, Sir?' he whispered.

Ruggles brought his finger back to his lips and bent down to Knot's ear.

'Very little so far, Lance Corporal,' he hissed. 'For whatever it was, it came to rest just outside of my line of sight. But I fear from the sheer weight of the tumbling package that it may well have contained a human body. We can only hope we have not arrived too late for Warrant Officer Karmacharya.' Knot grabbed hold of his lips and squeezed them together just in time to stymie a wail of distress. When it finally made it out, it resonated no more than the lament of a smothered mouse. The footsteps started up again, this time on the stairs. Ruggles screwed his eye back into the hole.

'Shit, shit, shit, shit, shit...' a voice intoned, in time with the hurried descending steps. From his position on the floor, Knot was desperate to see what Ruggles was watching – not just out of curiosity, but also because, having passed so close to the 'smock mill' during their zigzagging traverse of the yard, and having been able to confirm his suspicion that if indeed it was a mill, it was doing the best darned impression of an oak tree he could ever imagine seeing, he had begun to harbour doubts about the trustworthiness of the Captain's eyesight. As it was, however, the decomposition of the staircase had given them only one spy hole, and that was too high for Knot, even on tiptoe. So he watched as Captain Ruggles, on tiptoe himself, squirmed and threshed and batted with his arms, like some deranged orchestral conductor, at what he was witnessing above stairs.

After about a minute, a second door slammed and Ruggles turned back to face his companion.

'What is it, Sir?' said Knot. 'You look a little ruffled.' Ruggles leaned against the wall and let gravity slide him slowly downwards until he was seated beside Knot. He didn't speak.

'Was it a body, as you feared?'

Fixing the darkness before him, Ruggles said: 'No, Lance Corporal. Although under the circumstances, a cadaver would have been rather a sight for sore eyes.'

'I don't understand what could be worse, Captain, than the sight of the lifeless body of a fellow human being.' Ruggles waited again before speaking, inhaling deeply in the manner of a serial vomiter resigned to the next inevitable retch.

'Sometimes,' he went on, finally, 'it is not simply what one sees, but what one is forced to imagine that can be truly harrowing. Athena, she who governs our imagination, is a dangerous mistress, Lance Corporal. She can spirit you to the very heights of heaven and – as was just this moment the case, to the very depths of hell.'

Knot, who was having some trouble keeping up with the Captain's bevy of classical mistresses, began once again working the shiny cushions of his well-worn thumbs.

'Then, Sir,' he said, 'spare me all of the details and give me instead a stomachable précis of what you witnessed through that spy-hole.'

'Fear not, my dear Lance Corporal. I wouldn't dream of visiting the full extent of what I just saw even upon my worst enemy, let alone my faithful batman. Suffice it to say, that the package I took for a body bag contained some of the most horrendous instruments of torture that Lucifer has ever dreamt up.'

'And the torturer, Sir. From the weight of his footfall, one would image a fearful brute.'

'If only that were so, Lance Corporal. For at least when a man is devoured by a wolf or a bear he can take the smallest solace from knowing himself to be the victim of one of Mother Nature's physically formidable offspring. That cannot be so when one's devourer is a lamb.'

'A lamb, Sir?'

'The very picture of docility. A girl – pale as an egg and blonde as a rape field, Lance Corporal. She couldn't have been more than five years older than Dulcie and yet already so tarnished, already so comfortable in the uniform of the Gestapo.'

Neither man said anything for a while. Finally, Knot spoke up.

'She seemed in an awful hurry, Sir.'

'Indeed she was. There are barely enough hours in the day or night to satisfy the notorious Teutonic bloodlust. Just as a swift spends its whole life on the wing, so the Nazi must glide from one abomination to the next or his force leaves him.'

'Or her.'

'Quite right, in this case, Lance Corporal. No doubt our *Gestapette* is already gourmandising upon her next victim, without a thought for the horror she has left in her wake. A horror it is now our duty to face.'

'Must we, Sir?'

'We must, Lance Corporal. Do you need a hand up?'

'Almost there, old boy.'

'There?' Knot asked, between gasps. 'Where's there again?'

'Here!' Captain Ruggles said, jabbing a bony finger at his feet. They had arrived in a narrow hallway. It was windowless and grim, with five doors, all of them closed.

'And there are no more stairs to climb?'

'Not one! If our intelligence is correct, Karmacharya is being held behind this very door.'

Knot fixed the door for a moment and then, very abruptly, began to quake. For either his eyes deceived him, or the knot in the wood was rotating like a mesmerist's spiral. And not only that but the crack around the door was pulsing too. No, not pulsing… squirming! And not with light but… with darkness. Far more than just the absence of light, this had its own existence, its own force. Knot felt himself pale.

'Whatever's the matter?' the Captain asked.

The fingers of the darkness were reaching inside Knot's mouth now, tickling the depths of his throat. It was terrifying and yet he couldn't avert his gaze. Like a moth to a candle flame, the darkness held him ensorcelled.

'N… No, sir! Not that one, p… please.'

'Why ever not?'

'I… I've got a feeling, Sir.'

'A feeling?'

'A feeling, that's all. That we shouldn't open that door. We mustn't…' The Captain regarded his batman for a moment, then laid his hand on his shoulder.

'I understand. And it's true that what we might find behind that door, what they have done to dear old Karmacharya might prove to be the single most traumatic sight you have seen since we've been at war. But let me ask you this – if the sight of such torture traumatises you so, imagine how it must feel to be the subject of it. We owe it to Karmacharya to get him out of there. I, at least, owe it to him.'

'It's not that, Sir,' Knot tried again. 'It's something else. It's something…' here he paused, took his face in the palm of one of his fat hands and ground at his temples. Then, desperately: 'How do you even know that's the room, Sir? I would hasten that it's not even… There are *other* doors!'

The Captain once again lifted his shushing finger. Knot, desperate not to disobey further, chomped down hard on his lip.

'What do you see on that door?' Knot squinted.

'It looks like a rather large, terribly black kno—'

'Hole! The Captain interjected. 'A perfect rendering of the astronomical phenomenon of the black hole. It was Karmacharya who first showed me a similar picture, in one of the textbooks he used to bury his nose in as an antidote to my own inanity. I first saw this one several weeks ago when I was summoned upstairs by the Kommandant, and recognised it at once. How could this be anything other than the place?'

'I'm afraid, Sir, that once again I don't… Are you saying that Karmacharya painted it, as some kind of sign?'

The Captain considered this possibility for a moment before dismissing it with a shake of his head and returning to his original hypothesis.

'I'll forgive you only because you are from peasant and not military stock, Lance Corporal. Every soldier worth his salt knows that the black hole was once military argot for a prison. And one black hole was the most infamous of them all…'

Knot's face lit up with the joy of a breaching memory.

'The Black Hole of Calcutta, Sir!'

'The Black Hole of Calcutta! *Schwarzes Loch von Kalkutta*. The Teutonic sense of humour is notoriously nebulous, old boy. But even you can surely understand why a pun like this can lead us to only one conclusion. Calcutta, for heaven's sake! Karmacharya *must* be behind that door...'

Approaching the door, the Captain ran his fingers around the crack, squatted to peer through the keyhole, then took hold of the handle and gave it a hefty yank.

Knot yelped – '*sweet mercy!*' – but the door didn't budge. The Captain turned back to him.

'Am I able to count on your assistance here, old chap?' The Lance Corporal approached and stood sheepishly beside his master, using his walking canes to steady himself as he rolled his bulbish frame forwards. While he contemplated the Captain's question, he brought his hands together – making an isosceles triangle of his canes and the floor – and started vigorously rubbing his thumbs.

'Sir,' he said after a while. 'I accompanied you on our escape, on our adventure with the smock mills, as we hid from the torturess, and as we made our ascent to this point. I know at some times I have been a hindrance, but at other times, I fancy... at least, I hope... I have proven of some use to you. Indeed, I will even help you to bust open that god-forsaken door, if that's what you want from me. But, Sir, when it comes to going *inside* that room...' – looking askance at the door – '... I'm afraid you'll have to go on alone.'

The Captain looked at Knot for some time, but said nothing. The batman's oath required him to remain forever at his master's side, to face any danger his master faced, and to die alongside him if necessary. This was a clear dereliction of duty, worthy of instant dismissal from service.

The Captain tilted his head and smiled.

'Dear boy,' he said. 'It was never my intention that you should come in with me. Indeed, if we both go in, who will keep watch outside? Who will perform the vital, indeed the crucial duty of standing guard, of hooting like a female tawny owl to alert me to a coming danger? Who but you, my dear friend, is up to such a task of raising the alarm should I not return?'

Knot stopped rubbing his thumbs, took both canes in his left hand, lifted his right hand to his mouth and too-witted lustily through his clenched fingers.

'Attaboy!' said the Captain, clapping his batman on the back. 'A-ta-boy! Now, let's use the Nazis' cruelty against them and put that unsoldierly bulk of yours to good use.' The Captain picked up the length of rope and, after tying one end to the door handle, secured the other end tightly around Knot's waist.

'Tell me, is it secure about your gut?'

Knot tugged at the rope: 'Secure enough, Sir.'

'Then on the count of three...'

'On the count of three...' He planted his canes in the ground in front of him and leaned forward, taking up the slack on the rope.

'One...' Knot strained forward a step as the Captain, his gaze fixed on the door, crouched, a tiger ready to pounce.

'Two...' Another step. The door, or the handle, or the rope, or the batman, whinnied with the effort.

'Taking the strain...' the Captain growled. 'Ready for the final push?'

Knot, his face purple, groaned: 'R... Ready!'

'Three!'

As Knot took first one step forward, then another, then slid back as his feet slipped beneath him, the door handle squealed its last and snapped from the wood. He tumbled forward.

For a moment it looked as if the plan had failed. Then, almost shyly, the door cracked a few inches ajar. The darkness now came blazing out, tongues as black as Indian ink, raging through the crack. The Captain punched the air, just as the door flew open, the darkness raging in full view now. Knot clapped his hands over his eyes, refusing to look inside.

'The others!' the Captain barked above the roar of the darkness. 'You have to tell the others!'

'Righto Captain!' Knot shrieked back.

'Bravo! Bravo!' the Captain cried. '*Courage, mon vieux*! See you on the other side…' And with that he jumped into the closet.

The door slammed shut and the howling dropped away. Lying on the floor of the landing Knot scissored his fingers open a crack and looked up. The knot was still there, still turning, but was getting smaller, and quickly. Within seconds it would be gone. But that wasn't all – for the knot was now gyrating on a patch of bare wall. The door, a cause of such fear barely seconds earlier, had vanished too.

'The others…' Knot muttered, wobbling to his feet.

4

Dot came to, gasped, and almost retched as her lungs rejected the rancidness of baked air. Before anything, before any sense of where she was, of what had happened, she felt the tackiness of the skin between her thighs, the soupiness of the sheet under her buttocks, the cold, hard lino beneath that.

Pissed yourself again, have you, you stupid old cow – she thought, shifting from her back onto her side, away from the camphoric puddle – *when will you learn to...* The chastising thought trailed off as another one muscled in. Not a thought, a memory... Her gut somersaulted in protest at it. She balled up, hedgehog-like.

Why?

The day's events lay scattered about her mind. Rubble around a bomb-site. She surveyed them for a moment then, rolling her mental sleeves up, set about reconstructing them fragment by fragment...

Olive had shouted at them. That was the first link in the chain. She had shouted at them because... Well, because they had deserved it, Dot had to admit. Ever since the Captain had vanished, they had all to some extent surrendered to unreason. As if he had been the bulwark, the lone guard, holding madness back at the gates by absorbing its blows. And that wasn't all: his disappearance had left a vacuum in the ward, and Dot had watched with morbid fascination as the others had expanded to fill it, the Captain's character traits divvied up between them like the estate of a recently deceased *pater familias*. So Betty had become more rebellious, Smithy more mischievous. Even Lanyard had changed. He was spoiling for a fight so often these days – although that could have had as much to do with his anger and hurt over Windsor. And Olive? What about her?

An uneasiness descended on Dot as she realised that of all her fellow residents she felt she knew Olive the least. She had dismissed her on first sight – with rapier prejudice – as touchingly naive, comically paranoid, narrative light-relief. Neither Dot nor the others had made any effort to delve beneath the surface.

But now Olive had spoken of something she had found, upstairs, something important. After all this time clowning on the side-lines, she was forcing herself onto the board, interfering with the order of play. Perhaps it was nothing. But perhaps, too, it would be another lash of the cane, driving Dot's hoop forward, keeping it upright, ever trundling on, preventing it from leaning into the final, frenzied spin she so longed for...

Which was why, as Dot had wheeled herself across to Olive's bed, determined to coax her out from beneath the sheets, she was unsure herself whether she would caress it under the chin, or attempt to lop it off.

'Olive,' she said, gripping the frail ankle. 'Ol?'

'Leave me alone,' Olive snapped.

'Come on, Ol,' Dot said, dragging at the sheet until Olive's stubborn dinner-plate face was visible. Dot craned over her shoulder to check nobody was paying her any mind. 'Why don't you tell *me* what you found?'

'No point,' Olive said.

'Why not?'

'Because you're just like the others. You're not ready.'

Dot nodded. If Olive had decided to muzzle herself, for now, the threat she posed was minimal. Still, the insult stung.

'As you wish,' Dot said. She released Olive's ankle and began backing the wheelchair up.

'As I wish...' Olive muttered, more to herself than Dot.

'Pardon?' Dot clenched the wheels, stopping them dead.

'As I wish,' Olive said again, her face splitting into what looked like a grin. 'Well, isn't that a novelty?'

Dot had thought the dangerous waters were receding. She was wrong. They were rushing back in.

'What do you mean, Ol?'

She was laughing now.

'Almost half a century I was married, Dot. Strange, isn't it, to be buried by someone else for so long? Bullied, belittled… shagged over and over. Thank goodness we only had one kid. One boss above, and another one below – that was more than enough! Marriage always felt like a gap that I didn't know how to close. In the end, his dodgy ticker closed it for both of us, but it had gone on too long. I only came here because I didn't know what else to do. I was lost. I mean, I could hardly go back to Slocum's, could I?'

'No,' Dot said, although she had no idea who Slocum was. Olive was drifting, her gaze looking past Dot now, to the near four-score years laid out behind her. She smiled again.

'*Les filles* – that's what Nadja, the senior typist, called us. And we called her Nadja, even though her name was Natalie, because she preferred it that way. She had picked it up in one of those books she ordered, that came in brown envelopes from that place on the Charing Cross Road. That really impressed us back then.'

'Breton,' Dot said, through clenched teeth. Olive's blossoming in front of her, into something lurid and real, was too excruciating.

'Well, I wouldn't know where she was from. We all read too – dirty men's magazines that we took it in turns to pinch. As thick as thieves we were, a gang, a clique – and Slocum complained, but he loved it really, that dirty old albino bastard, keeping his office door ajar so that he could watch us working up each other's hairdos, or overhear us sharing private stories over endless cigarettes. It was so wonderful, but it could never have lasted. One by one the older girls floated off down the aisle. Even Nadja, who was Natalie again by then. Eventually it happened to me too, which was a shame really, when you think about it, because it was actually Tilly's turn…' Olive's smile had receded now and she was looking at Dot again, her fingers gripping the blanket's hem.

'It's so sad, Dot. We all lived so richly back then. Before our senses were dulled. That was why I always spiced up the stories I told them. I wasn't a liar. It was more complicated than that. How could I ever expect the others to understand, to really feel what I had felt, to really know what I knew, without gilding the lily a little?'

Olive stared at Dot, as if bumped from the mists of memory by a revelation of the utmost importance.

'What?' Dot asked, her voice creaking. 'What is it?'

Although she would never know if Olive had meant to answer, because it was at that moment that the cry had gone up:

'Inspection! Ward B!'

Dot's almost retched now as she remembered: a concerto of cramps, as if her mind was trying to expel the memories through her body. Perhaps that was why it had lingered so long on her conversation with Olive, distraction as a form of self-defence, a way of sparing her, for as long as possible, from the recollection of what had happened next.

The two of them, Tristan and the girl, had clattered into the room, armed with pots, pans and metal ladles, raising a hellish racket. Her ward mates had grumbled, then screamed and yelled as sheets and blankets were torn from them. Lanyard sprang from his bed like a sprite, clutching a pillow, before cowering in a corner and covering himself up with it. Olive took instinctive flight for the door, but her resurgent catalepsy snatched her legs out from beneath her and she collapsed in a heap. When Betty had not left her cot, a fierce dignity to her refusals, the metal brace was kicked out from under it, sending her rolling, slapping, like a beached seal to the floor.

Where was Smithy? That had been Dot's first thought. Surely now he would fight back, finally put some of that brute force to use? But who was she trying to kid?

Suddenly, Tristan was standing in front of her.

'Well look what we have here,' he said leaning forward so that his eyes were level with hers. They were heavily bloodshot, the pupils wildly dilated, the irises barely visible, two coruscating cerulean rims around holes of unfathomable darkness.

'Lady Strangelove,' he spat. 'Missus Ironside. The Lame Dame.' Dot looked away. 'Pushed around all day like the Queen of fucking Sheba. It's about time you were rehabilitated, wouldn't you say?' Dot clenched her jaw. Tristan repeated: 'Wouldn't. You. Say?'

Without a word Dot leaned forward in the wheelchair's sling and flicked the catch that secured the leg rest. Then, gripping her leg beneath the knee, she lifted the plaster boot and lowered it to the floor. Moving her hands to the armrests, she started rocking herself forward in the sling, until half of each buttock was hanging over the void. Her whole body was trembling now. At the effort already expended, and in anticipation of the effort to come. Straining at the armrests, and favouring her good leg, Dot lifted herself from the wheelchair. It must have only lasted seconds, but to Dot it felt like minutes, hours, lifetimes passed as she forced herself vertical. Whole civilisations might have been founded, bloomed, turned and fallen in the time it took her to stand. Her muscles were shrieking pain – how easy it would have been to drop back into the leather seat, to give in, to surrender to entropy. But if she did, she knew that would be her last act of agency, her signature at the bottom of life's contract. And although she had come to Green Oaks to reach that very state, to sign off, to wind down, at that moment it felt impossible for her to accept. There was just so much unfinished business...

Upright, she shifted some of her weight onto the plaster boot. Something inside it cracked loudly and the off-white surface fissured like baked earth. She lifted her head slowly until their eyes locked.

'*I wolde I hadde thy coillons in myn hond... Lat kutte hem of,*' she said.

Tristan laughed, a small interrogatory gurgle – '*Huh?*' – and took a step forward. He was breathing heavily through his nose, a flake of dried snot in his right nostril quivering like bunting in the summer breeze. She could have bitten his lips off right then, their faces were so close.

'I wish I had your balls in my hand... I'd cut them off,' she translated.

For a second Dot thought she had rattled him. The way his eyes opened wide and his head was cocked suggested, at the very least, that he was surprised. It didn't last long.

'If you think this is bad,' he whispered with faux-casualness, as if discretely making her privy to confidential information. 'You should see what I've got in mind for Ward C later.'

Dot froze. The confirmation of that elusive ward's existence grounded her with a thump. So she hadn't been mad all this time – at least not completely – and it wasn't a mere euphemism, as Betty seemed to believe. Ward C existed. Ward C was real. Which meant... Which meant... She blinked hard, several times. The implications were almost too much for her to process. Did that mean the Captain wasn't dead? Had she lifted that pillow from Leonard's face before it was too late?

She could sense the fight oozing from her and fatigue oozing back in, her paper-thin skin was too fragile a membrane to prevent the transfer. She should say something. Before it was too late.

'What...' she said a rogue quiver tugging at her voice. 'What have you got in mind?'

Tristan reached forward and laid a hand on her shoulder. His grip was firm, like a Cockateel's.

'For your two beaus, you mean?' he said, smacking his lips. 'Perhaps nothing. If you cooperate.'

He was only applying the lightest pressure, but Dot could already feel her knees giving way. Of course she would cooperate. What else could she do? The risks of resisting were just too great. Her mind's needle had jammed on Olive's words from several months earlier: *You know what they say, Dot? The house always wins...*

Beneath Tristan's hand she slumped to the floor.

'Jeepers! The carpet!'

Ruggles exclaimed, pushing hard against the

5

Tristan watched as Pat's furry belly waxed and waned. After a minute or so his left leg began twitching and Tristan worried he was about to awaken. But he didn't. The leg just twitched itself out and Pat rolled onto his side, his dumb, unconscious puss squashed into the fart-filled cleft of the old cushions.

It's for his own good.

On several occasions, before the Kalki delirium had knocked him off the rails, Tristan had wondered if he would ever need to use what he had come to know as the 'nuclear option' – revealing to Mister Cornish what had really become of the old Indian. He had assumed its utility would be to transform collective responsibility into something more… individual. Shifting the blame, after a blind and ailing Grey was discovered locked in the upstairs closet, onto Pat or Frankie. Or Agnes. Onto anybody but him.

He had called it the 'nuclear option', because he was sure it would be the moment everything exploded. He would never have guessed he would be using it to keep the team together…

One day he'll thank me.

There was no way any of them could leave once Kalki's disappearance was revealed to the world. Not Pat, not Frankie, not Cornish. Not Tristan either. They were all implicated in one way or another. Guilty only by association or incompetence, perhaps, but guilty all the same. They would be bound together, in a strange little four-way matrimony. *For better or worse.*

Perhaps, for want of other options, he and Frankie would end up fucking after all.

He opened the door as quietly as he could, left the staffroom and closed it again behind him.

He wasn't quite sure what he would say when Cornish asked – as he surely would – about what had become of Kalki's body, but the uncertainties this introduced would only heighten the sense of risk and the obligation for all of them to hold their tongues.

In sickness and in health...

He heard raised voices coming from Ward B. Recriminations probably, for the punishment he and Frankie had inflicted on them earlier. They would normally have been locked in for the night by now, but with the Captain out of the picture, Tristan had become a little lax. He'd see to them after he'd seen to Cornish.

After climbing the first few stairs, he froze...

There was nothing familiar at first about the mud-encrusted groundhog bowling towards him at an impressive gravity-aided clip. It was an extraordinary, harrowing sight, slowed down enough by the panic-centre in his brain so that he could watch it in excruciating detail. With two canes held aloft in one hand, the apparition was windmilling an open pot of honey with the other. Impossible to tell if he was in control or not, if each forward footfall, each rotation of the honey pot, was part of an elaborately choreographed attack-charge or, instead, a simple and desperate attempt to remain vertical.

Before Tristan could duck, the plastic tub connected, square with his jaw, and as consciousness left him, he felt his knees give way and his body crumple to the stairs.

From this day forward…

He must have only been out cold for a few seconds, because the first thing he saw when he opened his eyes was the old man finishing his descent, skidding into the hallway and promptly falling onto his arse.

Forget-me-Not. Tristan recognised him now. Impressive dementia. A terrifying black hole of a brain, that was slowly drawing in and crushing memories – new and old – out of existence. What the hell was he doing out?

His mouth overflowed with blood and he gagged. He coughed red onto the carpet. Moments later a tooth slumped onto his tongue. His head spun with the pain. Not again.

Forget-me-Not lifted himself to his knees then, rattlingly, to his feet… He looked about the hallway, from one door to another, to another. There were five for him to choose from, which looked like four too many. Frustrated he leaned back against the wall, propped his canes beside him and massaged his fleshy forehead with his free hand.

'It couldn't hurt,' he said, eyeing the honey pot. 'It could help. With the… the… the' – and plunging three fingers into the viscid goo he lifted a clod of it and trailed it into his mouth. He closed his eyes and worked his tongue over his lips. He was meticulous, working the crevices until the honey's vague gilding had been replaced by the clear shimmer of his spittle.

'Silk, silk, silk, silk, silk… And what do cows drink?' The effort of his reflections had carved deep crevasses in his forehead. 'Money… Money… Money… Money… Money. And what do bees eat?'

His eyes sprang open.

'Bee!' he cried. He closed the honey pot and started stropping his hand on his cardigan. Incanting 'Bee, bee, bee, bee…' his eye finally snagged on the large black letter painted on the door.

'*Carwious an… an… and Tai Tschi…*' he cried, wobbling into Ward B.

Things were falling apart, Tristan could see that now. Doors were unlocked, Feebies were on the loose, Pat was leaving… The tooth was still in his mouth. He spat it onto the palm of his hand where it lay in a puddle of saliva and blood. A fucking incisor. Typical.

He had to press the button. Now.

He was on the landing in three strides. At Cornish's door in another two. He stopped, took several deep breaths, and wiped his bloody lips with his sleeve.

'Mister Cornish,' he said, knocking. When no reply came, he knocked a second time, harder.

The door creaked open.

'Mister Cornish?' he said again, spreading the fingers of his left hand and easing the door open further with the tips. It squealed, as was only proper.

A sharp intake of breath. A flurry of blinks.

Then he stopped breathing. Stopped blinking.

He walked slowly towards the purple-faced effigy, cable-tied to the office chair.

'*Mister Cornish…*' he tried.

Inches away, he stared. Cornish stared back at him. Tristan looked away, looked down… At the body. It was horrible. Long gone to seed. The skin below the neck was the towel-grey of old underwear, and its layer of fuzz looked more like some extraterrestrial mould than anything human in origin.

Tristan swallowed hard and looked back up at the face. It was Cornish, there was no doubt. But transformed, swollen, the bulging eyes bloodshot, the fat tongue, an even deeper indigo than the rest of the face, lolling between his lips like a lazy hard-on.

Tristan reached out a pair of fingers to feel for a pulse. He hesitated before making contact, drew his fingers back, then steeled himself and touched him beneath the jaw. Only for the briefest moment, though… the sensation, the unearthly sponginess perhaps, reminded him of something and he drew his fingers back in shock. The moment contact ceased, Cornish's cadaver unleashed a long, loud fart.

Til death us do part…

Shit!

'*Pat!*' Tristan cried, staggering backwards. 'Pat!' he shrieked again from the landing, before suddenly falling silent. Hortense was staring at him, impassively, from Ward A. She tilted her head a few degrees, inviting an explanation.

'Dead!' Tristan shrieked. 'Dead! Murdered! Cornish!'

Without taking her eyes off him, and with an odd little smile, Hortense reached for the red emergency cord hanging beside her chaise-longue and gave it the heartiest tug her withered arm could manage.

'What the fuck's got into you?'

Tristan spun around. Pat was standing at the top of the stairs.

'Murder!' Tristan quivered again.

'Your mouth's gushing blood like a fucking hydrant.'

'R... r... rape!' A darkness settled onto Pat's face.

'Hortense?' he asked. Then: 'Tristan what the fuck have you done?'

'Ha!' Tristan choked, showering Pat with blood. 'Not me, dumb-dumb. And not Hortense,' he said, pointing off to the side. 'Cornish!'

Pat's gaze followed the invisible dotted line emanating from Tristan's index finger.

'Holy living...'

'Conspiracy!' Tristan interrupted.

'Wh... what?'

'The Captain! It must be. Forget-me-Not couldn't do this alone.'

'Tristan, no!'

Yes, he thought. *Yes, yes and yes!*

'Of course it's him. Who else could it be? This is my chance to...'

'No,' Pat shouted. 'This is your chance to nothing! A man's dead.'

'A man's always dead,' Tristan said. 'A man's always fucking dead, but an opportunity has to be taken when it comes.'

Tristan felt Pat's hands on his shoulders. Their faces were almost touching now.

'Listen,' he said. 'Listen to me, alright? The first thing we do is go downstairs and call someone. The police, I guess. Or an ambulance. I don't know. And they take it from there, OK?'

Pat put his arm over Tristan's shoulder and began leading him towards the stairwell.

'I mean… He's *really* gone and done it now.'

'Tristan?' Pat said. 'Come on. Please.'

Pat looked exhausted suddenly. Pale and drawn. Like a marathon runner who had abandoned the race at the twenty-five mile marker.

Halfway down the stairs, they stopped.

6

Dot couldn't tell for certain what happened after she had had fallen. Bringing her hands to her head – slowly, in case her movements drew further violent attention her way – she had crammed her fingers as deeply in her ears as they would go and waited for the fire to burn itself out. She had still heard some things – muffled shouts, screams, pleading. Almighty crashes as cots were overturned, and smaller crashes as keepsakes – the few that had been left to them – were cast to the lino, scattered, crushed underfoot. It didn't last long, no more than five minutes or so, although in line with cliché it had felt much longer. And as Dot had prayed to a God she didn't believe in for it all to end, one way or another, when it finally did the silence was even harder to bear.

Now, some hours later, Dot was still afraid to emerge from beneath the sheet. What had befallen them was, she knew, for all its violence, all its rage, the opening sally in a long campaign. What she understood now, and what the Captain and Betty must have understood long ago, was that given time, an untended pot always boils over. *Exposition, complication, climax, resolution.* Were they really fated to tread the same long-worn paths, re-enacting their own humdrum versions of vapid legends and stale myths?

Probably, yes. As far as myths went, she wasn't above the odd comparison or two herself. On the night she had left her bed in search of Leonard, Dot remembered thinking of herself as Theseus, and him as the Minotaur, a monstrous hybrid of man and disease. Now Orpheus and Eurydice felt a more apposite comparison, although with their genders switched. And Dot had made the same big mistake as Orpheus: she had looked back.

She shifted on the floor and pulled the sheet off her face. It was already dark, later, then, than she had thought. Still, there was enough light from the moon outside, now that the curtains had been pulled down, for her to assess the damage. Everything in the ward was on its head, and the place was deserted, the victim of a rampage by some crazed little demi-god in search of a lost penny. Piles of twisted blankets had transformed the floor into an unearthly moraine. Wheeled cot-legs spiked from the floor like strange metallic flowers. Curtains hung crookedly and torn. Assorted debris, souvenirs, life's clams, that had stuck to their owners for so many years, formed a bed of rubble stretching the length and breadth of the ward.

And suddenly – that bloody house up to its old tricks again! – she was no longer in Green Oaks but in the London of her childhood, in the junk shops and flea markets beneath the arches of one of the capital's bridges. She looked on, in silent fascination, but also with a kind of dread, as her mother bartered over the remnants of other people's lives. It was always strange to see her mother in situations several steps removed from the domestic. At home she was quiet, subservient, proper. Here she was assertive, staunch and brash. As a little girl, and no more, this transformation had frightened Dot every time it occurred, as if she feared that the jagged Mrs Hyde would never revert to pliant Madame Jekyll, although she always did. Now, a little girl again, but with the mind of an old woman – more than twice the age of the mother whose leg she was clinging to like a limpet – a truth dawned: there were never two women at all. Only one. Just one with depths as unfamiliar to Dot as Dot's own always had been, and always would be, to everyone else.

The vision showed no sign of retreating yet, and neither did Dot want it to. For there was something different this time. The night Green Oaks had transformed into a labyrinthine perversion of her bungalow she had been unsure whether to trust her senses. This time she had known from the start it was a vision. But she also felt that these new phantoms had not been stirred up to torment and confuse her, but instead to cradle and comfort. There was a tenderness to it, as if whatever malevolent sprite normally manipulated the levers and cranks of the Green Oaks carousel had been, temporarily, displaced.

She followed her mother from one stand to the next, from one arch to the next, grateful for being given the chance to witness this formidable woman in action with eyes mature enough to understand. She was a harsh critic of junk, but haggled fairly when she spied something of quality. She was warm with other women and commanding with the men, turning their lasciviousness into pikes she hurled deftly back at them. It was this incarnation, Dot realised now, that she had unconsciously emulated all her life, this that had been her model of strength and resilience. And she had honoured that model, she felt, for the most part. At least until the last few months…

'Sorry Mum,' she said, dipping her eyes. Her mother stopped digging through a pile of moth-eaten rugs, looked at Dot and smiled.

The vision began to fade.

As the bricks dissolved into plastered wall again, Dot understood something else that had passed her by at the time: much of the stock in these markets had been looted from houses destroyed during the Blitz. She had always felt oppressed by an awful gloominess during these visits and now understood what had caused it. For those who had been unable to bully their way onto the pages of history books, once their lives were over, all they left behind was a pile of trash, of useless knick-knacks. So easily scattered to the wind.

As Ward B returned Dot saw that, while they were not dead yet, for all of them this process had started long ago.

And then, as if in a *trompe-l'oeil* canvas, the landscape that had seemed devoid of life, in the blink of an eye, a shift of focus, became animate. What, minutes earlier, her eye had passed over as a faggot of blankets, it now saw clearly as Betty, lying on the floor, her legs hidden beneath a thin mattress and the slits of her swollen eyes glimmering as she fixed a point on the ceiling. And that wasn't a curtain, but a pair of legs… Olive's legs! Dot couldn't tell if she was peering out of the window or just hiding there, vainly hoping she would be passed over if there was a second visitation. But where were the others? The CareFriends hadn't closed the door behind them this time, perhaps they had finally followed the Captain's lead and bolted... Although, what would have been the point? They all understood something the Captain never had: there was nowhere else for them to go. Green Oaks was the world and the world was Green Oaks.

'Bet,' Dot said. When no response came, she raised her voice a little. 'Betty?'

'I knew it, Dot. I knew it would end like this.' She was addressing Dot, but her encrusted eyes remained fixed on that point on the ceiling. 'Without the Captain we had nobody to absorb the blows for us. Father Patterson said as much. That was why he wanted to help us. Before... before...' Betty exhaled a tortured gurgle – not quite a sigh, not quite a groan. 'Violence like that can never be contained, Dot. Not forever. Its appetite can only grow... until it consumes everything. Its victims, of course, but the perpetrator too. That's the only comfort. The little bastard will get his.'

A creaking arose from beneath one of the cots and, seconds later, Smithy dragged himself out. He was topless, exposing the remains of a once huge torso, the muscles old and flaccid, but still with something to prove – the old Shire Horse whose impossible choice lay between the too-heavy plough and the knacker's yard. He crawled towards Betty, across the floor.

'Fine time to put in an appearance,' Betty scolded him. 'And get up on your feet and walk like a bloody man, why don't you? Lord save us!'

Smithy obeyed, slowly righting himself. Dot could almost feel the rust grinding in his joints.

'I heard what you said, Bets. But look, it's not over. We're here. We're alive. We haven't been consumed. We...'

'You!' Betty bellowed. '*You* haven't been consumed. And have you bothered to ask yourself why you were spared that humiliation, that degradation? Have you asked yourself that you useless slab of gristle?'

'I was *here*, Bets!' Smithy shouted back, his face and neck crimson.

'For all the bloody good you did!' Betty thundered. 'They wouldn't touch you of course, not since you showed your strength and booted that child's tooth out. But they also knew – just as we all did, just as you've now proved – that you wouldn't step up to stop them either. Jesus Christ, Alain, you bloody coward! What would it take for you to…'

'Smithy?' It was Olive. Her emergence from behind the curtain triangulated the scene, adding an unpredictable dimension to proceedings. Smithy, his chest heaving, turned to her.

'*What*, Olive?'

She looked from Smithy to Betty, then back to Smithy again.

'A word, if you will.'

Smithy was confused. He looked to Betty, as if for permission, but his lover didn't respond, her anger far too severe. If she wouldn't give him the green light, then what about the others? Lanyard? He too had appeared – Dot wasn't sure from where – but looked even more broken, even more defeated than the rest of them. What a terribly brutal way to be proven so wrong. And Dot? Betty's words had hit their mark, she refused to meet Smithy's gaze.

'Just a word,' Olive said again. When Smithy didn't respond, she approached him, took hold of his forearm and led him a few steps from the others towards the door.

'I have to show you something,' Dot heard her say. Smithy looked back over his shoulder, then nodded. Dot squinted, determined to make out as much as she could across the fog of myopic no-man's-land. Olive pulled something from the pocket of her nightie. It was long, thin, and ivory-coloured, and tapered at one end. Smithy eyed it, baffled. Dot squinted – was that a bone?

'One second,' Olive said. 'It's come loose from the clip.' She reached in her pocket again and this time drew out a folded square of paper. It was clear that she was unsure of the effect it would have, and she watched Smithy carefully as he unfolded it, then held it at arm's-length to better take it in.

His great shoulders began trembling.

'Where did you find this?' struggling to keep his voice from cracking.

'Upstairs,' Olive said. 'In Cornish's office.' Her voice was cool, calm, Dot noticed. Almost too much so.

'Did *he* do it?'

'I think so, and it wasn't the only one. There were *dozens*, just like this one, by all of the staff.' From across the room Dot couldn't make out what was on the paper, all she could see was a dark-blue ballpoint swirl. Some kind of sketch, perhaps? Whatever it was, she didn't like it, didn't like the effect it was having on Smithy. The CareFriend's threat batted frantically about the inside of her head. *You should see what I've got in mind for Ward C later.*

'All of them, of me... of *us*?' Smithy asked.

'Not all, Smithy, but lots.'

'And all of them, like this? So... *filthy*?'

'All of them,' Olive confirmed. For some reason, at that moment she turned and looked straight at Dot, as if waiting for her to step in, to dispel some myth, to expose some lie.

'No!' Smithy jack-knifed straight. 'No! No! No!'

The blue touch-paper lit, Olive stepped back, retiring to a safe distance. Would he explode, furiously, a Catherine Wheel of sparks and anger? Or had he been left alone too long in the dark and dank? Would he just fizzle out?

Smithy strode towards the door. Then he stopped, turned... and now he was looking at Dot. He was awaiting her permission. But why her? Was it unanimity he wanted? He knew the others were onside, even Lanyard, but perhaps he harboured doubts about Dot.

If so, they were doubts that would prove well-founded. She couldn't endanger Leonard, no matter if it meant sacrificing everyone else. Even the Captain...

'What about...'

At that moment, there was a clatter from the hallway, and a sudden presence at the door. A short, balding, fat fellow, breathing heavily.

He was wearing muddy pyjamas and carrying two canes, which he held in his left hand, and a bucket of something in his right, that seemed to be dripping blood. There was a wild look in his eyes, as if he was straddling the border between reality and delirium. And yet he looked so happy. He was peering into the ward. Past Smithy, past Betty, past Olive and Lanyard and had fixed his gaze on Dot, huddled on the floor.

'You remember,' she whispered.

'Once-in-a-blooming-coupling, Dotty!' the apparition cried, his mouth cracking into a proud grin. All eyes in the ward were flitting between this new interloper and Dot. She could feel that her facial muscles had loosened, and her lip was starting to quiver. Any moment, she would lose control and sob...

But instead, she laughed, almost choking on the unfamiliar bubbling-up. Although almost as quickly, her face hardened again. Not with indifference or intransigence anymore, but with determination.

From the hallway, the crazed old grandfather clock started its irregular chiming. One, two, three, four, five...

'Feeding time,' the apparition mumbled.

'You heard the man, Smithy,' Dot said.

Smithy replied with a workman-like nod. The apparition walked past him, past all the others and towards Dot. She watched his approach through eyes clouded with tears.

'Leonard,' she managed, finally.

'Lance Corporal Leonard Knot, loyal batman to Captain Ruggles,' he corrected. 'Reporting for duty.'

Dot choked back another laugh: 'Is that so?'

Holding out her arms to him, Leonard crouched down and leaned in for a hug, as if it was the most natural action he could perform, as if every muscle in his body remembered the gesture. His head came to rest in the fleshy cup between her breast and shoulder. She ran her fingers through what was left of his hair.

'I'm so sorry, Leonard,' she whispered. 'So, so sorry.'

'No, no, no. Ssh!' Leonard said, looking her in the eye. 'We've come all the way to Bognor. Let's just enjoy our honeymoon.'

After helping Dot back into the wheelchair, Leonard pushed her out into the hallway where the others had followed Smithy. They arrived just in time to hear a commotion from upstairs, and a clatter of footsteps. Seconds later, the two male CareFriends staggered from the landing into the stairwell, their faces contorted with physical exertion and existential horror, one of them, Tristan, was sluicing blood from the mouth.

Halfway down the stairs, they stopped...

Whatever had spooked them on the floor above, now they had something new to worry about. Looking across the hall they saw Smithy, his huge muscular torso shimmering with sweat, shoulders square, back straight, staring them down.

Before either had a chance to react, Smithy started walking towards them. Slow but determined strides. Neither of them moved. They couldn't, Dot realised. Something was holding them in place. The authority of this old warrior, perhaps, or the menace of his imminent explosion? Impossible to know, although its effectiveness was also impossible to deny. The clock, apropos of nothing, chimed again. Smithy's lip curled into a terrifying smile.

From the corner of her eye Dot saw the girl, Frankie, slouch from the staff room. At first she looked irritated, bored, but when she saw what was happening her face cracked with mild interest.

'*Smithy!*'

Dot tried to shout, to alert him to the girl's presence, but nothing came out. When Smithy was only a few steps away from his petrified quarry Dot looked on despairingly while Frankie, as casually as if stubbing out a cigarette, poked her toe under the corner of the old rug and gave it a small flick, curling it along its length. Smithy, blind to this, made no effort to avoid the new obstacle, clipped it with his toe, stumbled and lost his balance. As cartoon law dictates for all large, dense objects before they fall, Smithy's body hung in the air for a beat, then crashed to the floor like a bull at the end of a corrida, his chin cracking on the bare wood of the bottom stair, inches from the CareFriends' feet.

Tristan was the first to react. Colour, albeit a strange, inhuman one, a kind of green-grey, returned to his cheeks. He wriggled his shoulders, as if feeling his way back into his body after some time separated from it, then hopped down the final step and crouched, his face beside Smithy's.

'Nice try, you stupid old duffer,' he spat into Smithy's ear, bubbles of bloody saliva erupting between his lips with every word. 'But it was never going to be enough.' He straightened up and addressed the others. 'Now get back to your ward!'

If Dot could have slid out of the wheelchair and slumped to the floor, she would have. She wanted only to erase what had happened from her mind. It was too hard to bear. It wasn't just that Tristan had won. Tristans normally do. Neither was it how Smithy had failed, had been cut down the moment – the very moment! – he had decided to stand up for himself... for them all. She was too used to seeing duplicitous Fortune launch her attacks from life's blind-spot for that to rattle her. No, what terrified her was the thought of what would happen next. To her, to Leonard, to all of them.

She looked away from Smithy's still-splayed body, first to the others, and then, when their blank, hopeless expressions proved too painful, to the hallway itself, to the cracked plaster and crumbling mouldings, to the discoloured walls that marked the limits of her world. The malevolent sprite was clearly back in the driver's seat...

'How could you?' Dot said, closing her eyes.

Before either had a chance to react, Smithy started walking towards them. Slow but fiercely determined strides. Neither of them moved. They couldn't. Something was holding them in place. The authority of this old warrior, perhaps, or the menace of his imminent explosion? Impossible to know, although its effectiveness was impossible to deny. The clock, apropos of nothing, chimed again. Smithy's lip curled into a terrifying smile.

As he was advancing, Frankie slouched from the staff room. At first she looked irritated, bored, as if interrupted, but when she saw what was happening her features cracked with mild interest...

Dot's head was spinning. How could this be? Smithy had been plucked from the floor, rewound, re-placed, and was advancing on the CareFriends again as if the humiliation of a few seconds earlier had just been wiped from the slate. She felt sick. Her body was rejecting this repeat performance as if it was a virus, forcing it out through the pores of her skin.

Dot looked across at the others. Were they seeing this too? She couldn't tell, although their eyes were trained on Smithy with an attention that suggested this rift in time was an exquisite torture devised for her alone. How many repetitions would she be forced to watch?

Jeepers! The Carpet!

A slither of a second before Frankie was due to slip her toe under the rug, however, something happened. Dot wouldn't have been able to explain it if asked, but for an instant she felt a strain in the room around her, a tension, a concentrated energy, primed for release like the string of an archer's bow. The whole room, the whole house, perhaps the whole world trembled. The walls around her seemed to flex. It was so intense, she feared she would pass out...

Then came the release. Frankie's feet slapped together and lifted, both of them, from the floor as she pivoted about the axis of her pelvis, spinning ninety degrees. She yelped – '*Ah! Agh!*' – and slapped to the floor like a decked fish.

And nobody noticed! They were all too transfixed by Smithy's advance – now gloriously uninterrupted. A few feet from his target, he dipped his shoulder and, with the grace of a rugby forward, rammed into Tristan's gut, scooping the CareFriend up onto his shoulder before the two of them dropped, hard and heavily, onto the stairs.

Pat dodged the impact and wasted no time setting off across the hallway. With barely a backwards glance at his fallen colleague he took hold of Frankie, dazed from her own inexplicable tumble, pulled her to her feet in one fluid motion, and the two of them were out of the door and halfway down the driveway before anyone had the chance to stop them.

Smithy hoisted Tristan – writhing, though with little real fight – back onto his shoulder, strode across the hall, flung open the rubber room door and hurled the bewildered youth inside, before closing it and bolting it shut.

Then he turned to the others. He looked as surprised as they did. Dazed, as all revolutionaries look at the moment of victory – unable to believe what has happened. In barely five minutes everything had been overturned, and none of them quite knew how. No matter, that was for the historians to argue over. Or not. Green Oaks, suddenly, was theirs now...

Without a word, Smithy walked towards them. As he reached the edge of the rug, his toe caught on it. He looked down and smoothed away the kink with his foot. With an expression on his face Dot found utterly inscrutable, Smithy took Betty in his arms and rested his old, heavy head on her shoulder.

On the floor above, the closet door opened. For a few seconds a high-pitched sound, almost a shriek, could be heard, the sound of air rushing into a vacuum. Entropy at work. Then, a lanky pyjama-wearing old man was ejected – spat! – through the door and onto the landing. A dead heap of bones.

Dead?

No, not quite. Watch:

Limbs distended, a mouth gasped.

Fall in chaps.

One two three... ah!... four!

Book Six

Gripping the Zimmer's bars tightly, Dot shifted her weight onto her left foot and then, tentatively, tipped over onto her right. The ankle twinged, stabbed… but held! After so much time under plaster her right leg had taken on an existence quite removed from the rest of her body. It was mannishly furry and pale and, while all of her muscles had withered, her right calf had atrophied to such an extent that if someone had told her Doctor Frankenstein had passed in the night and replaced her lower leg with a goat's, she would have accepted this explanation without too much protest. Wasted though it was, it was recovering.

Ward B was empty this morning. She remembered, vaguely, hearing the others awake, exchange a few jokes, a few barbs, and then, alone or in pairs, leave the room. Now that all the doors were left unlocked – all but one, anyway – it was difficult to keep them in one place, except when they were sleeping. Set free, they had explored Green Oaks, discovered rooms, upstairs and down, that had previously existed for them only as closed or locked doors. The morning after the CareFriends had been chased from Green Oaks, Olive had once again shaken Dot awake.

'Oh, Dotty, you have to see it. It's wonderful!'

'Hmm… Olive? What time is…? What are you…?'

'The toilet, Dotty. In the staffroom. The seat. It's made of *wood*.'

Or it was the stash of food in the kitchen, or Cornish's library, of books and music, or the carpet and faux-coal fireplace in Ward A. Everything seemed wondrous, everything new. The Hadean wasteland had transformed, overnight, into Aladdin's cave. Lanyard, after a few hours of tinkering, had fixed the chairlift, and they had queued like impatient children at a fairground to try it out. Now, barely ten minutes passed without the new calm, drained of its eeriness, being broken by that dilapidated whirr, carrying one of them up or down the stairs.

For Dot, however, it was the phone in Cornish's office that had been the greatest boon of their newfound freedom. As soon as the Captain and Smithy had shifted the bloated corpse of the unfortunate director, she'd nestled into the office chair, picked up the receiver, and let her fingers trace that familiar old dance across the keypad.

'Knot!' The imperiousness with which the small boy answered the phone had always made her smile.

'Kristoph?'

'Ja?'

'It's Granny. Is your daddy home?'

Thomas must have been standing beside his son because his voice rang out immediately.

'Mum?' Then, whispering. 'What the bloody hell? We've been trying to call you for months. Does nobody ever answer the phone in that place? I almost contacted the police. You've no idea how…' At which he had broken down in great, heaving sobs.

Dot had apologised, explained, her voice acting as an emollient to her son's distress. She had wept too. The tears had been rolling before the call connected, but now they were charging down her cheeks in happy torrents. It was so unlike Thomas to cry and, after a while, he had gathered himself.

'How's Dad?' he asked. Dot had thought back to earlier that evening when Leonard, mud-caked and ecstatic had barrelled into the ward.

'He's fine,' she'd said. 'Well, as fine as can be expected.'

The weight back on her left foot now, she shuffled the Zimmer forward a good six inches and repeated the process, her arms trembling with the strain. A part of her was surprised she was even walking again, that a body as old as hers could be both disintegrating and, simultane-ously, executing a dogged recovery. The body couldn't hold back the tide forever, of course, but something in her admired it for trying now. Admired the delusion and the fight. More fool her for ever thinking that she could choose to draw the line.

Her thoughts turned abruptly to Leonard and the Captain.

Where were they this morning?

'The trick,' Captain Ruggles said as he bound the two oak twigs together, 'is to twist the grass before knotting it. That increases the strength enormously.'

Lance Corporal Knot was lying on the grass, watching the only cloud in the clear blue sky slowly unpick itself to nothing. A long blade of grass was arcing from between his lips.

'Twist the grass,' he echoed, vacantly, 'before knotting it.'

'Exactly!' Ruggles said, hopping to his feet. He leaned over the long mound of earth and thrust his makeshift cross, complete now, into one end. Then he pulled it out again, walked the length of the mound, and thrust it into the other end, before pulling it out again.

'I suppose it's no use asking you which end was his head and which his feet?' he said, turning to the Lance Corporal. No answer. The Captain shrugged and plunged it into the middle of the mound. 'He's lucky to get a cross at all, if you ask me. A lot of more deserving men have received a lot shoddier treatment during this god-awful war.' His gaze lifted to the first floor of the guard house. 'Much, much more deserving.'

The cross was somewhat lopsided and the Captain reached down to straighten it. It was presumptuous of him, he knew, to assume the Kommandant would want his grave marked with a cross. Perhaps he wasn't a Christian at all. He certainly hadn't acted like one. Then again, the mind could be remarkably plastic. It could, like a French waiter, balance all kinds of apparently contradictory beliefs on its tray, without ever toppling over.

Perhaps, though, he'd still have preferred a swastika. Well, tough luck! There was no way Ruggles would sully his hands by making one, or this newly liberated earth by laying one upon it.

Lance Corporal Knot hoisted himself into a sitting position.

'The war?' he asked, as if angling for a memory that was refusing to bite. 'Is it won now, then? Is it over? Is it tea time? I didn't hear mother calling…'

'Impossible to say, old boy,' Ruggles answered, straightening up. He brushed himself down and looked out over the war-ravaged desert. 'Communications are down at the moment, so I have no way of contacting headquarters. Whether it's over or not, though, and whether we win or lose in the end, what we did here will go down in history. Dirk Shavings will be proud of us when he hears about this, you mark my words. Really! Whoever heard of prisoners taking over the camp? The insane taking over the asylum, that's a worn out old trope… But this? And to think, all that time I was planning an *escape*…'

In the hallway, Dot saw Lanyard, on his knees in front of the grandfather clock. The door was open and an array of components, including the long, delicate pendulum, had been laid meticulously on the carpet.

'Dot, dear!' Lanyard said, turning and wiping his greasy hands on his trousers. 'How's the Zimmer working out for you? Did we get the height right? I can easily shave off a few more centimetres if need be.'

Dot shunted forward a few inches.

'No, no, Lanyard. It's just perfect like this.'

Lanyard almost looked disappointed.

'Well, that or anything else, just ask,' he said.

'You look like you've got your hands full already,' Dot said, nodding at the clock.

'Oh this? No, no. I should have this done by noon. The caretaker actually kept a fine toolbox.' The tools were lying beside the clock parts, arranged with surgical precision.

'I can see that.'

'I think I found what the problem was,' he said. 'Should have it working tickety-boo in no time. It so frustrates me when things don't work as they should.'

Of all of them, it was Lanyard who had undergone the most dramatic transformation. Dot sensed a lingering shame about how he had acted before, and an effort to make amends. That couldn't be the only explanation, though. The change was simply too great.

'Where are you off to, anyway?' A shifty look fleeted across Lanyard's face. Dot tried to disguise her own shiftiness when she replied:

'Oh, I'm just taking a little stroll. You know how it is.'

'Maybe you should pop your head around the door of C, check everything's alright in there.'

Ward C. Just across the hall. Where it always must have been, Dot was forced to admit. And yet… Why had it proven so difficult for her to locate? Where had she thought that door led? Had she even noticed that door at all? Even though only a couple of days had passed since her reunion with Leonard, Dot found it hard, almost impossible, to think herself back into her mind as it was before. That was the problem when things got turned on their heads: all reference points were lost.

Still, there Ward C was, and Lanyard mentioning it had made Dot suspicious.

'Why? Is nobody keeping an eye?'

'Betty, I think,' Lanyard said, turning back to his work. 'But you know how it gets in there. It's always nice to have company.'

Okay – she thought, glaring at Lanyard as he hunched back over his work – *I'll go to Ward C, but only because my original destination can wait.* She smiled. *It can wait and wait and wait…*

She arced off course and, a couple of minutes later, made it into Ward C. The first thing she noticed was that Leonard wasn't home.

'Don't worry!' Betty said, intuiting from her chair beside the door. 'He's with the Captain. Important mission, apparently.'

'Betty! What have you got on?'

'A nurse's cap. I found them in the stores,' Betty said, shifting the origami hat so that it perched squarely on top of her head. 'When I do something, I like to do it properly. And I'd thank you for at least making some effort to hide your amusement.'

'You look splendid, Bet,' Dot said. 'Everyone looks splendid.'

It was true. Dot had insisted that Ward C be their priority and now, a few days later, the place was unrecognisable from how they had first found it. Betty had recruited the Captain, Olive and Smithy – the most able-bodied of the lot – to clean and disinfect the room, to strip and change the sheets, to open the windows, to bathe the poor sods as much as they were able. She couldn't tell if it made much difference to the residents themselves, but she hoped it did. Either way, at least they all looked like real people again.

'Snap!' An old, olive-skinned man slammed a card down on the half-eaten Monopoly board, sending a shower of plastic counters to the floor. The small woman sitting across the table from him applauded.

It had been Betty's idea, just yesterday, to give them the games, and they had taken to them with real enthusiasm. The fact that they were incomplete, unplayable, didn't seem to matter. The haphazardness of the games seemed to gel perfectly with the haphazardness of their minds. The Jack of Hearts overtook Colonel Mustard to pass Go and collect several jigsaw pieces for his trouble. Why, in the end, *shouldn't* that make sense? Stranger things had been known to.

There would be darker days ahead, of course. When someone fell ill, or when the food or drugs ran low, and Dot wasn't sure yet how they would handle things. But she was trying not to worry too much about that for now.

'I'll relieve you after lunch, Bet,' she said, clomping Windsor's old Zimmer around a full hundred-and-eighty. Betty batted the air.

'Whenever you're ready, my darling.'

Just as she was about to leave the ward, Betty took hold of Dot's wrist and looked sternly at her.

'I need you to do me a favour, Dot.'

'What's that?' The grip tightened.

'Help me keep an eye on Alain.'

'An eye on Smithy? Is he alright?'

'Oh he's fine. But I'm worried he's getting just a little too big for his boots.'

Dot had noticed a certain cockiness to Smithy since that night, but had been more than willing to forgive him it.

'And I do wish he wasn't acting so proud about his newly loosened bowels.'

Dot smiled.

'We do have him to thank, though. Without him, none of this…'

'Come on, Dot,' Betty interrupted. 'You must be able to see that Alain's actions were the symptom of something, not the cause. I'd been trying to get him to do something for ages. Who'd have thought it would be an act of rudeness, of social indiscretion that would finally make him crack?'

Well, not Dot for one. Then again…

'Don't get me wrong,' Betty went on. 'I'm glad he's proud of himself. God knows it's been a long time coming, but…' she paused, as if afraid of betraying a confidence. 'The way he sighed and rolled his eyes when I mentioned Ward C earlier. Just keep an eye on him, will you? We don't want history repeating itself here.'

'Of course, Bet. Don't worry too much, eh?'

Out of the ward, Dot reset her course for her original destination. The rubber room window was dark. She ignored Lanyard this time as she crossed the hallway, attentive for any movement, any flicker of light. To offset the slowness of her progress, she thought back to what she had seen yesterday, the first time she had paid that room a visit.

To begin with he had looked so small, so helpless, balled up in the far corner. How the mighty fall, she had thought, watching the boy sleep. The menace he had once embodied for her had leaked out of him, pooled on the floor like a rancid puddle of piss. It was as if he had been a man possessed, and the events of the previous night, when Smithy had hoisted him on his shoulder, strode to the rubber room, tumbled him in and bolted the door, had acted as some kind of exorcism. He was an empty vessel, a wreck of his former self.

They couldn't keep him forever, of course. She knew that. But deciding what to do with him, when to release him, that would be difficult. It was De Tocqueville, she thought she remembered, who had said that in a revolution, just as in a novel, the most difficult part to invent was the end. Luckily this was not really one and certainly not the other. The end would most likely just invent itself.

She'd knocked on the window, knocked until he stirred. Then, as he ungummed his eyes, she'd pressed her face up against the pane of glass so he could see exactly who was watching him, exactly how the tables had been turned. At first he'd looked confused, then desperate, begging her with outstretched hands to set him free. Perhaps he had her down as one of the least wronged. Perhaps she was. She'd smiled – a vicious sneer, one she hadn't known she was capable of – and slowly shook her head. At that he had grown enraged and hurled the pewter bowl against the door. Dot had only smiled more broadly, maybe she had even laughed… It felt good to be cruel. The pretence to goodness, to sanity, took its toll after a while. She had been engrossed by the boy's predicament, revelling in it, so much so that she hadn't noticed someone approaching her from behind, laying his bony hand on her shoulder.

'Private?' the Captain had said, softly. With the presence of another her pleasure had evaporated. It was replaced with a savage shame and she'd blushed. She didn't know why. Wasn't Ruggles the one most sinned against by this brute? Shouldn't he be enjoying it as much as she was?

'Dinner's ready,' he said, pulling her gently away from the door.

Despite yesterday's embarrassment, though, Dot couldn't stop herself from visiting Tristan again. It reassured her to know that the source of so much of their discomfort and humiliation was locked away like that. She could allow herself a little peek…

Flicking the light switch, she pressed her face to the glass. This morning, though, she couldn't see him. She lifted her hand from the Zimmer and knocked on the window. Nothing. She knocked harder.

'Hey!' she said when there was no reply. 'Boy! Show yourself!'

Still nothing.

'You don't want to eat today, eh?'

She was fingering the bolt. What she was doing was stupid. He'd be lying in wait for just such carelessness, ready to pounce as soon as the door was opened.

'Well, we'll see…'

Because to see was just what Dot needed. Knowing he was in there, suffering, just wasn't enough. She had to see it on his face. She'd be quick. Unbolt the door silently, push it open then pull it shut again. Just enough for a quick glimpse. Just enough to look the cocky young bastard in the eye.

The door was already unbolted. Her body was one step ahead of her mind. And why shouldn't it be? It had suffered just as much.

'Boy!'

She knew as soon as the door was open a crack that the rubber room was empty. She threw it open wide. Nothing. A dirty dish, a spoon, a stale smell, but no Tristan.

'Lanyard!' She craned her head round, but the duplicitous swine had slunk off somewhere. 'Betty!' No answer.

'Betty!' she croaked again. 'Where is the little bugger?'

From upstairs a scratchy recording of a trumpet sounded like a clarion call.

'What is going on here?' she said… to herself, since nobody else seemed to be listening. 'Who on earth would let him go?'

Captain Ruggles had found the photo of Dulcie in the Guards' mess room. It had been torn in two along the crease, and was flecked with the detritus of food waste from its time languishing in the bin. After a few meticulous minutes with a damp sponge and sticky tape, Ruggles had restored his totem to some semblance of its old form. And yet, it had lost something too. Some of its power, some of its hold over him. Ever since he had been spat from that room upstairs, his memory wiped clean of what had come to pass therein, and had discovered what his fellow prisoners had accomplished while he was away. Ever since then he had found himself thinking less about Dulcie. Less? No, not less exactly, but certainly differently. His single-bloody-mindedness had softened, almost evaporated, the longing to see her, to hold her, was still there, but it didn't gnaw as ferociously, didn't hurt as much...

He took the picture out of his shirt pocket and examined it again. Dulcie. There she was. Or at least, there she had been. When he looked at it now it almost felt as if he was looking at it the wrong way through a telescope. The distance between them felt composed of more time, more years, more life than he dared even imagine.

Captain Ruggles sat down on the damp grass beside the Lance Corporal.

'Tell me, L.C. Do you have children yourself?' Lance Corporal Knot yanked the tuft of grass he had been fingering from the ground. For a moment Ruggles wondered if he had even heard him. Then the batman's face creased into a smile and his eyes pricked with tears.

'Kristoph,' he said. 'My little boy.'

The chairlift ground to a halt at the top of the staircase. Clunking the Zimmer from her lap onto the floor, Dot righted it, checked that it was steady, and hefted herself from the seat. Her arms trembled with the effort as she rocked her weight onto her good leg.

The music was coming from the Director's office. It was an insufferably playful ditty, all trumpets and violins, rancid with mi-siècle optimism. Someone was signing along:

> '*Toot-a-shanjay deepwee yeah,*
> *Ella a day sure kew regard over nets,*
> *Yadu leelas yardayman tandoos,*
> *Solami le so yeah va parrot-err...*'

It was Olive massacring the lyrics, singing as though she had pebbles in her mouth, joyfully unconcerned with corralling her gobbledegook into line with her French duelling partner. If the disappearance of the CareFriend hadn't disturbed her so much, Dot might have even found it endearing. As it was...

'Olive!'

'*Boom! Aster du your fait boom…*'

'Olive, can you turn that racket down?'

The music choked off with a click. Olive was sitting at Cornish's desk, two piles of cardboard folders in front of her, as well as the portable stereo.

'What's the matter, Dot?' Olive asked with a smile. 'You don't like… erm…' she picked up the CD case, squinted. 'Charles *Trennet*?'

'What are you doing?'

'Filing,' she said. 'You really wouldn't believe the mess all this was in. Not even alphabetised.'

'What's in the files?'

'These are resident files. Our files. Personal details, medical records, family contact details, behaviour reports.'

Concrete information. Real details. Would getting her hands on these finally calm Olive down, or just be more grist to her mill? Dot herself was tempted to find out how well the stories she had imagined for them all mapped onto reality. She saw her own there – Dorothy Knot – and felt suddenly defensive towards its contents. Olive leaned in conspiratorially.

'Did you know the Captain was never even in the army?'

'I had my suspicions,' Dot said, picking up the Captain's file. 'Are you sure you should be looking at all this? I mean, shouldn't it be…' – she flipped it open – 'Confidential?'

'If we don't, how will we know who should take what medicine?'

Dot glanced at the first page of the Captain's file.

First name: Dylan. Surname: Ruggles. Other names: None.

'Funny…' she said to herself.

'What's funny?' Olive asked, but Dot didn't really hear her.

Next of kin. Wife: Celia (deceased). Children: Dulcie Andrews (né Ruggles).

There was a phone number under his daughter's name with a note: *Weekdays after 6. Weekends.* This had been struck through with red ink and beside it, in block capitals: *ONLY IN CASE OF EMERGENCY/DEATH.*

Below this was a witheringly concise summary of Ruggles' life. His place of birth (*Meanwell*), his education (*Grammar*), and his employment history as a clerk, then accountant for the gas board.

'Undistinguished,' Dot muttered to herself, rolling the folder into a tube and sliding it into her pocket.

'Erm. Are you taking that, Dot?' Olive asked. 'Are you sure you should?'

'Why not?' Dot snapped. 'People seem to be doing what they want around here.' Olive opened one of the files and pretended to read. When it had become clear Dot was waiting for her reply she said, 'So... you heard?'

'I saw, Ol,' she said. 'I didn't hear. I saw. Who let him go?'

Despite her best efforts Olive's eyes flickered to Dot's pocket.

'Impossible!' she said. Then: 'Why would he?'

Olive shrugged.

'You'll have to ask him.'

'That's exactly what I intend to do, as soon as I find the little shit,' Dot said, already clomping the Zimmer towards the door.

'Hold it, Lance Corporal! Hold it, now! Just a moment longer!'

'You said that two minutes ago...'

'Ha! You remembered that well enough, didn't you? Now hold steady, I said.'

Lance Corporal Knot teetered left, then teetered right again while Captain Ruggles, mounted on his shoulders, crucified himself to maintain balance. He wasn't helped in his quest by the battered old saucepan in his left hand and the huge ball of twine in his right.

After a few precarious seconds, the Lance Corporal determinedly stamped his feet into the grass, steadying their crippled totem-pole.

'Attaboy, L.C.! This is the last one now, I promise. There's hardly any room left on the sail as it is.'

Lance Corporal Knot mumbled something.

'What's that, L.C.?'

'It's a bloody branch!' he cried, almost sending them reeling again. 'Not a sail. It's a tree, sir! An oak. Not a smock mill. I just don't understand how you can't see that!'

'My dear friend,' the Captain said, dandling his fingers through the remains of Knot's hair. 'If these are indeed oak trees as you have repeatedly claimed – and not just today – would they really be able to do that?'

Gripping the Lance Corporal firmly by his pate, Ruggles snapped his head a sharp ninety degrees to the right.

Knot stared, blinked, rubbed his eyes with his paws like a cartoon bear and blinked again. There was no denying it, the four great boughs of the second oak tree were... rotating! Cutting great circles against the clear blue sky the branches – for they were still branches to his eyes, not sails, replete with smaller branches and scads of rustling leaves – were sweeping groundwards then thrusting skywards, unaware of the aberration of nature they represented.

'Done!' Captain Ruggles said, ignoring the Lance Corporal's shock. He tapped his mount's skull. 'You can let me down now, L.C.'

Lance Corporal Knot, keeping an eye on the rotating branches, crouched shakily, allowing Captain Ruggles to execute a splendid commando roll before springing to his feet.

'A fine job, old friend,' he said. Knot followed his gaze to the cluster of pots and pans dangling from the branches. 'Just as I envisioned it.'

'You'll forgive me, sir,' the Lance Corporal said, 'if I ask you to remind me just what exactly these wind chimes are for.'

'I will and I do, L.C.,' the Captain said, brushing blades of grass from his fatigues. 'What we have constructed here is a rustic but ruthlessly efficient early warning system. Hand me the ladle will you? And observe!' Knot complied and the Captain lifted the ladle and struck one of the pans with it. A metallic note shattered the calm of the morning.

'Imagine the racket we'll be able to conjure up with all these pots and pans. Should the axis launch any kind of counter attack, whoever is acting as our lookout will stir up an unholy din, rallying all of our troops.' The Captain paused and looked out over the desert of razor-wire and churned earth. 'Although I hope with every sinew in my body, old boy, that we'll never have to use it.'

★

Sure to cover all bases before boarding the chairlift again, Dot left Cornish's office and eyed the three other doors on the landing. The first looked to be little more than a closet, but she had to make sure. It was plain, except for a small, black knot in the wood, the size of a spy-hole. Taking hold of the handle, she pushed the door open.

Nothing. A bucket, a couple of mops, a broom, and a few aerosol cans, weapons in the war against flies, cockroaches and moths. She closed the door tightly.

Now for Ward A.

What had happened there on the night they took over Green Oaks scared them all. Things had quietened down. Tristan had been locked up and the other CareFriends had disappeared with a speed and determination that had reassured them that they weren't coming back. At least not right away. Exuberant but exhausted, they had taken to their beds.

It was past midnight when she had been woken by a noise. A deep, monstrous rumbling, the approach of heavy vehicles. The counter-attack – that was her first thought. Well, it had been fun while it had lasted, but the blowback was sure to be fierce.

The vehicles had stopped right outside their windows, the brutal glow of the headlights illuminating the ward. Dot had heard the crackle of a radio, the back-and-forth between whoever was outside and some distant control centre.

Dot had sat upright in bed, and noticed that all the others had too, even Olive, who had dragged her sheet up so only her eyes and the top of her head were visible.

The front door had flown open. Four figures then strode into the hallway carrying two stretchers. They had scanned the hallway, paying no attention to the seven pairs of terrified eyes in Ward B, then hurriedly climbed the stairs. Barely a minute later they had thudded back down, their stretchers sagging with two fossilised old creatures, their heads as soft and wrinkly as a pair of scrotums. Dot had never seen them before. They had been asleep, or unconscious, unaware of what was happening to them and why.

The stretcher-bearers had hustled out the door, the last one casting a final gaze about the ground floor, unconcerned with the fact he was being observed. The door had closed, the rumble of the vehicles risen up then died away.

Silence had reigned again for a brief moment before a woman's desperate cry split the air.

'What about me?' it had lamented. 'What about me?'

It was that same voice Dot heard now, its authority restored.

'Olive!' it cried. 'My bunions!'

At which the string-bean went scudding past Dot on the landing.

The door to the guardhouse opened and the sickly Private – who had been bereft of a certain vim since the demise of the Field Marshall – emerged from the gloom of the building. It was that gloom, in part, that was keeping Ruggles outside in the resplendent sunlight. It was as if, during his time in the upstairs closet, his eyes had been so bombarded with darkness, so scoured, so attacked – and not merely deprived of light, this was something quite different – that now, whenever he caught sight of a shadow, or a dingy corner, his body resonated with the repressed memories of the struggle.

Nobody had asked him about it because nobody, except his loyal but forgetful batman, knew that he had gone in there in search of dear old Karmacharya. And he hadn't volunteered any information, either. It wasn't proper, he knew, for a man of his rank and standing to turn himself inside out over matters like this. As a Captain he had to be a finely tuned body and a supple reasonable mind, but that was it. He couldn't dally with that soupy in-between world.

Still, he hadn't emerged completely unchanged. Or rather, he'd felt, at first, that he had, but the world seemed to have other ideas. It was difficult for Ruggles to articulate. Things looked different, cast in a new light, impermanent somehow, less authentic, falser. As he'd grappled to pin down the thought, he'd tried out different similes for size. He thought first of the farm set he had played with as a child – wooden animals, buildings and trees. He thought too of the theatre, of the painted flats used to jemmy enormous and extravagant cityscapes into the constricted space of the proscenium arch stage, of how the audience, suspending their disbelief, would refuse to let their minds even contemplate the existence of the wings, where actors huddled before making their entrances, exchanging one costume for another. Along similar lines he also thought of the Punch and Judy fit-ups of his family trips to Swanage and Brighton, of how impossible it had seemed to him as a little boy that a single man – the Professor – was controlling all the puppets, manipulating the swizzle in his mouth to spirit forth a dozen different voices. All of the similes had one thing in common: make-believe, charade… He couldn't escape such thoughts, or their obvious implications. If the world was a farm set, who was the wanton boy manipulating the pieces? If the world was a theatre, where were the wings, where the backstage, and who were the actors really? And if it was a fit-up, what did the Professor actually look like?

Captain Ruggles didn't see the Private at once. It was only when the wind slammed the door shut behind him that Ruggles turned, all thoughts of farm sets and theatres and fit-ups scattering like a plague of spooked rats.

'Ah! Here he is, our Royal Engineer!' The new arrival looked confused for an instant, then glowed.

'Dylan,' he said, adding, 'it is alright if I call you that?' Ruggles nodded his assent. 'Have you seen Dot this morning? Dot, uh, Private Thingy? Your friend, with the ankle?'

'All my friends have…' Ruggles began, before his brain knitted together the descriptive elements into a coherent image. 'Not yet, Private. Why do you ask?'

'I just thought you'd like to know that… well, that she knows.'

'Knows?'

'That you let the boy go.'

Captain Ruggles, who had crouched to bridge the distance between him and the diminutive Private, straightened up, looked away, then looked back again, his regard birdishly intense.

How did she know? How did any of them know? He had conducted the operation with the utmost secrecy, posting Lance Corporal Knot as his lookout and… He glared at his batman, reclining on the grass, tugging tufts of it out with his fat hands and showering them into the air above him. Of course. Who else?

'What use was he to us, anyway?' he said, defensively. 'He was only a lowly foot soldier. A lever-puller, a button-pusher. He had orders and was following them. He was a weak'un, not a bad'un. Better all round to just show the boy a bit of humanity, don't you think?'

He wasn't telling the Private everything, of course. The explanation he had just furnished him with was drawn from the file marked *Post-Factum*. He couldn't tell him how it had really happened, how he had awoken in the middle of the night, had gone, almost against his will, to the lock-up and had looked in, seen the boy-soldier asleep and broken his heart over him. The decision to release him had been made at that moment. The scaffold of justification… that had come later.

'I just thought you should know,' the Private said. 'Anyway.'

'Anyway,' Ruggles echoed. For a moment the two of them watched the Lance Corporal as he continued his assault on the lawn.

'Tell me,' Ruggles said, leaning in so that the Lance Corporal, who wasn't listening anyway, wouldn't be able to hear. 'I've been watching you these last few days, and your dexterity with a drill, your skill with a screwdriver. It's quite remarkable. Which makes me deduce this whole Private act is little more than a cover story.'

The Private nodded, but said nothing. Ruggles went on.

'What I mean to ask is – and just between commissioned officers, of course – what rank are you really, old boy?'

He leaned in, an overly sincere look on his face. He licked his lips before speaking:

'Well. Just between commissioned officers. I'm a Commander.'

Captain Ruggles clapped his hands over his mouth to contain the gasp, his eyes almost shooting from their sockets. As the shock faded he removed the hands and used them to bat air towards his blushing cheeks.

'M... I... 6?' he mouthed, breathlessly.

The Commander tilted his head to one side and nodded. In possession of himself again Captain Ruggles snapped to attention and offered his hand. The Commander took it.

'A genuine, genuine pleasure to work with' – his voice dipping to a whisper – 'MI6. A real and genuine and authentic and veritable pleasure!'

'At ease, please!' the Commander said, extracting his hand from Ruggles'. 'I think... we can drop the formalities somewhat now, don't you?'

'Whatever you say, Sir. I mean... Mate!' Ruggles said, grinning. 'Although would you care to inspect the early warning system Lance Corporal Knot and I have improvised this morning? I'd value your professional opinion.'

The Commander sighed.

'I suppose you won't leave me in peace until I do?'

'Excellent, right this way then.'

The Commander examined the pots and pans, tried to strike one of them, but couldn't reach high enough, so let the Captain demonstrate for him.

'Fine work, Captain,' he said. '*Erm*... very... very...'

'Thank you Commander. Neither is the arrangement of the pots merely random. I have long maintained an interest in acoustics and have studied the various forms and compositions of the utensils, so as to...'

'... very, *er*, fine...'

'... so as to, generate the... generate the highest... the highest volume... Is everything alright, Sir? Mate!'

Something had distracted the Commander. He was fixing the horizon, squinting.

'What's that?' Captain Ruggles followed the direction of his gaze, but saw nothing.

'What's what?'

'That!' He pointed out over the hills. And maybe, yes, Captain Ruggles did see something there. Arranged on the lip of a distant hill, a line of black spots that he hadn't noticed before.

'Lance Corporal!' he bellowed. Knot, who had been napping on the grass, sprang awake and rocked to his feet.

'Sir?'

'Do me the favour of lending me your spectacles, won't you?' Without giving the Lance Corporal a moment to respond, Ruggles plucked them from his face, shoving the ladle into the blinded soldier's hand. Holding the glasses at arm's length, he angled the lens between his fingers, squinting too now.

'Blow me,' his arm dropped limply to his side.

'What is it?' the Commander asked.

'Tanks,' Ruggles mumbled. 'Eight or nine tanks. Panzer Fours.'

'You mean cars, don't you, Dylan? But we have no idea whether they're friendly or not. Perhaps…'

'Oh cars, cars! To hell with your cars! Why must everyone contradict me all the time? I tell you they are tanks because tanks are what I see, Commander. Tanks. Not Cars. Tanks. *Axis* tanks. Panzer Fours.'

The Commander steadied himself against the tree.

'Then what are we to do?'

'Lance Corporal?' the Captain barked, in control of himself once again. 'Hand me the ladle!'

The howler that night had been Hortense. Long after the other residents of Ward A had been evacuated, she could still be heard sobbing alone in her ward. Why she had been left was a mystery to Dot, although it must have had something to do with money. There was really very little that didn't.

It was Olive who had reached out to Hortense that first morning. After Betty had prepared a steaming vat of porridge, Olive had first invited her to join them, and when she had refused – politely, timidly – she had taken two bowls upstairs and they had eaten breakfast together.

'I used to meet women like that all the time when I stitched dresses in Selfridges,' Olive said, casually dropping a detail of her life BGO. 'Inside their castles, with their courtiers, they are queens, and have the attitude to match. But as soon as they're forced outside, they crumble. She's upset at having been left behind, but she won't cause any trouble.'

Olive was right. Hortense kept to herself, adopting Olive as a kind of housekeeper, a go-between, and a confidante. Olive seemed to relish the role, steeped as it was in the classic mistress-maid dynamic, in which the real power lay not with the person who assumed herself in charge, but with the sly and manipulative underling.

By the time Dot had crossed the landing Olive had already settled in and the two of them were chirruping away.

'… difficult to say Mum at this stage but I'm…'

'… the bunion, dear… work the bunion, not the corn… alphabetically…'

'… afraid for the coming days… a hierarchy is forming that may not be conducive to…'

'… the scissors, please, what did I tell you… always the scissors, never the clippers…'

'Good morning!' Dot knocked on the doorjamb, unsure why. They looked up, brief flashes of irritation followed quickly by false, toothy smiles. Olive, sitting on a footstool now, Hortense's bare and ugly talons resting in her lap, patted the feet to reassure her new friend. Still, Hortense executed a kind of physical retreat, becoming noticeably limper in the plush cushioning of her *chaise-longue*.

'What brings you up here?'

Dot prickled. Why shouldn't she come upstairs?

'I'm looking for the Captain, as Olive well knows.'

Hortense perked up, intrigued by the new twist to events. Olive gave her a fill-you-in-later kind of look.

'Betty saw him do it, apparently,' Olive said. Dot wondered why Olive hadn't told her this a few minutes earlier, but quickly understood. She was showing off to her new friend. 'Says he spent almost an hour standing at the rubber room window yesterday, just watching the boy. Said it was strange. Sometimes he was looking through the glass, other times he seemed to be watching his own reflection in it. Muttering to himself too, but she couldn't hear what he was saying. Then he slowly undid the bolt, whispered something, then turned and strolled off as if nothing had happened. The little bastard wasted no time in escaping, of course. But don't worry, Dot. I don't think we'll be seeing him again.'

That, Dot thought, wasn't the point. She still couldn't understand what had possessed the Captain. Had he spent so long living in that fantasy world, embedded deep in the trenches of his own delirium, just to do something so inconsistent now? If he really believed there was a war on, there was no way he'd have let the boy go. Now she had his file, she had a good mind to seek him out, sit him down and force him to recognise, force him to understand the absurdity of his charade. She turned, about to do just that, when Olive stood up.

'In fact, Dot, I've been meaning to speak with you about something else. Do you mind?'

'A minute won't make much of a difference, I suppose,' Dot said.

'Excuse us for a moment, Mum,' Olive said to Hortense, gesturing to Dot to join her in the ornate armchairs by the fireplace. Beautiful old pieces of furniture, Dot thought as she sat down, but my did they stink of piss.

'What is it?' Olive glanced at the door before leaning towards Dot.

'Smithy,' she said.

'Smithy?' Dot echoed, remembering her earlier conversation with Betty.

'I've been thinking it over, Dot, and it all makes sense…' she paused, waiting for some kind of agreement or acknowledgement.

'What makes sense?'

'He planned it all.'

'Stop, Olive.' Dot knew this trope well enough. Same story, different characters. Same poles, new horses.

'No, I'm serious, hear me out. He chose his time perfectly, can't you see that?'

'I'm not sure he chose anything, Olive. I'm not sure he thought too much about it at all.'

'Wrong, Dot! Wrong! Think was *all* he did. Think and plan and plot. Who had the most to gain once the CareFriends were gone? Who else had the strength to kill Cornish?'

It was true that the director's unsolved death bothered Dot. Of all the potential suspects – Smithy, the Captain, Tristan, Frankie and Pat – she couldn't imagine any of them capable of it, not really. There was Leonard too, of course. He had been roaming the halls of Green Oaks just before the body was discovered…

'There's talk of a girl,' Dot said.

'A girl!' Olive squawked. 'Listen to yourself, Dot. A girl?'

'I admit it sounds unlikely.'

'Unlikely? Impossible! There's always a motive. You just have to be brave enough to look for it.'

'Or crazy enough to invent it,' Dot said. 'And besides, Olive. It was you who showed Smithy the sketch…'

Before Dot could finish, the air exploded with the clamour of metal being beaten. She hopped from her armchair and bounded across to the window.

'What on earth is it?' Dot called to Olive over the din.

'It's the Captain,' Olive said. 'And Lanyard, and your Leonard too. They're in the garden.' Olive pulled her robe tightly around her body. All of the fight, all of the certainty she had been pouring forth only moments earlier had run dry. 'Bloody hell, Dot, I think something's wrong.'

By the time Dot had left Ward A, struggled onto the chairlift with the Zimmer on her lap, vibrated down the stairs, righted herself and shuffled through the door into the garden, most of the others were already outside. Olive had overtaken her on the stairs, while Betty had dropped what she was doing, swaddled herself in a cardigan and anorak, and come to investigate what lay behind the Captain's racket. Leonard was there too. Sitting on the ground he was covered in blades of grass. He looked at her, as he had been looking at all of them, kindly, but without a glimmer of recognition. This hurt, in a way, but she knew it wasn't his fault. His path had skewed sharply away from the one they had set off on together, and did so too long ago, for her to expect that it could ever swing back into line. Perhaps her own path had likewise skewed and she just hadn't noticed. Or had it been wishful thinking for her to imagine any two people could really share a common path at all? How different a story they might both have told about their marriage. How different a story all of the residents, all of the staff, might have told about Green Oaks. What was omitted was as important as what made it in. The despicable convenience of the blanks we leave.

Seeing the gathered crowd, the Captain stopped battering his demented mobile, dropped the ladle and came to join their huddle. He shook each of the new arrivals by the hand:

'Private,' he said, gripping Dot's hand firmly, as if he feared she might slip away. She thought about taking him to task for releasing the CareFriend, but then thought: what's the point? He'd just spin her some war story, give her some explanation involving military intelligence, or tactics... and then what? She'd just have to accept it as she always had...

Or would she? She felt the rolled cardboard file in her pocket. She reached down and fingered its rough edges. Confront him with the facts of his real life, there in black and white, and perhaps he would emerge from the fog, perhaps she'd be able to reel him in by reciting his date of birth, the name of his late wife or by – but could she? – by giving him the phone number with which, after all this time, he could be reunited with Dulcie. Speaking with Thomas had helped her, after all, brought her back, in a sense.

The Captain's hand came to rest on her own and gripped it. It was trembling.

'I've got something you should see,' she said, wriggling her hand beneath his. His fingers tightened over hers, and he was glaring at her, with an intense sadness.

'What?' he asked, although it rang like a please. A please don't.

'But I need you!' she wanted to say. 'We need you… if we're going to get through this. Put that tactical mind of yours to work in this world, the real world, and maybe you really will be able to make a difference. Maybe you'll actually be able to help us.'

The 'us', she knew, did not mean all of them. It was an exclusive us, a selfish us. It meant her and Leonard. The others, bless them, but in the end they could all go hang. She needed the Captain to come back to reality for them.

She tried to pull the file from her pocket but the Captain's hand held hers stubbornly in place. She resisted for a moment, then capitulated.

Oh, forget it! What did it matter, really, which world he lived in… except to her? Dragging him back, kick and biting, would be for her and her alone. An act of pure egotism, a wanton act of destruction, bombing Oz as if it was Dresden. With the Captain's hand still on top of her own, she buried the file deeper in her pocket.

'Nothing,' she said.

'Thank you,' the Captain said, letting go of her hand. He was still watching her although his expression had changed. She felt as if she wasn't looking at Captain Dylan Prometheus Ruggles, British Army First Airborne Division, but at the other Dylan Ruggles, he of no middle name, no military rank. Undistinguished. She wanted to tell him that it was this man, not the other one, that she would like to get to know, this one that had reunited her with Leonard, this one that was the hero. What she actually said surprised even herself. Not the fact that she had said it, but the fact that she was sure it was true… although since when?

'You know.'

'What in the name of Jumping Jehoshaphat is going on here?'

Smithy's bellowing denied Dot the reaction, the acknowledgement, she craved. He must have just come from a hot shower. Steam was rising from the cleft of his bathrobe and his skin was prickled red. He was wearing a towel-turban too, that twisted from his head like the Tower of Babel. There was a new cockiness to his stride, despite his bizarre appearance.

'You just interrupted the most tremendous shite!'

Betty rolled her eyes full circle and turned to him.

'I've a good mind to send you packing with language like that, Alain,' she said.

'If something's happening, Bet, I of all people…'

'Of *all* people!' Betty hooted it like a lion seal. Olive was eyeballing Dot.

'Captain,' Smithy said, locking the muscles in his face to prevent his humiliation from surfacing. 'Would you do me the honour?'

The Captain stepped away from the group.

'I'll do you all the honour,' he said. 'Look!' He pivoted on his heels and threw his arm up so that it was extending towards the horizon. 'It's time for the counter attack!'

The Captain's intended moment of drama was scuppered by the enfeebled eyes of the others. Some of them strained forward, others fumbled for spectacles on cords around their necks.

'What is…?'

'Do you see?'

'What's he… pointing at?'

Olive reached inside her coat and pulled out an old pair of theatre binoculars.

'They were Cornish's,' she said, adding. 'I hadn't planned on keeping them.'

'Give those here, woman!' Smithy snatched the binoculars and anchored them below his overhanging brow. Betty clenched her fists, kissed her teeth.

'Cars!' he barked, almost involuntarily. 'Six or seven of them. People too.'

'Anyone you recognise?' Dot said. The Captain flashed her a guilty glance.

'Not really. A few blokes in suits, a good dozen bovver-boys, skinheads.' He lowered the binoculars. The shower's blush had vanished. He was suddenly very pale. 'Christ, I think the Captain's right. I think this is the counter attack.'

Deflated, he plodded towards Betty. Dot swiped the binoculars from him. As Smithy leaned up against Betty she said:

'I don't know what *you* want,' but wrapped her arms around him anyway.

It took Dot a moment to locate the rank of cars. There were seven, not six, and they had spilled their human load onto the roadside verge. Bovver-boys was an apposite choice of words. These boys were clearly bent on bovver. Dot counted eleven of the buzz-cut slabs of meat, trussed into bomber jackets, combat trousers and boots. They stood in a gaggle, chatting, smoking, occasionally jostling for what she assumed to be their own iteration of alpha-supremacy. They had things, objects, weapons, stuffed in their belts. The binoculars weren't good enough for her to tell exactly what – batons probably, or canisters of pepper spray, or... She took a couple of deep breaths in an attempt to calm her nerves.

And yet despite the aggressive countenance of these thugs, it was the three men in suits that inspired the most fear in Dot. Perhaps it was the cut of their tailoring, wide at the shoulders, pinched at the waists, that gave them such an air of menace, or the shimmer of product in their hair. Or perhaps it was simply what they represented, some kind of brutal, steamrollering efficiency. A grim inevitability. The others, a dozen or so, were a more disparate band. She wondered if one middle-aged couple might be the same who had come to visit Olive a few months back. There was also a woman dressed in widow's weeds. Mrs Cornish? Had word already reached her of her husband's demise? A chill spiked Dot, as if the sun had just passed behind a cloud. But there were no clouds today. Just endless blue.

As she completed her sweep, she snagged on a final figure. Frankie, sitting cross-legged on the bonnet of one of the cars. She was wearing her CareFriend smock, but only for form. It was unbuttoned halfway down her chest. Beneath it she was wearing a black tee-shirt with a print of that cartoon coyote, jeans, and on her feet a pair of heavy black boots, loosely laced. A camera hung on a strap around her neck.

'You little bitch,' Dot whispered. And yet, something in her couldn't condemn the girl. She stood, somehow, outside of the realm of Dot's condemnation. She couldn't help but feel that Frankie might just as easily be standing with them, facing up to the coming onslaught. That whatever side she was on didn't matter to her, only that there was going to be a fight, that she would have to be on one side, and that circumstances, in their dumb wisdom, had dictated she stand that side of the line.

The girl reached into the smock and pulled out her own binoculars, much bigger, much more powerful than Dot's. She made a sweep of her own horizon and – although, could it really be so? – came to rest when her vision alighted on Dot. Although mediated by eight thick lenses, Dot had the distinct feeling that their eyes met, that they were looking directly at each other. Frankie's face cracked into a smile. It wasn't malevolent. In fact it was almost friendly. Then, lifting one hand from the binoculars, and still smiling, she waved...

'They're advancing!' the Captain cried. 'This is it!'

He was right. The line of cars, now just black spots to her again, were snaking off the hump of the hill and winding, like a procession of ants, along the road towards Green Oaks. They'd be upon them in a matter of minutes.

'I took the liberty of barricading the gateway,' the Captain said. 'It should hold them off for a moment at least.'

Dot considered that they could be wrong. That those people could be coming to help them. Maybe they were coming to re-impose order at Green Oaks, but would do so in a kind and compassionate way. Was that that outcome so implausible?

She almost laughed at herself. That after all this time, all this life, she could still find a shred of optimism left to allow such a thought. Allow it. Entertain it. But never take it seriously. She didn't know how it worked exactly, but she understood, deep in her knotted guts, that human instinct was finely tuned in to the menace of an approach. Whether it was a snaking procession of cars, or a passenger plane on a clear blue autumn sky. Somehow, even if the brain fought against it, the body just knew...

And yet she wasn't sad. She was hardly even frightened. For wasn't this just the way of things? The decline, the slide, was coming. You couldn't fight it, perhaps, but you could thumb your nose at it. You could, as that old drunken Welsh mystic (another Dylan!) had it, rage, rage against the dying of the light… And then, at some point there would be calm. All of this movement, all of this commotion would stop, all the energy would have run down, run out. Entropy – that word, that dear word! – would have done its work at last.

She looked at her friends. Betty and Smithy propped up against each other, four thick arms offering succour – if they went down, it would be as one and the earth would quake. Lanyard, poor, sad Lanyard, his thumbs hooked in his waistband, watching the cars advance, an expression that said he was determined to hang on to the shreds of dignity he had only recently reclaimed… but wasn't sure how. Olive and her complicated certainty that this was part of someone's, anyone's, grand scheme… She looked at the Captain. For perhaps the only time since she had known him, he looked afraid, terrified even, stripped rudely of the certainty of victory.

And then there was Leonard, covered in grass, smiling like a Hindu statuette as he stared into the bliss of oblivion. His hands between his legs, fiddling with. Oh, god! He wasn't…

The first car, a bull-barred four-wheel-drive, pushed cockily through the Captain's barricade at the gate and the cars began their final climb towards the house.

'*Ooh! Oh Mmm!*' Leonard's hand had dived between his fly and was working to draw his member out. He was attracting attention. Smithy and Betty were smiling indulgently at Dot. She should probably go and stop him, but what about the Captain? What was decorum worth when a friend needed comforting?

Dot walked over to the Captain and took hold of his hand. He was trembling, and gripped her so tightly she suffered an immediate attack of pins and needles. A wind was picking up too, driving the birds into a flocking frenzy. It was only right that it should, really. She saw it first in the dirty plastic roses on the lattice, then felt it curling about her ankles. It was almost soothing. She found herself thinking that, if they wanted to, they could lean into it and, against all odds, against all physics, it would support them.

'I tried, Private,' the Captain said.

'Oh, that's it. That's hitting the spot!'

'I know you did.'

'I really thought we could win. This isn't how adventures end. They end with white picket fences, with reconciliations. Things don't happen by... by *accident*.'

'*Mmmmm!*' Leonard moaned.

Dot grinned. Then she laughed. She couldn't help herself. For the first time in a long time she laughed from the pit of her belly. It wasn't the laughter of joy, though. It was the laughter of defiance. Defiance of the absurd scandal that life was. Always had been. Always would be. What else was there to do but laugh?

The others turned to look at her. They were confused at first, but then, one by one, and perhaps without fully understanding why, they began laughing too. It was as if they had finally got the universe's corny joke, played on them all. Even Leonard. Even he was laughing. Only the Captain wasn't.

'Private?' he asked.

'Oh, my dear friend,' she said. 'We *did* win. Can't you see that? This is us winning...'

'So why do I feel like the ground is crumbling beneath me?'

'Because it is. But it's okay.' Dot saw that the others were holding hands too now. Smithy cleared his throat:

'Anyone for a few verses of Kumbayah?'

Dot laughed even harder.

'But...' the Captain tried to ask. Dot let their fingers interlock. 'Weather balloons?' he whispered, his face hopeful.

'No. Not this time,' Dot said. 'We don't need them this time.'

For a moment the Captain looked scared again, but only for a moment. They leaned into the wind.

'Just don't let go, Dylan,' she said.

Captain Ruggles will return in a brand new adventure. Soon.

Only in

AIR SOULS!

On newsstands the 5th of every month.

A.N.B
PARIS
2010—2016

ACKNOWLEDGEMENTS

To everybody who read a draft or two along the way – Coline Abert, Jean-François Caro, Linda Fallon, Svetlana Lavochkina, Amy Sackville, Antony Topping – thank you, if this book works it's because of you. To Sam Jordison and Eloise Millar, thank you for helping make this the book I always hoped it would be. To Stephen Crowe and Melanie Amaral, thank you for making Ruggles beautiful. To Susan Tomaselli, thank you for giving him his first public outing. To Andrew Gallix, thank you for not asking my permission. To Will Wiles, thank you for the advice and support. To Ben Brown, thank you for the Chaucer. To Sylvia Whitman, David Delannet and everyone at Shakespeare and Company, thank you for the welcome. To my parents, Angela and Graham, thank you for never telling me to stop. To my brother Darran, thank you for everything. And, of course, to Audrey – thank you for raising an island of meaning from the ocean of chaos.

Friends of Galley Beggar Press

Galley Beggar Press would like to thank the following individuals, without the generous support of whom our books would not be possible:

Edward Baines
Jaimie Batchan
Kianna Behrami
Alison Bianchi
Hilary Botten
Patricia Borlenghi
John Brooke
Ellie Bury
Stuart Carter
Paul Crick
Alan Crilly
Paul Dettman
Janet Dowling
Gerry Feehily
Andrew Fenwick
Robert Foord
Lorena Goldsmith
Neil Griffiths
Drew Gummerson
George Hawthorne
David
    Hebblethwaite
Penelope Hewett
    Brown

Diana Jordison
Lesley Kissin
Wendy Laister
Jackie Law
Elizabeth Lee
Sue and Tony Leifer
Philip Makatrewicz
Anil Malhotra
Tom Mandall
Adrian Masters
Jarred McGinnis
Malachi McIntosh
James Miller
Richard Myers
Linda Nathan
Catherine
    Nicholson
Seb Ohsan-
    Berthelsen
Eliza O'Toole
Keith Packer
Radhika Pandit
Roger Partridge
Sarah Passingham

Emma Pheby
Alex Preston
Polly Randall
Jack Gwilym
    Roberts
Richard Sheehan
Matthew Shenton
Ashley Tame
Justine Taylor
Sam Thorp
Colleen Toomey
Emma Townshend
Anthony Trevelyan
Stephen Walker
Steve Walsh
Rosita Wilkins
Bronwen Wilson
    Rashad
Bianca Winter
Ben Yarde Buller
Carsten Zwaaneveld